Edward Walford

Juvenal

Edward Walford

Juvenal

ISBN/EAN: 9783337365820

Printed in Europe, USA, Canada, Australia, Japan

Cover: Foto ©Andreas Hilbeck / pixelio.de

More available books at **www.hansebooks.com**

J U V E N A L

EDWARD WALFORD, M.A.

LATE SCHOLAR OF BALLIOL COLL., OXFORD; AUTHOR OF
'THE HANDBOOK OF THE GREEK DRAMA,' ETC.

WILLIAM BLACKWOOD AND SONS
EDINBURGH AND LONDON
MDCCCLXXII

CONTENTS.

JUVENAL.

CHAPTER I.

LIFE OF JUVENAL.

IF the saying be true, that the greater the poet is, the less are we likely to know of him from his own writings, Juvenal ought certainly to occupy a very high place among the poets of Rome. In this respect he offers a most complete contrast to Horace, who has left us in his various poems an account of himself—his character, habits, and pursuits, his successes and his failures—almost as complete as, and far more instructive than, many a professed biography. Juvenal, on the other hand, never allows the personality of the poet to obtrude itself in any way on the reader's notice. In reading Horace, we can never lose sight of the cultivated, genial man of the world, who indeed makes his puppets play before us, but allows them to speak only with his own voice, to utter his own words. In Juvenal, the subject entirely overshadows the identity of the poet ; we read him, but we no more think of the writer as we read, than we should allow a vision of the blind old bard to roam on the plain of the Scamander, and preside at the death of Hector or at the games around the tomb of Patroclus.

All that we know of Juvenal, beyond those allusions to himself, or to contemporary history, which may be found scattered up and down throughout his writings, is contained in the volume of memoirs attributed to Suetonius. The sum and substance of what we read in his pages is as follows :—

"Junius Juvenalis, the son or the alumnus (it is uncertain which) of a rich freedman, practised declamation till near middle life, more for amusement than by way of preparing himself for school or forum. Afterwards, having written a clever Satire of a few verses on Paris the pantomime, and a poet of his time, who was puffed up with his paltry six months' military rank, he took pains to perfect himself in this kind of writing. And yet for a very long time he did not venture to trust anything even to a small audience. But after a while he was heard by great crowds, and with great success, several times ; so that he was led to insert in his first writings those verses which he had written first :—

'What ! will you still on Camerinus wait,
And Bareas ? will you still frequent the great ?
Ah ! rather to the player your labours take,
And at one lucky stroke your fortunes make !'
                                        —Sat. vii. 90.

" The player was at that time one of the favourites

at court, and many of his supporters were daily pro-
moted. Juvenal, therefore, fell under suspicion as one
who had covertly censured the times ; and forthwith,
under colour of military promotion, though he was
eighty years of age, he was removed from the city,
and sent to take command of a cohort which was
stationed in the furthest part of Egypt. That sort of
punishment was determined upon as being suited to a
light and jocular offence. Within a very short time
he died of vexation and disgust."

This notice, meagre as it is, and probably not
original, is yet more authentic and fuller than any
other account we can find in the literature of the
period. The facts which can be gleaned and the in-
ferences which can be drawn from Juvenal's writings
with regard to his personal career, are if possible more
scanty and less to be depended upon. To such an
extent is this the case, that even such questions as
whether the poet ever visited Egypt, and if so, at
what period of his lifetime, and in what capacity, are
left in complete uncertainty. The dates of his birth
and of his death are alike disputed ; events to which
he is supposed to allude are ascribed by different
authorities to the reigns of the different Emperors from
Nero to Trajan ; and the very text of the author has
been interpolated and revised to suit one or other of
the views from time to time in vogue to such an extent, that the authenticity of well-nigh half the work
has been disputed by some one commentator or more.

The upshot of all this is, that the only facts with
regard to Juvenal on which we can implicitly rely are,

that he flourished towards the close of the first century; that Aquinum, if not the place of his nativity, was at least his chosen residence ; and that he is in all probability the friend whom Martial addresses in three epigrams.

There is, however, a far more interesting question, to which we may yet be enabled to give an answer by a careful study of the Satires of Juvenal, and that consists in the consideration of the gradual development of the high moral qualities with which our poet was endowed. We have elsewhere endeavoured to point out how we may trace the fierce and almost truculent satire of his youth gradually softening down to the gentler temper of his mature years. In these he is not indeed blind to the vices of mankind; but, taking a larger and more philosophic view of human life, he is more anxious to point out how those vices may be remedied, by an earnest pursuit after virtue ; and how God seldom fails in the end to reward the good for their righteous dealings, and to punish the wicked for their sins.

" Though the mills of God grind slowly, yet they grind
    exceeding small ;
Though with patience He stands waiting, with exactness
    grinds He all."

We can also see how his whole life was one continued protest against the encroachments of foreign and especially of Grecian customs; against the influx of those wealthy but low-born, low-bred foreigners who, by dint of their huge fortunes, and supported by court favour, were successfully disputing with the ancient Roman families the few privileges which were still left them. " Must I," he exclaims with indignant scorn,

" Let him seat first, and on the chief couch lie
    At feasts, whom to our Rome the same wind brought
    That brought us figs and prunes ? goes it for nought
    That we Aventine air first breathed, and, bred
    In Rome, were with the Sabine olive fed ?
                                —Sat. iii. 81.

Yet even in this respect there is a material change in the tone which he adopts in his more advanced age. The diatribes against foreigners are less frequent, and their place is taken by earnest and lofty moral precepts, weighty alike with the experience of a long life, and with the disinterested zeal of a philanthropist and philosopher. Of his æsthetic tastes, though little disposed to speak much of himself, Juvenal has allowed pretty frequent traces to appear in his writings. From these we may gather that he had, in greater measure than most Romans, a love of the country, a " romantic " sympathy with and longing for nature and the picturesque, which we may add to the other hints we find in his works of tastes and feelings that are generally considered to be distinctive marks of a modern as opposed to a classical tone of thought : traces of a love of country scenery and quietude for its own sake, and not only as a refuge from the turmoil and vices of an overgrown capital. It is with heart-felt joy, then, that Juvenal shakes the dust of Rome from off his feet, and escapes from the profligacy and

hollowness of the imperial city, in which even the
face of nature cannot avoid the sophisticating touch of
an artificial æstheticism. A notable example of this
fact we have at the very gates of Rome :—

> " Here we view
> The Egerian grots—ah, how unlike the true !
> Nymph of the spring, more honoured hadst thou been
> If, free from art, an edge of living green
> Thy bubbling fount had circumscribed alone,
> And marble ne'er profaned the native stone."
>
> —Ibid., 17.

Far better than all this parade, in the poet's eyes, is
the beauty of simple Gabii :—

> " Bleak Præneste's seat,
> Volsinium's craggy heights, embowered in wood,
> Or Tibur, beetling o'er prone Anio's flood !"
>
> —Ibid., 191.

There the true farmer's life may yet be enjoyed by the
husbandman; blessed, indeed, if he only had eyes to
see the real happiness of his lot !

> " There wells by nature formed, which need no rope,
> No labouring arm, to crane their waters up,
> Around your lawn their facile streams shall shower,
> And cheer the springing plant and opening flower.
> There live delighted with the rustic's lot,
> And till with your own hands the little spot—
> The little spot which yields you large amends,
> And glad with many a feast your Samian friends."
>
> —Ibid., 226.

To such a quiet home as this Juvenal would gladly
retire with a friend of congenial tastes, and recall for a
short space the mode of life that once was led by all

the citizens of Rome. Let us then accompany Persicus
as he goes to accept the poet's invitation, and with him
make our way from the din of the Suburra to the quiet
country homestead, hidden behind the oak-clad hills of
Latium. The bridges over the Tiber, with their throng
of beggars, seated each on his woven mat of rushes, is
left behind; the roar of the street traffic, the hoarse
voices of the drovers and waggoners, the hum of the
circus and of the crowded theatre, grow indistinct; and
we no longer hear the prancing of the train of the rich
man's mules, or the ringing of their iron hoofs in his
paved and shady portico. We pass together through
the Capene gate, dripping with the waters of the
conduit that passes overhead, bringing a supply of
water from the distant hills into the imperial city.

> " Here Numa erst his nightly visits paid,
> And held high converse with the Egerian maid :
> Now the once-hallowed fountain, grove, and fane,
> Are let to Jews, a wretched, wandering train,
> Whose furniture's a basket filled with hay,—
> For every tree is forced a tax to pay ;
> And while the heaven-born Nine in exile rove,
> The beggar rents their consecrated grove."
>
> —Ibid., 12.

Passing beneath this vaulted gate, the road led
down the world-renowned Appian Way, the well-
known burying-place of the mighty dead at Rome.
For many miles the broad straight road was lined on
the right hand and on the left by huge marble monu-
ments, stretching away in an unbroken series till they
grew smaller and smaller, and at length vanished in

the distance.   Yet even here—in this place, of all
others, most sacred to the memories of a departed greatness—modern depravity was not ashamed to obtrude
its brazen face of extravagance and vice :—

> " See, by his great progenitors' remains
>   Fat Damasippus sweeps, with loosened reins :
>   Good consul ! he no pride of office feels,
>   But stoops, himself, to clog his headlong wheels.
> ' But this is all by night,' the hero cries :
>   Yet the moon sees ! yet the stars stretch their eyes
>   Full on your shame !   A few short moments wait,
>   And Damasippus quits the pomp of state :
>   Then mounts his chariot in the face of day,
>
>   Whirls with bold front his grave associate by,
>   And jerks his whip to catch the senior's eye."
>   —Sat. viii. 146.

It will hardly be necessary to remark here, that this
driving in public was looked on as a gross offence
against morality and common decency ; indeed, as an
act scarcely less disgraceful than to engage in the fights
of the amphitheatre, or to play a low part on the stage.
And thus the satirist lashes on the same page the de-
bauchee Matho, or the renegade patrician, and the man

> " Who spent on horses all his father's land,
>   While, proud the experienced driver to display,
>   His glowing wheel smoked o'er the Appian way."

Meanwhile we follow along the road, and reach Aricia's
hill, and its proverbial throng of beggars.   These, then
no less than in the present day, took advantage of the
steep incline to crowd round the passing carriage, and

demand, even with threatening words and gestures, the alms that they seemed to consider due to them. At this point we leave the broad Campagna Romana which we have hitherto been traversing, to climb with Juvenal's friend the range of hills among which his secluded farm was situated, shunning the glare and heat of the plain no less than the feverish jealousies and intrigues of the city. But what were the scenes that might there be seen, and what the poet's frugal way of life, he shall himself set forth in his letter of invitation to this rural retreat.

The eleventh satire is written in the form of a letter to a friend, Persicus, inviting him to supper at the poet's farm. The introductory lines are occupied with an attack on the extravagance and luxury of the Romans, and the numerous shameful bankruptcies that were attributable to indulgence of the palate. He then seizes the occasion, and shows the superiority of the good old times, when every man measured his appetite by the simple requirements of nature, nor ever thought to spend more than a small part of his moderate income on the pleasures of the table :—

> " Enough : to-day my Persicus shall see
> Whether my precepts with my life agree ;
> Whether, with feigned austerity, I prize
> The spare repast, a glutton in disguise,
> Bawl for coarse pottage, that my friends may hear,
> But whisper ' sweetmeats !' in my servant's ear.
> For since, by promise, you are now my guest,
> Know, I invite you to no sumptuous feast,
> But to such simple fare, as long, long since,
> The good Evander bade the Trojan prince.

Come then, my friend, you will not, sure, despise
The food that pleased the offspring of the skies ;
Come, and while fancy brings past times to view,
I'll think myself the king, the hero you.

Take now your bill of fare ; my simple board
Is with no dainties from the market stored,
But dishes all my own. From Tibur's stock
A kid shall come, the fattest of the flock,
The tenderest too, and yet too young to browse
The thistle's shoots, the willow's watery boughs,
With more of milk than blood ; and pullets drest
With new-laid eggs, yet tepid from the nest,
And 'sparage wild, which, from the mountain's side.
My housemaid left her spindle to provide ;
And grapes long kept, yet pulpy still, and fair,
And the rich Signian and the Syrian pear ;
And apples, that in flavour and in smell
The boasted Picene equal, or excel :—
Nor need you fear, my friend, their liberal use,
For age has mellowed and improved their juice.

How homely this ! and yet this homely fare
A senator would, once, have counted rare ;
When the good Curius thought it no disgrace
O'er a few sticks a little pot to place,
With herbs by his small garden-plot supplied—
Food, which the squalid wretch would now deride,
Who digs in fetters, and, with fond regret,
The tavern's savoury dish remembers yet !'

Time was when on the rack a man would lay
The seasoned flitch against a solemn day ;
And think the friends who met with decent mirth
To celebrate the hour which gave him birth,
On this, and what of fresh the altars spared

(For altars then were honoured), nobly fared.
Some kinsman, who had camps and senates swayed,
Had thrice been consul, once dictator made,
From public cares retired, would gaily haste,
Before the wonted hour, to such repast,
Shouldering the spade, that, with no common toil,
Had tamed the genius of the mountain soil.—
Yes, when the world was filled with Rome's just fame,
And Romans trembled at the Fabian name,
The Scauran, and Fabrician ; when they saw
A censor's rigour e'en a censor awe,
No son of Troy e'er thought it his concern,
Or worth a moment's serious care to learn,
What land, what sea, the fairest tortoise bred,
Whose clouded shell might best adorn his bed.—
His bed was small, and did no signs impart
Or of the painter's or the sculptor's art,
Save where the front, cheaply inlaid with brass,
Showed the rude features of a vine-crowned ass ; *
An uncouth brute, round which his children played,
And laughed and jested at the face it made !
Briefly, his house, his furniture, his food,
Were uniformly plain, and simply good.

Then the rough soldier, yet untaught by Greece
To hang, enraptured, o'er a finished piece,
If haply, 'mid the congregated spoils
(Proofs of his power, and guerdon of his toils),
Some antique vase of master-hands were found,
Would dash the glittering bauble on the ground ;
That in new forms the molten fragments drest
Might blaze illustrious round his courser's chest,
Or, flashing from his burnished helmet, show
(A dreadful omen to the trembling foe)

* The head was crowned with vine leaves, the ass being sacred
to Bacchus.

The mighty sire, with glittering shield and spear,
Hovering, enamoured, o'er the sleeping fair,
The wolf, by Rome's high destinies made mild,
And, playful at her side, each wondrous child.

Thus, all the wealth those simple times could boast,
Small wealth ! their horses and their arms engrossed ;
The rest was homely, and their frugal fare,
Cooked without art, was served in earthenware :
Yet worthy all our envy, were the breast
But with one spark of noble spleen possest.
THEN shone the fanes with majesty divine,
A present god was felt at every shrine !
And solemn sounds, heard from the sacred walls,
At midnight's solemn hour, announced the Gauls,
Now rushing from the main ; while, prompt to save,
Stood Jove, the prophet of the signs he gave !
Yet, when he thus revealed the will of fate,
And watched attentive o'er the Latian state,
His shrine, his statue, rose of humble mould,
Of artless form, and unprofaned with gold.

Those good old times no foreign tables sought ;
From their own woods the walnut-tree was brought,
When withering limbs declared its pith unsound,
Or winds uptore and stretched it on the ground.
But now, such strange caprice has seized the great,
They find no pleasure in the costliest treat,
Suspect the flowers a sickly scent exhale,
And think the ven'son rank, the turbot stale.
Unless wide-yawning panthers, towering high—
Enormous pedestals of ivory,
Formed of the teeth which Elephantis sends,
Which the dark Moor, or darker Indian, vends,
Or those which, now, too heavy for the head,
The beasts in Nabathea's forest shed—

The spacious ORBS support : then they can feed,
And every dish is delicate indeed !
For silver feet are viewed with equal scorn,
As iron rings upon the finger worn.

    To me, for ever be the guest unknown,
Who, measuring my expenses by his own,
Remarks the difference with a scornful leer,
And slights my humble house and homely cheer.
Look not to me for ivory ; I have none :
My chess-board and my men are all of bone ;
Nay, my knife-handles ; yet, my friend, for this,
My pullets neither cut nor taste amiss.

    I boast no artist, tutored in the school
Of learned Trypherus,* to carve by rule ;
Where large sow-paps of elm, and boar, and hare,
And phœnicopter, and pygargus rare,
Getulian oryx, Scythian pheasants, point
The nice anatomy of every joint ;
And dull blunt tools, severing the wooden treat,
Clatter around, and deafen all the street.
My simple lad, whose highest efforts rise
To broil a steak in the plain country guise,
Knows no such art ; humbly content to serve,
And bring the dishes which he cannot kerve.
Another lad (for I have two to-day),
Clad, like the first, in homespun russet grey,
Shall fill our earthen bowls : no Phrygian he,
No pampered attribute of luxury,
But a rude rustic :—when you want him, speak,
And speak in Latin, for he knows not Greek.

---

* "Trypherus, and the professors of the art of carving, employed wooden models of the dishes to be carved. The parts
of these were slightly fastened together, so that the pupil could
separate them with a blunt knife."—J. E. B. Mayor.

Both go alike, with close-cropt hair, undrest,
But spruced to-day in honour of my guest ;
And both were born on my estate, and one
Is my rough shepherd's, one my neatherd's son.
Poor youth ! he mourns, with many an artless tear,
His long, long absence from his mother dear ;
Sighs for his little cottage, and would fain
Meet his old playfellows, the goats, again.
Though humble be his birth, ingenuous grace
Beams from his eye, and flushes in his face ;
Charming suffusion ! that would well become
The youthful offspring of the chiefs of Rome.—
He, Persicus, shall fill us wine which grew
Where first the breath of life the stripling drew,
On Tibur's hills ;—dear hills, that many a day
Witnessed the transports of his infant play.

But you, perhaps, expect a wanton throng
Of Gaditanian girls, with dance and song,
To kindle loose desire ; girls, that now bound
Aloft with active grace, now, on the ground,
Quivering, alight, while peals of praise go round.

. . . . . .

My feast, to-day, shall other joys afford :
Hushed as we sit around the frugal board,
Great Homer shall his deep-toned thunder roll,
And mighty Maro elevate the soul ;
Maro, who, warmed with all the poet's fire,
Disputes the palm of victory with his sire :
Nor fear my rustic clerks ; read as they will,
The bard, the bard, shall rise superior still !

Come then, my friend, an hour to pleasure spare,
And quit awhile your business and your care ;
The day is all our own : come, and forget

Bonds, interest, all ; the credit and the debt ;
Nay, e'en your wife :

.　　　.　　　.　　　.　　　.

Yet, at my threshold, tranquillise your breast ;
There leave the thoughts of home, and what the haste
Of heedless slaves may in your absence waste ;
And, what the generous spirit most offends,
Oh, more than all, leave there, UNGRATEFUL FRIENDS.

But see ! the napkin, waved aloft, proclaims
The glad commencement of th' Idæan games,
And the proud prætor, in triumphal state,
Ascends his car, the arbiter of fate !
Ere this, all Rome (if 'tis, for once, allowed,
To say all Rome, of so immense a crowd)
The Circus throngs, and—Hark ! loud shouts arise—
From these I guess the GREEN has won the prize ;*

* The race in its first institution was a simple contest of two
chariots, whose drivers were distinguished by white and red live-
ries : two additional colours, a light green and cerulean blue,
were afterwards introduced ; and as the races were repeated
twenty-five times, one hundred chariots contributed every day to
the pomp of the Circus. The four factions soon acquired a legal
establishment and a mysterious origin, and their fanciful colours
were derived from the various appearances of nature in the four
seasons of the year ; the red Dog-star of summer, the snows of
winter, the deep shades of autumn, and the cheerful verdure of
the spring. Another interpretation preferred the elements to
the seasons, and the struggle of the green and blue was supposed to represent the conflict of the earth and sea. Their
respective victories announced either a plentiful harvest or a
prosperous navigation, and the hostility of the husbandmen
and mariners was somewhat less absurd than the blind ardour
of the Roman people who devoted their lives and fortunes to
the colour which they had espoused. Such folly was disdained
and indulged by the wisest princes ; but the names of Caligula,
Nero, Vitellius, Verus, Commodus, Caracalla, and Elagabalus,

For had it lost, all joy had been supprest,
And grief and horror seized the public breast ;
As when dire Carthage forced our arms to yield,
And poured our noblest blood on Cannæ's field.
Thither let youth, whom it befits, repair,
And seat themselves beside some favourite fair,
Wrangle, and urge the desperate bet aloud ;
While we, retired from business and the crowd,
Stretch our shrunk limbs by sunny bank or stream,
And drink at every pore the vernal beam.
Haste, then : for we may use our freedom now,
And bathe, an hour ere noon, with fearless brow—
Indulge for once :—Yet such delights as these,
In five short morns, would lose the power to please ;
For still, the sweetest pleasures soonest cloy,
And its best flavour temperance gives to joy.

—Sat. xi. 56, *sqq.*

were enrolled in the blue or green factions of the Circus : they fre-
quented their stables, applauded their favourites, chastised their
antagonists, and deserved the esteem of the populace, by the
natural or affected irritation of their manners. The bloody and
tumultuous contest continued to disturb the public festivity till
the last age of the spectacles of Rome ; and Theodoric, from a
motive of justice or affection, interposed his authority to protect the greens against the violence of a consul and patrician,
who were passionately addicted to the blue faction of the Circus.
—Gibbon's Decline and Fall, ch. xi.

CHAPTER II.

" THE true end of satire," says Dryden, " is the amend-
ment of vices by correction." This definition of satire
is no doubt too narrow, and by taking up too lofty a
stand-point would altogether exclude those writings
whose highest aim it is to "shoot folly as it flies,"
seeking less to expose the crimes or to reform the
manners of the age, than to provide amusement for
the idle reader, and, while so doing, endeavouring to set
up a standard of taste and criticism to be developed
by instances of failure where such failure can but
provoke a smile, and by more or less cynical epigrams on the *gaucheries* of our less cultivated neighbours. Nevertheless, the words which we have just
quoted, considered from another point of view, draw
an excellent distinction between true satire and that
spurious branch of satirical writing whose object it is
rather to gratify personal pique or lust for revenge by
the ridicule or defamation of a private enemy, than to
check public foibles by wit and sarcasm. Addison
points out with admirable clearness the contrast be-

A. C. vol. xiii.   B

tween the true satirist and the mere writer of lam-
poons, while explaining the difference between the
mode of criticism which he intended to pursue in the
' Spectator,' and that which was only too prevalent
among authors of every rank in his time. " If I attack
the vicious, I shall only set upon them in a body, and
will not be provoked by the worst usage I can receive
from others to make an example of any particular
criminal. It is not Lais or Silenus but the harlot or
the drunkard whom I shall endeavour to expose, and
shall consider the crime as it appears in the species,
not as it is circumstanced in the individual." In these
words we may discover a test that shall enable us to
distinguish between the mere scurrilous productions
of Grub Street and writings animated by the true fire of
genius. The difference is obvious. Yet we frequently
find that the satirist is confounded in popular esteem
with the common libeller ; many people, even among
those whose culture might lead one to expect from
them a more liberal judgment, being apparently unable to discriminate between the malice of the literary
vitriol-thrower and the sarcasm of the poet who seeks
to strike a good blow in the war of virtue against vice,
of wit against folly, without the slightest wish to hurt
the self-esteem or wound the vanity even of those
whose many failings lay them most open to the shafts
of ridicule. If we were asked what is in our opinion
the most distinctive mark by which satire may be
separated from lampoon, we should point to the strain
of good-natured pleasantry that is never long absent
from the best satire—a quality that, by enabling a

man to assume a position of superiority similar to that
which the physician is enabled to hold towards his
patient, gives the satirist an immense advantage over
his less even-tempered antagonist, and, whether in
attack or defence, may be counted one of the most
effective weapons in his armoury. Such an one, by
preserving a certain impartiality and frankness in his
opinions and conversation, is able far more readily
to command the respect and attention of his hearers.
In illustration of this we may repeat the old anecdote
told by Steele of a humorous fellow at Oxford. When
he heard that any one had spoken ill of him, he used
to say, " I will not take my revenge of him till I have
forgiven him." What he meant was this : that he
would not enter the lists until his temper was so
thoroughly under his control that there would be no
danger of his laying himself open to repartee, by allow-
ing his anger to outrun his judgment. Dryden himself was fully aware of the necessity of keeping all
violence in check, and of subjecting all outbursts of
pique and animosity to the strictest rule of moderation
and good taste. True, he did not always act upon this
rule, and sometimes he seems to think that savage undis-
criminating invective is the highest aim of the satirist.
It is not, however, in such passages that he has been
counted most successful, but rather in those in which,
with the greatest delicacy of touch, he mocks ·at the
ridiculous pretensions of vanity, or rallies the eccentri-
cities of genius. One of the most exquisite examples
of this method is the character of Buckingham in his
" Absalom and Achitophel." Dryden himself, in his

"Discourse on Satire," selected this as one of the brightest gems of his poems; and he there supports his judgment by the following arguments:—"The character of Zimri, in my Absalom, is, in my opinion, worth the whole poem; it is not bloody, but it is ridiculous enough; and he for whom it was intended was too witty to resent it as an injury. If I had railed, I might have suffered for it justly; but I managed my own work more happily, perhaps more dexterously. I avoided the mention of great crimes, and applied myself to the representing of blind sides and little extravagances, to which, the wittier a man is, he is generally the more obnoxious." We can only regret that Dryden, as well as many other satirists, both ancient and modern, did not more faithfully adhere to the excellent maxims which he here inculcates. It is a failure in this respect that has doomed so much of the satire of the contemporaries of Juvenal, no less than of those of Dryden, to the oblivion it so well deserved. Epigram and sarcasm, however witty, if guided by mere personal spite or party feeling, must of necessity lose their interest when the object against whom they were directed has perished.

It would of course be wholly unfair to reproach any writer who lived in the time of the Roman Empire for not reaching the standard of unprejudiced and goodnatured criticism that is to-day aimed at by the satirist of men and manners—a style with which we are all well acquainted in the writings of Thackeray, an author who, of all others, acted up to his own dictum, that "if fun is good, truth is better, and love is best of all." Other times, they say, other manners. The society of Rome under Domitian was not one to be curbed by a silken thread, and the thicker-skinned Romans could hear without flinching attacks on their lives and conduct that would be unendurable to a man living in these later days. Nor should we forget that in ancient Italy life was very much more public than it is under our own customs, and that thus much which we should now consider an unpardonable breach of confidence and of good manners would hardly be open to objection where every man lived constantly under the eyes of his neighbour, and the privacy necessitated by modern ideas of self-respect and decorum was quite unknown. Juvenal was thus by no means under the same obligation as would now be universally acknowledged and enforced among ourselves, to abstain from criticising the vulgar display that offended him at the dinner-table of Vino, or the unwieldy gait of Matho; the gluttony of Crispinus, or the prosaic epics of Codrus. Where the whole body of citizens divided their day between the bath, the forum, and the circus, the poet could not tear away the curtain that protects family life from the vulgar gaze, for the simple reason, that what we now mean when we speak of family life had really no existence.

Again, we must remember that, under the repressive system pursued by the imperial government, political satire, as such, was impossible. The actions of the divine descendant of the Julian line might either be accepted in silence or greeted with gratitude and applause; but criticism—that is to say, adverse criticism—on the political topics of the day was altogether forbidden. Where such criticism is found, it is always directed against the dead, while the present occupant of the purple is never mentioned except to be praised. The laws of treason, that served to punish or prevent all attempts to break down the hedge of majesty that encircled the throne, were strained to the utmost; whilst those laws which protected the reputation of the private citizen were, on the principle of compensation, not so strictly enforced.

Nevertheless, though we may regret that Juvenal did not more entirely refrain from singling out as the objects of his satire individuals of obscure station in the rank and file of society, we must yet grant this much to his memory, that, so far as we can see, he was seldom guided in his selection of victims by personal considerations. It is not his private enemies that he has honoured with an unenviable immortality; nor does he seem to have dragged forward any man into the fire of general ridicule or odium except as an example of the evil consequences of some particular vice or folly.

His method was, in fact, in this respect, similar to that pursued by Horace's father and eulogised by his son, who has left us the following example of his father's teaching :—

" ' Look, boy !' he'd say, 'at Albius' son, observe his sorry
    plight ;
And Barrus, that poor beggar there ! say are not these a
    sight

To warn a man from squandering his patrimonial means ?'
When counselling me to keep from vile amours with common queans—
'Sectanus, ape him not!' he'd say; or, urging to forswear
Intrigue with matrons when I might taste lawful joys
elsewhere—
'Trebonius' fame is blurred since he was in the manner
caught.'"

It is, moreover, quite unnecessary to agree with the
crowd of learned commentators, and maintain that every
proper name introduced by Juvenal must needs refer to
some real personage, though many no doubt did so
refer. But the acumen that seeks to discover an actual
owner for the term *Bubulco Judice,* or, as we should
say in English, "Judge Bumpkin," is apt to overshoot
the mark ; and we shall probably be nearer the truth
if we look on Matho, Mævia, or Crispinus, and many
of the other names that figure in these pages, as being
just as historical as the Marquis of Steyne or Mrs
Rawdon Crawley.

With regard to Juvenal's true rank as a poet, opinions
have differed as widely as have the judgments passed on
any other writer. While one class of critics, among
whom we may mention the historian Gibbon, cannot
find words to express their admiration for a style so
perfect that not a single word could be added or removed without loss,—a style matched only by the noble
sentiments of patriotism and religion that it teaches,
and the lofty moral strain in which it is pitched,—
others look on his writings as among the most corrupt
productions of a vicious age, overloaded by a spurious

loftiness of manner, the result of a pedantic and inflated mode of thought acquired in the schools of rhetorical declamation. In the judgment of this class of critics, the naturally vicious disposition of the author may be traced in his forced and artificial praise of virtue, no less than in his choice of subjects. The candid and impartial critic will, as usually is the case, find that the truth lies somewhere between the two extremes. While it cannot be denied that the effect of an early training in the rhetorical schools may often be traced in a somewhat turgid and exaggerated diction,—in a too free use of ornament, by which the sense is occasionally rather overloaded than illustrated — though there are passages where a declamatory style is carried beyond the limits that a cultivated taste would have assigned,—we shall yet not be going beyond the bounds of strict truth when we assert that, for impassioned eloquence of the highest order, for the power by which the orator is able to enlist all the sympathies of his hearers, Juvenal has seldom been equalled. True, this "rapid and resistless sway of torrent genius" does not necessarily imply poetic faculties of the highest order, and is perhaps the mark rather of the orator than of the poet. However that may be, superlative excellence in qualities that exercise so strong a sway over the judgment and passions of men will never fail to deserve and to obtain general applause for their possessor. Such excellences as these, where no small portion of the effect is gained by the choice of expressions, or even by the collocations of the words, it is of course more than usually difficult to reproduce in a translation ; and it is with some hesitation that we give the following passage as an example of Juvenal's style, when appealing to the deepest feelings of his audience. The subject of the passage is the punishment which a guilty conscience brings on its possessor :—

> " At night, should sleep his harassed limbs compose,
> And steal him one short moment from his woes,
> Then dreams invade ; sudden before his eyes
> The violated fane and altar rise ;
> And (what disturbs him most) your injured shade
> In more than mortal majesty arrayed,
> Frowns on the wretch, alarms his treacherous rest,
> And wrings the dreadful secret from his breast.
> These, these are they, who tremble and turn pale
> At the first mutterings of the hollow gale ;
> Who sink with terror at the transient glare
> Of meteors, glancing through the turbid air.
> Oh, 'tis not chance, they cry ; this hideous crash
> Is not the war of winds, nor the dread flash
> The encounter of dark clouds, but blasting fire
> Charged with the wrath of heaven's insulted sire !
> That dreaded peal, innoxious, dies away ;
> Shuddering, they wait the next with more dismay,
> As if the short reprieve were only sent
> To add new horrors to their punishment."
>   —Sat. xiii. 217.

Nor is Juvenal less a master of the humorous style, when, touching on a lighter theme, he adopts the mock-heroic vein, and laughs at the state council of Domitian and the Fathers of Rome, met to consider what shall be done with a mighty turbot—a present to the Emperor.

The fish was of unparalleled size, and the difficulty to be solved was this : in all the palace

> " No pot was found
> Capacious of the turbot's ample round."
>
> —Sat. iv. 72.

The council is therefore summoned in all haste to the Emperor's presence, where the fish lay. Pegasus was there, and Crispus—

> " Of gentle manners and persuasive tongue ;",.

Acilius, and Rubrius, and Montanus ;

> " Crispinus followed, daubed with more perfume—
> Thus early !—than two funerals consume !"

then Pompey and Fuscus, Viento and Catullus—

> " A base, blind parasite, a murderous lord,
> From the bridge-end raised to the council-board ;
> Yet fitter still to dog the traveller's heels,
> And whine for alms at the descending wheels.
> None dwelt so largely on the turbot's size,
> Or raised with such applause his wondering eyes ;
> But to the left (oh, treacherous want of sight !)
> He poured his praise—the fish was on the right !"
>
> —Ibid., *sqq.*

After a little preliminary conversation, in which each noble senator strives to outdo his neighbour in abject flattery of their common lord and master, the important matter is brought forward for decision :—

> " The Emperor now the important question put—
> ' How say ye, Fathers,—shall the fish be cut ?'
> ' Oh, far be that disgrace !' Montanus cries :
> ' No ; let a pot be formed of amplest size,
> Within whose slender sides the fish, dread sire !

May spread his vast circumference entire.
Bring, bring the tempered clay, and let it feel
The quick gyrations of the plastic wheel.'
But Cæsar, thus forewarned, ' Make no campaign
Unless your potters follow in your train !'"

—Ibid., *sqq.*

The very luxury of servile obsequiousness could go
no further ; and all having approved the plan, the
council is dismissed, and the anxious citizens are reas-
sured that it was no threatened invasion of barbarians
that had caused all this amount of trepidation in the
imperial cabinet.

Another talent with which Juvenal is pre-eminently
endowed, is that of bringing up before the reader's
eyes a graphic picture of the scene which he describes.
Whether he tells of Codrus living in his garret among
his dovecots, with but one bed, and that too short for
his short wife, and six pipkins on a cupboard for all
his stock of furniture ; or of the pomp of triumph, with
its crushed helms and battered shields, and streamers
borne from vanquished fleets ; whether he describes
the wrinkled old man, toothless and blear-eyed with
age ; or the scene on a ship's deck when tossed by the
angry sea, and shrouded in a black storm-cloud ; a feast
in a palace, or a drunken brawl in the streets,—we always have the same power manifested ; a power by
which we are made conscious of seeing and feeling
that which the poet would have us see and feel. What
could be finer or more powerfully expressed than the
following passage, in which the mingled joy and fear of
Rome at the disgrace and death of Sejanus, the hated

minister of Tiberius, is photographed to the very life
for all future ages ?—

"The statues tumbled down
Are dragged by hooting thousands through the town ;
The brazen cars torn rudely from the yoke,
And, with the blameless steeds, to shivers broke.
Then roar the fires ! the sooty artist blows,
And all Sejanus in the furnace glows ;—
Sejanus, once so honoured, so adored,
And only second to the world's great lord,
Runs glittering from the mould in cups and cans,
Basons and ewers, plates, pitchers, pots, and pans.
' Crown all your doors with bay—triumphant bay !
Sacred to Jove—the milk-white victim slay ;
For, lo ! where great Sejanus by the throng—
A joyful spectacle !—is dragged along.
What lips ! what cheeks !   Ah, traitor ! for my part,
I never loved the fellow—in my heart.'
' But tell me,—why was he adjudged to bleed ?
And who discovered, and who proved the deed ?'
' Proved !   A huge wordy letter came to-day
From Capreæ.' 'Good ! What think the people ?' 'They !
They follow fortune, as of old, and hate
With their whole soul the victim of the state.
Yet would the herd, thus zealous, thus on fire,
Had Nurscia met the Tuscan's fond desire,
And crushed the unwary prince, have all combined,
And hailed Sejanus master of mankind !

.   .   .   .   .   .

' But there are more to suffer.'   ' So I find ;
A fire so fierce was ne'er for one designed.
I met my friend Brutidius ; and I fear,
From his pale looks, he thinks there's danger near.
What if this Ajax, in his frenzy, strike,
Suspicious of our zeal, at all alike ?'

'True. Fly we, then, our loyalty to show,
And trample on the carcass of his foe,
While yet exposed on Tiber's banks it lies.'
'But let our slaves be there,' another cries.
'Yes, let them (lest our ardour they forswear,
And drag us pinioned to the bar) be there.'"

—Sat. x. 58.

With regard to the charge of immorality, already
alluded to, if it were not for the high characters that
many of the detractors from the poet's fame have
borne, both for critical acumen and integrity of character, we should be tempted to say with Gifford,
"that there is something of pique in the singular
severity with which he is censured;" that, feeling his
high morality as a censure on themselves, "they seek
to indemnify themselves by questioning the sanctity
which they cannot but respect, and find a secret
pleasure in persuading one another that this dreadful
satirist was at heart no inveterate enemy to the licen-
tiousness which he so vehemently reprehends." The
coarseness which does undoubtedly deface his pages in
more than one instance must not be confounded with
immorality, or even with indecency. It is the result
of the times far more than of the individual temperament of the writer ; and the same coarseness will be
found not only in the pages of Horace and Persius,
but also of philosophers like Seneca and Pliny, to say
nothing of such writers as Martial and Petronius.
If, however, it is complained that the fault lies not
so much in the subjects, or even in the expressions,
as in the undercurrent of thought, in hints and innuen-

does,—we can only reply, that the volume is read by many who see no such moral defects, and that there are few writers on moral subjects against whom the same insinuations might not be made with equal justice.

As to the subjects that are treated by Juvenal, their name in truth is legion. Of some of the more prominent among these we have already spoken, and we shall illustrate them in other chapters. For the rest, the general scope and mode of treatment,—the way in which one subject is made to lead on to another, and how allusions to social life and the events of contemporary history and politics are introduced,—may be gathered from the First Satire.

In it the poet gives his reasons for writing satire, and lays down a kind of outline that is subsequently filled up. Of part of this satire we here give a translation, both because it enumerates the subjects that are treated of at greater length elsewhere, and as giving an example of the general spirit of the poet, and setting forth in emphatic language many of his peculiar likes and dislikes. We may however, perhaps, be allowed to repeat here what we have elsewhere laid down with regard to the continual development visible in Juvenal's moral life,—that it is in the later, and not in the earlier, satires that his philosophy may best be traced. It is not till his later years that he shows a readiness to see what there is of good in all that surrounds him; that he lays aside the destroying club of Hercules, in order to build up on the ground that has thus been cleared an ethical system that has been declared by some authorities to equal, as far as might be without the aid of revelation, the more complete code of morality which we owe to Christianity.

After a few lines by way of introduction, in which he playfully describes his dread of the whole herd of reciters of poetry, and his resolve to be revenged upon them in kind, Juvenal proceeds to give the reasons that determined him to write satire rather than any other kind of poetry :—

> "But why I choose, adventurous, to retrace
> The Auruncan's route, and, in the arduous race,
> Follow his burning wheels, attentive hear,
> If leisure serve, and truth be worth your ear.
>
> When the soft eunuch weds, and the bold fair
> Tilts at the Tuscan boar, with bosom bare ;
> When one that oft, since manhood first appeared,
> Has trimmed the exuberance of this sounding beard,
> In wealth outvies the senate ; when a vile,
> A slave-born, slave-bred vagabond of Nile,
> Crispinus, while he gathers now, now flings
> His purple open, fans his summer rings ;
> And, as his fingers sweat beneath the freight,
> Cries, 'Save me—from a gem of greater weight :'
> 'Tis hard a less adventurous course to choose,
> While folly plagues, and vice inflames the Muse.
> For who so slow of heart, so dull of brain,
> So patient of the town, as to contain
> His bursting spleen, when, full before his eye,
> Swings the new chair of lawyer Matho by,
> Crammed with himself ! then, with no less parade,
> That caitiff's, who his noble friend betrayed,
> Who now, in fancy, prostrate greatness tears,
> And preys on what the imperial vulture spares !

Whom Massa dreads, Latinus, trembling, plies
With a fair wife, and anxious Carus buys.

  .   .   .   .   .

 Ye gods !—what rage, what frenzy fires my brain,
When that false guardian, with his splendid train,
Crowds the long street, and leaves his orphan charge
To prostitution, and the world at large !
When, by a juggling sentence damned in vain
 For who, that holds the plunder, heeds the pain ?)
Marius to wine devotes his morning hours,
And laughs in exile at the offended Powers :
While, sighing o'er the victory she won,
The Province finds herself but more undone !

 And shall I feel that crimes like these require
The avenging strains of the Venusian lyre,*
And not pursue them ?—shall I still repeat
The legendary tales of Troy and Crete ;
The toils of Hercules, the horses fed
On human flesh by savage Diomed,
The lowing labyrinth, the builder's flight,
And the rash boy, hurled from his airy height ?
When what the law forbids the wife to heir,
The adulterer's Will may to the wittol bear,
Who gave, with wand'ring eye and vacant face,
A tacit sanction to his own disgrace ;
And, while at every turn a look he stole,
Snored, unsuspected, o'er the treacherous bowl !

 When he presumes to ask a troop's command
Who spent on horses all his father's land,
While, proud the experienced driver to display,
His glowing wheels smoked o'er the Appian Way :—
For there our young Automedon first tried
His powers, there loved the rapid car to guide.

* The allusion is to Horace, who was born at Venusium.

Who would not, reckless of the swarm he meets,
Fill his wide tablets, in the public streets,
With angry verse ? when, through the mid-day glare,
Borne by six slaves, and in an open chair,
The forger comes, who owes this blaze of state
To a wet seal and a fictitious date ;
Comes, like the soft Mæcenas, lolling by,
And impudently braves the public eye !
Or the rich dame, who stanched her husband's thirst
With generous wine, but—drugged it deeply first !
And now, more dext'rous than Locusta, shows
Her country friends the beverage to compose,
And, 'midst the curses of the indignant throng,
Bears, in broad day, the spotted corpse along.

Dare nobly, man ! if greatness be thy aim,
And practise what may chains and exile claim :
On Guilt's broad base thy towering fortunes raise,
For Virtue starves on—universal praise !
While crimes, in scorn of niggard fate, afford
The ivory couches, and the citron board,
The goblet high-embossed, the antique plate,
The lordly mansion, and the fair estate !

Oh, who can rest—who taste the sweets of life,
When sires debauch the son's too greedy wife !

    .   .   .   .   .

No : INDIGNATION, kindling as she views,
Shall in each breast a generous warmth infuse,
And pour, in Nature and the Nine's despite,
Such strains as I, or Cluvienus,* write !

E'er since Deucalion,† while, on every side,
The bursting clouds upraised the whelming tide,

---

* Cluvienus was a contemporary poet, or rather poetaster, of whom nothing more is known than his name, here immortalised by Juvenal.

† According to Ovid (Metamorph., Book I.), Deucalion and

Reached, in his little skiff, the forkèd hill,
And sought, at Themis' shrine, the Immortals' will ;
When softening stones grew warm with gradual life,
And Pyrrha brought each male a virgin wife ;
Whatever passions have the soul possest,
Whatever wild desires inflamed the breast,
Joy, Sorrow, Fear, Love, Hatred, Transport, Rage,
Shall form the motley subject of my page.

    And when could Satire boast so fair a field ?
Say, when did Vice a richer harvest yield ?
When did fell Avarice so engross the mind ?
Or when the lust of play so curse mankind ?—
No longer, now, the pocket's stores supply
The boundless charges of the desperate die :
The chest is staked !—muttering the steward stands,
And scarce resigns it, at his lord's commands.
Is it a SIMPLE MADNESS, I would know,
To venture countless thousands on a throw,
Yet want the soul, a single piece to spare
To clothe the slave, that shivering stands and bare !
    Who called, of old, so many seats his own,
Or on seven sumptuous dishes supped alone ?—
Then plain and open was the cheerful feast,
And every client was a bidden guest ;
Now, at the gate, a paltry largess lies,
And eager hands and tongues dispute the prize.
But first (lest some false claimant should be found)
The wary steward takes his anxious round,
And pries in every face, then calls aloud,
' Come forth, ye great Dardanians, from the crowd ! '

Pyrrha were the progenitors of the human race after the flood.
The story is, that they took up stones and threw them over
their heads ; and that these stones became the first men and
women of the new creation.

For, mixed with us, e'en these besiege the door,
And scramble for—the pittance of the poor !
'Despatch the Prætor first,' the master cries,
'And next the Tribune.' 'No, not so,' replies
The Freedman, bustling through ; 'first come is still
First served ; and I may claim my right, and will !—
Though born a slave ('tis bootless to deny
What these bored ears betray to every eye),
On my own rents, in splendour, now I live,
On five fair freeholds !   Can the PURPLE give
Their Honours more ? when, to Laurentum sped,
NOBLE Corvinus tends a flock for bread !—
Pallas and the Licinii, in estate,
Must yield to me : let, then, the Tribunes wait.'
Yes, let them wait ! thine, Riches, be the field !—
It is not meet, that he to HONOUR yield,
To SACRED HONOUR, who, with whitened feet,
Was hawked for sale, so lately, through the street.
O gold ! though Rome beholds no altars flame,
No temples rise to thy pernicious name, ·
Such as to Victory, Virtue, Faith are reared,
And Concord, where the clamorous stork is heard,
Yet is thy full divinity confest,
Thy shrine established here, in every breast.
  But while, with anxious eyes, the great explore
How much the dole augments their annual store,
What misery must the poor dependant dread,
Whom this small pittance clothed, and lodged, and fed ?
Wedged in thick ranks before the donor's gates,
A phalanx firm, of chairs and litters, waits :
Thither one husband, at the risk of life,
Hurries his teeming, or his bedrid wife ;
Another, practised in the gainful art,
With deeper cunning tops the beggar's part ;
Plants at his side a close and empty chair :
'My Galla, master ;—give me Galla's share.'

'Galla!' the porter cries; 'let her look out.'
'Sir, she's asleep.   Nay, give me;—can you doubt?'

What rare pursuits employ the client's day!
First to the patron's door their court to pay,
Next to the forum, to support his cause,
Thence to Apollo, learnèd in the laws,
And the triumphal statues.

> .   .   .   .   .   .

Returning home, he drops them at the gate:
And now the weary clients, wise too late,
Resign their hopes, and supperless retire,
To spend the paltry dole in herbs and fire.

Meanwhile their patron sees his palace stored
With every dainty earth and sea afford!
Stretched on the unsocial couch, he rolls his eyes
O'er many an orb of matchless form and size,
Selects the fairest to receive his plate,
And, at one meal, devours a whole estate!—
But who (for not a parasite is there)
The selfishness of luxury can bear?
See! the lone glutton craves whole boars! a beast
Designed by nature for the social feast!—
But speedy wrath o'ertakes him: gorged with food,
And swollen and fretted by the peacock crude,
He seeks the bath, his feverish pulse to still,
Hence sudden death, and age without a Will!
Swift flies the tale, by witty spleen increast,
And furnishes a laugh at every feast;
The laugh, his friends not undelighted hear,
And, fallen from all their hopes, insult his bier.
    NOTHING is left, NOTHING for future times
To add to the full catalogue of crimes;
The baffled sons must feel the same desires,
And act the same mad follies, as their sires.

VICE HAS ATTAINED ITS ZENITH :—Then set sail,
Spread all thy canvas, Satire, to the gale.
 But where the powers so vast a theme requires ?
Where the plain times, the simple, when our sires
Enjoyed a freedom which I dare not name,
And gave the public sin to public shame,
Heedless who smiled or frowned ?—Now, let a line
But glance at Tigellinus, and you shine,
Chained to a stake, in pitchy robes, and light,
Lugubrious torch, the deepening shades of night ;
Or, writhing on a hook, are dragged around,
And with your mangled members plough the ground.
 What ! shall the wretch of hard, unpitying soul,
Who for THREE uncles mixed the deadly bowl,
Propped·on his plumy couch, that all may see,
Tower by triumphant, and look down on me ?
 Yes ; let him look.   He comes ! avoid his way,
And on your lip your cautious finger lay ;
Crowds of informers linger in his rear,
And, if a whisper pass, will overhear."

—Sat. i. 19.

The practice of delation here alluded to was a topic
which could hardly have been avoided by any satirist
who took the reign of Domitian for his theme.   This
odious custom—one of the most intolerable evils of the
Roman Empire—had its rise in a trait of character
which was in itself innocent, if not praiseworthy.   Even
in the days of the Republic, it had not been unusual
for young men who wished to take a place among the
leading politicians of the day to commence their public
career by impeaching before the people of Rome any
among her more powerful citizens who, during their
tenure of office, had transgressed the laws or had harshly

ruled over their province. Such conduct was considered no less honourable to the accuser than serviceable to the state ; and it was by such means that men like Crassus, Cicero, and Cæsar first earned the applause of their fellow-citizens. It is, however, clear that such a mode of procedure was eminently liable to abuse, as indeed the event but too soon proved.

The fact is, that as early as the days of Augustus, many men of honourable birth, forgetful of what was due to their own reputation and the glorious traditions of their family, had not been ashamed to prostitute their intellect by a persecution, thinly veiled by an observance of legal forms, of any private enemies of the emperor. Under the successors of Augustus, the practice, though sometimes discountenanced, spread on the whole with fearful rapidity, till, in the time of Domitian, the Terror reigned throughout the Empire. "The best and noblest of the citizens were still marked out as the prey of delators, whose patrons connived at enormities which bound their agents more closely to themselves, and made his protection more necessary to them. The haughty nobles quailed in silence under a system in which every act, every word, every sigh was noted against them, and disgrace, exile, and death followed upon secret whispers."

This system it is against which Juvenal has inveighed in his most telling manner. At one time, in his more humorous vein, he mocks at the way in which this self-appointed police swarmed even in places where they might have been least expected ; at the paltry annoyance of the inquisitor, almost too ridiculous to be hated, which thought no matter too unimportant for his attention. A fisherman near Ancona has caught an enormous turbot—the same which figured at Domitian's supper-party, already mentioned *—but can hardly be congratulated on his luck. And the reason is soon made obvious :—

" The mighty draught the astonished boatman eyes,
  And to the Pontiff's † table dooms the prize :
  For who would dare to sell it ? who to buy ?
  When the coast swarmed with many a practised spy,—
  Mud-rakers, prompt to swear the fish had fled
  From Cæsar's ponds, ingrate ! where long it fed,
  And thus, recaptured, claimed to be restored
  To the dominion of its ancient lord !
  Nay, if Palphurius may our credit gain,
  Whatever rare or precious swims the main
  Is forfeit to the crown, and you may seize
  The obnoxious dainty when and where you please.
  This point allowed, our wary boatman chose
  To give—what else he had not failed to lose."
                                    —Sat. iv. 45.

Elsewhere Juvenal pours out his indignation more openly on such men as

      " Pompey, practised to betray,
  And hesitate the noblest lives away ; "—Ibid., 110.

men who, under the guise of friendship, would worm out the secret thoughts of their neighbour, and then betray him who had put confidence in their loyalty. Such men were Carus, Massa, Messalinus, and, above all, Reg-

* See above, page 25.

† Among the various titles assumed by the early Roman emperors was that of Pontifex Maximus, or Supreme Pontiff.

ulus, whose infamous reputation earned for him the title
of " prince of informers."

In the remaining lines of this first satire Juvenal
contrasts the satirical with other kinds of poetry, and
comes to the conclusion, after an argument with a
supposed interlocutor, that the former, if the more
dangerous, is also the more honourable to the poet.

> " Bring, if you please, Æneas on the stage,
> Fierce war with the Rutulian prince * to wage ;
> Subdue the stern Achilles ; and once more
> With ' Hylas !' ' Hylas !' fill the echoing shore ;
> Harmless, nay, pleasant, shall the tale be found—
> It bares no ulcer, and it probes no wound.
> But when Lucilius, fired with virtuous rage,
> Waves his keen falchion o'er a guilty age,
> The conscious villain shudders at his sin,
> And burning blushes speak the pangs within ;
> Cold drops of sweat from every member roll,
> And growing terrors harrow up his soul :
> Then tears of shame, and dire revenge succeed—
> Say, have you pondered well the advent'rous deed ?
> Now, ere the trumpet sounds, your strength debate
> The soldier, once engaged, repents too late.
>
> 　　Yet I MUST write : and since these iron times,
> From living knaves preclude my angry rhymes,
> I point my pen against the guilty dead,
> And pour its gall on each obnoxious head."
> 　　　　　　　　　　　　—Sat. i. 162.

　　* Turnus.　See Virgil's Æneid, *passim.*

CHAPTER III.

The characters of Horace and Juvenal, the two principal Roman satirists—the only two whose writings, as they have come down to us, are in themselves worthy of much study—appear to invite, while at the same time they defy, comparison.

The themes on which they wrote were also to a great extent the same, yet treated from so different a point of view that it is difficult to find any sentiment repeated in the two.

Horace affords by no means an exception to the rule, that the men of the truest wit are always of a melancholy, not to say an unhappy, temperament. Throughout his works there is always a tinge of a pessimist feeling, a tendency to take a despondent view of his own career, and of the state of society in which he moved, which, though often disguised, is constantly cropping up under various guises, and in passages where one would hardly expect to meet it. His farm is charming, yet he cannot bear to live at a distance from Rome; in Rome he pines for the air and scenery of the country. Restless when at home, and deriving nothing but discomfort from his travels, he harps on his failing health, on the sickness and death of his friends, on the inconstancy of one or other of his mistresses. In spite of all this, he does not feel what it is that is really wanting to him. Throughout his life his great object was to—

" Snatch gaily the joys which the moment shall bring,
And away every care and perplexity fling."

The one thing needful to make his life a truly happy life—the conscious striving after some great ideal, or the pursuit of some worthy end—was a quality of whose absence he seems never to have been aware ; and thus his life—a life that, worthily guided, might have accomplished great things—was idly frittered away. Whether he appears as the love-sick poet, or as the favoured friend of the emperor's favourite ; as the amateur farmer, or as the neophyte in philosophy ; as the scoffer at superstition, or as the repentant religionist,—there is always an oppressive conscious- ness of something wrong, a shrinking anxiety as to the future, and a despondency with regard to the present, which is scarcely less apparent in the lines in which he tries to shake off the feeling than in those in which he yields to it. Most of all we may notice it in his latest poems. In these he yields more than elsewhere to the depressing effects of failing health, and the loss of the friends and companions of his childhood. To multiply instances of this fact were idle ; indeed the greater part of his writings might be cited as examples

of this trait in Horace's literary character. One or two
passages from his works shall suffice here as instances :

> "Both thou and I
>> Must quickly die,
>> Content thee, then, nor madly hope
> To wrest a false assurance from Chaldæan horoscope.

> Use all life's powers :
>> The envious hours
>> Fly as we talk ; then live to-day,
> Nor fondly to to-morrow trust more than you must or may."
>> —I. Od. xi.

Again, in addressing a friend, Dellius :—

> "It recks not whether thou
>> Be opulent, and trace
> Thy birth from kings, or bear upon thy brow
>> Stamp of a beggar's race ;
> Be what thou wilt, full surely must thou fall,
> For Orcus, ruthless king, swoops equally on all.
> Yes, all are hurrying fast
>> To the one common bourne ;
> Sooner or later will the lot at last
>> Drop from the fatal urn
> Which sends thee hence in the grim Stygian bark,
> To dwell for evermore in cheerless realms and dark."
>> —II. Od. iii.

In very similar language he addresses Posthumus :—

> "Land, home, and winsome wife must all be left ;
>> And cypresses abhorred
>>> Alone of all the trees
>>> That now your fancy please
> Shall shade his dust, who was a little while their lord."
>> —Ibid.

It was, perhaps, a result of the general feeling of his times, rather than of his own temper, that he dwelt so frequently on the certain deterioration of the human race :

> " How time doth in its flight debase
> Whate'er it finds ? "

Yet it is fully in accord with the general undercurrent of the poet's own feelings, whether he is looking forward to his own death, or reminding a friend of the uncertainty of life and the helplessness of man against the powers of Fate, or deploring the death of Virgil. If he speaks of the spring, it is to tell us how short-lived it is; if of its flowers, to show how soon they fade away.

Juvenal, on the other hand, if we may be allowed to judge of him from such evidence as is afforded by his writings, was animated by feelings of a wholly different nature. In his earliest satires we may notice a fierceness which almost degenerates into savage, cynical onslaught on the whole social system of the day. In the seventh satire, while there is less of this fierce ungovernable temper, there are more decided traces of melancholy and despondency than we shall find in his other writings. But this defect is shaken off as the poet advances in years, and in the latest poems there is less of the satirist and more of the philosopher. No longer content with a disheartened criticism on the failings and shortcomings of human life, on the vanity of all around him, Juvenal now aims at holding up before our eyes the charms of

virtue, and the true dignity and happiness of the good
man's life. In these his later writings the poet shows
how high lineage may be worthily adorned by a true
and honourable career.

> " Oh, give me inborn worth ! dare to be just,
> Firm to your word and faithful to your trust,
> These praises hear, at least deserve to hear ;
> I grant your claim, and recognise the peer.
> Hail ! from whatever stock you draw your birth,
> The son of Cossus or the son of Earth,
> All hail ! in you exulting Rome espies
> Her guardian Power, her great Palladium rise ;
> And shouts like Egypt when her priests have found
> A new Osiris for the old one drowned ! "
>   —Sat. viii. 25.

He now dwells on the pleasures of simple tales and
of a country life, pointing out how " its best flavour
temperance gives to joy." He teaches how a man
should live, and how he should train up his children
in the way in which they should go. He reminds the
parent that " reverence to children as to heaven is
due ; " shows how it is from a sound education that
all honourable conduct must arise, and that luxury is
by no means necessary for a contented spirit.

> " What call I then enough ?   What will afford
> A decent habit and a frugal board ;
> What Epicurus' little garden bore,
> And Socrates sufficient thought before.
> These squared by nature's rule their harmless life—
> Nature and wisdom never are at strife."
>   —Sat. xiv. 315.

Holding in view this growth in Juvenal's moral

life, it has well been said that "the satirist whose
aim is merely negative and destructive—who only
pulls down the generous ideas of virtue with which
youth embarks on its careers—is simply an instrument
of evil; and if his pictures of vice are too glowing,
too true, the evil is so much the greater; but if he
pauses in his course to reconstruct, to raise again our
hopes of virtue and point our steps toward the goal of
religion and morality, he may redeem the evil tenfold.
Thus the later satires of Juvenal more than compensate for the earlier; and for the service which he has
in them done to mankind our reverential gratitude is
due." *

Besides all the effects of these differences of character,
there are in the writings of Juvenal and Horace many
instances of a different mode of treating their subject-
matter, which we must attribute far more to the effects
of the changed political and social conditions under
which they lived and worked, than to any traits in
their individual mode of thought.   In that age which
we are accustomed to call Augustan (an age, be it said,
whose weakness and crime was but scantily veiled by
the flimsy tinsel of a spurious refinement), the effects
of that social revolution and anarchy through which
the world had but lately passed, and in which it was,
indeed, to a certain extent still involved, may be but
too readily traced in the customs and modes of thought
of the people of the day, as depicted in the writings of
contemporary authors that still survive.   For half a
century before the battle of Actium, the Roman world

* Merivale's Roman Empire.

had been torn to pieces by civil strife, and harassed by
repeated proscriptions, while its fairest provinces had
been depopulated by the clash of opposing armies, by
the hateful strife of brother with brother, in which

> "Roman against Roman bared his blade,
> Which the fierce Parthian fitter low had laid."

And though, in spite of all this, the armies of the great
Republic had still marched victoriously in all directions;
though the frontiers of the Roman commonwealth had
still been continually thrust out further and further
from the vast metropolis; though the pomp of the
stately triumph might year after year be seen winding
its length up the sacred way to celebrate an ever-
lengthening list of victories over distant nations, whose
very name and habitation were scarcely known to the
sovereign people under whose sway they were now to
live ; though Fortune still seemed to wait patiently the
order of her most highly favoured state,—the day had
gone for ever in which the Roman could burn with
pride and pleasure as he contemplated the successes
of the Republic, of which it was each man's greatest
boast to be a citizen.   Even before the rise of Augustus,
few thinking Romans, however patriotic, could conceal
from themselves the fact, that Roman virtue and
Roman success had found a common grave in vice and
luxury.   The days of high aspirations and of noble
deeds of patriotism had now gone by.   Men who,
under more happy auspices, might have been capable
of great actions, sank into a life of idle, empty frivolity,
of mere dilettanteism in religion as in art, in morality

as in politics. These melancholy features of decay may easily be traced in all the authors of the age, scarcely veiled by a superficial appearance of pride in the great events of their day, and of exultation in the fortune and the destiny of Rome. Men felt that the old order of things had passed away, and felt it without regret. Like the lotos-eaters of Tennyson, they were content to live on without honour, so they might exist in luxury and sluggish peace ; they said in their lives, though possibly not in their words,—

" Let us swear an oath, and keep it with an equal mind,
  In the hollow Lotos-land to live, and lie reclined
  On the hills, like gods, together, careless of mankind."

The day for action—for doing and daring—had gone by ; and now the dead calm of the *Pax Romana* was spread over the face of the earth. Already in its moral and intellectual bearing the condemnation passed by Tacitus on his fellow-countrymen of a later age was justified. " They make a desert and they call it Peace." Hence, feeling the emptiness of their own times, the total absence of any field in which a spirit cast in the old heroic mould could find a worthy sphere of action, it was impossible that the writers of the age should find scope for any thoughts of really noble import. Most assuredly is it true that the literature of any period can have no life except that which it may have as the echo of the active existence of the nation. In such nations, then, as are destitute of political life, no literature of any noble kind can exist, unless the poet is borne back in his imagination to times when decay had not yet tainted the national growth. And this is the only kind of inspiration which we can find in the writers of the age of Augustus. The burden of Horace, Virgil, and Livy is all the same. "Who shall restore us the years that are past?" By no author was this sentiment more distinctly enunciated than by Livy, when in the preface to his 'History' he sets forth his reasons for recounting the past glories of Rome, and for telling the tale of the foundation and spread of her rule. "One reward of this my toil," he says, "will be that, for a time at all events, I shall be enabled to forget the desolation which has come upon our nation — our nation that has now reached a pitch of iniquity at which it can bear neither its vices nor yet the remedies for them." In Virgil, though we shall not be able to find in his poems any so distinct assertion of the effeteness of the age in which he lived, we may yet distinctly trace the effects of the same despairing acquiescence in the state of his countrymen, the same hopelessness of their political future. It is always to the Past that Virgil points back when he would arouse the enthusiasm of his hearers for the theme he lays before them. The age of the seven ancient kings, of the mighty Fabii, of the Fabricii, of the Decii, and Gracchi, that was the age on which the Poet might look back with mingled pride and reverence ; but with the death of Cato a veil of separation must be drawn between themes that inspire hope, and joy, and the poet's sacred song, and themes which may not be touched. The present generation might indeed be conscious of having hurled back the threatened invasion of the swarthy Egyptian queen, of having crushed Antonius, and dashed the pirate Sextus to the ground. But were not the latter brothers? and was it not a disgrace, worse than any victory could blot out, that the great Rome of Mars and Romulus should have trembled before a woman's threats?—should have heard with panic fear the barking of Anubis, and the shaking of the rattle of the Nile?

And now the victory had come, but it had been followed by a universal peace, containing within itself the seeds of a listless disease—a disease that was already chilling the whole body politic into a lethargy, where no lofty resolve could be developed, no patriotic aspirations had any room. It is in the Georgics only, in which, as the apostle of the country, he inculcates the homely virtues of a farmer's life, that Virgil is able to emancipate himself from the melancholy with which he is elsewhere weighed down, and holds out to the Romans of his own day the hope of emulating, to some extent at least, the noble characteristics of their forefathers.

The effect of the same political phenomena was somewhat different on Horace, even as his character differed from that of Virgil. In him there was none of that enthusiasm which might have led Virgil, had he lived in the twelfth century, to found an order of monks or of knighthood. In Horace sound common-sense took the place of high-flown romance. Himself in his philosophy a professed Epicurean, he could, under no circumstances, have inspired any real love or admiration for the good and holy. But besides all

this, his moral and physical surroundings were such as
would have kept back a man of far purer and more
intense feelings from any stirring exhortation to
patriotism, or stinging rebuke of frivolity and vice.
And so, in a court which, beyond all other courts, was
given up wholly and entirely to the pursuit of the fleeting follies of the hour; in which all attempts to
shake off the golden chains of pleasure were met with
open ridicule or half-contemptuous praise; in which
the main object of each man's life was to float pleasantly,
if listlessly, with the current; where each day that had
witnessed the discovery of some new path of pleasure
was accounted well spent,—a court poet and a courtier
such as Horace had not the energy to strike out manfully
against the stream. One of the main aims of Augustus
was to hide the fetters in which he had bound the
nobles of the land,—to mould the Romans by persua-
sion and example, rather than to force their wills by
direct command. No ruler than he ever knew better
how seldom it is that men will fight to retain the substance, if only they are allowed to enjoy the form and
shadow of that which they profess to admire and to
love; how much easier it always is to govern men by
the dictates of fashion and custom, than to establish
a custom by law and ordinance. In this endeavour
to lead those whom a less shrewd politician might
have attempted to coerce, he found a most valuable
coadjutor in Horace. Contented by disposition, by
education a man of the world rather than a philosopher; a man with few pretensions to profound
learning or any great insight into the tenets of even

the Epicurean philosophy, of which he was a professed adherent,—Horace was yet sufficiently versed in the commonplaces of the sect to be able to clothe in *quasi* philosophical language his disparagement of political ambition, or his sneers at any indecorous vice or folly, while inculcating the precepts of the gardens, and setting forth the advantages of an unambitious life, undisturbed by any outbursts of temper or of misplaced zeal, a pursuit of pleasure chastened by temper, and bounded by the dictates of moderation. He was thus peculiarly fitted to be the preacher of this new life of Rome, of this golden age of tinsel and mediocrity. He was ever ready at the earliest hint of Mæcenas to divert, by a pleasant laugh, any threatened outburst of political ambition or republicanism that might yet linger about the court of his patron, or to scoff down any offensive and unbecoming display of old-fashioned boorishness, or of vulgar ostentation. Did Iccius prepare an expedition to the golden East to increase the store in his overflowing treasury,—he was pleasantly reminded how much more choiceworthy was the study of Socrates than any pomp of barbaric splendour; did Hirpinus or Grosphus yearn to play a more active part in the politics of the day, or seem to grow restless under his golden chain,—the poet was ready to contrast the quiet happiness of a voluptuary's life with the uncertainty and toil of that of the warrior or politician, filled as they were with anxieties and cares which the divine race of Iulus was alone fitted to support. Nor was Horace less ready to crush with a sar-

casm bordering on the licence of pasquinade the folly
of Rufillus, or the senseless extravagance of the *parvenu* Nasidienus. Even when, taking a more serious
view of life, he wrote as a moralist, or even as a religious reformer, it is difficult to believe that he is not
acting a part. When we read in one page " that the
gods live a life careless of mankind, and that if nature
works any wondrous woe on earth, it is not they who
send it down from heaven in their wrath," there is a
hollow ring in the words,—

> " Ye Romans, ye, though guiltless, shall
> Dread expiation make for all
>   The laws your sires have broke,
> Till ye repair with loving pains
> The gods' dilapidated fanes,
>   Their statues grimed with smoke !
>
> Ye rule the world because that ye
> Confess the gods' supremacy ;
>   Hence all your grandeur grows !
> The gods, in vengeance for neglect,
> Hesperia's wretched land have wrecked
>   Beneath unnumbered woes."
>   —III. Od. vi. (T. Martin.)

The rhythm, indeed, may be perfect, and the expressions such as to leave nothing to be desired ; but we
miss that impressiveness which nothing but the writer's
faith in what he says can give, however grandly and
sonorously his verses may roll in our ears. While
Horace is thus always a trifler on the surface of
life, opening up no deep questions, seldom really in

earnest either in praise or blame, Juvenal goes far
deeper, and is infinitely more vigorous and manly,
both in his thoughts and in his language. Nor is the
cause of this far to seek. In the days of Horace, despotism, tempered by the exquisite skill of Augustus,
seldom if ever wounded the susceptibilities of the most
jealous ; the forms of republicanism were carefully kept
up ; and it was ostensibly as the servant of the people
and of the senate that the emperor guided the wheels
of the state. And yet in that earlier day, even had
the real facts of personal rule been more openly displayed, people would still have acquiesced in them with
scarcely a murmur. Wearied out with the endless
and bloody disputes of half a century, there were few
Romans who were not ready to purchase rest and freedom from the chances of revolution at any cost which
did not bring with it a direct loss of personal dignity
or comfort. As long as he was allowed to give an
ostensibly independent vote in the divisions of the
senate, to force his advice on the ears of the emperor,
and even to make a show of calling him to account for
his action, the descendant of the Fabii or Cornelii was
satisfied to wear in silence the badge of political
slavery. Even the dregs of the city population were
gratified when their consent was asked (as Augustus
took care that it always should be asked) before the
consul was finally invested with the insignia of office,
albeit they knew too well that that consent could not
be refused. Rest was the cry of the nobles and of the
people, and rest it was that Augustus was able and
willing to provide.

" For ease he doth the gods implore
 Who, tossing on the wide
 Ægean billows, sees the black clouds hide
The moon, and the sure stars appear no more
 The shipman's course to guide.
For ease the sons of Thracia cry,
 In battle uncontrolled ;
 For ease the graceful-quivered Median bold,—
That ease which purple, Grosphus, cannot buy,
 Nor wealth of gems or gold.

For hoarded treasure cannot keep
 Disquietudes at bay,
. Nor can the consul's lictor drive away
The brood of dark solicitudes that sweep
 Round gilded ceilings gay."   —II. Od. vi.

But if the great Augustus once take his stand on the
Capitol, and look forth with benignant aspect on the
expectant world, all shall at once be changed, and the
desire of every heart shall be satisfied to the full.

" While Cæsar rules, no civil jar
 Nor violence our ease shall mar,
 Nor rage, which sword for carnage whets,
 And feuds 'twixt hapless towns begets.
 .   .   .   .   .   .

 And we, on working days and all
 Our days of feast and festival,
 Shall with our wives and children there,
 Approaching first the gods in prayer,
 Whilst jovial Bacchus' gifts we pour,
 Sing, as our fathers sang of yore,
 To Lybian flutes, which answer round
 Of chiefs for mighty worth renowned—
 Of Troy, Anchises, and the line
 Of Venus, evermore divine."   —IV. Od. xiv.

But this repose could only be purchased at the cost of a neglect of the most important events of the day—a price which was indeed willingly paid. And while bestowing on them a careless approval or a mere sentimental condemnation, the writers of the time were satisfied if they could rouse themselves into a forced and but half-real enthusiasm for the history of the glorious past. Their chains, wreathed with flowers, were not felt ; they had hearkened to the voice of the charmer, and the whole soul of Rome was lulled into a repose fatal to any greatness of aim or steadiness of purpose.

In the years that elapsed between the time of Horace and that of Juvenal, a great change had come over the political horizon. The cruelty and treachery of Tiberius had succeeded to the frankness and affability with which Augustus had always made it his aim to amuse his subjects, or rather his equals, as he delighted to call the patricians of Rome. But the cruelty and treachery of Tiberius might be borne, as being the manifestation of a character which, however misdirected and depraved, was yet strong, and had a foundation of qualities that might command respect. It was less easy to bear with the caprices of Caligula and his herd of actors, gladiators, and prostitutes. Claudius, though less depraved than either of his predecessors, could neither engage the affections nor deserve the esteem of his people, and died unlamented and unavenged when his wife sent him—

> " A palsied, bedrid sot, with gummy eyes
> And slavering lips, heels foremost to the skies."
> —Sat. vi. 622.

Even the caprice and tyranny of Nero were less insupportable than the senseless folly of a prince who could be so lost to all sense of dignity, and of that decorum which was in a Roman's eyes so indispensable to the good name of any public character, as to sing openly on the stage amid troops of hired actors and public slaves, and compete with the lowest foreigners for the applause of the mob of Athens or of Rome. How could even that majesty which surrounds a throne protect an emperor, if his every action proclaimed him fit only for a position that the very meanest of his subjects might hardly count an honourable way of life ?

> " Lo ! these the arts, the studies that engage
> The world's great master ! on a foreign stage
> To prostitute his voice for base renown,
> And ravish from the Greeks a parsley crown."
> —Sat. vii. 224.

The disgraceful scenes which followed thickly on each other during the brief reigns of Galba, Otho, and Vitellius, could not but open the eyes of the blindest and most self-complacent to the real facts of the case. No man could now even endeavour to persuade himself that he, as a Roman, was in any way less a slave to the emperor than the meanest sycophant of Greece or the most uncultured Mauritanian boor. Hence many who would have been satisfied with any salve to their dignity, however vain—with any veil to cover the iron hand that ruled them, however transparent that veil might be—felt themselves compelled, now that the last shred of disguise that had served to conceal their

real state had been rudely torn away, to vindicate their
honour by denunciations of tyranny, if not by plots
against the tyrant. The gilding which had decked
the bars of the cage had been worn away, and the
prisoner, though not more closely confined than before,
beat his wings against prison walls whose undisguised
restraint now first allowed its pressure to be felt. It
was this changed feeling that in part brought about
the change in the views on politics taken by Juvenal
as contrasted with Horace. Horace, as *par excellence*
the court poet, conspired with the head of the court to
make everything run pleasantly, to smooth down all
asperities. To expatiate on what was pleasant was his
cue, and to dwell rather on the minor follies of his
neighbours than on those vices which might bring real
discredit on the time and on the government. Juvenal,
though he lived at a time in many respects more de-
graded and less refined than that of Horace, had yet this
advantage, that he plainly saw the vices under which
men laboured, and did not shrink from naming them
openly, and from exhibiting them in their undisguised
hideousness—the first distressing but necessary step
towards compelling men to apply the suitable remedies. This seems to be the reason why Juvenal has
frequently been stigmatised as an immoral poet, and
unfavourably contrasted in this respect with Horace—
most unjustly, in our opinion. The truth is more
nearly this, that Juvenal, from his very hatred of vice,
is more frequently led into coarseness of expression
than Horace ; while the latter seems sometimes almost
to sympathise with vice while he stigmatises it, or at

all events to satirise more severely what was repulsive
or indecorous in the clownish folly of the boor, than
the refined but not less mischievous gallantry of the
man of fashion. In short, he would doubtless have ad-
hered to that most unfortunate dictum of Burke, when
he assigned as a reason for regretting the departure of
the age of chivalry the fact, that in those days "vice
itself had lost half its evil by losing all its grossness."

But we should be very wrong in attributing this
outward faultiness of expression to any inferiority in
his moral sense; rather let us say that, while Horace
was not wholly unwilling to strip vice of all its grossness, though to do so was to present it in a more baneful
if less repulsive form, his rival, with truer purpose and
more honest judgment, chose rather in his portraiture of
it to add to than to detract from the loathsome disease
that had aroused his indignation. The same action
might thus be represented under two wholly different
aspects. For while Horace, by the glamour of his un-
rivalled art, would present to his hearers a pleasant and
not ungraceful peccadillo, Juvenal would dash on a
few touches with a master-hand, which would startle
by the hideousness of crime where we had before seen
only a venial offence. Perhaps some one or two
instances, culled at random, will make our meaning
plainer. For example, when Horace would lay claim
to religious feeling, and takes upon himself to censure
the irreligion of the age, it is difficult to persuade one-
self that he is not writing to order; and even where he
proclaims the sovereignty of heaven, and rebukes the
godlessness of the times as the source of all the woes

of Rome, he does not conceal his belief in a blind fate superior to Jove himself, driving him on, and mocking the desires of men; nor can he entirely divest himself of a certain sympathy with those who would palliate their sins by accusing the injustice of heaven. Juvenal, on the other hand, earnestly proclaims the guidance of an omniscient and benevolent deity or deities. To them let man trust his fortunes :—

> " Their thoughts are wise, their dispensations just,
>   What best may profit or delight they know,
>   And real good for fancied bliss bestow :
>   With eyes of pity they our frailties scan ;
>   More dear to them than to himself is man."
>   —Sat. x. 347.

Again, Horace would laugh at conjugal infidelity, and dissuade from it as often dangerous in its results ; yet he appeals to no high moral law, but rather aims his shafts at the inconvenience of detection than at the sin of success. How different the feeling which prompted the line,—

> " Trebonius caught must lose both fame and name," —

from that which moved Juvenal when he wrote,—

> "Grant me a soul
> That reckons death a blessing, yet can bear
> Existence nobly with its weight of care ;
> That anger and desire alike restrains,
> And counts Alcides' toils and cruel pains
> Superior far to banquets, cruel nights,
> And all the Assyrian monarch's soft delights."

In the former passage we have indeed sound advice,

as far as it goes, but the motive merely such as might
be supplied by the most heartless man of the world—
such as Major Pendennis might have preached to his
nephew in Pall Mall; while in the latter we find precepts of morality set forth as high and disinterested as
those which guided the life of Zeno or Parmenides, of
Socrates or Plato.

When we come to compare these two writers as poets,
it will be no easy matter to light upon a common standard by which to measure their respective merits. No
two men could well be found whose genius is so completely different. Juvenal is a poet by virtue of his
fierce passions; of a loathing for vice which bears him,
as it were, beyond himself, and drives him, fit or unfit,
to pour forth his soul in a torrent of eloquent invective,
which cannot but bear the most phlegmatic hearer
along with it.

> "If nature will not verse command,
>   Still Indignation shall at least indite,
>   Such lines as I or Cluvienus write."
>   —Sat. i. 80.

Juvenal, in short, is a poet far more of the heart than
of the brain. Surrounded on all sides by openly triumphant vice, while he saw the righteous man everywhere begging his bread; writing amid scenes which
could not but make his heart bleed for his country,
amid tragedies, at the hearing of which a man's ears
might well tingle,—Juvenal had neither the time nor
the inclination to bestow such care on his writings as is
necessary to all poetry before it can really claim the admiration due to perfect execution. Horace might well

turn and turn again each metaphor, and polish to the utmost those sweet love-songs which he alone could write ; and pause and pause again till he had expressed each trite observation on human life, each panegyric on the old Republic, in language that can never be surpassed. Fabius, Fabricius, and Hannibal, Alcides and Romulus, were no eager claimants for praise or blame ; the fount of Bandusium, or the golden locks of Pyrrha's hair, were not the less bright because the odes in their honour lay year after year in the poet's desk. But how could one whose soul had indited the indignant patriotism of the third satire, or the lofty sarcasm of the sixth, while he, day after day, looked on the flagrant immorality of Roman society, bear to suppress the lines in which he scathes—

> " The slave-born slave-bred vagabond of Nile,
> Crispinus, both in birth and manners vile,
> Pacing in pomp with cloak of Tyrian dye,
> Changed oft a day for needless luxury."
> —Sat. i. 26.

Or again,—

> " The rich dame, who stanched her husband's thirst
> With generous wine, but—drugged it deeply first !
> And now, more dext'rous than Locusta, shows
> Her country friends the beverage to compose,
> And, 'midst the curses of the indignant throng,
> Bears, in broad day, the spotted corpse along."
> —Sat. i. 69.

We should thus be looking in his writings for what Juvenal never professed to give us, if we expected to find in them anything that could be compared to the

consummate art of the Odes of his predecessor. It was
not such minstrelsy that Juvenal had either the wish
or the power to imitate ; it was only as a satirist that
he took Horace as his model :—

> " And shall I feel that crimes like these require
>   The avenging strains of the Venusian lyre,
>   And not pursue them ?"
>
> —Sat. i. 52.

Yet even here it is not easy to compare the two
authors. Their aims and method were wholly different. Indeed, as far as we can judge from the description we have of Lucilius's manner, and from the fragments of his writings that remain, it is to him far
more than to Horace that we should compare Juvenal.

Their respective methods have thus been well described and contrasted by Persius :—

> " Yet old Lucilius never feared the times,
>   But lashed the city and dissected crimes ;
>   On Lupus, Mutius, poured his rage by name,
>   And broke his grinders on their bleeding fame.
>   And yet arch Horace, when he strove to mend,
>   Probed all the foibles of his smiling friend ;
>   Played lightly round and round the peccant part,
>   And won, unfelt, an entrance to his heart ;
>   Well skilled the follies of the crowd to trace,
>   And sneer with gay good-humour in his face."
>
> —Sat. i. 115.

With few exceptions, the Satires of Horace can
hardly be said to deserve the title that is given them.
They are rather witty discourses on the manners of the
day, or on the topics current in the town, written with

no definiteness of aim, but passing on from point to point as fancy led. Thus in one page Horace gives an amusing account of his education, in the next he indulges in a good-natured laugh at the philosophers of the time; again returning to himself, he tickles our fancy with an account of his journey to Brundusium, or of his adventure with a bore in the Sacred Way. But nowhere does he aim at being more than a good-natured if slightly cynical critic; and he laughed at vice as being vulgar and ungentlemanly, not as a foul stain on human nature. To Juvenal, on the other hand, we can most aptly apply his own description of Lucilius, and indeed it would be difficult to find one more appropriate to these poems :—

> "But when Lucilius, fired with virtuous rage,
> Waves his keen falchion o'er a guilty age,
> The conscious villain shudders at his sin,
> And burning blushes speak the pangs within ;
> Cold drops of sweat from every member roll,
> And growing terrors harrow up his soul."
>
> —Sat. i. 165.

CHAPTER IV.

MORALS AT ROME.

THE avarice and venality everywhere rampant at Rome —the influx of new customs and of new religions—the deterioration of the old Roman type of character, and the substitution for it of an insidious compound of refinement and hypocrisy, of mental culture combined with moral degradation—the sudden rise of low-born foreigners to the highest places in the Empire through a vile pandering to the appetites of their rulers—the growth of a spurious philosophy, which, under a specious show of morality, tended to obliterate the eternal distinctions between right and wrong,—such are some of the main faults of his age which it was Juvenal's self-appointed task to lash with no sparing hand. Of all the sights which met his gaze at Rome, there is not one that seems to have jarred more sharply on his whole nature than the high and utterly undeserved position reached by more than one foreigner, either himself an emancipated slave, or if not this, at least the son of one who had held such a condition, by the most ignoble of all roads. Conservative to the backbone, and a true Roman in sentiment and by birth, it is clear that Juvenal is speaking straight from his heart when he denounces the affected manners and insolent assurance of Crispinus—"the slave-born slave-bred vagabond of Nile"—or the ostentatious display of his newly-acquired riches by one

> "That oft since manhood first appeared
> Has trimmed th' exuberance of his sounding beard;"
> —Sat. i. 25.

winning their way upwards to wealth and power, not by force of statesmanship or a fine sense of honour— by the judge's discrimination or the soldier's courage —but by pleasing manners, and by their insight into the mysteries of the kitchen and of the cellar, of the theatre and of the circus. These foreign courtiers pointed out a road to affluence and dignity which their Roman competitors were not slow to follow. Besides, this was the only course by which a Roman of noble birth might hope to be permitted to live on in safety, and preserve his family from destruction. Honest advice—the outspoken opinion of a friendly censor—was fatal at Cæsar's court. So Crispus knew. He, wise in time, dragged out a life of comfort, if without honour or self-esteem: Crispus,

> "Of gentle manners and persuasive tongue:
> None fitter to advise the lord of all,
> Had that pernicious pest, whom thus we call,
> Allowed a friend to soothe his savage mood,
> And give him counsel wise at once and good.
> But who shall dare this liberty to take,
> When, every word you hazard, life's at stake?

Though but of stormy summers, showery springs—
For tyrants' ears, alas ! are ticklish things.
So did the good old man his tongue restrain ;
Nor strove to stem the torrent's force in vain.
Not one of those who by no fears deterred,
Spoke the free soul, and truth to life preferred.
He temporised—thus fourscore summers fled,
Even in that court, securely o'er his head."
                                        —Sat. iv. 80.

Yet even such self-debasement was not always rewarded by success. The emperor of that vicious court was quick to suspect a superior ; a suspicion to be followed by jealousy, a jealousy soon fatal to its object. Too common, alas ! must have been the fate of the noble yet timorous citizen, who, in spite of all disguises, was, like Acilius, detected, and who

          " Unjustly fell, in early years,
A victim to the tyrant's jealous fears :
But long ere this were hoary hairs become
A prodigy among the great at Rome ;
Hence had I rather own my humble birth,
Frail brother of the giant brood, to Earth.
Poor youth ! in vain the ancient sleight you try ;
In vain, with frantic air and ardent eye,
Fling every robe aside, and battle wage
With bears and lions on the Alban stage.
All see the trick; and, spite of Brutus' skill,
There are who count him but a driveller still ;
Since, in his days, it cost no mighty pains
To outwit a prince, with much more beard than brains."
                                        —Sat. iv. 95.

Yet even more unendurable than the insolent airs of a Crispinus or the ostentatious wealth of Matho, or the many other parasites and voluptuaries who plume themselves on outshining the ancient families of the Palatine, is the outrageous conduct of Marius. He, though found guilty of extortion in the government of his province, escaped all real punishment by his shameless bribery of the court; and now, setting infamy at defiance, revels in luxury in his easy exile, while his late subjects and prosecutors bemoan them over their dearly-bought victory of the judgment-hall. With him we may well class those perjured guardians

> " Who, proud with impious gains,
> Choke up the streets, too narrow for their trains ;
> Whose wards by want betrayed to crimes are led,
> Too vile to name, too fulsome to be read."
>
> —Sat. i. 45.

Yet, in spite of all, they are able, by the connivance of venal and avaricious judges, to brave it openly in the sight of Rôme and of the world :—

> " Wouldst thou to honour and preferments climb ?
> Be bold in mischief, dare some mighty crime.
> On guilt's broad base thy towering fortunes raise,
> For virtue starves on universal praise."
>
> —Sat. i. 72.

It is this same avarice that has led to the present reckless extravagance of the gambling-table : gambling, which, though checked by the strictest laws, is now so prevalent that men go forth accompanied by their stewards and treasurers, prepared to stake their whole livelihood—all their family estates and ancient heirlooms—on the fall of the dice, though they grudge the

cost of a cloak for their slave who is shivering in the
cold.   Even the ostentation so dear to the heart of
the *parvenu* is checked by avarice.   But who shall
wonder at this, seeing that it is now according to their
wealth that men take their social position in the state,
not according to their lineage or their noble qualities?
nay more, even in the courts of law it is the same.
There, if anywhere, one would think that moral qualities would rank first ; but no !

> "Produce at Rome your witness : let him boast
>   The sanctity of Berecynthia's host,*
> Of Numa, or of him,† whose zeal divine
> Snatched pale Minerva from her blazing shrine.
> To search his rent-roll first the bench prepares,
> His honesty employs their latest cares :
> What table does he keep, what slaves maintain,
> And what, they ask, and where is his domain ?
> These weighty matters known, his faith they rate,
> And square his probity to his estate."
>
> —Sat. iii. 137.

Yet worse than this, children, taught by their parents
to shun every other vice, are actually brought up to
pursue this fault of avarice as though it were a praiseworthy quality :—

> " For this grave vice, assuming Virtue's guise,
>   Seems Virtue's self to undiscerning eyes.

* "Berecynthia's host :"—P. Cornelius Scipio Nasica, who,
for his great merits, and the exemplary conduct of his life, was
chosen by the senate to escort the image of Cybele when it was
brought from Pessinus to Rome.   Cybele is here called Berecynthia, from the name of a mountain in Phrygia where she was
worshipped.

† Æneas, who rescued the Palladium from the flames of Troy.

> The miser hence a frugal man they name ;
> And hence they follow with their whole acclaim
> The griping wretch who strictlier guards his store,
> Than if the Hesperian dragon kept the door.
> Add that the vulgar, still a slave to gold,
> The worthy in the wealthy man behold ;
> And reasoning from the fortune he has made,
> Hail him a perfect master in his trade."
> —Sat. xiv. 109.

It was to the influx of Greeks and other foreigners that this was to a great extent due. These conquered countries no doubt had brought in a culture and refinement of manners quite new to their victors ; but along with this culture were introduced a train of those vices that are almost invariably found among vanquished races—mean, low, sneaking vices, very different to those prevalent among a harder and more warlike race, such as were their Roman masters. And yet, by virtue perhaps of this very weakness, they have a strong, not to say irresistible, tendency to lead their captors captive, and stupefy their minds with the insinuating enervating poison which is their essential character. This process may be traced recurring again and again in the history of central Asia, from the earliest times to the present day. There one horde after another descends from the hill-country, conquering the enervated inhabitants of the plains, only in their own turn to form part of the same cycle of deterioration, decay, and subjugation, being ensnared by the luxurious and effeminate customs of those whom they had vanquished.

So now in Rome the ancient virtues of the simple countrymen of Mars, choked by the overgrowth of

foreign habits and of foreign morals, served but as a
foundation on which these new-fangled importations
might take a firmer growth, as a substratum of
intensity to the pernicious whole :—

" Whence shall those prodigies of vice be traced ?
    From wealth, my friend,"—

from that eager, restless making haste to be rich which
is the peculiar curse of our day,—a passion which,
strong by nature and sucked in by children with their
very mother's milk, is yet further fostered by the teaching of the tutor, by the precept as by the example of
the parent,—as witness the advice here enforced on a
son by his own father :—

" Hides, unguents, mark me, boy, are equal things,
    And gain smells sweet from whatsoe'er it springs.
    This golden sentence, which the powers of heaven,
    Which Jove himself might glory to have given,
    Will never, never, from your thoughts, I trust,—
    ' None question whence it comes, but come it must.'
    This, when the lisping race a farthing ask,
    Old women set them as a previous task ;
    The wondrous apophthegm all run to get,
    And learn it sooner than their alphabet."

What wonder, then, if the old simplicity of life,
that helped to develop the virtues of honesty, generosity, courage, and steadfastness of purpose, the ancient crown and glory of the conquering race of
Romulus, are rapidly vanishing from among us ? How
can we expect such qualities to be cherished, now that
a man takes rank not by his own intrinsic worth, but

by the amount of his account with his banker, by the number of acres that he owns? Every day you may see your slaveling lord take precedence of the scion of some princely house, simply because "more ground to him alone pertains than Rome possessed in Numa's pious reign!"

> "Since *then* the veteran, whose brave breast was gored
> By the fierce Pyrrhic or Molossian sword,
> Hardly received, for all his service past,
> And all his wounds, two acres at the last,
> The meed of toil and blood! yet never thought
> His country thankless or his pains ill bought.
> For then his little glebe, improved with care,
> Largely supplied, with vegetable fare,
> The good old man, the wife in childbed laid,
> And four hale boys that round the cottage played,
> Three free-born, one a slave ; while on the board
> Huge porringers, with wholesome pottage stored,
> Smoked for their elder brothers, who were now,
> Hungry and tired, expected from the plough.
> Two acres will not now, so changed our times,
> Afford a garden-plot ; and hence our crimes !
> For not a vice that taints the human soul
> More frequent points the sword or drugs the bowl
> Than the dire lust of an ' untamed estate.'
> Since he who covets wealth disdains to wait:
> Law threatens, conscience calls,—yet on he hies,
> And this he silences, and that defies ;
> Fear, shame, he bears down all, and with loose rein
> Sweeps headlong o'er the alluring paths of gain !"
>   —Sat. xiv. 161.

And how could this be a subject of wonder, however much it might alarm and distress the lover of his country, when the possession of a huge estate was the one thing indispensable to any man who aimed at making himself a name,—when every avenue by which a man might hope to rise to eminence, or even to retain a position of mediocrity, was closed to him who refused to burn his incense as a devotee to the vile money-worship of the day? Flattery, meanness, hypocrisy, sycophancy, cruelty, rapacity, low cunning, and a tongue speaking false things,—such were the qualities which would fix a man's footsteps firmly on the rounds of the ladder leading to wealth and social position. The vision which the fancy of Maud's lover pictured to his heated imagination was then realised, and more than realised, in Rome :—

" *Those* were the days to advance the works of the men of
    the mind,
When who but a fool would have faith in a tradesman's
    ware or his word ?

   .   .   .   .   .

Sooner or later I, too, may passively take the print
Of the golden age—why not ? I have neither hope nor
    trust ;
May make my heart as a millstone, set my face as a flint,
Cheat and be cheated, and die—who knows ? we are ashes
    and dust."

For these are days—

" When only the ledger lives, and only not all men lie."

" What's Rome to me ? " exclaims the poet's friend ;
" what business have I there,—

    " I who can neither lie nor falsely swear,
      Nor praise my patron's undeserving rhymes,

> Nor yet comply with him, nor with his times?
> I neither will nor can prognosticate
> To the young gaping heir his father's fate.
> Others may aid the adulterer's vile design,
> And bear the insidious gift and melting line.
> For want of these town virtues, thus alone
> I go, conducted on my way by none."
>
> —Sat. iii. 41.

But though strangers poured into Rome from every nation, as to a common mart, for their hateful wares,— though

> " Sicyon, and Amydos, and Alaband,
>   Tralles, and Samos, and a thousand more
>   Thrive on his indolence, and daily pour
>   Their starving myriads forth ; "
>
> —Sat. iii. 69.

yet it is from Greece that the great high priests of lust and iniquity of every kind come most fully equipped for their task,—most thoroughly initiated in all the ways which lead men insensibly to glide in flower-dressed barks down that stream whose end is the blackness of death, though its banks are gay and its waters sweet. Yes,—the home of Socrates and of Demosthenes has now fallen so low that even the coarsest Roman may well cast his stone at her, as at the great nurse and producer of all that is most vile on earth. A consummate master in all the arts which may pander to this luxurious age, the Greek knows but too well how to make himself acceptable, or even necessary, to his patron :—

> " A flattering, cringing, treacherous, artful race,
>   Of torrent tongue and never-blushing face,

A Protean tribe one knows not what to call,
Which shifts to every form, and shines in all,—
Grammarian, painter, augur, rhetorician,
Rope-dancer, conjurer, fiddler, and physician ;
All trades his own your hungry Greekling counts,
And bid him mount the sky, the sky he mounts." *
                                        —Sat. iii. 75.

The drift of this passage will be familiar to many of
our readers, from Dryden's character of the Earl of
Shaftesbury in his " Absalom and Achitophel," to
which it bears a strange similarity.   Indeed, we can
hardly doubt that those lines were written by him
with Juvenal's description of the Greek ringing in
his ears :—

" Some of their chiefs were princes of the land ;
  In the first rank of these did Zimri stand ;
  A man so various, that he seemed to be
  Not one, but all mankind's epitome :
  Stiff in opinions, always in the wrong ;
  Was everything by starts, and nothing long ;
  But, in the course of one revolving moon,
  Was chymist, fiddler, statesman, and buffoon."

Nor did it now avail the Roman client that he was
ready to humble himself in the very dust, to accept
any office however menial, to be the mouthpiece of
any flattery however fulsome.   He might indeed cringe
as low as his Greek rival, but he had not the graceful
manners and the ready wit that could alone make this
debasement of himself acceptable :—

* A less complimentary version of the line will occur to many
of our readers :—

   " And bid him ' go to hell'—to hell he goes."

> " We too can cringe as low and praise as warm,
>   But flattery from the Greek alone has charm ; "
>   —Sat. iii. 92.

for " Greece is a theatre where all are players," and
not one of its children but could easily supplant, by
the plausibility of his manners and his natural apti-
tude for deceit, the most experienced Roman parasite.
As in the time of Pericles, so now, the Greeks, but
especially the Athenians, surpassed all men in the ver-
satility of their genius, and their power of adapting
themselves to each circumstance as it might arise.
Thus the same qualities which, in their more glorious
days, had guided them to the highest place in political
life and in the arts, could now but lead them to explore the lowest depths of servility and moral degradation.

Perhaps even worse than these other innovations
were those that had been introduced into the religious
sphere of Roman life. The national religion of Rome,
in its proper form, differed from that of the Greek in
being of a far more abstract and ideal nature,—not
appealing to men's minds by a concrete personification
of that which they worshipped, still less by a corporeal
representation of the deity, but binding the soul of the
worshipper to an adoration of that which was spiritual
and universal in nature. Without any real sympathy
for the allegorical mythology which was nevertheless
soon grafted on it from the more artistic worship of
Greece, this purer form of religion lost all hold on its
followers as soon as that earnest belief which was indispensable to its continuance began to be called in ques-

tion by the growing scepticism of the times. When its
binding force had thus been weakened, it no longer had
any power to resist the influx of all the foreign forms
of worship which poured into Italy from the surrounding nations. Among these, those which struck most deep
root into the heart of Rome were the element-worship
of the Syrian and the mysterious cult of the deities of
the Nile. The pure religion of the Jews seems also
to have had powerful attractions for the imagination
of the Romans; and though it was seldom, if ever,
rightly understood by them—though its followers seem
sometimes even to have been involved with the Egyptian
priesthood in the punishment of a common proscrip-
tion, as being disturbers of the peace of the city and
as relaxing the purity of female manners—it frequently
met with an amount of consideration at the hands of
the government which was but seldom granted to foreign
creeds. In the age of Juvenal, however, it was from the
Nile and from the Orontes, above all other places,
that issued forth the superstitions which were the most
fatal to purity in manners and to faith in religion.
Along with these came in troops of fortune-tellers from
Armenia or from Commagene, of Chaldæan astrologers
and of Syrian seers, who, at one fell sweep, took a firm
hold on the whole Roman people, but especially on the
women. The descendants of the ancient matrons of
Rome, types of modesty and matronly décorum, claim-
ing even in the days of Cæsar to be not only free from
all guilt but also above all suspicion, now gladly em-
braced these foreign superstitions as an easy means of
indulging their every passion. Guided by some Ara-

barces, the wife would roam the streets by night, in open contempt of common decency and of her husband's orders. A slave to superstition, she would shrink at nothing which the object of her prayers might command :—

> " Should milk-white Io bid, from Meroë's isle
> She'd fetch the sunburnt waters of the Nile
> To sprinkle in her fane ; for she, it seems,
> Has heavenly visitations in her dreams.
> Mark the pure soul with whom the gods delight
> To hold high converse at the noon of night !
> For this she cherishes above the rest,
> Her Io's favourite priest, a knave professed,
> A holy hypocrite, who strolls abroad
> With his Anubis, his dog-headed god."
>
> —Sat. vi. 526.

The same account might stand for the wild votaries of Bellona or of Anubis, of Osiris or of Cybele. All these had the one common quality of reckless disregard of that which was by others deemed most binding, an intolerance of any restraint which might be placed on the whim of the hour. Closely connected with this degeneracy in religion was that further progress in iniquity on which we have elsewhere dwelt,—the wholesale poisoning of husbands by their wives, and of fathers by their children.

CHAPTER V.

THE same practical cast of intellect which has made the Romans the great lawgivers of all ages, which has spread their code throughout the civilised world, has had other not less marked if less important effects on their social history.

It is to this prevailing mode of thought that we must attribute the fact, that no original philosopher of any mark ever rose among the Romans. Their writers had indeed remarkable clearness of perception, and the power of setting forth with great force and accuracy any idea that they had once fully grasped in their own minds; but beyond this the Roman did not go. He had neither the wish nor the ability to solve the many metaphysical problems which lay in his way—to resolve into their ultimate elements the many complex psychological phenomena with which it was necessary to grapple before the superstructure of Ethics could be based on a firm foundation. Such questions were attractive to the Greeks, and to them he left them, content to draw his axioms at second-hand from the vast repertory which had been amassed since the days of Socrates, and to build them without question into his own edifice.

Such a philosopher is Juvenal : or, if we may take his own account of his philosophical lore as accurate, he was even less instructed than most Roman writers on the subject in the tenets and opinions of the various schools of philosophy. Hear him as he prepares to give advice and consolation to a repining friend :—

> " Hear in turn what I propose,
> To mitigate, if not to heal your woes ;
> I, who no knowledge of the schools possess,
> Cynic, or Stoic, differing but in dress.
> Or thine, calm Epicurus, whose pure mind
> To one small garden every wish confined.
> In desperate cases able doctors fee,
> But trust your pulse to Philip's boy—or me."
>
> —Sat. xiii. 120.

Juvenal then goes on to point to the everyday life that surrounded them, to ask in what way his friend thought himself worse off than many of his neighbours, on what grounds he claimed exemption from such misfortunes as are part of the common lot of mankind. No high flights of philosophy do we see here, but plain common-sense ; the advice of a shrewd and kindly man, such as Horace's Ofella might have given.

One thing that we may notice in the passage quoted above, is a pretty obvious disparagement of the teachings of professed philosophers. Juvenal seems, in fact, to have looked with considerable suspicion on the professors of the various schools, as being mere hypo-

crites, who hoped to be able to accomplish their vile
purposes behind the shield of a sanctified life unde-
tected, or at all events with comparative impunity:—

> "Turn to their schools :—yon grey professor see,
> Smeared with the sanguine stains of perfidy !
> That tutor most accursed his pupil sold !
> That Stoic sacrificed his friend to gold !
> A true-born Grecian ! littered on the coast,
> Where the Gorgonian hack* a pinion lost."
> —Sat. iii. 114.

Though he thus declined to enroll himself under any
sect,—

> "To swear obedience to a guide's behests,"—

the bias of Juvenal's mind had yet an obvious prepos-
session towards the doctrines and tenets of the Stoics.
This was the only school of philosophy which ever took
a firm hold on Roman society. There is indeed an
apparent exception to this statement in the history of
the closing years of the Republic, and of those which
witnessed the foundation of the Empire. But the
Epicurism which then spread so rapidly through Italy
had no real foundation—did not call forth to itself the
deeper sympathies even of its professed adherents.
The movement was rather political than philosophical,
and had its rise in the desire of men to find a plausible
reasoning with which to delude both themselves and
others into the belief that the reason why they thus
abandoned all interest in political life was not their

---

* "Gorgonius caballus ;" a periphrasis for "Pegasus," who is
said to have alighted on Mount Helicon.

own subjection to a master who would brook no rivalry and no equals, but the advice of a calm and chastened judgment bidding them abandon all such cares and anxieties, as things which brought but trouble and weariness of spirit, and interfered with man's true end, —an intelligent pursuit of happiness.

Stoicism, on the contrary, was in perfect harmony with the real instinct of every true Roman,—the desire to be up and doing. For though, theoretically, this sect set before men an aim of immaculate perfection, the attainment of which alone was in any way praiseworthy, while that which fell below this perfection by however small a degree was utterly and entirely bad, yet its actual working, as modified by the practical genius of the Roman, was to recognise each step towards a good life as a distinct and tangible gain; while it asserted boldly that virtue was its own reward, that no wicked man could be happy, however successful in his wickedness :—

> " Man, wretched man, whene'er he stoops to sin,
> Feels, with the act, a strong remorse within—
> 'Tis the first vengeance : conscience tries the cause,
> And vindicates the violated laws ;
> Though the bribed Prætor at their sentence spurn.
> And falsify the verdict of the Urn." *
>
> —Sat. xiii. 1.

Juvenal is never wearied of dwelling on this great

* The Urn, that is, into which the votes of acquittal or condemnation were put by the *judices,* or jury, at a criminal trial, and which was afterwards inspected by the prætor or magistrate.

doctrine, and of repeating it again and again in slightly different forms :—

> " Virtue alone is true nobility.
> Oh, give me inborn worth ! dare to be just,
> Firm to your word and faithful to your trust ;
> These praises hear, at least deserve to hear,
> I grant your claim, and recognise the peer."
>
> —Sat. viii. 24.

Hence there is something above and beyond the mere fruition of life, and this it is which we must treasure up beyond all else :—

> " Be brave, be just ; and when your country's laws
> Call you to witness in a dubious cause,
> Though Phalaris plant his bull before your eye,
> And, frowning, dictate to your lips the lie,
> Think it a crime no tears can e'er efface,
> To purchase safety with compliance base ;
> At honour's cost a feverish span extend,
> And sacrifice for life life's only end.
> Life ! 'tis not life : who merits death is dead,
> Though Gauran oysters for his feasts be spread,
> Though his limbs drip with exquisite perfume,
> And the late rose around his temples bloom ! "
>
> —Sat. viii. 80.

A corollary to this doctrine is clearly the following. No mere misfortune can ever call for exceeding bitter sorrow. As long as the man preserves himself from contamination of that which is foul, he cannot reach any very low depth of woe. By his own act, by his own voluntary desertion of the true aim of life, and by that alone, is it possible that a man should drink his cup of misery to the dregs.

The want of happiness, so prevalent, is thus the natural consequence of the inherent blindness of men. By it they are led to pursue eagerly the unreal phantoms of wealth, rank, power, and so forth, while neglecting that which alone can satisfy the wants of the soul, man's godlike part. If men could but see what is really their chief good, we should no longer hear on every side prayers offered up for all those idle accoutrements of the body which may indeed be enjoyed, but often bring only dissatisfaction to their owners, and can at all events be dispensed with without inconvenience, while the *man* himself—he for whom all these are desired—is passed over as though he were merely a lay figure on which these paraphernalia might be set off to the greatest advantage. Yet who shall wonder at the senseless folly of mankind if he do but consider their education? From his earliest youth the one precept dinned most assiduously into the ears of the Roman child is —get unto thyself wealth, and all other things shall follow :—

" None question whence it come, but come it must."
—Sat. xiv. 117.

Later on, when the child has grown into the boy, he goes to school, but still the teaching is equally faulty. What shall it profit a man to know—

" Who nursed Anchises ; from what country came
   The step-dame of Archemorus, what her name ;
   How long Acestes flourished, and what store
   Of generous wine the Phrygians from him bore ? "
—Sat. vii. 234.

Or to be able with all the subtleness of a master in the
schools to balance, point by point, the conduct of Hannibal's affairs, and to be able to decide—

> " Whether 'twere right
> To take advantage of the general fright,
> And march to Rome ; or by the storm alarmed,
> And all the elements against him armed,
> The dangerous expedition to delay,
> And lead his harassed troops some other way."
> —Sat. vii. 161.

With the natural tendency of all men to be hurried
into that vice opposite to the one which they wish to
shun, Juvenal carried his disregard of physical science
into a truly Socratic extreme. Seeing the excessive
weight given to questions, interesting, indeed, but not
indispensable to the conduct of a good and honest life,
he would entirely neglect every science except that of
Ethics :—

> " Whip me the fool who marks how Atlas soars
> O'er every hill on Mauritania's shores,
> Yet sees no difference 'twixt the coffer's hoards
> And the poor pittance a small purse affords ! "
> —Sat. xi. 23.

In this condemnation of useless knowledge Juvenal
would seem to include all mythological lore, whether
imported from Greece or of native growth. Though
he does not speak of them in the same tone of con-
temptuous hatred which he uses with regard to the
gods of Syria or of Egypt, we may yet trace in his
manner a good-natured and patronising tone when he

speaks of Jupiter or Mars, of Juno or Venus, very different to that which a true believer would deem fit to use : very different to that which he himself uses when speaking of the unknown and beneficent god who guides the affairs of mortals :—

> "Whate'er they [Chaldeans] say, with reverence she receives,
> As if from Hammon's secret forth it came ;
> Since Delphi now, if we may credit fame,
> Gives no responses, and a long dark night
> Conceals the future hour from mortal sight."
>
> —Sat. vi. 553.

Or again, speaking of the golden age :—

> " There was indeed a time
> When the rude natives of this happy clime
> Cherished such dreams : 'twas ere the king of heaven
> To change his sceptre for a scythe was driven ;
> Ere Juno yet the sweets of love had tried,
> Or Jove advanced beyond the cares of Ide.
> 'Twas when no gods indulged in sumptuous feasts,
> No Ganymede, no Hebe served the guests ;
> No Vulcan, with his sooty labours foul,
> Limped round, officious, with the nectared bowl ;
> But each in private dined : 'twas when the throng
> Of godlings now beyond the scope of song,
> The courts of heaven in spacious ease possest,
> And with a lighter load poor Atlas prest.
> Ere Neptune's lot the watery world obtained,
> Or Dis and his Sicilian consort reigned ;
> Ere Tityus and his ravening bird were known,
> Ixion's wheel, or Sisyphus's stone :
> While yet the Shades confessed no tyrant's power,
> And all below was one Elysian bower ! "
>
> —Sat. xiii. 38.

As a moral teacher Juvenal takes up a high standpoint. Virtue alone is true happiness, is alone worthy of our earnest pursuit. But this virtue, in what does it consist; how are we to attain to it? Briefly, by doing unto others as we would that others should do unto us. Such conduct may indeed fail to meet with its due reward, yet in the long-run it will usually deserve and obtain the esteem and kindly offices of your fellow-men. But even if this be not the case, that inward peace of mind which no man can take away is sure to follow an honest endeavour after that which is right, even as the contrary course will most surely be punished by the tortures of a violated conscience. We have a memorable example of the soothing power of conscious uprightness in the death of Socrates, cheerful under the most grievous wrongs :—

> " That old man by sweet Hymettus' hill,
>   Who drank the poison with unruffled soul,
>   And dying, from his foes withheld the bowl."
>   —Sat. xiii. 185.

Do not then, O man, if thou hast suffered any wrong at the hand of a false friend, consider it as anything very strange or grievous ; still less allow thyself to be carried away by a spirit of anger or revenge, and so lose thine own peace of mind. Rather give him over to his own conscience ; his punishment will be greater than any thou couldst have called down on him :—

> " Trust me, no tortures which the poets feign
>   Can match the fierce, the unutterable pain,
>   He feels, who, night and day devoid of rest,
>   Carries his own accuser in his breast."
>   —Sat. xiii. 196.

Nay more,—

> " In the eye of heaven a wicked deed
> Devised, is done ;"
>
> —Sat. xiii. 209.

and even the intended, though unperpetrated, wickedness shall have its own reward. While for him who
goes beyond the desire, and brings his purpose to actual
accomplishment, retributive justice will surely lie in
wait :—

> "This thou shalt see ; and while thy voice applauds
> The dreadful justice of the offended gods,
> Reform thy creed, and, with an humble mind,
> Confess that heaven is neither deaf nor blind."
>
> —Sat. xiii. 247.

But how is this justice to be reached ? How shall
our children learn to eschew the evil and to choose the
good ? By example, answers the poet—by the reform
of your own sinful practices, of your own wicked lives,
ye that are fathers and mothers in Rome ! How can
ye hope for a chaste and noble offspring, when on
every side your children look on sights too foul for
words to tell ?—

> " Swift from the roof where youth, Fuscinus, dwell,
> Immodest sights, immodest sounds expel ;
> The place is sacred ; far, far, hence remove,
> Ye venal votaries of illicit love !
> Ye dangerous knaves who pander to be fed,
> . And sell yourselves to infamy for bread !
> Reverence to children as to heaven is due :
> When you would then some darling sin pursue,
> Think that your infant offspring eyes the deed,
> And let the thought abate your guilty speed ;

> Back from the headlong steep your steps entice,
> And check you tottering on the verge of vice."
> —Sat. xiv. 44.

An evil habit, when once formed, is with difficulty broken off; and the child will most certainly rather follow the example of the parent if he sees him indulging in luxury, than his precept when he bids him choose the narrow and difficult path that leads to virtue. If the father gambles or spends his fortune on the luxuries of the table, will not his son be a dicer and a glutton? If he sees his father cruelly maltreat his slaves, of what avail will be all precepts to gentleness and humanity? Or how can the daughter of a licentious mother become a chaste and faithful wife?—

> " One youth, perhaps, formed of superior clay,
>   And warmed by Titan with a purer ray,
> May dare to slight proximity of blood,
> And, in despite of nature, to be good :
> One youth,—the rest the beaten pathway tread,
> And blindly follow where their fathers led."
> —Sat. xiv. 33.

We may trace a progressive change in Juvenal's moral being, and a sustained advance from his earlier to his later writings. At first he can see nothing but what is evil. Like David before him, he thinks that " there is none that doeth good, no, not one." The very philosophers who aspire to lead mankind are murderers and perjured witnesses ; nay, they add this to their other faults, that they are hypocrites as well as debauchees. The present days are wholly corrupt, and it is only in the far-distant past that we can see traces of a purity and virtue now long forgotten. Now, alas ! it is neither by noble birth or noble conduct, by genius or by virtue, that men rise. The caprice of a blind fate drives us hither and thither, and determines our position in life :—

> " Oh, there's a difference, friend, beneath what sign
> We spring to light, or friendly or malign !
> Fortune is all : she, as the fancy springs,
> Makes kings of pedants and of pedants kings.
> For what were Tullius and Ventidius,* say,
> But great examples of the wondrous sway
> Of stars, whose mystic influence alone
> Bestows on captives triumphs, slaves a throne ? "
>
> —Sat. vii. 194.

Soon, however, this pessimist view of the affairs of men is modified. Strive, cries the poet, to make yourself a name ; rise from the lowly station in which your fortune may have placed you ! What though you have no ancient blood in your veins ?—you may well build yourself an honourable reputation :—

> " Virtue alone is true nobility."

See then that you aim at this alone, and value not your life above that which alone can give to your life any real value. Men, indeed, may sometimes be ruined by the will of God, but such ruin will never come undeservedly. It is because men so often aim, not at virtue, but only at the reputation which it brings,

---

* Servius Tullius, who rose from a servile position to be king of Rome ; and P. Ventidius Bassus, who, starting in life as a hirer of mules, was taken up by Julius Cæsar, and became successively tribune and prætor, pontifex and consul.

that we see them fail so miserably. God loves men, and would always, did their vices or their folly permit it, bring them to happiness and honour. Be brave, then, be honest and diligent ; then shall victory most assuredly crown your efforts. Nor need we look far for examples of the truth of what I here lay down. How often in the history of Rome have men of humble birth come forth in time of danger, and, nobly risking all, even to the death, or disgrace worse than death itself, stood between their country and defeat, and built themselves a glorious name ! Nor, alas ! is the opposite case to this unknown. Some of Rome's proudest sons have ere now by their own acts sunk themselves into such a depth of infamy as to be ready to bear the flaming torch of rapine into their country's breast :—

" Cethegus, Catiline ! whose ancestors
    Were nobler born, were higher ranked, than yours ?
    Yet ye conspired, with more than Gallic hate,
    To wrap in midnight flames this helpless state,
    On men and gods your barbarous rage to pour,
    And deluge Rome with her own children's gore,—
    Horrors which called indeed for vengeance dire,
    For the pitched coat and stake and mouldering fire !
    But Tully watched, your league in silence broke,
    And crushed your impious arms, without a stroke.
    Yes, he, poor Arpine, of no name at home,
    And scarcely ranked among the knights at Rome,
    Secured the trembling town, placed a firm guard
    In every street, and toiled in every ward :
    And thus, within the walls, the *gown* obtained
    More fame for Tully than Octavius gained
    At Actium and Philippi, from a sword
    Drenched in the eternal stream by patriots poured :

For Rome, free Rome, hailed him with loud acclaim
The ' Father of his Country,'—glorious name !
Another Arpine, trained the ground to till,
Tired of the plough, forsook his native hill,
And joined the camp, where, if his adze were slow,
The vine-twig whelked his back with many a blow ;
And yet, when the fierce Cimbri threatened Rome
With swift and scarcely evitable doom,
This man, in the dread hour, to save her rose,
And turned the impending ruin on her foes !

.   .   .   .

The Decii were plebeians ! mean their name,
And mean the parent stock from which they came ;
Yet they devoted, in the trying hour,
Their heads to earth and each infernal power,
And by that solemn act redeemed from fate
Auxiliars, legions, all the Latian state,
More prized than those they saved, in Heaven's just esti-
    mate !
And him who graced the purple that he wore
(The last good king of Rome), a bondmaid bore !"
                       —Sat. viii. 230.

Men talk of Fortune as though she barred the way.
But what is Fortune?—a mere idle name, to him who
has the courage to meet and wrestle with her :—

    " The path to peace is virtue. We should see,
      If wise, O Fortune, nought divine in thee :
      But we have deified a name alone,
      And fixed in heaven thy visionary throne."
                       —Sat. x. 263.

In his succeeding Satires we can see how Juvenal lays
down what we might almost call a complete ethical system. He shows what virtue is, and how by habit the

practice of it gradually becomes easy and natural to man. Especially we may notice how he forbids cruelty to slaves, grasping fully the Stoical doctrine of the equality of all men. " I am a man," he says with Terence, "and think that there is nothing human but claims my sympathies." Hence, how detestable an example the father sets before his son when he punishes the slightest offence of his attendant with savage severity !—

> " Does Rutilus inspire a generous mind,
>   Prone to forgive, and to slight errors blind,
>   Instil the liberal thought that slaves have powers,
>   Sense, feeling, all as exquisite as ours,
>   Or fury ? He, who hears the sounding thong
>   With far more pleasure than the syren's song."
> —Sat. xiv. 15.

It is one of the principal merits of the Stoic philosophy, that by dwelling so emphatically on the real equality of all men in the eye of nature, it did much towards making the lot of Roman slaves more tolerable. This doctrine Epictetus enforces in a practical if homely discourse : " ' When you call for hot water, and your slave does not answer, or brings it lukewarm, or is not to be found in the house, if you pass the matter over, is not this well-pleasing to the gods ?' ' How then can I bring myself to pass it over ?' ' Slave, will you not bear with your own brother, who has Zeus for his ancestor, who is born as a son from the same seed and from the same heavenly stock ? . . . Bear in mind who you are, and whom you rule,—your kinsmen, your brothers, the offspring of Zeus.' "

It is this bond of sympathy, this feeling of a common fate and of common hopes, says Juvenal, that is the most distinguishing mark of man :—

> " Nature, who gave us tears, by that alone
> Proclaims she made the feeling heart our own ;
> And 'tis her noblest boon.　　.　　.　　.
> 　.　　.　　.　　.　　This marks our birth
> The great distinction from the beasts of earth !
> And therefore—gifted with superior powers,
> And capable of things divine—'tis ours
> To learn and practise every useful art,
> And from high heaven deduce that better part,
> That moral sense, denied to creatures prone
> And downward bent, and found in man alone !
> For He who gave this vast machine to roll,
> Breathed life in them, in us a reasoning soul,
> That kindred feelings might our state improve,
> And mutual wants conduct to mutual love."
> 　　　　　　　　　　　— Sat. xv. 131.

CHAPTER VI.

LITERARY men in the days of Juvenal held a somewhat anomalous position, very different to that which is at present occupied by authors ; and it is necessary, unless we would allow many of the allusions that are found in Juvenal to remain unintelligible, to make the effort necessary to realise the hopes and prospects, the difficulties and disappointments, which lay before the aspirant to literary fame in the reign of Claudius or of Domitian. We all, of course, know the many avenues by which the young writer can now lay his work before the public ; the numerous magazines, the daily prints, the circulating library, and the advertising publisher, will occur to every one's mind. In ancient Rome there were none of these resources ; in fact, the reading public, as we now understand the term—the public to which the writer looks for the reward of his labour—had no existence.

The absence of printing, and the restricted sphere to which education was limited, would be sufficient to account for this ; still, the difference in the conduct of everyday life that was thus brought about was so vast, that it is by no means easy to appreciate it sufficiently. We shall, however, receive considerable assistance in the endeavour to bring before our eyes the life of the Roman author of the first century A.D. if we contemplate the position of his representative in the modern London, during the epoch of the Stuarts or the early part of the Hanoverian dynasty. Differences there still will be, and important differences; yet many of the main features of the pictures will bear a pretty close resemblance to each other.

In the time of Domitian, as in the time of Charles, education, as we now understand the word, was limited to a very narrow class. In both these ages the circulation of books was, as compared with what we are now accustomed to, insignificant in the extreme. Few men, even among those that made some pretensions to a literary reputation, owned a larger library than may now be found in the parlour of a country inn. In part this change may, of course, be attributed to the invention of printing, and its effect on the facilities of circulation, but still more is it a secondary result brought about by the spread of education among the masses. In fact, these two results of printing, or even more perhaps of cheap and abundant paper, have acted and reacted on each other, cheap literature spreading education ever more generally among the people, and this more general education causing a greater and greater demand for literature, and so tending to facilitate the production of it and lessen the cost. Nevertheless, the difficulties and expense of bringing out a small edition of a new work in ancient Rome will probably be much overrated by the superficial observer. With the cheap and abundant slave-labour that was then at command,—labour too, we must remember, of considerable skill, and well adapted by practice and education for this description of work,—it is pretty clear that an edition such as we have mentioned could be sent out by the bookseller of the "Forum" quite as rapidly and at as cheap a rate as could have been accomplished by the publisher of Dryden or of Pope. Let us then consider how the work would be set about. Imagine an extensive room furnished with desks and writing materials sufficient to accommodate from fifty to a hundred writers; at each desk a slave is seated, many if not all of them highly educated, as education went in those days. When all is ready, a reader chosen for his loud voice and distinct articulation proceeds to read forth, it may be, a collection of Martial's Epigrams, newly sent in from Spain, or a fresh edition of the Odes of Horace that the general public has been calling for.

Quickly and neatly the hands of the writers run down the smooth papyrus, keeping pace with the measured intonations of the reader. When the roll had been filled up, it would be coiled round a stick or reed of the appropriate length, and finally, after being neatly cut, so as to reduce all the folds to an even surface, it would be smoothed down with pumice-stone and the base dyed black. It was then ready to be placed in its envelope of parchment that served to preserve it from injury, and also to receive the title that

was usually attached to it in the shape of a small strip
of papyrus, with the name of the book written on it in
deep red characters.   Then the work might either be
sent at once to those who had ordered it, or be exposed
for sale on the stall of the Sosii—the great booksellers
of the day at Rome.   We might expect that such a
work, by the aid of abundant slave-labour, would be
produced at a reasonable rate.   And the conclusion
that we might have arrived at by *a priori* reasoning is
supported by direct contemporary evidence.   We read in
Martial, that a small volume of poems neatly finished and
enclosed in a parchment case might be sold at a price
corresponding to a few pence of our present currency,
in fact much the same as would now be asked for a
volume of the same size.   Publication such as this,
seems, however, seldom to have been adopted, except
by an author whose reputation was already such as to
secure a rapid sale of the whole edition, or one whose
private means were sufficient to defray the expense in
case of failure.   It was an avenue to fame closed to the
unknown or poor author.   Such a one might, however,
hope to earn protection, and open the purse of some
more wealthy citizen, some aspirant to the reputation of
Mæcenas, by a fulsome dedication of his work to the
man whose assistance he desired.   Such dedications
were highly prized by those to whom they were
offered, and frequently an author of repute would look
for pecuniary gain more to the present he received as
a reward for the preface of his book than to the price of
the copyright of the entire work.   Yet this was not
always the case.   Often the Roman poet would be as

much disappointed in his patron as Johnson was in the expectations which he grounded on the countenance of Lord Chesterfield. The end of these expectations is described by that author himself in most touching language, which has been often quoted before, but will bear repetition here :—

"Seven years, my lord, have now passed since I waited in your outer room, or was repulsed from your door; during which time I have been pushing on my work through difficulties of which it is useless to complain, and have brought it at last to the verge of publication, without one act of assistance, one word of encouragement, or one smile of favour. Such treatment I did not expect, for I never had a patron before. . . .

"Is not a patron, my lord, one who looks with unconcern on a man struggling for life in the water, and, when he has reached ground, encumbers him with his help ? The notice which you have been pleased to take of my labours, had it been early, had been kind ; but it has been delayed till I am indifferent and cannot enjoy it ; till I am solitary and cannot impart it ; till I am known and do not want it.".

Very similar in the thought that underlies it is the following passage from Juvenal. Indeed, if we did not know that Juvenal was himself a man of fair fortune, and thus independent of such assistance, we might think that, like the letter of Johnson, his lines too had been prompted by the bitterness of a personal rebuff. He has just been deploring the unhappy position of authors in an age in which Cæsar alone "the drooping Nine regards;" in which, but for his munificence, the poet would do better to turn cobbler or

crier, or learn some other similar handicraft, than continue to work at his' unappreciated art :—

> " But if for other patronage you look,
>   And therefore write, and therefore swell your book,
>   Quick, call for wood, and let the flames devour
>   The hapless produce of the studious hour ;
>   Or lock it up, to moths and worms a prey,
>   And break your pens, and fling your ink away:
>   Or pour it rather o'er your epic flights,
>   Your battles, sieges (fruit of sleepless nights)—
>   Pour it, mistaken man, who rack your brains
>   In dungeons, cock-lofts, for heroic strains ;
>   Who toil and sweat to purchase mere renown,
>   A meagre statue and an ivory crown !
>   Here bound your expectations : for the great,
>   Grown wisely covetous, have learned of late
>   To praise, and only praise, the high-wrought strain,
>   As boys the bird of Juno's glittering train."
>   —Sat. vii. 22.

There is another feature of the literary history of this
period repeated in modern history. Just as Dryden
found that fame, and nothing more, was likely to be his
reward for such poems as " Absalom and Achitophel,"
or his Tales and Fables, and therefore turned to writing for the stage as a more lucrative branch of literature, unfitted though he was, and knew himself to be,
for dramatic composition, both by education and the
natural bent of his genius,—so Statius earned his livelihood, not by his epic poems, though it is to them that
he owes his reputation, but by the sale of tragedies,
whose very names are to us unknown. His " Thebaid "
he recited amidst universal applause, and the judgment

of posterity has fully ratified the enthusiasm of his own
days :—

> " Yet, while the seats rung with a general peal
>   Of boisterous praise, the bard had lacked a meal,
>   Unless with Paris * he had better sped,
>   And trucked a virgin tragedy for bread.
>   Mirror of men ! he showers with liberal hands
>   On needy poets honours and commands :—
>   An actor's patronage a peer's outgoes,
>   And what the last withholds, the first bestows ! "
>   —Sat. vii. 85.

This is indeed very much what one would have expected from an *a priori* consideration of the circumstances under which these poets lived. The many-
headed multitude did not yet call in sufficient numbers
for a supply of literary food to enable writers to rely
on a widespread popularity as a reward of their labours. The author still looked for his fortune—nay,
it might be for the very necessaries of life—not to the
subsidies of the publisher, but to the open-handed
largesses of the emperor, or of some Mæcenas of the
day.

It was in order to gain the degree of notoriety
that was necessary to insure the countenance of his
patron that the custom of the author reciting in
public his own works came into vogue. This was indeed the only way in which, in days destitute alike of
the circulating library and of the critical review, an
unknown author could bring his works forward to be

---

* A Roman actor of the day, and an especial favourite of the
emperor.

tried at the bar of taste and criticism. This custom
had even in the days of Horace taken deep root in
literary circles.   In the succeeding century, however,
it had spread far and wide, and the risk of being at
any time compelled to listen to the second-rate effu-
sions of some would-be poet of your acquaintance
seems to have been recognised as one of the draw-
backs on town-life.   Thus Juvenal, though in a
but half-serious passage, sets this grievance down as
the climax of the annoyances heaped on the Roman
citizen :—

> " What desert land,
> What wild uncultured spot can more affright,
> Than fires wide blazing through the gloom of night,
> Houses with ceaseless ruin thundering down,
> And all the horrors of this hateful town,
> Where poets, while the dog-star glows, rehearse
> To gaping multitudes their barbarous verse ! "
>
> —Sat. iii. 6.

Pliny indeed spoke of the practice as not devoid of
its own advantages, and regretted that his countrymen
did not show themselves more ready to become acquainted in this manner with the literature of their
own day.*   Juvenal, like a true member of the irritable
tribe, spoke with far less indulgence of the customs of
his brothers of the pen.   He had indeed formed a high
ideal for himself of what a real poet should be, and
confessed that in his days there was none such to be
found.   Virgil and Horace had left behind no succes-

* See, on this subject, 'Pliny's Letters,' vol. xi. of this
Series, Ch. 7, " Public Readings."

sors on whom their mantle might fitly fall, though but too many competitors would fain have grasped the magic wand :—

    " The insatiate itch of scribbling, hateful pest,
       Creeps, like a tetter, through the human breast,
       Nor knows, nor hopes a cure ; since years which chill
       All other passions but inflame the ill !
       But He, the bard of every race and clime,
       Of genius, fruitful, ardent, and sublime,
       Who from the glowing mint of fancy pours
       No spurious metal, fused from common ores,
       But gold to matchless purity refined,
       And stamped with all the godhead in his mind;
       He whom I feel, but want the power to paint,
       Springs from a soul impatient of restraint,
       And free from every care ; a soul that loves
       The Muses' haunts, clear founts and shady groves."
                  —Sat. vii. 51.

With such a lofty standard before him, we can hardly be surprised if Juvenal vented his spleen on the crowd of mediocre poets that lived and wrote around him: especially when they insisted not only on writing —an innocent amusement enough—but on compelling their friends to listen while they read their prosy epics, or the comedy that would raise far less hearty a laugh than the bathos of the tragedy. Like Martin Scribblerus, the poetasters of the day were in no difficulty with regard to a plot. The old fables, though worn threadbare, might surely serve yet once again as pegs on which to hang some fresh turn of fancy, some newly-framed conceit. So on the game went, till at last it might be said with truth,—

> " None knows his home so well
> As I the grove of Mars, and Vulcan's cell
> Fast by the Æolian rocks !   How the winds roar ;
> How ghosts are tortured on the Stygian shore ;
> How Jason stole the golden fleece, and how
> The Centaurs fought on Othrys' shaggy brow."
>   —Sat. i. 8.

But while thus holding up to ridicule the folly of the tribe, and endeavouring to divert the writers of the day from barren themes on which even true genius might have toiled in vain—from ploughing the light sand, and sowing seed where none could ever grow— Juvenal was not less ready to set forth their wrongs, and protest in indignant verse against the injustice with which the poet was treated, the undeserved contumely that was heaped upon him.   True, the man who had to earn his own bread showed but scant wisdom when he essayed to mount the hill of Helicon, or wandered by the rills of Aganippe.   This, however, was no excuse to the wealthy *parvenu*, the would-be literary dictator. What right had he to entice the man of letters to pay his court to him, and to increase by his homage the reputation of his train, and then refuse to pay him his reward ?—

> " Hear now what sneaking ways your patrons find
> To save their darling gold ;—they pay in kind !
> Verses composed in every muse's spite,
> To the starved bard they in their turn recite ;
> And if they yield to Homer, let him know
> 'Tis that he lived a thousand years ago."
>   —Sat. vii. 36.

Such conduct, however, we can only deplore,—no

judge can interfere ; and the poet indeed to a certain extent brought it on himself by his foolish credulity, and he must bear a double penalty,—for how is it possible for him to indite any lofty strain while half starved, and harassed by anxiety as to how he shall procure his next day's meal ?—

> " No ; the wine circled briskly through his veins,
> .When Horace poured his dithyrambic strains."
>
> —Sat. vii. 62.

And even Virgil would have had no readers, had he been continually distressed with household cares. The snakes which he wreathes round his fierce Fury would in that case

> " Have dropt in listless length upon the ground,
> And the still slumbering trump groaned with no mortal sound."
>
> —Sat. vii. 70.

Unenviable as the poet's lot is shown to be, that of the historian is even more worthy of our pity. He gets no greater recompense for his work. And as for his labours,—

> " More time, more study they require, and pile
> Page upon page, heedless of bulk the while ; "
>
> —Sat. vii. 99.

though all this extra material, and the necessary books of reference, demand an outlay that his slender purse can ill afford. So with the rest of the learned walks of life. Take the lawyer. If, after endless toil, he win a cause, he is rewarded by an empty crown of bays, or perhaps

> " A rope of shrivelled onions from the Nile,
> 　A rusty ham, a jar of broken sprats,
> 　And wine, the refuse of the country vats." *
> 　　　　　　　　　　　—Sat. vii. 119.

That is to say, if he is a poor man; for the wealthy
lawyer is another example of the fact, that unto him
that hath shall be given.

And here, it may be remarked, we have another
of those parallels between life in the present day and
life at Rome under the Cæsars. Just as, in London, a
doctor is said frequently to drive himself into a practice by setting up a brougham and making a show of
a vast connection on nothing a-year, so the Roman
lawyer who wished to thrive had learned to simulate
an unreal success, as knowing that men are ever ready
to encumber with their help those who have made
it clear that they stand in no need of it. It was no
uncommon plan for the young jurisconsult to go about
followed by a hired train of slaves, and, though penni-
less, to make a show of buying all the luxuries and
superfluities of life :—

> " And some, indeed, have thriven by tricks like these ;
> 　Purple and violet swell a lawyer's fees ;
> 　Bustle and show above his means conduce
> 　To business, and profusion proves of use.
> 　Could our old pleaders visit earth again,
> 　Tully himself could scarce a brief obtain,
> 　Unless his robe were purple, and a stone,
> 　Diamond or ruby, on his finger shone."
> 　　　　　　　　　　　—Sat. vii. 135.

* It would seem that in Juvenal's time it was not unusual
to give a lawyer at Rome a reward in kind in the place of any
money fee.

The rhetorician's case is yet more desperate than the rest. Worse paid than his compeers, his work is of a dismal sort, such as would drive the meanest soul to rebel. Week after week he listens to the same class droning out their prosy declamations, till in despair he throws up the task, and, giving up all claim to payment, declines to continue the thankless trade.

In the account of the grammarian's woes we meet by the way with an interesting allusion to Virgil and Horace, showing that they had already become standard books for school use, had already come to be dog's-eared by the schoolboy's thumb, — a fate that has been theirs for an unbroken period of eighteen centuries.

It is, then, part of the grammarian's or schoolmaster's task to guide his scholars through the pages of the 'Æneid' or the 'Odes,' rising up early and lying down late to rest; and as payment for all this toil, besides being ready on all occasions with every branch of possible and impossible knowledge, he shall be rewarded at the year's end with as much as a fencer gains in a single hour. Such, at all events, was the case at Rome in the days of the Emperor Nero.

CHAPTER VII.

THE social position of women in the days of Juvenal, and the relation of the sexes to each other, are subjects which could not but force themselves on any thinking mind,—could not but be a cause for the deepest anxiety to every patriotic Roman citizen. From the earliest days of Roman history, women had held a much higher place in the family than has usually fallen to their lot among a but partially civilised people. Though, of course, subordinate to the man with regard to her position in the state, and, according to strict law, subject absolutely to the will of her husband, the wife was not looked on habitually as by any means his slave, but rather as a friend and an equal,—as one who should be treated with affectionate respect and esteem. And, indeed, in her own province,—the management of the interior economy of the household, — the Roman wife was permitted to exercise full authority over all the inferior members of the family.

Precluded by custom from any prominent appearance in public, the matron at Rome was yet by no means confined to her own apartments, as was usually the case in Greece. On the contrary, as long as she conducted herself with decorum and propriety, she was permitted to take her place among men at public banquets and on other festive occasions, or, accompanied by her children, to be a spectator of the dramatic performances of the theatre,—a custom which Juvenal mentions as one of the remnants of the good old days that was still in his time kept up in the country :—

" There, when the toil foregone and annual play
  Mark, from the rest, some high and solemn day,
  To theatres of turf the rustics throng,
  Charmed with the farce that charmed their sires so long ;
  While the pale infant, of the mask in dread,
  Hides in his mother's breast his little head."

—Sat. iii. 172.

Thus the Roman wife, though by law as much given up to her husband's control as were his children or even his slaves, yet by custom enjoyed a position of comparative independence and equality. For, irrespective of that personal influence which a woman cannot fail to acquire over any man with whom she spends so large a portion of her life, and of whose children she is the mother, public opinion would not fail to express a very decided censure on any husband who should have exercised the power given him by law over his wife with any harshness or disregard of justice.

But in the days of Juvenal there were other causes which had conspired to place women in a position of far greater independence as regarded their husbands. During the later times of the Republic, the ancient and solemn form of religious marriage, by which the wife passed as it were into her husband's family, and became subject to him, even as a child was subject to his father, had fallen into desuetude. The ceremony was long and inconvenient, and the increasing levity of women would not brook so complete a loss of independence. So entirely had this ceremony gone out of fashion in the time of Tiberius, that, according to the testimony of Tacitus, considerable difficulty was on one occasion experienced during that reign before a chief priest could be found whose parents had, as the religious canon required, been joined together according to the forms of this most ancient and binding rite. In the place of this old covenant of marriage, a new custom gradually arose by which the woman did not cease to be a member of her father's household, but was, in technical language, merely intrusted as a temporary deposit to her husband. As a consequence of this, the position of women tended to become one of great practical independence ; for while the husband had no legal authority with which to back his wishes or his commands, the head of the family to which his wife belonged by birth would naturally hesitate to interfere with the conduct of one who had to all intents and purposes become a member of a different family. The very fact of this independent position of the weaker sex would in itself have gone far to shock the feelings of Juvenal, who of all Roman writers with whom we are acquainted was the most conservative, and clung most fondly to the manners and customs of his fathers, under which Rome had learned to rule the nations of the earth. But matters did not end here. The practical change in the conduct of women was even greater than the change that had developed itself in their legal position. Many causes had been at work to bring this change about.

The education which the Roman considered proper and decorous for his daughters was the same now as it had been in the early days of the Republic, when, amid a tribe of herdsmen and shepherds, the highest praise that could be placed as an epitaph on the tomb of a deceased matron, was the statement that she who lay beneath had led a sober and a pious life, had regulated her household with diligence, and had presided ably at the spinning-wheel, untouched by foreign manners, careless of what occurred abroad; and, finally, that she had been the wife of only one lord and master, and had never sought a second matrimonial alliance.

Innocence such as this, grounded on simple habits, and preserved by ignorance, might indeed be maintained among the rude farmers of Latium—among the citizens of what was then merely the capital of an Italian tribe. But when once the highly cultivated nations of the East began to pour their treasures into the open bosom of the queen of the Mediterranean, such innocence and such ignorance could no longer be of any avail, even had men been in earnest in their endeavours to preserve them. "Conquered Greece led her conquerors captive" in morals no less than in philosophy and in art; and now the softer manners and

the looser morals of the Ægean were transferred to
the hills among which Curius had tilled his farm, and
Camillus driven his oxen :—

> " Our matrons then were chaste,
> When days of labour, nights of short repose,
> Hands still employed the Tuscan wool to toss ;
> Their husbands armed, and anxious for the State,
> And Carthage hovering near the Colline gate,
> Conspired to keep all thoughts of ill aloof,
> And banished vice far from their lowly roof.
> Now all the evils of long peace are ours ;
> Luxury, more terrible than hostile powers,
> Her baleful influence wide around has hurled,
> And well avenged the subjugated world !
> Since poverty, our better genius, fled,
> Vice like a deluge o'er the State has spread.
> Now, shame to Rome ! in every street are found
> The essenced Sybarite with roses crowned,
> The gay Miletan and the Tarentine,
> Lewd, petulant, and reeling ripe with wine !
> Wealth first, the ready pander to all sin,
> Brought foreign manners, foreign vices in ;
> Enervate wealth, and with seductive art,
> Sapped every home-bred virtue of the heart."
>
> —Sat. vi. 287.

When the Roman magistrate returned to his native
city from his temporary command in Asia or in Greece,
he returned with his morals as much debased as his
taste was raised by the mode of life practised among
the luxurious and effeminate citizens of Athens and of
Miletus.   It was from these towns, or from such towns
as these, that the whole apparatus of life at Rome was
borrowed ; from them that the whole tribe of slaves

was drawn, whose business it was to flatter the pride or gratify the idle appetites of their lords and masters. To such a depth had fallen the descendants of Miltiades, of Leonidas, of Demosthenes, and of Pericles, that, to use words which we have already quoted in a previous chapter, the Roman satirist could deservedly style them—

> " A flattering, cringing, treacherous, artful race,
> Of torrent tongue and never-blushing face ;
> A Protean tribe one knows not what to call,
> Which shifts to every form, and shines in all."
> —Sat. iii. 73.

Among the other productions of Greece which thus bore down the old Roman simplicity, among the most noteworthy were the Hetæræ. One of the worst results of the very slender education, if education it might indeed be called, to which the honourable daughter of Rome might aspire, was to force on all Roman citizens, whom the call of duty or of pleasure had introduced to foreign and more refined customs, a comparison between his own uncultivated wife and the accomplished women with whom he associated in his Grecian or Asiatic home. This class, called into greater prominence through the whole of Greece, but especially so in Athens and in Corinth, owing to the very subordinate position that the legitimate wife of the Greek citizen was allowed to occupy, cannot with justice be compared to any similar class in our present state of society. Though bound by no legal or formal tie to their protector, yet, as we may gather from the accounts that have come down to us of the intercourse of Pericles and Aspasia, as well as from other sources, the connections thus formed were no mere temporary *liaisons,* but were observed with fidelity on one side, and were rewarded by unremitting, often by unselfish, affection on the other. We may take Aspasia as a type, though an unusually noble type, of her class; a class which, combining rare personal charms with intellectual attractions of the highest order, usurped, and not without reason, the place reserved, under happier auspices, for the legitimate wife. It was in their endeavour to outrival the influence of these courtesans, without, however, aiming at that higher culture to which this influence was in a great measure due, that the Roman matrons were hurried into those excesses which Juvenal has immortalised; and to the description of them he has devoted the whole of his longest and most carefully elaborated poem.

Another cause of the anomalous relations of the sexes during the second century A.D. may be found in the widely-spread and growing disinclination to marriage. This was to the moralist one of the worst features of the times. As early as the year 400 B.C. we hear of fines being levied by the censors on many Roman citizens, if they had not taken to themselves a wife before reaching a reasonable age; shortly after this, official speeches are recorded, as spoken by men of rank who bewailed the necessity of marriage, while calling on the citizens to take up manfully that burden so grievous, and yet so necessary, for the good of the State.

During the civil wars, and the general deterioration

of manners consequent on them, the evil here alluded to increased to an alarming extent—so much so, indeed, that one of the principal aims of the legislation of Augustus was to diminish the untoward proportion of unmarried men, to check the disinclination to marriage which, according to a statement in one of the authors of the period, threatened to extinguish the entire stock of the old Roman families. But the legislation of the emperor was scarcely of more avail than were the songs of Horace and of other court poets, who at the bidding of their prince hymned the praises of a married state, albeit they showed but little inclination to put their teaching into practice in their own cases. This distaste for marriage itself was yet further increased, if not justified, by the extraordinary demands made by any wife who happened to bring with her as dowry a large addition to her husband's property. Such a one would not only arrogate to herself absolute control of her own estate, and an unbridled licence of action in things both small and great,—a freedom to violate all customs, and cast aside the last shred of womanly modesty,—but would even claim to dictate to her husband his conduct and his mode of life. Well indeed might the poet exclaim in his wrath :—

> " Sure of all ills with which mankind are curst,
> A wife who brings you money is the worst."
> —Sat. vi. 139.

In this as in other paths of vice, it was in the most lofty rank that virtue was most openly outraged by women. It was not necessary at Rome, under

Nero or Domitian, for amorous widow-hunters of the
type of "Colonel Chartres" or the "Duke of Roussillon"
to lay their toils with craft and skill in order to catch
their victims.　The matrons themselves would save
them all that trouble, for at all events in that day it
was quite as true as in the age of Pope or of ourselves,
that

"Every woman is at heart a rake."

Of all the tragedies which have been recorded in the
annals of the earlier years of the Roman Empire, there
is none, perhaps, so striking as the intrigue of Messalina and Silius,—none which shows in plainer colours
how utterly dissolute the society must have been in
which such horrors could be perpetrated, not indeed
with impunity, but apparently without exciting any
strong feeling of disgust.　The tale of this the last of
the amours by which Messalina dishonoured her husband, and led the way on to the very extravagance of
vice, is related by the historian Tacitus in almost the
same words as Juvenal has employed :—

> "But Silius comes.　Now be thy judgment tried,
> Shall he accept, or not, the proffered bride,
> And marry Cæsar's wife ?　Hard point, in truth :
> Lo, this most noble and most beauteous youth
> Is hurried off, a helpless sacrifice
> To the lewd glance of Messalina's eyes !
> Haste, bring the victim : in the nuptial vest
> Already see the impatient Empress drest,
> The genial* couch prepared, the accustomed sum
> Told out, the augurs and the notaries come.

* "Lectus genialis."　It has been supposed that a figure of

'But why all these ?'   You think, perhaps, the rite
Were better known to few, and kept from sight
Not so the lady : she abhors a flaw,
And wisely calls for every form of law.
But what shall Silius do ! refuse to wed ?
A moment sees him numbered with the dead.
Consent, and gratify the eager dame ?
He gains a respite till the tale of shame
Through town and country reach the Emperor's ear,
Still sure the last—his own disgrace to hear.
Then let him, if a day's precarious life
Be worth his study, make the fair his wife ;
For wed or not, poor youth, 'tis still the same,
And still the axe must mangle that fine frame !"

—Sat. x. 329.

It is against such deeds as these, and to hold up to
infamy women who took such enormities as their
model, that Juvenal pours forth the invective of the
satire we are now considering.   The poem is itself
addressed to one Ursidius, a friend to Juvenal, on the
occasion of his intended marriage.   After a brief
proem, in which the poet, by way of introduction,
bewails the lost simplicity of the golden age—

" When the race that broke
Unfathered from the soil and opening oak
Lived most unlike the men of later times,
The puling brood of follies and of crimes ;"

—Sat. vi. 11.

he plunges at once "*in medias res*," according to the
Horatian maxim, apostrophising his friend on the
folly he is about to commit :—

the man's " Genius " or guardian spirit was carved on his marriage-bed.

" Even now the ring is bought,
Even now—thou once, Ursidius, hadst thy wits,
And now to talk of wiving !   O these fits !
What more than madness has thy soul possest ?
What snakes, what furies, agitate thy breast ?
Heavens ! wilt thou tamely drag the galling chain,
While hemp is to be bought, while knives remain !"
                                              —Sat. vi. 27.

After this tirade, Juvenal proceeds to justify at
length his advice by an enumeration of the social
disadvantages of the married state, and of all the
many faults of women which the intending husband
risked experiencing in the person of his wife.   In the
first place, the married man would not fail to lose the
turtle and the turbot,—

" And all the dainties which the flatterer still
Heaps on the childless to secure his will."
                                              —Sat. vi. 39.

This same legacy - hunting was one of the chief
banes of Roman life under the Empire, and it went
far towards making true friendships impossible, by
raising suspicions against every man who seemed to
desire the society of any one who had property to
leave in his will.   And there was a double incentive
to this eager seeking after legacies.   Not only was the
money itself a prize, but it was considered to be in
some sort a stigma on a man's character if he were
passed over unmentioned in the will of an acquaintance.   Hence the wealthy and childless old man was
surrounded, from rise of morn till set of sun, by crowds
of parasites ready to perform for him the most menial

services, while even his affluent friends poured in presents of delicate fish and other dainties, in hopes of being remembered in the rich man's testament—presents and attentions which neither the poor man nor yet the father of a family could hope to receive. Hear in what manner the poet seeks to set at rest the question of his own disinterestedness, on the occasion of his entertaining a friend at a feast in his country villa :—

> " Nor think, Corvinus, interest fires my breast :
> Catullus, for whose sake my house is drest,
> Has three sweet boys, who all such hopes destroy ;
> And nobler views excite my boundless joy.
> Yet who besides on such a barren friend
> Would waste a sickly pullet ? who would spend
> So vast a treasure where no hopes prevail,
> Or for a *father* sacrifice a quail ? "
>
> —Sat. xii. 93.

Juvenal next goes on to consider the infatuated partiality of many a noble dame for actors, gladiators, and other public performers—a partiality often proved by the truest of all praise, imitation. For some women, says the poet,—

> " Sicken for action, and assume the airs,
> The mask, and thyrsus of their favourite players ; "
>
> —Sat. vi. 69.

nay, even descend as combatants into the arena,—

> " Where the bold fair
> Tilts at the Tuscan boar with bosom bare."
>
> —Sat. i. 22.

Many women, too, who did not so outrageously unsex

themselves, were yet ready to abandon all that they should have held most dear, and sacrifice their name and fame for the sake of some outcast player or gladiator :—

> " Hippia, who shared a rich patrician's bed,
> To Egypt with a gladiator fled,
> While rank Canopus eyed with strong disgust
> This ranker specimen of Roman lust.
> Without one pang the profligate resigned
> Her husband, sister, sire ; gave to the wind
> Her children's tears ; yea, tore herself away
> (To strike you more) from Paris * and the Play."
>
> —Sat. vi. 82.

Then look at the reckless extravagance, so prevalent as to be almost universal, that prompts the sex to squander their husbands' fortunes on useless trifles. See Ogulnia, the woman of fashion, as she leaves her house; contemplate her actions through the day, her costly dress, her numerous attendants, her worthless and ruinously expensive bargains, and then answer whether any fortune can support such a heavy and so constant a drain upon it. But, like the insatiable leech, the woman will never lose her hold so long as a single farthing can be extracted from the funds of her much-enduring husband :—

> " Whene'er Ogulnia to the circus goes,
> To emulate the rich she hires her clothes ;
> Hires followers, friends, and cushions ; hires a chair,
> A nurse, and a trim girl with golden hair,
> To slip her billets : prodigal and poor,
> She wastes the wreck of her paternal store

* See note above, p. 101.

On smooth-faced wrestlers,—wastes her little all,
And strips her shivering mansion to the wall !"

—Sat. vi. 352.

Men may indeed be led into extravagant profusion, but usually they have more or less thought for the morrow; while the fair sex, if once they enter on the headlong course, without a pause and without delay plunge on and on, as though no power could reduce the heap of gold from which they draw. In other cases the same peculiarity may be traced, the same inability to preserve the bounds of moderation, though these bounds alone can preserve even the ornaments and little elegances of everyday life from degenerating into flaws, if not into more serious faults. As an example of this, we may take the affectation of mixing up Greek words with Latin, a custom carried to such a length that no lady with any pretension to taste will allow herself to use anything but this nondescript jargon,—much as some people in our own day inter-lard their English with French names and phrases :—

" 'Tis now the nauseous cant that none is fair
Unless her thoughts in Attic terms she dress ;
A mere Cecropian of a Sulmoness ! *
All now is Greek ; in Greek their souls they pour,
In Greek their fears, hopes, joys,—what would you more ?
In Greek they clasp their lovers."

—Sat. vi. 185.

* Sulmo, a town of the Peligni, in which the poet Ovid was born, is here taken for any provincial place. The women of Sulmo, in spite of their country breeding and their coarse country accent, gave themselves the airs of thoroughbred Athenians, who are here, as elsewhere, styled Cecropians, from Cecrops, an early king of Attica.

The same ignorance of what bounds should be observed allows women to become the very caricature of themselves when they engage in public life, and enter into competition with men in masculine professions and pursuits. Thus many women are eager to refine upon—

> " The finest subtleties of law,
> And raise litigious questions for a straw.
> They meet in private, and prepare the bill,
> Draw up the instructions with a lawyer's skill,
> Suggest to Celsus where the merits lie,
> And dictate points for statement or reply.
> Nay more, they fence ! Who has not marked their oil,
> Their purple rugs, for this preposterous toil ?
> Room for the lady !—lo ! she seeks the list,
> And fiercely tilts at her antagonist,
> A post ! which with her buckler she provokes,
> And bores and batters with repeated strokes,
> Till all the fencer's art can do she shows,
> And the glad master interrupts her blows."
>
> —Sat. vi. 242.

Nor is the wife a less skilful combatant when, casting aside those weapons which she but now usurped, she takes up her true part, and, in the curtain lecture, with ready wit baffles all the complaints her husband may make, or turns the tables upon him by fierce rejoinder against his own unfaithfulness, or by tears of well-feigned rage at his neglect :—

> " 'Tis night ; yet hope no slumbers with your wife ;
> The nuptial bed is still the scene of strife :
> There lives the keen debate, the clamorous brawl,
> And quiet ' never comes that comes to all.'

Fierce as a tigress plundered of her young,
Rage fires her breast and loosens all her tongue ;
When, conscious of her guilt, she feigns to groan,
And chides your loose amours to hide her own ;
Storms at the scandal of your baser flames,
And weeps her injuries from imagined names,
With tears that marshalled at their station stand,
And flow impassioned as she gives command.
You think those showers her true affection prove,
And deem yourself so happy in her love !
With fond caresses strive her heart to cheer,
And from her eyelids kiss the starting tear :
But could you now search through the secretaire
Of this most loving, this most jealous fair,
What amorous lays, what letters would you see—
Proofs, damning proofs of her sincerity !"

—Sat. vi. 286.

Truly "Mrs Caudle" was flourishing even in the days of Juvenal! So was also she who is now called bluestocking. Though no title had then been given her, the marks by which she may be known are most graphically set forth in this poem. Here we may unmistakably trace the features of one who would in the present day have gone in for competitive examinations, and essayed to mount the lecturer's desk or the professor's chair; nor, indeed, does she seem to have been more of a favourite a thousand years ago than now :—

" But she is more intolerable yet,
    Who plays the critic when at table set ;
    Calls Virgil charming, and attempts to prove
    Poor Dido right in venturing all for love.
    From Maro and Mæonides she quotes
    The striking passages, and, while she notes

Their beauties and defects, adjusts her scales,
And accurately weighs which bard prevails.
The astonished guests sit mute : Grammarians yield ;
Loud Rhetoricians, baffled, quit the field.

.   .   .   .   .

Oh never may the partner of my bed
With subtleties of logic stuff her head,
Nor whirl her rapid syllogisms round,
Nor with imperfect enthymemes confound !
Enough for me, if common things she know,
And boast the little learning schools bestow.
I hate the female pedagogue, who pores
O'er her Palæmon* hourly ; who explores
All modes of speech, regardless of the sense,
But tremblingly alive to mood and tense ;
Who puzzles me with many an uncouth phrase
Of some old canticle of Numa's days,
Corrects her country friends, and cannot hear
Her husband solecise without a sneer."

—Sat. vi. 434.

Another parallel between our own days and those of
Juvenal may be found in the matter of women's dress,
and more particularly in the elaborate head-gear, which
would seem to have varied but little in the intervening
centuries.   Or perhaps it would be truer to say that
the fashion, after going through a cycle, has now returned to the point whence it set out.   Listen then to
the description of a belle of the first century A.D., preparing for engagement.   Her handmaids stand around
her, and, under the guidance of an old nurse of experience and judgment, who by virtue of her age is pre-

---

* Palæmon the grammarian, and teacher of no less a pupil
than Quintilian.

sident of the council, toil to complete the work of
decoration :—

> "So warm they grow, and so much pains they take,
> You'd think her honour or her life at stake !
> So high they build her head, such tiers on tiers,
> With wary hands they pile, that she appears
> Andromache before : and what behind ?
> A dwarf, a creature of a different kind."
>
> —Sat. vi. 500.

Hitherto, however, the charges brought forward have
been only of a comparatively venial nature—offences
against taste and good breeding : now we are introduced
to faults of a darker hue; to vices which have stamped
that era, to all time, as one pre-eminent above all other
epochs in recklessness and superfluity of naughtiness.
Here, as the poet heaps on charge after charge, we
stand aghast at the disclosures of avarice, superstition,
cruelty, and murder—of crimes which argue a heart
saturated to the core in vice, a heart dyed deep in
iniquity.

The charge for cruelty is easily made good. It
needs but to consider the conduct of the Roman
lady towards her unfortunate household. The idlest
caprice of the mistress is often gratified by the most
wanton torture of one or other of her dependants :—

> " There are who hire a beadle by the year
> To lash their servants round ; who, pleased to hear
> The eternal thong, bid him lay on, while they
> At perfect ease the silk-man's stores survey,
> Chat with their female gossips, or replace
> The cracked enamel on their treacherous face.

.   .   .   .

> The wretched Psecas, for the whip prepared,
> With locks dishevelled and with shoulders bared,
> Attempts her hair ; fire flashes from her eyes,
> And—' strumpet ! why this curl so high ?' she cries ;
> Instant the lash without remorse is plied,
> And the blood stains her bosom, back, and side."
>
> —Sat. vi. 480.

The same woman, goaded by superstition, and unmindful of all decency and of her country's religion, will hurry to the vile and unhallowed worship of Cybele or Io, of Osiris or Anubis, and squander the remains of her fortune in bribes and presents to their foul effeminate priests, or to the scarcely less hateful Jewish fortune-tellers. For,—

> " Though Delphi now, if we may credit fame,
> ` Gives no responses, and a long dark night
> Conceals the future hour from human sight ;"
>
> —Sat. vi. 555.

yet Syrian sages and Chaldæan priests can still be bribed to foretell that which shall, or shall not, come to pass. The more thoroughly these men have transgressed all laws human as well as divine, the more eagerly will they be sought after by the chaste and honourable Roman matron:—

> " No juggler must for fame or credit hope
> Who has not narrowly escaped the rope,
> Begged hard for exile, and by special grace
> Obtained confinement in some desert place—
> To him your Tanaquil applies in doubt
> How long her jaundiced mother will hold out,
> But first, how long her husband ?".
>
> —Sat. vi. 562.

Perchance you think this is the lowest depth that can be reached. Not so. Behold the wretch who is herself a proficient in the black science. She will never do anything, great or small, without first consulting the manual of astrology that hangs ever at her side :—

> " She, deep in science, now allows her mate
> To go or stay ; but will not share his fate,
> Withheld by trines and sextiles ; she will look,
> Before her chair be ordered, in the book
> For the fit hour."
>
> —Sat. vi. 573.

Even the poor rival their betters. Though unable to employ a prophet of their own, they have recourse to the wandering priest, the strolling quack seer. And by him they are guided in all the decisions of life.

'Tis, however, but a single step further to call in the philtre-monger, and by the aid of some Thessalian witch

> " To subdue the will
> Of an uxorious spouse, and make him bear
> Blows, insults, all a saucy wife can dare."
>
> —Sat. vi. 610.

And what remains after this ? What further crime is yet untried ? Murder ! And why not that ? Has not Agrippina showed how an obnoxious husband may be despatched ? And is not Locusta ready, with her slow and secret poisons, to remove any too long-lived husband or parent from the path of love or of avarice ? But why call for the help of Locusta ?—now that the art of the most skilled professional poisoner has been outdone by many a Roman matron who—

"More dext'rous than Locusta, shows
Her country friends the beverage to compose,
And, 'midst the curses of the indignant throng,
Bears in broad day the spotted corpse along."
—Sat. i. 71.

Nor is this mere fiction, or even exaggeration—the real facts are as bad, if not worse ; and the guilty wretch, far from being shamed into secrecy, openly avows and glories in the crime :—

"Lo ! Pontia cries aloud—
'No, I performed it. See the facts avowed—
I mingled poison for my children, I !
'Twas found upon me ; wherefore then deny ?'
'What ! two at once, most barbarous viper, two ?'
'Nay, seven, had seven been mine : believe it true.'"
—Sat. vi. 638.

Thus, exclaims the poet, all the horrors which were invented of old by the tragic poets are actually performed before our eyes :—

"Abroad, at home, the Belides* you meet,
And Clytemnestras † swarm in every street ;
But here the difference lies ; those bungling wives
With a blunt axe hacked out their husbands' lives,
While now the deed is done with dexterous art,
And a drugged bowl performs the axe's part.
Yet if the husband, prescient of his fate,
Have fortified his breast with mithridate,

* The fifty daughters of Danaus, king of Argos, who all, except one, killed their husbands in a single night.
† Clytemnestra, the wife of Agamemnon, is said to have killed her husband on his return from the siege and capture of Troy.

In such a case, reserved for such a need,
Rather than fail, the dagger does the deed."
—Sat. vi. 655.

We have dwelt rather at length on this Satire, and given a rather long *résumé* of its matter, for several reasons. Not only is it the longest poem that Juvenal wrote, and composed with more than ordinary care, and as such worthy of attention if only from a literary point of view ; but it also bears on one of the most important questions of the times—on one that in great measure lay at the root of that disintegration of society which, growing from year to year, finally led to the disruption of the Roman Empire, and with it of the whole structure of Western civilisation, as so well expressed in the words of Horace :—

" Our times, in sin prolific, first
The marriage-bed with taint have cursed
And family and home ;
This is the fountain-head of all
The sorrows and the ills that fall
On Romans and on Rome."

The greater portion of the poem will, however, call neither for explanation nor for comment. The superstitions of women, their faithlessness, their lavish use of cosmetics, and all the apparatus of the perfumer's art, their craving after novelty, and their subservience to the dictates of fashion, have always formed a part of the commonplace of the Satirist, among all societies in which the sex has played a prominent part. These, though now and again (as, for instance, in the reigns of Nero, Claudius, or Domitian) attracting a larger share of attention, are in all essential points invariable, and admit of no very great variety in the way of treatment. With regard to the crimes of poisoning and witchcraft, and especially the use of philtres, the parallel cases of the Countess of Somerset and the Duchess of Brinvilliers will occur to every one.

The one branch of the Satire to which no parallel can be quoted in the history of any civilised nation is the custom of fighting in the public arena. This, the latest and most extraordinary fantasy of the sex, is, as we have seen, more than once alluded to by Juvenal; and incredible as the charge might otherwise be held, the most sensational accusation of the Satirist is fully supported by the independent evidence of more than one historian of the time. Tacitus, in his history of the reign of Nero, writes : " In the same year were exhibited gladiatorial shows on a scale no less magnificent than those of previous years ; but many women of noble birth, and many senators, disgraced themselves by appearing in the arena." Suetonius also expressly asserts that women took part as combatants on the occasion of some shows being celebrated in the reign of Domitian. The practice was not put down till the reign of Septimus Severus, when a decree was passed making such indecent exhibitions for the future illegal.

It is difficult to understand how such a state of things could ever have been tolerated by any Roman government ; and scarcely less difficult to realise the state of society in which any woman—above all, any woman of rank—could voluntarily engage in such encounters, and not forfeit, to say nothing of her own self-respect, not only her position in society, but even every claim to be looked on as a woman at all. We shall perhaps not be wrong if we attribute the phenomenon, in part at least, to the reaction consequent on the relaxation of a strictly enforced code of propriety, followed, as in our own history at the time of the Restoration, by a general growth of extravagance and immorality, such that any outrage on common decency could hardly fail to meet with pardon and applause, as being a virtual protest against the puritanical notions of a detested *régime*. As to the apparent indifference of the government on the subject, it may be explained as being but a part of the hereditary policy of the Empire. From the days of Augustus it seems to have been a maxim with the government to allow great latitude to the people both in the discussion of religious questions, and also in social matters generally, in the hope that these might act as safety-valves, and give a vent to the more active spirits of the day, and so postpone the clash between the government and the governed. Moreover, the general prevalence of suicide, which about this time came to be almost a fashion, made it well-nigh impossible for the emperor to keep a firm rein on any determined spirit. When a man or woman has once so ceased to cling to life as to be ready to summon death as a happy release from any momentary trouble or annoyance, how shall any power restrain them from doing that which seems right in their own eyes, except by a system of universal coercion, which it would of necessity be wholly impossible to maintain ?

CHAPTER VIII

It may be remembered by some of our readers that Martial, the contemporary and the friend of Juvenal, in addressing to him one of his Epigrams, condoles with the poet on his mode of life in Rome, as compared with the ease and comfort of a Spanish farmer's existence. From many passages in his poems there can be no doubt that Juvenal fully felt all the discomforts of a life in the capital, though, perhaps, like our own Johnson, he would not have been willing to part with those discomforts on the condition of having to submit to a long absence from the great focus of all social and political life. In the time of Juvenal, Rome had long ceased to be the mere capital of an Italian state : it was the great metropolis of the world, the centre to which flocked all needy adventurers, all men who hoped to raise their fortunes or to escape from the hands of justice.

" Long since the stream that wanton Syria laves
Has disembogued its filth in Tiber's waves,

Its language, arts ; o'erwhelmed us with the scum
Of Antioch's streets, its minstrel, harp, and drum.
Hie to the circus ! ye who want to prove
A barbarous mistress, an outlandish love ;
Hie to the circus ! There in crowds they stand,
Tires on their head, and timbrels in their hand."
—Sat. iii. 62.

There was, however, one striking peculiarity that
calls for notice as regards the constitution of that
population. There was in Rome no middle class.
The upper layer of society consisted partly of old
Roman families, who clung to the ancient cradle of
their race with a patriotic fondness, and were besides,
for the most part, connected with the carrying on of
the government ; partly of the retinue of the court, the
favourites of the emperor, and his wealthy freed-
men. In the lower part was to be found the
" Plebs Romana." The name was still retained, but
it was now by no means the same honourable title
which it had been in former times. The Roman citizens had long since ceased to have any political
honour or responsibility, and now even their influence in the world of politics was gone. Their approval, when it was thought worth asking, might be
had at the price of a gratuitous admission to the
amusements of the circus or of an extra gladiatorial
show :—

" For since their votes have been no longer bought,
 All public care has vanished from their thought ;
 And those who once, with unresisting sway,
 Gave armies, empire, everything away,

For two poor claims have long renounced the whole,
And only ask—the Circus and the Dole." *

—Sat. x. 77.

Besides these, the lower part of the city swarmed with
needy foreigners from every part of the Mediterranean
coasts, who had come to Rome to live by their wits,
and attracted also, in many cases, by the dole of corn,
and the free admission to the circus, the theatres, and
the baths—the "Panis et Circenses" of the Roman
rabble. It was from among this class that were drawn
the clients of the great houses, who thronged the court-
yard of the patron under whom they had enrolled themselves from the very earliest hour possible. Juvenal,
indeed, would seem to imply that among this crowd of
needy suppliants might often be found men of consular
family, who in rank and lineage far surpassed their
protectors :—

> " ' Come forth, ye great Dardanians, from the crowd ! '
> For mixed with us e'en these besiege the door,
> And scramble for—the pittance of the poor !
> ' Despatch the Prætor first,' the master cries,
> ' And next the Tribune ! ' "

—Sat. i. 100.

But in this we can hardly look on him as a trustworthy witness, for we know from other sources that
the emperors were most unwilling to permit any of the
ancient families to fall into utter decay, and were
ready to prevent such a calamity by large presents
from their own private treasuries.

---

* For a description of the "sportula " or " dole," the reader
is referred to p. 136.

These two sections of society occupied, as a rule, utterly distinct parts of the town. The poorer classes were huddled together in the lower parts of the city— in the valleys, that is, which occupied the low lands on the south side of the Tiber, and separated the seven hills of Rome one from the other. The houses in these parts were built to a great height, frequently beyond what was by any means safe :—

> "Half the city here by shores is staid,
> And feeble cramps that lend a treacherous aid ;
> For thus the stewards patch the riven wall,
> Thus prop the mansion tottering to its fall :
> Then bid the tenant court secure repose,
> While the pile nods to every blast that blows."
> —Sat. iii. 193.

But lofty as were the houses, they supplied but scanty accommodation for the vast population which desired to find accommodation within them. The result was that, as in the poorer districts of the large towns of our own day, whole families were forced to be contented with a single room to serve every purpose. True, this was of less consequence in a southern climate, where during the greater portion of the year an outdoor life was the most healthy as well as the most pleasant ; nevertheless the hardship was felt, and at times felt severely. It is not, however, on the inhabitants of these tenements that Juvenal pours out his fiercest satire. He does indeed blame them, but the blame is for the most part mixed with pity, as for men who were rather what the circumstances of their lives made them, than those who had established their own position and were responsible for it. No, it was on the upper classes—on the self-styled "lords of the earth"—that he pours out the vials of his wrath. These, when they lived at home, occupied mansions of a very different description, not built alongside of the narrow and crooked city lanes, but situated within their own grounds, on the slope or summit of some one of the hills of Rome—sumptuous palaces, where the haughty occupants lived undisturbed by the turmoil of the city, except when, in the early morning, their own peculiar clients attended at a sort of levee, to which the first two hours of the day were devoted, there to receive the "sportula," or daily dole, which it was customary for the wealthy "patronus" to deal out to any client who chose to apply for it. This "dole" had originally been a light meal, which was provided by the "patronus" in the main hall of his mansion; but in time, as motives of ostentation took the place of real hospitality, instead of the meal a portion of food was given to each man. This was carried away in baskets ("sportulæ"), either at the time of the morning levee or in the afternoon, according to the convenience of the recipient. It was, however, not unusual to substitute for this dole of food a small sum of money—somewhat less than a shilling. Thus only the chosen few had the honour of taking their meal with the master of the house, and that only by special invitation. This shabby avarice of the wealthy is one of the first quarrels which Juvenal has with them. How different, he exclaims, is their conduct from that of former days !—

> " Then plain and open was the cheerful feast,
> And every client was a bidden guest ;
> Now at the gate a paltry largess lies,
> And eager hands and tongues dispute the prize.
> But first (lest some false claimant should be found)
> The weary steward takes his anxious round,
> And pries in every face."
>
> —Sat. i. 95.

After the first two hours of the day had been thus spent, the noble Roman would go forth, if a senator, to the senate-house, or else to the forum, and there transact either his own business or that of the State, and would there be ready to plead the cause of any client who might be engaged in a lawsuit.

Thus, till eleven o'clock, the day was devoted by all Romans, who had any pretensions to an active life, to their more serious pursuits. At eleven our citizen would return home, attended by many a client who had followed him in hopes of an invitation to the evening meal. Vain hope, at all events in most cases :—

> " Returning home, he drops them at the gate ;
> And now the weary clients, wise too late,
> Resign their hopes, and supperless retire
> To spend their paltry dole on herbs and fire."
>
> —Sat. i. 32.

The next hour was sacred to the mid-day siesta ; and from eleven till twelve the whole town was wrapped in unbroken silence. The siesta over, Rome woke up again to pleasure and idleness, except in the few cases where arrears of the morning's work had to be made up. Now, if you wished, you might go and hear Codrus bawl out his "Theseid" to an unwilling audience, or more pleasantly spend an hour listening to the sweet modulations of Statius's voice, as he read out parts of his unfinished "Thebaid" to a delighted crowd. This was the time when poets and historians would, if they could by any means assemble an audience, declaim their works in public in hopes of founding a reputation ; while others, whom frequent failure had made desperate, waited till the bathing-hour, and would then assault the ears of the disgusted but helpless bathers. Or, if you wished, you might now repair to the circus, and, under the guidance of the great censor of manners, watch with indignation

"Mœvia, with naked breast, transfix a Tuscan boar." *

—Sat. i. 22.

Or the high-born Gracchus, or some other noble, step forth :—

"No sword his thigh invests,
No helmet, shield—such armour he detests,
Detests and spurns, and impudently stands
With a poised net and trident in his hands.
The foe advances. Lo ! a cast he tries,
But misses, and in frantic terror flies
Round the thronged cirque ; and, anxious to be known,
Lifts his bare face, with many a piteous moan."

—Sat. viii. 200.

Else you might go to the theatre, and there see

* For an account of the active part taken by the Roman women in the games of the Amphitheatre, the reader is referred to p. 130.

"The hired Patrician's low buffoonery;
Laugh at the Fabii's tricks, and grin to hear
The cuffs resound from the Mamerci's ear!"
—Sat viii. 190.

It was, however, seldom that a patrician would be seen on the stage; even the most reckless would hesitate before breaking with the prejudice dearest to the Romans in so open a manner. It was bad enough that any free-born citizen should disgrace himself by public acting—a profession which Roman usage had always limited to slaves and foreigners; but that one of patrician race should do so was in a manner an insult to the entire nation. Not even the example of Nero, who, when emperor, sang and played on the public stage, could reconcile the Romans to such a breach of ancient custom; and, in truth, it was this very singing and acting of his that more than aught else led to Nero's unpopularity and downfall.

"Who, Nero, so depraved, if choice were free,
To hesitate 'twixt Seneca and thee?
Whose crimes, so much have they all crimes outgone,
Deserve more serpents, apes, and sacks than one.*
Not so, thou say'st; there are, whom I could name,
As deep in guilt, and as accursed in fame;
Orestes slew his mother. True, but know,
The same effect from different causes flow:
A father murdered at the social board,
And Heaven's command, unsheathed his righteous sword.

* The old Roman law commanded that the convicted parricide should be sewn up in a sack with a viper, an ape, a dog, and a cock, and then cast into the sea.

Besides, Orestes, in his wildest mood,
Poisoned no cousin, shed no consort's blood,
Buried no poniard in a sister's throat,
Sung on no public stage, no Troicks wrote.
This topped his frantic crimes—this roused mankind ;
For what could Galba, what Virginius find
In the dire annals of that dismal reign
Which called for vengeance in a louder strain ?
Lo, here the arts, the studies that engage
The world's great master, on a foreign stage
To prostitute his voice for base renown,
And ravish from the Greeks a parsley crown !"
                                   —Sat. viii. 212.

As a rule, therefore, the parts in a play would all be
taken by Greeks, who were, by the natural bent of
their nation, exquisitely adapted for the stage.

From the public spectacle the citizen would make
for the baths of Agrippa. Entering them, he would
be provided at the State expense with spacious bath-
rooms, supplied with hot or cold water, and attendants
ready to his call. Outside these lay enclosed spaces,
where he might join in a game of ball, or take more
violent exercise in the gymnasium or palestra, as a
preparation for the bath. Here an hour or more
would be spent, partly in the water, partly in the
marble-paved halls, watching the other bathers, or
listening to some poet who mouthed out his last work
till the columns echoed again, hoping for a more
lenient audience among men exhilarated by the freshness of the air and water, and who were conscious of
having ended the work of the day. Here, too, might also
be heard the latest extravagance of the philosophy of

the day, the last ingenious turn given to the tenets of
Epicurus or to the arguments of Zeno. The bearded
Stoic, in his long mantle, followed by a small knot of
admirers, would pace around, and prove that the Stoic
was alone happy, and, by virtue of his philosophy,
alone fit ruler over his fellow-men; while the more
practical Epicurean laid down precepts for the pursuit
of happiness, professing only to teach men how to
pluck the blossom of the fleeting hours. From the
bath our client, if he were fortunate enough to have
obtained in the morning an invitation to sup with his
patron, would make the best of his way to his mansion upon the Esquiline hill. To reach it he would
have to thread the maze of the narrow and tortuous
lanes of the Suburra, past many brawling taverns,
where a few drinkers had already assembled for their
evening bout; in between the rumbling carts and the
shouting drovers, who would chafe at each delay in
the route in no gentle language. He might cast a
glance in passing at the troop of professional beggars,
seated each on his square of matting, trying to impose
on the passer-by with their various tricks and unblush-
ing effrontery; or—a fresh proof that there is nothing
new under the sun—

> " The ingenious sailor,
> Who shows, where tears, where supplications fail,
> A daubing of his melancholy tale."
> —Sat. xiv. 300.

And now he would be violently jostled on one side by
the surging crowd, as it parted in haste to make way

for the litter of some wealthy patrician, and to avoid
the blows of his tall Liburnian slaves as they laid
about them right and left to open a lane for their
master, or trampled down those who were too weak to
resist, or too slow to avoid them.   Meanwhile the
client,—

> " By the throng
> Elbowed and jostled, scarce can creep along,
> Sharp strokes from poles, tubs, rafters, doomed to feel,
> And plastered o'er with mud from head to heel."
> —Sat. iii. 244.

Nor was the progress through these narrow lanes un-
attended with danger to life or limb.   Drivers of carts
and vans seem to have been as reckless then as they
now are :—

> " Hark ! groaning on, the unwieldy waggon spreads
> Its cumbrous load, tremendous !   O'er our heads
> Projecting elm or pine, that nods on high,
> And threatens death to every passer by.
> Heavens ! should the axle crack, which bears a weight
> Of huge Ligurian stone, and pour the freight
> On the pale crowd beneath, what would remain,
> What joint, what bone, what atom of the slain ?
>
> .   .   .   .
>
> Meanwhile, unconscious of their fellows' fate
> At home, they heat the water, scour the plate,
> Arrange the strigils, fill the cruse with oil,
> And ply their several tasks with fruitless toil ;
> For he who bore the dole, poor mangled ghost,
> Sits pale and trembling on the Stygian coast,
> Scared at the horrors of the novel scene,
> At Charon's threatening voice and scowling mien,

Nor hopes a passage, thus abruptly hurled,
Without his farthing, to the nether world."

—Sat. iii. 254.

Approaching nearer to his patron's house, our friend
Trebius meets a string of clients less fortunate than
himself, bearing away the dole which was given in the
morning. The viands themselves are kept hot in a
portable kitchen, and the whole apparatus

" With steady neck a puny slave must bear,
And lest amid the way the flames expire,
Glide nimbly on, and gliding fan the fire."

And now Trebius has at length reached his goal, to
find, however, only too soon, that it is but little pleasure he may expect from this banquet ; and yet it must
stand for payment in full of many a menial service, of
much slavish flattery.

In the first place it is clear that he has been asked,
at the last moment, merely to fill up a place which a
late excuse had left empty, and to make sport for the
more favoured guests. The very servants know the
difference between the needy client and the wealthy
friend, and make Trebius feel his position at every opportunity. The guests having taken their places, and
their hands and feet having been washed by the attendants, wine is handed round to whet the appetite.
And what wine it is !—rank, heady, ropy, served in a
cracked and worthless cup, while Virro himself quaffs
from a chased and jewelled goblet a choice vintage iced
with snow from the top of Mount Soracte. Course

after course follows, and in all the same contrast is observed :—

> " A lobster introduced in state
> Stretches enormous o'er the bending plate !
> Proud of a length of tail, he seems to eye
> The humbler guests with scorn, as, towering by,
> He takes the place of honour at the board,
> And crowned with costly pickles greets the lord."
>
> —Sat. v. 80.

While the poor client has but a mangy crab to eat with his coarse and gritty bread—

> " Black mouldy fragments which defy the saw,
> The mere despair of every aching jaw,
> While manchets, of the finest flour, are set
> Before your lord."
>
> —Sat. v. 68.

Then a red mullet is carried in, but not for Trebius ; for him a half-starved pike and rancid oil must suffice. Meanwhile, to add insult to injury, your sour and ill-cooled wine is poured out by a hideous raw-boned Moor,

> " Whose hideous form the stoutest would affray,
> If met by moonlight near the Latian way."
>
> —Sat. v. 52.

A contrast indeed to the fair youth who waits on his patron—a youth

> " So dearly purchased that the joint estates
> Of Tullus, Ancus would not yield the sum,
> Nor all the wealth of all the kings of Rome.
> A page who costs so much will ne'er, be sure,
> Come at your beck ; he heeds not, he, the poor,

But of his youth and beauty justly vain,
Trips by them with indifference and disdain."
—Sat. v. 56.

The custom of having these beautiful slaves as personal attendants was introduced to Rome from the
luxurious courts of the conquered East ; and the enormous price paid for such youths is a frequent topic
in the writings of the time.   Nor was the extravagance
indulged in, to gratify the ruling fashion of the dining-
table, less prodigious.   Not only was every sea swept to
produce fish of a more delicate flavour than those supplied by the North Mediterranean, but even the very
expense of a dish was an irresistible recommendation
to the rich *parvenus* who now occupied the chief places
at Rome.   For instance, we are told of a small fortune
being paid down for a mullet of six pounds weight,
though, except for the rarity of its size, it was no more
worthy of the price than any other fish.   Such ostentation, however, was one of the weakest points in the
Roman character, aptly satirised by Cleopatra, when, at
her famous banquet, she dissolved a priceless pearl in
vinegar, and quaffed an emperor's ransom at a draught.

The banquet, however, proceeds through a long suc-
cession of dishes ; a fresh relay of fish comes on—a
lamprey from the Sicilian straits balanced by skinny
eels, a goose's liver, a capon, a wild boar, huge mush-
rooms from the plains of Africa, haunches of venison,
hares and pullets, apples bright of hue

" As those which in Alcinous' garden grew,"
—Sat. v. 151.

come on the table ; but none will ever reach Trebius.
At a side table,

> " To put your patience to the test,
> Lo ! the spruce carver, to his task address,
> Skips like a harlequin from place to place,
> And waves his knife with pantomimic grace,
> Till every dish be ranged, and every joint
> Severed, by nicest rules, from point to point.
> You think this folly—'tis a simple thought.
> To such perfection now is carving brought,
> That different gestures by our curious men
> Are used for different dishes—hare and hen."
>
> —Sat. v. 120.

At last, mortified and insulted in every way, he must
retire, his hunger but half satisfied, from the board,
while the rest of the company go to another chamber,
and close the evening with deep potations, and gambling deeper still.

We will, however, leave them crowned with roses or
parsley to elect the king of the drinking-bout, and
cool their palates with the iced vintages of Greece and
Asia, and follow Trebius on his homeward journey to
his solitary room in the Suburra—a journey not without its own peculiar dangers.　As in modern Edinburgh, so in ancient Rome, night was the time chosen
by the careful housewife for throwing her slops from
the upper windows into the open drain that ran through
the street beneath.　And not only slops, but other
harder if more cleanly *débris,* descended from the many-
storied pile—

> " Whence heedless garrettiers their potsherds throw,
> And crush the unwary wretch that walks below !

Clattering, the storm descends from heights unknown,
Ploughs up the street, and wounds the flinty stone.
Pray then, and count your humble prayer well sped,
If pots be only—emptied on your head."

—Sat. iii. 274.

This danger escaped, there was another which he who traversed the city by night had to encounter. The streets of imperial Rome swarmed with a race of bloods similar to the Mohawks and Hectors who, towards the close of the last century, wandered forth " flown with insolence and wine," breaking windows, upsetting sedans, beating quiet men, and offering rude caresses to pretty women. The encounter of one of these with our poor client, as he treads his way homeward, husbanding the last glimmer of the modest lantern that guides his steps, is described with great humour by Juvenal.

First, there is a graphic sketch of the bully as he struts along the street looking for his prey, but carefully avoiding the patrician and his well-armed flambeaux-bearers' train. When the solitary plebeian comes on the stage, " Stand !" cries his antagonist; and then follows a scene somewhat like that of the wolf and lamb in the fable. The client tries to avoid the unequal contest by slavish obsequiousness in vain :—

"'Whence come you, rogue ?' he cries. 'Whose beans
  to-night
Have stuffed you thus ? What cobbler clubbed his mite
For leeks or sheep's-head porridge ? Dumb, quite dumb !
Speak, or be kicked ! Yet once again, your home,

Where shall I find you ?   At what beggar's stand,
Temple, or bridge, whimpering with outstretched hand ?'
Answer or answer not, 'tis all the same,
He lays me on, and makes me bear the blame.
Before the bar for beating him you come ;
This is the poor man's liberty at Rome.
You beg his pardon, happy to retreat
With some remaining teeth to chew your meat."
—Sat. iii. 292.

Suppose all these dangers past, there is still the un-happy chance of a fire in his poor home, which may burn his little all, and leave him to beg his livelihood in cold and hunger through the street, happy to have escaped with his bare life. Of course in such narrow streets, flanked by such lofty houses, a fire would spread with fearful rapidity, and the difficulty of escape would be great indeed ; and, in fact, we are often told of widespread conflagrations at Rome in which the loss of life was enormous, even greater than that of property ; the means of quenching a fire being miserably insufficient, and amounting to little more than a few buckets of water flung on by the hands of the neighbours or of the night-watch, except in those desperate cases where the fire was kept within bounds by cutting off, as a last resource, the supply of food, and the neighbouring houses fell a prey to the hand of man instead of the fire.

Finally, nocturnal marauders and highwaymen swarmed in the streets of Rome, ready to set the police at defiance in the most open way, and to spread terror throughout whole districts of the city :—

" The hardened in each ill,
To save complaints and prosecution, kill.
Chased from their woods and bogs, the Paddies come
To this vast city as their native home,
To live at ease, and safely skulk in Rome."
—Sat. iii. 305.

Well indeed might Juvenal exclaim that he preferred even the desert crags of Prochyta to Rome,
where honesty and noble birth, justice and religion,
were alike crushed and laughed to scorn by the
treachery of the venal Greek—by the adulation of the
slavish parasite !

CHAPTER IX

OF all English writers who have either imitated or translated the Satires of Juvenal, Johnson is undoubtedly the one to whom must be assigned the highest rank. Whether we weigh these imitations on their own intrinsic merits, or as reproductions of the spirit of the original, no competent judge can deny them a high place in the roll of literary fame. Johnson has left imitations of two of the Satires of Juvenal—the second and the tenth—under the respective titles of "London," and "The Vanity of Human Wishes." Of these his "London" is in every way the less worthy of notice. It is pitched in a decidedly lower tone than the imitation of the tenth satire ; and though a fine poem, it contains few passages of any remarkable merit. It will always be read with pleasure, but it will hardly rouse the enthusiasm of the reader, who will not consider that the touches of humour and pathos which the poem certainly contains, compensate for a certain want of natural flow, a tendency to adopt artificial and unreal sentiments, that is far more

apparent here than in the original. The praise of a
country life was not by any means a theme on which
Johnson could be expected to write in his best style.
He had not studied human nature except as developed
in the town. He knew little of the country, and that
little did not encourage him to seek for more knowledge. Fleet Street was to him far more attractive
than any rural solitude, and the view from Temple
Bar more beautiful than the loveliest scenery of Wales
or Scotland. This fact is sufficient to account for the
weakness of the lines in which Johnson glorifies the
country at the expense of the town : lines that remind us of Claude's pictures, where rural simplicity is
exemplified by nymph-like shepherdesses, courted by
musical and perfumed swains. Here, for instance, is a
sketch of the life that the poet's friend is made to
propose to the man who, weary of the crimes and
follies of the metropolis, should seek for quiet and
repose in the seclusion of some country retreat as yet
unpolluted by the vices of civilisation—

"There prune thy walks, support thy drooping flowers,
 Direct thy rivulets, and twine thy bowers ;
 And, while thy grounds a cheap repast afford,
 Despise the dainties of a venal lord :
 There every bush with Nature's music rings,
 There every breeze bears health upon its wings ;
 On all thy hours security shall smile,
 And bless thine evening walk and morning toil."

It is not easy to say what sort and manner of men
Johnson here has before his eyes. Certainly the
description is not like anything that he would have

met with in any Welsh county, or indeed in any
part of England.

"London," as is well known, was written by Johnson during a short stay that he made in Hampstead
for the benefit of his health in the year 1738; and in
that quiet suburban village he may have persuaded
himself that he really was sated with the pleasures
and pursuits of London, and weary of its ceaseless turmoil.   Soon, however, very far from abjuring the
metropolis, which was to him a centre of attraction,
he returned to his old love, clinging to her allurements
more closely than ever.   Few will now be found to
doubt that this poem, though it contains many sonorous lines, and shows a very considerable command of
language, was very much overrated at the time of its
first publication.

The plot of the satire is briefly as follows: The poet,
upon the occasion of the departure of an imaginary
friend from the din of the city to some distant country
solitude, praises his resolution while regretting the loss
of his companion; the friend rejoins, justifying his
design and setting forth the advantages which he will
derive from his choice.   The statement of these reasons forms the bulk of the poem.   The friend whom
Johnson introduces has been pretty generally identi-
fied with that unfortunate man Savage, who, about
this date, left London for Wales, there to live on the
charity of his friends.   The design was indeed well
carried out by Johnson, but it would be probably
quite impossible to attain to excellence in the task
which he here set himself to accomplish.   His genius

was fettered by the conditions that he had imposed upon it, and by trying to observe too close a similarity between his own poem and the model on which he worked, he was forced to sacrifice much plausibility in the plot and propriety of illustration in a vain attempt to grasp at once two aims which were wholly incompatible. He might have produced an excellent translation of Juvenal's satire. He might have taken that satire as his text and written a poem really his own, which, while the general scope might have been borrowed, would yet have been cast in a fresh mould, and illustrated with scenes and characters more appropriate to the times in which the plot was laid. What he actually did write has neither the merits of a translation nor the piquancy and spontaneity of an original poem.

In reading Juvenal we cannot fail to see that the poet, though perhaps hardly sincere in the contempt which he pours on the active life of Rome, is yet writing out of the fulness of his heart, as he criticises with an impetuous flow of sarcasm things that he has seen with his own eyes and heard with his own ears. When we read Johnson's version we cannot get rid of the feeling that many of his ideas are not really called for by the exigencies of the poem, and would never have found a place there had it not been for the desire not to omit any stroke of satire or political allusion that had been made a point of in the original. We may especially notice as an example of this unfortunate mode of treatment the description of Greenwich at the opening of the poem. This would seem to be

introduced simply in order to match the account of
the grove and fountain of Egeria, and in order that an
indirect sort of parallel may be hinted at between the
inspired Nymph of Numa and the Virgin Queen.   So,
again, the burning of the house of Arturius, and the
humorous assertion that the many contributions he
received from his friends, as marks of sympathy for his
loss, made him even more wealthy than before, though
quite in accord with Roman manners, will hardly
justify to the English reader the introduction of
Orgilio's similar misfortune and good luck.   Many
parts of Johnson's poem are, however, quite free from
this blemish; especially those passages where the
thought is one that is, from its nature, equally appli-
cable to all times.   Looking at his own life, at his own
disappointed hopes and blighted career, Johnson
might well exclaim that, in his time, just as in that of
Juvenal,

> " This mournful truth is everywhere confessed,
>   Slow rises worth by poverty depressed."

From his own experience he could furnish many
examples of the keen sting left behind by the sarcasm
of a rich fool which the hungry author did not dare
resent.   Often must he have felt in his own person,
that—

> " Of all the griefs that harass the distressed
>   Sure the most bitter is a scornful jest ;
>   Fate never wounds more deep the generous heart,
>   Than when a blockhead's insult points the dart."

The most successful parts of the satire are, however,

unquestionably those in which Johnson pours out his
indignation upon the French, in imitation of Juvenal's
invective against the Greeks; or where he describes
the unseemly brawls or the murderous encounters that
might have been seen almost nightly by any man
whom business or pleasure detained till late in the ill-
lighted streets of London. Such scenes he must often
have himself witnessed in his midnight rambles; and
the lines in which he satirises the Mohawk of the
Strand, are little if at all inferior to Juvenal's ren-
contre between the poor plebeian and the patrician
fire-eater :—

> " Some fiery fop, with new commission vain,
> Who sleeps on brambles till he kills his man ;
> Some frolic drunkard, reeling from a feast,
> Provokes a broil, and stabs you for a jest.
> Yet ev'n these heroes, mischievously gay,
> Lords of the street, and terrors of the way ;
> Flushed as they are with folly, youth, and wine,
> Their prudent insults to the poor confine ;
> Afar they mark the flambeau's bright approach,
> And shun the shining train, and golden coach."

The imitation of the tenth satire is a poem in every
way superior to " London." In the ten years that
intervened between the production of these two satires,
Johnson's powers as a writer had made decided progress, and " The Vanity of Human Wishes " was a subject on which he always wrote with vigour and elegance.
In this .poem, too, Johnson shows himself a far less
close imitator, and is thus able to give his genius a
wider range. The lines no longer seem to labour under
the cramping demands of a translation ; and Johnson

is here able to show that he was endowed with a fair
share of the poet's divine breath.   Like Juvenal, he
introduces his subject by a few lines deploring the
unhappy fate of man, who, deluded by hope and fear,
by desire and hate,

"Shuns fancied ills, and chooses airy good;"

who is so little able to guide his own life that those
things which he longs for most eagerly will often,
when attained, bring nothing but misery and ruin in
their train.   This is the general theme of the satire ;
and in proof of its truth are adduced many examples
of men whose ambition has been baffled by that which
seemed to be their chiefest boast, whose pride has been
brought down to the very dust through the qualities
in which they had most gloried themselves.

First, the fall of Cardinal Wolsey is given as a parallel to that of Sejanus in Juvenal.   Here the palm of
superior merit must undoubtedly be awarded to Juvenal.   His graphic and impassioned account of the
tumultuous scenes in the streets of Rome immediately
after the condemnation and death of the hated favourite,
is incomparably grand.   We seem to see the houses
all decked with laurel branches as for a victory ; to
hear the anxious hum of the crowds of citizens, as they
collect half in joy, half in terror, at the awful rapidity
of the blow, and swell into a universal roar of execration
as the hated features of Sejanus are recognised.   Everywhere are his statues hurled from their pedestals and
rolled into the bonfires roaring ready for their prey ;
while his lifeless and mutilated corpse is itself dragged

amid ignominy and derision through the streets, exposed to the mean insults of the cowardly populace,
that was but one short day before ready to shout "long
life and prosperity to Emperor Sejanus."

Johnson has here failed to reach the high excellence
of his model, yet his failure is not ignominious. The
description of the great prelate as he stood forth in all
the haughtiness of power, rivalling the king himself in
the magnificence of his retinue and the authority of his
command, is with considerable skill made to lead up to
the sudden catastrophe by which the whole edifice of
dignity and wealth is in a moment swept away.

> " In full-blown dignity, see Wolsey stand,
>   Law in his voice, and fortune in his hand :
>   To him the Church, the realm, their powers consign,
>   Through him the rays of regal bounty shine,
>   Turned by his nod the stream of honour flows,
>   His smile alone security bestows :
>   Still to new heights his restless wishes tower,
>   Claim leads to claim, and power advances power ;
>   Till conquest unresisted ceased to please,
>   And rights submitted left him none to seize."

The blindness of man is next exemplified by the
miserable portion that awaits the aspirant to literary
fame. Here Johnson's pathetic enumeration of misfortunes and rebuffs that the author must expect— of
his hunger and nakedness—of his shifts to satisfy the
bare demands of nature—of the patron's cruel coldness,
and the yet more cruel neglect of the learned—of the
emptiness of success that comes only when success has
lost its charms, and has no longer any value for one

who has outlived the enthusiasm of youth, and in the desolateness of old age has none to whom he might impart the pleasure of gratified ambition—is full of the truest and most touching pathos. Very far superior in execution, it must be owned, is the whole passage to Juvenal's somewhat frigid lamentation over the fate of Demosthenes and Cicero.

> " When first the college rolls receive his name,
> The young enthusiast quits his ease for fame ;
> Resistless burns the fever of renown,
> Caught from the strong contagion of the gown :
> O'er Bodley's dome his future labours spread,
> And Bacon's mansion trembles o'er his head.
> Are these thy views ?   Proceed, illustrious youth,
> And Virtue guard thee to the throne of Truth !
> Yet, should thy soul indulge the gen'rous heat
> Till captive Science yields her last retreat ;
> Should Reason guide thee with her brightest ray,
> And pour on misty Doubt resistless day;
> Should no false kindness lure to loose delight,
> Nor praise relax, nor difficulty fright ;
> Should tempting Novelty thy cell refrain,
> And Sloth effuse her opiate fumes in vain ;
> Should Beauty blunt on fops her fatal dart,
> Nor claim the triumph of a lettered heart ;
> Should no disease thy torpid veins invade,
> Nor Melancholy's phantoms haunt thy shade ;
> Yet hope nor life from grief or danger free,
> Nor think the doom of man reversed for thee ;
> Deign on the passing world to turn thine eyes,
> And pause awhile from Letters, to be wise ;
> There mark what ills the scholar's life assail,
> Toil, envy, want, the patron, and the gaol.
> See nations, slowly wise and meanly just,
> To buried merit raise the tardy bust.

> If dreams yet flatter, once again attend,
> Hear Lydiat's life, and Galileo's end."

We can hardly resist the impression that it is to himself that Johnson is here alluding, especially in the
lines beginning with " Should no disease,"—lines that
feelingly tell of his own ill-health and many privations,
of the despondency that continually checked his re-
liance on himself, and the melancholy fear of death
against which he so often and so earnestly strove in
vain. In any case he has here this advantage over
Juvenal, that he describes scenes and events that came
under his own observation. He does not, like the
Roman, write on themes that had long since become
the commonplace of every ambitious poetaster, a subject of declamation in all the schools of Rome. The
same advantage in the choice of his examples still
stands Johnson in good stead when he illustrates the
vanity of military success and of the warrior's fame by
the ruin and death of Charles of Sweden. That prince,
to whose marvellous victories and still more portentous
ruin Europe still paid the tribute of terror or of
admiration, was as yet a name of power to evoke the
wonder and the sympathy of men. When Juvenal
wrote, three hundred years of eventful history had
elapsed since the battle of Zama, and the memory of
the day when Rome had trembled before the armies of
Hannibal was now scarcely sufficiently distinct to
thrill with real emotion the heart of any citizen of the
Empire. Juvenal has also here this additional difficulty to overcome : patriotism would not allow him
to dwell on the great victories of Hannibal over the

Romans, though the contrast that he might have thus brought out would have added much in dramatic interest to the tale of his defeat and inglorious death. Johnson was hampered by no such scruples; and for loftiness of thought and majesty of diction, the lines in which he describes the brief though brilliant career of the ill-starred monarch, have seldom been surpassed. The whole passage is well worth quoting.

"On what foundation stands the warrior's pride,
How just his hopes, let Swedish Charles decide ;
A frame of adamant, a soul of fire,
No dangers fright him, and no labours tire ;
O'er love, o'er fear, extends his wide domain,
Unconquered lord of pleasure and of pain ;
No joys to him pacific sceptres yield,
War sounds the trump, he rushes to the field ;
Behold surrounding kings their powers combine,
And one capitulate, and one resign ;
Peace courts his hand, but spreads her charms in vain ;
'Think nothing gained,' he cries, 'till nought remain,
On Moscow's walls till Gothic standards fly,
And all be mine beneath the polar sky.'
The march begins in military state,
And nations on his eye suspended wait ;
Stern Famine guards the solitary coast,
And winter barricades the realms of Frost ;
He comes, nor want nor cold his course delay;—
Hide, blushing Glory, hide Pultowa's day :
The vanquished hero leaves his broken bands,
And shows his miseries in distant lands ;
Condemned, a needy supplicant to wait,
While ladies interpose and slaves debate.
But did not Chance at length her error mend ?
Did no subverted empire mark his end ?

Did rival monarchs give the fatal wound ?
Or hostile millions press him to the ground ?
His fall was destined to a barren strand,
A petty fortress, and a dubious hand ;
He left a name, at which the world grew pale,
To point a moral or adorn a tale."

In the remainder of the poem there is a distinct falling off from the high standard that Johnson has here reached ; and Juvenal has everywhere the advantage over his imitator, in the general train of thought and the vividness of his illustrations, no less than in the grace and dignity of his language.   The picture of the helpless and imbecile grey-beard, in which he would show how vain and foolish is the oft-repeated prayer for length of days, has never been surpassed for graphic power.   No less vivid and life-like is the description of the ill-omened marriage of Silius to Messalina—a warning to mothers, terrific in its awful catastrophe, that a prayer granted to the full is but too often a cruel curse.   Once at least had that beauty that is so earnestly desired for every child hurried its unfortunate possessor to a shameful and untimely end. Yet his death, though early, came too late to save a noble name from the stain of guilt.   Himself married, he did not shrink to marry Cæsar's wife in the face of Rome and of the sun, and to become an actor in a crime that was before unknown even in the guilty Court of Rome.   We have elsewhere given Juvenal's description of this scene.   In the place of this thrilling episode, Johnson can offer us only a collection of trite commonplaces on the lonesomeness of old age and the instability of female virtue. Yet more; in the concluding lines of the poem, where Johnson again imitates Juvenal more closely, and his subject is the efficacy of prayer, and the trust that we should repose in a kind and omniscient Deity, Johnson has failed to approach the lofty precepts and the truly religious tone of the heathen moralist. The one couplet of the entire passage that is most adequate to the subject is an almost literal translation of two lines of Juvenal; and we seek in vain for any traces of that superiority in this respect which we would naturally have been led to expect from one who wrote from the vantage-ground insured to him by a knowledge of the teaching and examples of Christianity. On the whole, however, in spite of occasional flaws, we may safely assert that these two imitations have reached a degree of excellence rarely attained in works of this description. Johnson seldom falls very far behind his model. He never allows himself to become insipid or prolix, while sometimes the copy is decidedly superior to the original itself. There is, indeed, one failing common to both the Latin and the English poet that tends much to obscure and even to invalidate the argument as a whole. As Gibbon has clearly pointed out, Juvenal altogether failed to draw the obvious distinction between those apparent goods, such as warlike fame and absolute command, which cannot fail to bring discontent and unhappiness in their train, and those which, like length of days or personal beauty, may well prove a real blessing to those to whose portion they fall, and who use them aright.

Of translators, properly so called, there are not many that will call for notice. The Satires of Juvenal do not seem to have attracted, at any rate not in England, the same attention that has been bestowed on the writings of Horace. Whatever the reason may be, it was not till the middle of the seventeenth century that the two versions edited. by Barten Holyday and Sir Robert Stapylton appeared almost contemporaneously. Of the latter it is not necessary to say much. He was little qualified, either as a scholar or as a poet, to do justice to the task he had undertaken; and his volumes are now seldom read, never admired. The translation of his literary rival has had a longer term of existence, though it can hardly be said that even it was ever really popular. Holyday was indeed deficient in some of the qualifications necessary to the translator. What Dryden said of him is true, that the poetry of Juvenal has always escaped his grasp, and that his version is often more difficult to understand than the original itself. His learning and industry were considerable, but the object he aims at is one which, from its very conditions, it is impossible to reach; and his attempt to give a word-for-word translation in rhyme has met with the failure that might have been foreseen to be its inevitable result. As an example of the style in which he wrote, we here give a few lines from the 10th Satire describing the fall of Sejanus. These may be compared with Gifford's rendering of the same passage that we have quoted elsewhere :—

" Hark, the fires snap ! the rout's adored head lacks
  Nor blast nor furnace : huge Sejanus cracks !
  Of the world's second face are formed strange matters,
  Water-pots, basins, frying-pans, and platters !
  Crowned be the doors with bays ! a bull, chalk-white
  And large, led to Jove's Capitol ! O sight !
  Sejanus dragged ! O joy ! his lips, his wan
  Face saw y'? Believe't, I never loved the man."

And this is neither better nor worse than his average manner throughout the volume. Of his Notes and Illustrations we must speak far more highly; and at the period when they were published they were looked on as a contribution of considerable importance towards the elucidation of the Latin poets. Yet even here, it is the matter far more than the manner in which it is expressed that calls for admiration; and the same absence of taste, and of ear for harmony of sound, is everywhere conspicuous. It is amusing to turn from his forced rhymes and halting prose to his preface, where he excuses at some length, though not apparently without a certain amount of complacency, his own flirtation with the Muses. "As for publishing poetry," he writes, "it needs no defence, there being a divine rapture in it, if my Lord Verulam's judgment shall be admitted." In spite, however, of the claim that Holyday thus urges for the indulgence that is granted to the poet, it is clear that he wrote rather for the convenience of the scholar than for the entertainment of the general reader, who indeed very soon turns with disgust from the inartistic rhymes and ill-constructed sentences in which are united all the disadvantages of rugged prose and of still more rugged verse. In spite, then, of the learning and industry displayed by the accomplished archdeacon, a new version of Juvenal was before long demanded, or at all events welcomed, by the public.

Towards the close of the seventeenth century Dryden was absolute dictator of the literary world, and a new translation was published under his auspices. This work, supported by his authority and the reputation that he then enjoyed, met with a considerable share of popularity. Dryden himself translated the 1st, the 3d, the 6th, and the 10th Satires, besides an introductory essay of some considerable length, written in the form of a dedication to the Earl of Dorset of his day, in which he takes occasion to review the history and the scope of satire. In spite, however, of the conspicuous position which Dryden then held, and of his high character as a poet, the merits of the volume were not great. The lines, indeed, are often powerful and sonorous, and almost always correct, while the finer passages seldom fail to leave a distinct impression on the mind. The general style, though by no means equal either in force or elegance to that of Dryden's original poetry, is terse and vigorous; and if the expressions are sometimes familiar, or even coarse, the interest is never allowed to flag, and every page is enlivened by the play of wit and the ornament of epigram or antithesis. Nevertheless, no one who reads these satires but will feel that they in some sort fail to satisfy the expectations that he might justly have indulged. When the greatest master of English satire set himself the task of translating into his own language the works of the first satirist of Rome, we should have grounds for expecting that the result would be a volume of no slight merit ; that it would take a high, if not the highest, place among works of that description, especially when we remember that Dryden excelled far more in command of language and delicacy of judgment than in any peculiar gift of imagination or fancy. Who, one is tempted to ask, more fit than the founder of the English critical school of poetry to excel in a task in which perfection must be attained far more by practised skill in versification, and a nice discrimination in the choice of expressions, than by any of the rarer and more precious gifts of the inspired poet ? A luxuriant imagination might indeed make a translator impatient of the trammels cast on him by the necessity of following closely his original, and thus render him *pro tanto* a less competent workman than one far inferior to him in poetic genius.

And yet, in spite of these great and obvious qualifications, both positive and negative, Dryden has not even attained that degree of success which would seem to be within the reach of many men of but slight literary capacity. This failure is due in part, at least, to an inadequate conception of the end that a trans-

lator ought to propose to himself. Until the time of
Dryden, there had scarcely been any English render-
ings of the poets of Greece and Rome that would in
the present day meet with the slightest degree of
applause. Some writers, like Holyday, had rendered
success impossible for themselves by attempting an
exactly literal translation into rhyming verse. Others,
such as Cowley, mistook licence for liberty, and barely
imitated the poems which they professed to translate.
Dryden himself was in some danger of falling into this
latter error. He saw clearly the faultiness of Holyday's version, and was himself, as he distinctly tells
us, ready to sacrifice the scholar to the poet whenever
it should seem to him impossible to seize at once both
the exact meaning and the poetry of his author.
"The common way we have taken," he says, speaking
of himself and his colleagues in the undertaking, " is
not a literal translation, but a kind of paraphrase ; or
somewhat, which is more loose, between a paraphrase
and an imitation."

The least pleasing form of all in which this licence
shows itself is the laxity into which Dryden has only
too often permitted himself to fall, of using terms
that must necessarily, by their meaning and their
associations, call up a train of modern ideas quite alien
to any that could have presented themselves to
Juvenal's mind. For example, such lines as—

" When he dares hope a colonel's command ;"

or—

" Board-wages and a footman's livery ;"

or again—

" A hundred hungry slaves with their Dutch-kitchens
      wait ; "

or—

    " A third is charmed with the new opera notes ; "

or—

    " The ghostly sire forgives the wife's delights,"—

can hardly be accepted as representing any form of
Roman thought.   So, again, to translate *Porticus* by
the Mall, or *Seres* by *France*, is to hurry the reader
over twenty centuries of time, from the Rome of
Domitian to the London of the Restoration.   In
spite of these failings, however, Dryden's version is in
some ways the best that we have in the English
language ; at all events, it has the merit of having
been written by a true poet.   The more modern
translations of Gifford and Hodgson have this merit,
that they follow the Latin text more faithfully than
any previous attempts.   Both of them bear the traces
of careful and accurate study, and the scholarship of
both is thoroughly sound ; while the versification, if
not always of the highest class, is always elaborated
with diligence, and seldom sins against the maxims of
good taste.   They may be read and appreciated both
by the scholar and by those who can hope for no
closer acquaintance with the writings of Juvenal.
Still, neither the one nor the other has reached
that high standard of excellence which we have now
been taught to expect.   No one has yet done for
Juvenal what the late Professor Conington did for
Virgil, or Lord Derby for the Iliad of Homer.   Till

such a translation shall appear, the English reader must perforce be contented with an imperfect acquaintance with him, whose verse—to use words applied to Cowper and Johnson—

> " May claim—grave, masculine, and strong—
> Superior praise to the mere poet's song."

END OF JUVENAL.

PRINTED BY WILLIAM BLACKWOOD AND SONS, EDINBURGH.

PLAUTUS AND TERENCE

BY THE

REV. W. LUCAS COLLINS, M.A.

AUTHOR OF

'ETONIANA,' 'THE PUBLIC SCHOOLS,' ETC.

WILLIAM BLACKWOOD AND SONS

EDINBURGH AND LONDON

MDCCCLXXIII

NOTE.

THESE pages are much indebted to M. Guizot's volume entitled 'Menandre; Etude Historique, &c. :' also to Mr Dunlop's 'History of Roman Literature.'

No attempt has been made to avoid roughness in the metre of the translations from Plautus and Terence; they can hardly be, in this respect, more irregular than the originals.

W. L. C.

CONTENTS.

PLAUTUS AND TERENCE.

CHAPTER I.

INTRODUCTORY—THE ANCIENT COMIC DRAMA.

THE Comedies of Plautus and Terence are all that
remains to us of the Roman Comic Drama. It is
impossible to deal with the works of these writers,
even in so slight a sketch as is contemplated in
this volume, without some previous reference to the
Greek originals from which they drew. For the
Roman drama was, more than any other branch of
Roman literature, an inheritance from Greece; one of
those notes of intellectual sovereignty which that marvellous people impressed upon their conquerors. The
plays which, during five hundred years, from the days
of the Scipios to those of Diocletian, amused a Roman
audience, had as little claim to be regarded as national
productions as the last happy "adaptation" from the
French which enjoys its brief run at an English
theatre.

But when we speak of Greek Comedy in its relation
to the Roman Drama, we must not form our idea of

Comedy from the plays of Aristophanes. It so happens that he stands before us moderns as the sole surviving representative, in anything like discernible shape, of the comic drama at Athens. But his brilliant burlesques, with their keen political satire, their wealth of allusion, their mad extravagance of wit pushed even to buffoonery, have not much more in common with the plays of Plautus and Terence than with our modern parlour comedy as we have it from Mr Robertson or Mr Byron.

It has been said, when we parted from Aristophanes in a former volume of this series, that the glories of the old Athenian comedy had departed even before the great master in that school had put his last piece upon the stage. The long War was over. The great game of political life no longer presented the same intense excitement for the players. Men's lives and thoughts had begun to run in a narrower channel. As a political engine, there was no longer scope or occasion for the comic drama. And again, it was no longer easy to provide that costly and elaborate spectacle,—the numerous Chorus, highly trained and magnificently costumed, the machinery, the decorations, and the music,—which had delighted the eyes of Athenian playgoers none the less because their intellect was keen enough to appreciate every witticism of the dialogue. It must be remembered that the expense of mounting a new play—and this must always have been considerable where the theatres were on such a vast scale—was not a matter of speculation for author or manager, as with us, but a public charge undertaken in turn by the richer citizens; and in which those who sought popularity, in order to advance their own political claims, vied with each other in the liberality of their expenditure. But at the close of the Peloponnesian War, many a noble family found itself impoverished by the long and terrible struggle, and the competition for public office had probably lost much of its charm. The stage followed the temper of the nation : it became less violently political, less extravagant and more sedate. Shall one venture to say that, like the nation, it lost something of its spirit? There was method, we must remember, in the mad licence of Aristophanes. Bitter as he was against his political opponents, it was an honest bitterness, and Cleon was his enemy because he believed him to be the enemy of the state. Socrates and Euripides were caricatured in the most unsparing fashion, for the amusement of the audience, and it was convenient for a professional jester to have two such well-known characters for his subject ; but he had always the apology that he really believed the teaching both of the philosopher and of the tragedian to have an evil influence upon public morality. There was a certain earnestness of purpose which gave respectability to the Aristophanic comedy in spite of its notorious offences against decency and good manners.

The new style of Comedy, which was the original of that of Plautus and Terence, and which developed in later times into what we call Comedy now, did not perhaps fully establish itself at Athens until nearly half a century after the death of Aristophanes. But the germ of it may be found in the later tragedies of Euripides. His heroes, and even his gods, are as unlike as possible to the stately figures who move in the dramas of

Æschylus.   He may call them by what names he
pleases, but they are the personages of ordinary life.
His drunken Hercules, in his beautiful drama (tragedy
it can hardly be called) 'Alcestis,' is as really comic as
any character in Menander's plays.   His unsparing
satirist Aristophanes, in his 'Frogs,' when he introduces Æschylus and Euripides pleading before Bacchus
their respective claims to the chair of tragedy, makes
it one of the charges against the latter that he had low-
ered the whole tone of tragedy : that whereas Æschylus
had left the ideal men of the drama "grand figures,
four cubits high," his rival had reduced them to the
petty level of everyday life—poor mean gossips of the
market-place.*   He allows Euripides indeed to plead
in his defence that while the elder tragedian had given
the audience nothing but high-flown sentiment and
pompous language which was quite above their compre-
hension, he had brought before them subjects of common
household interest which all could understand and
sympathise with.   Both accusation and defence were
true.   Euripides had violated the severe simplicity of
classic tragedy : but he had founded the domestic
drama.

The oligarchy of Rome would scarcely have permitted
to the writers for the stage the licence of personal satire
which the Athenian democracy not only bore with,
but encouraged and delighted in.   The risk which
Aristophanes ran from the political partisans of Cleon
would have been as nothing, compared with the perils
of the comic dramatist who should have presumed to

* Frogs, 953, 910.

take the same liberty with any members of the "old great houses" of Rome. There had been at least one example of this in the fate of the poet Nævius. We know very little, unfortunately, of what his dramas may have been like, for in his case we have remaining to us only the merest fragments. But he seems to have made an attempt to naturalise at Rome the old Aristophanic style of comedy. A plebeian by birth, and probably a democratic reformer in politics, he had ventured upon some caricature of, or satire upon, the members of the great family who bore the name of Metellus, and who, as he complained, were always holding high office, fit or unfit. "It is fatality, not merit," he said, in a verse which has been preserved, "that has made the Metelli always consuls of Rome." The family or their friends retorted in a song which they chanted in the streets, the burden of which was, in effect, that "Nævius would find the Metelli a fatality to him." They very soon got him imprisoned, under the stringent libel laws of Rome : and,—since that was not enough to break his spirit—for he is said, after his release, to have written comedies which were equally distasteful in high quarters,—they succeeded at last in driving him into banishment. We hear of no more ambition on the part of Roman dramatists to assume the mantle of Aristophanes. They were content to be disciples in the later school of Menander, and to take as the subject of comedy those general types of human nature under which no individual, high or low, was obliged to think that his own private weaknesses were attacked.

CHAPTER II.

MENANDER was born at Athens, B.C. 342, of a family in which dramatic talent was in some degree hereditary, for his uncle Alexis had written comedies of some repute. It would appear that the faculties which make the successful comic writer commonly develop themselves at an early age ; for Menander, like his predecessor Aristophanes, won his first prize for comedy when he had barely reached manhood : and the same may be remarked as to the early and rapid success of some of our modern humorists.* But this youthful triumph was not followed, as might have been ex-

---

* Of course he did not escape the charge of presumption and precocity from older candidates. He had to defend himself on this occasion, like Pitt, from "the atrocious crime of being a young man." His defence, if we may trust the anecdotist, was by a parable. He brought upon the stage some new-born puppies, and had them thrown into a vessel of water. Blind and weak as they were, they instinctively tried to swim. "Athenians," said the young author, "you ask how, at my years, I can have the knowledge of life which is required in the dramatist : I ask you, under what master and in what school did these creatures learn to swim ? "

pected, by many such victories. He wrote more than a hundred comedies, and he only won the crown eight times. He was beaten in the contest, again and again, by his elder rival Philemon. Of this writer's plays nothing but the merest fragments remain to us, and we are thus unable to form any opinion as to the justice of the popular verdict. But critics who probably had the means of comparing the performances of both authors, do not hesitate to impute this preference of Philemon to Menander by the contemporary public to other causes than the comparative merits of the rivals. Quintilian goes so far as to say that the wonderful genius of Menander robbed all his contemporary dramatists of what might have been their reputation, and that "the blaze of his glory threw their merits into the shade."

The honours which were refused to the poet by his fellow-citizens were liberally offered him by powerful patrons elsewhere. Demetrius "Poliorcetes" both protected him when he occupied Athens and invited him to his court when he had seated himself upon the throne of Macedonia : and Ptolemy Lagus, when he founded his celebrated library at Alexandria, would gladly have imported the living dramatist as well as the manuscripts of his predecessors' works. Menander refused the invitation, though the king offered him "all the money in the world;" but whether it was, as he declared, because he could not tear himself from a certain fair lady at Athens, or because he found that the invitation had been extended to his rival Philemon, may not be so certain.

But it is said that the injustice of his fellow-citizens

broke the poet's heart. In his bitter mortification
at one undeserved defeat (so goes the story) he threw
himself into the sea off the wall at the Piræus, and was
drowned, while yet in the fulness of his powers—not
much over fifty years of age. The authority is suspicious, and the act is very little in accordance with
the philosophy of Menander, as we gather it from the
remains of his plays. A contemporary and probably a
personal friend of Epicurus (they were born in the
same year), he seems to have adopted heartily the easy-
going optimism of that much-abused teacher. To take
human life as it was; to enjoy its pleasures, and to
bear its evils cheerfully, as unavoidable : not to expect
too much from others, as knowing one's own infir-
mities ; to remember that life is short, and therefore
to make the most of it and the best of it, not to
waste it in vain regrets ;—this is the philosophy of
Menander's comedies, which on these points are occasionally only too didactic. The whole secret of it lies,
he says, in three words—" Thou art man."

" The sum of all philosophy is this—
    Thou art a man ; than whom there breathes no creature
More liable to sudden rise and fall." *

This is the principle on which, by the mouth of his
various characters, he is continually excusing human
weaknesses, and protesting against the unreasonable-
ness of mortal regrets and expectations :—

    " Being a mortal, ask not of the gods
        Escape from suffering ; ask but to endure ;
        For if thou seekest to be ever free

        * Meineke, Menandri Reliq., 188.

From pain and evil, then thou seekest this,—
To be a god, or die." *

One does not wonder that Horace, when he shut himself up in his country villa in December, to escape
from the noisy riot of the Saturnalia at Rome, took
with him into his retirement a copy of Menander as
well as of Plato. No doubt he read and appreciated
the philosopher; and the manuscript looked well upon
his table when his friends called. But we may be
sure that the dramatist was his favourite companion.
In him Horace found a thoroughly congenial spirit;
and we shall probably never know how far he was
indebted to him for his turn of thought.

Menander's private habits seem to have been too much
those of an Epicurean in the lower sense of the term;
and if Phædrus is to be trusted in the sketch which he
gives of him in a couple of lines, he had a good deal
of the foppishness not uncommon to popular authors.
Phædrus describes him as "scented with delicate per-
fumes, wearing the fashionable flowing dress, and
walking with an air of languor and affectation." †

It is possible, indeed, that the philosophic and didactic character of Menander's comedies may have been
one reason why they failed so often to win popular
applause. Horace himself must have been the poet of
the court, and of what we call "Society," rather than
of the million. The comedy of manners, which deals
with the problems of domestic life—and such is the
comedy of Menander—had not so strong an attraction

* Meincke, Menand. Rel., 203.   † Fabul., v. 1.

for the multitude as the uproarious farce which formed
so large an ingredient of the Old Comedy. So far as we
can judge from the mere disjointed fragments which
alone have survived, there was very little of broad fun or
of comic situations in the plays of Menander.   It was
in the finer delineation of character, as is admitted by
all his critics, that he most excelled.   He had studied
carefully, and reproduced successfully, the various
phases of that human nature which was the Alpha and
Omega in his philosophy.   The saying of the wise
man of old—" Know thyself "—was a very insufficient
lesson, he considered, for the dramatist.

> " It was not, after all, so wisely said,
>   That precept—' Know thyself;' I reckon it
>   Of more advantage to know other men." *

How real the characters in his dramas appeared to those
who had the best means of judging may be gathered
from the terse epigram ascribed to the grammarian
Aristophanes, the librarian of Alexandria, who lived
about a century after him :—

> " O Life, and O Menander ! speak, and say
>   Which copied which ? or nature, or the play ?"

There certainly does not seem to have been that variety
in the characters introduced which we expect and find
in the modern drama.   But life itself had not then the
variety of interest which it has now : and the sameness
of type which we observe in the persons of the drama
probably existed also in society.   It must be re-

* Meineke, Menand. Rel., 83.

MENANDER. 11

membered also that, owing to the immense size of
the theatres, every performer wore a mask in which
the features were exaggerated, just as he wore buskins
which increased his stature, in order to make his face
and figure distinctly visible to the distant rows of the
audience. These masks necessarily presented one fixed
expression of features; they could not possibly be
made to display the variable shades of emotion which
a real comedian knows how to throw into his face ;
nor could the actor, if he was to preserve his identity for
the audience, change his mask together with his mood
from scene to scene. This difficulty would naturally limit
the dramatic author's sphere of invention : he would feel
that he had to confine himself to certain recognised
generalities of character, such as the mask-moulder could
contrive more or less to represent, and that the finer
shades of distinction which, in spite of so much that is
identical, distinguish man from man, must be left for
the descriptive poet, and were outside of the province
of the author who worked for the stage. The
cold severity of Greek tragedy did not suffer much
from this limitation of the actor's resources : the level
and stately declamation of the text might be accomplished perhaps as well with a mask (which was even
said to increase the volume of sound) as without it.
So also, in the Old Comedy of Aristophanes and his
contemporaries, the exaggerated style of their humour
found apt expression in the broad grotesque which the
mask-maker and property-man supplied,—just as they
do now in our burlesques and extravaganzas. The
delicate play of features and expression which are
so essential to the due impersonation of some of the

most original characters in our modern drama was
plainly impossible to an actor who wore a mask : one
might as reasonably look for it from a company of
Marionettes.   The manufacturer of masks for the
ancient comic drama worked according to fixed rules,
which were perfectly well understood both by the
performers and by the audience.   There was a tolerably
large repertory of these contrivances always at the
disposal of the stage-manager : but each mask had its
own specific character ; its features were so moulded as
to be typical of a class.   We are told with great par-
ticularity that about the period during which these
comedies were placed upon the stage, there were nine
different characters of masks representing old men, ten
for younger characters, and seven for slaves.   For the
women, three varieties were considered enough for the
older personages, the matrons and nurses of the scene.
The young ladies, as was their due, were better provided for ; no less than fourteen varieties of face were
kept in stock for them.   And the mask, in their case—
unlike some masks which are still worn on the stage
of real life—was made not to conceal but to indicate
the character of the wearer, and even her age.   There
was to be found, in the theatrical wardrobe, the face
and head-dress, all in one, which denoted "the
talkative young woman," and the "modest young
woman ;" the one who was still fairly on her promotion,
and the one who was past her prime ; there was a
special mask for the young lady "with the hair," and
one still more peculiar, the "lamp" head-dress, as it
was called, for the young lady whose hair stood up-
right like a lamp.   There was the head-dress "with

the gold band," and that with " the band of many colours ;" and, if we did not know that in the classical comedy, as on our own stage in former times, even the female parts were taken by men, we might have fancied that there was some jealous rivalry as to the right to wear these latter distinguished costumes. The advantage of the system, if any, was this : that the moment the performer appeared upon the scene, the audience had the key to the character.*

The range of characters which were available for the purposes of the dramatist was limited again by the nature of the scenic arrangements. By long theatrical tradition, intelligible enough amongst a people who led essentially an outdoor life, and where the theatre itself was, up to a comparatively late period, open to the sky, all the action of these dramas was supposed to take place in the open air. In the comedies which we are now considering, the scene is commonly a public street,—or rather, probably, a sort of " place " or square in which three or four streets met, so that there was (as has been more than once attempted on the modern stage) a virtual separation of it into distinct parts, very convenient in many ways for carrying on the action

* Should any English reader be inclined to smile, with some degree of superciliousness, at these simple contrivances of the earlier drama, let him remember there was a time when a provincial actor in an English strolling company would borrow of some good-natured squire a full-bottomed wig and lace ruffles in which to perform the part of—Cato ; without which conventional costume it was thought no audience could recognise the "noble Roman." George Harding tells us an amusing story of the Eton amateurs of his day impressing a cast-off wig of the Vice-Provost's for the purpose.

of the piece. A party coming down one street towards
the centre of the stage could hold a separate conversation, and be quite out of the sight of another party in
the other street, while both were equally visible and
audible to the spectators. This will help to explain
the stage directions in more than one scene in the
comedies of Plautus and Terence. But this limitation
of the locality of the scene limited also the range of
characters. These were usually supposed to be resi-
dents in the neighbourhood, and occupants of some of
the houses in the street. Practically, they will be
very often found to be members of two neighbouring
families, more or less closely connected, whose houses
occupied what we should now call the right and left
wings of the stage. Occasionally (as in the 'Aulularia'
and 'Mostellaria' of Plautus) the scene changes to the
inside of one of the houses, or a temple which stands
close by ; but such scenes are quite exceptional, and
in those cases some kind of stage chamber appears to
have been swung round by machinery to the front.

For these reasons, perhaps, as well as for others,
the principal characters in the repertory of the
"New" Comedy are few, and broadly marked. They
seem to have occurred over and over again with but
little variation in almost every piece. There are
the fathers, heads of families, well-to-do burghers,
occupying their house in the city, and commonly
having a farm in the adjacent country besides, but
seldom appearing to have any other particular occupation. Their character is almost always one of two
recognised types,—either stern and niggardly, in which
case they are duly cheated and baffled by their spend-

thrift sons and their accomplices : or mild and easy,
when they go through the process of having their
purses squeezed with less resistance and less suffering.
There is the respectable mother of the family, who is
sometimes the terror of her husband and sometimes
tyrannised over by him. One or two sons, and sometimes a daughter—to which number the household of
comedy seems limited—make up the family group.
The sons are young men about town, having apparently
nothing to do but to amuse themselves, a pursuit
which they do not always follow after the most reputable fashion. Then there are the slaves, on whom
depends in very great measure the action of the piece.
It is very remarkable how in Greek comedy, and in
the Roman adaptations from it, this class supplies
not only the broadly comic element, but the wit
of the dialogue, and the fertility of expedient which
makes the interest of the drama. They are not
brought upon the stage merely to amuse us by their
successful roguery, or by its detection and consequent
punishment, by their propensity to gormandise and
their drunken antics,—this kind of "low comedy
business" is what we might naturally expect of them.
But in witty repartee, and often in practical wisdom,
they are represented as far superior to their masters.
And this ability of character is quite recognised by the
masters themselves. They are intrusted, like Parmeno
in the 'Eunuchus' of Terence, with the care of the sons
of the house, even at that difficult age when they are
growing up to manhood, during the father's absence
abroad : or like his namesake in the 'Plocium' of
Menander, and Geta in the 'Two Brothers' of Terence,

they are the trusted friend and mainstay of a struggling family. It is by no means easy to explain satisfactorily this anomalous position. The slave no doubt in many cases, owing the loss of his personal liberty to the fortunes of war, being either a captive or a captive's child, might, although a foreigner, be of as good birth and hereditary intellect as his master. In many households he would go to the same school, and enjoy the same training in many ways as the young heir of the family : he would be taught many accomplishments, because the more accomplished he was, the more valuable a chattel he became. But was it also that these Athenian citizens, from whom Menander drew, held themselves somewhat above the common practical business of life—in short, like the Easterns in the matter of dancing, considered that they "paid some one else to do their thinking for them " in such matters? The witty slave occupied a position in those households somewhat akin to the king's jester in late times—allowed to use a freedom which would not have been suffered from those of higher rank, but limited always by the risk of condign personal chastisement if he ventured too far. The household slave was certainly admitted to most of his master's secrets ; admitted, it must be remembered, almost of necessity, as many of our own modern servants are—a condition of things which we are all too apt to forget. He might at any moment by his ability and fidelity win, as so many did, his personal freedom, and became from that moment his master's friend ; not, indeed, upon terms of perfect equality, but on a much nearer level than we in these days should be willing to allow. No stronger instance of this need be sought than that of Cicero's freedman Tiro, between whom and his master we find existing an affection almost fraternal. The slave who had gained his freedom might rise—for it was Terence's own case—to be a successful dramatist himself, and to sit down at table with such men as Scipio and Lælius. The anomaly is that a man who stood in such confidential relations to his master, and with such possibilities in his future, should feel himself every moment liable, at that master's slightest caprice, to the stocks and the whip. But it is an anomaly inherent to the institution of slavery itself; and no worse examples of it need be sought than are to be found in the annals of modern slave plantations.

In the few fragments of Menander which remain to us we find the poet adopting, as to the slave's position, a much higher tone than we might have expected, and which is very remarkable in a writer who would certainly never have dreamed of the abolition of a system which must have appeared to him a necessity of civilisation. It is a tone, be it said, which we do not find in his Roman imitators, Plautus or Terence. He plainly feels slavery to be an evil—a degradation to the nature of man. His remedy is a lofty one—freedom of soul :—

" Live as a free man—and it makes thee free." *

The young men are, as has been said, usually very much of the same type, and that not a very high one : hot-blooded and impulsive, with plenty of selfish good-nature, and in some cases a capacity for

* Meineke, Menand. Rel., 269.

strong and disinterested friendship. We have too
little opportunity of judging what Menander made of
them; but in Terence they have commonly the re-
deeming point of a strong affection for their parents
underlying all their faults, though it does not prevent
them from intriguing with their slaves to cheat them
in order to the gratification of their own passions or
extravagance. Yet their genuine repentance when detected, and the docility with which they usually accept
their father's arrangements for them in the matter of
a wife, are a remarkable proof of the strength of the
paternal influence. The daughter of the family may be
said (in quite a literal sense) to have no character at
all. She is brought up in something stricter than even
what Dryden calls "the old Elizabeth way, which was
for maids to be seen and not heard;" for she is never
seen or heard, though we are always led to believe that
she is an irreproachable young lady, possessing a due
amount of personal charms, and with a comfortable
dowry; which combined attractions are quite sufficient
to make one of the young gentlemen happy—sometimes at very short notice—in the last scene of the
play. But it was not etiquette for an unmarried
woman at Athens to make her appearance in the public
streets—and in the streets, for the reasons already
given, the action of the piece invariably takes place.
Of some of the ladies who do appear on the stage the
same remark as to character (in a different sense) might
be made; and if something less were seen and heard
of them, it might be better.

This entire absence of what we should call love-
scenes, places these dramas at an enormous disadvantage

before the modern reader. Yet in one direction, a great approach to modern ways of thought had been made in this New Athenian Comedy. Love, with the dramatists of this school, is no longer the mere animal passion of some of the older poets, nor yet that fatal and irresistible influence which we see overpowering mind and reason in the Medea of Euripides, or in the Dido of Virgil. It has become, in Menander and his followers, much more like the love of modern romance. It is a genuine mutual affection between the sexes, not always well regulated, but often full of tenderness, and capable of great constancy. Still, the modern romance is not there. It was very well for ancient critics to say that Menander was emphatically a writer of love-dramas—that there was no play of his which had not a love-story in the plot : and it is true, if we may judge from the Latin adaptations, that his comedies usually ended in marriage. But a marriage with a bride whom the audience have never been allowed to see, and for whose charms they must take the bridegroom's word, has not a very vivid interest for them. The contrivances by which, in order to suit what were then considered the proprieties, the fair object is kept carefully out of sight while the interest in her fortunes is still kept up, will seem to an English reader a striking instance of misplaced ingenuity.

If, however, in these comedies of ancient domestic life we miss that romance of feeling which forms so important an element—if it may not rather be said to be of the very essence—of the modern drama, we escape altogether from one style of plot which was not only the reproach of our old English comedy-writers, but is still too common a resource with modern writers of fiction, romantic or dramatic. The sanctities of married life are not tampered with to create a morbid interest for audience or reader. The husband may sometimes be a domestic tyrant, or his wife a scold, and their matrimonial wrangles are not unfrequently produced for the amusement of the audience; but there is little hint of any business for the divorce court. The morality of these comedies is lax in many respects, chiefly because the whole law of morality was lower on those points (at least in theory) in the pagan world than it is in the Christian: but the tie of fidelity between husband and wife is fully recognised and regarded. In this respect some advance had been made, at least so far as popular comedy was concerned, since the time of Aristophanes. His whole tone on such points is cynical and sneering; and when he lashes as he does with such out-spoken severity the vices of the sex, it seems to be without any consciousness of their bearing upon domestic happiness. The wife, in his days at least, was not the companion of her husband, but a property to be kept as safe as might be, and their real lives lay apart. Some considerable change must have taken place in these relations at the time when Menander wrote, if we may judge from scattered expressions in his lost comedies. He is not, upon the whole, complimentary to marriage, and he makes capital enough out of its risks and annoyances; he does not think (or perhaps professes not to think) that good wives are common.

" Needs must that in a wife we gain an evil,—
Happy is he who therein gains the least." *

* Meineke, Menand. Rel., 190.

But, if a really good wife can be found, he admits
with the wise Hebrew king that "her price is above
rubies." Verses like the following, salvage from the
wreck of his plays, passed into proverbs :—

> " A virtuous woman is a man's salvation."
> " A good wife is the rudder of the house."

He is honest enough, too, to lay the fault of ill-assorted
marriages at the door of those who have to choose in
such a matter, as much as of those who are chosen ; in
this, as in other things, he recognises a certain law of
supply and demand.

> " What boots it to be curious as to lineage—
> Who was her grandfather, and her mother's mother—
> Which matters nought ? while, for the bride herself,
> Her whom we have to live with,—what she is,
> In mind and temper, this we never ask.
> They bring the dowry out, and count it down,
> Look if the gold be good, of right assay,—
> The gold, which some few months shall see the end of ;
> While she who at our hearth must sit through life,
> We make no trial of, put to no proof,
> Before we take her, but trust all to chance."*

The gibes which he launches against women seem
to have been not more than half in earnest. He probably borrowed the tone from Euripides, of whom he
was a great admirer, and whose influence may be
pretty clearly traced in the style and sentiment of his
comedies.

We usually find, then, the chief parts in the comedy
filled by the members of one or two neighbouring

* Meineke, Menand. Rel., 189.

families.   Of the other characters who are introduced,
two of the most common, and therefore, we must suppose, the most popular, are the Braggadocio and the
Parasite.   The former is usually a soldier of fortune
who has served in the partisan wars in Asia, under
some of those who were disputing for the fragments of
Alexander's empire ; who has made money there, and
come to Athens—as a modern successful adventurer
might go to Paris—to spend it.   He has long stories to
tell of his remarkable exploits abroad, which no one
is very well able to contradict, and to which those
who accept his dinners are obliged to listen with such
patience as they may.   His bravery consists much
more in words than deeds : he thinks that his reputation will win him great favour from the ladies, but
on this point he commonly finds himself very much
mistaken.   How far such a character was common at
Athens in Menander's time, we cannot say: he appears,
with variations, in at least five of his comedies of which
fragments have reached us, and in no less than eight
out of the twenty which remain to us of Plautus.   He
would evidently present salient points for the farce-
writer, and it is not surprising to find him reproduced, no doubt an adaptation from these earlier
sketches, as the " Spanish Captain " of Italian comedy,
or the " Derby Captain " of our own.   He is the Don
Gaspard of Scarron's ' Jodelet Duelliste,' Le Capitaine
Matamore of Corneille's ' L'Illusion Comique,' and the
Bobadil of Jonson's ' Every Man in his Humour.'   In
Spain or Italy he is perhaps more in his natural place
—for these military adventurers were not uncommon in
the Continental wars of the fifteenth and sixteenth cen-

turies—than he is in the plays of Plautus or of Terence,
who transferred him bodily from their Greek original :
for the Romans themselves were not likely to furnish
examples of him, and no hired mercenary would have
ventured to swagger in those days at Rome. To a
Roman audience this could only have been one of those
conventional characters, made to be laughed at, which
an easy public is very often willing to accept from an
author's hands. He is sometimes accompanied by the
Parasite, who is content to eat his dinners on condition
of listening to his military reminiscences, and occasionally drawing them out for the benefit of others,—acting, in short, generally as his humble foil and toady.
This is a character almost peculiar to the comedy of
this school, and which has not found its way much
into the modern drama. In the Athens of Menander,
and in the Rome of Plautus and Terence, when life
was altogether more in public, and when men of any
moderate position seldom dined alone, the character,
though not in the exaggerated form which suited the
purpose of the comic dramatist, appears to have been
sufficiently common. Athenæus, from whose curious
' Table-Talk ' we learn so much about the social life of
those times, notes three distinct classes of the Parasite. There was the professed talker—the narrator of
anecdotes and sayer of good things—who was invited to " make sport " for the guests who might be too
grand or too dull to amuse each other ; and this useful
class of " diner-out " is not altogether unknown in
modern society. This variety of the character seems
to have not unfrequently " read up " carefully in preparation for the display of the evening, as modern

professors of the art of conversation have been reported
to do. " I will go in and have a look at my common-
place-books, and learn up some better jokes," says
Gelasimus in the 'Stichus' of Plautus, when he is
afraid of being superseded by some new pretenders.
There was, again, the mere toady and flatterer, of
whom we shall see a specimen presently in one of the
fragments of Menander, as well as in the comedies of
Plautus; * and of whom we have some historical examples fully as ludicrous as any inventions of the stage,
if the biographers of Philip and Alexander of Macedon
are to be trusted. We are told, that whenever King
Philip ate anything sour or acid, and made wry
faces at it, his flatterer Cleisophos went through exactly
the same grimaces; when the king hurt his leg,
Cleisophos immediately put on a limp; and when the
king lost his right eye by the arrow at Methone, the
courtier appeared next morning with the same eye
bandaged up. It is also said that to wear the head a
little on one side became quite the fashion in the court
of Alexander, because he himself had a slight deformity
of the kind. Another variety of the parasite was the
still meaner humble companion, who carried messages
and did little services of all kinds, sometimes worse
than menial, for his richer patron.

An amusing soliloquy of one of these hungry guests
who is waiting for his dinner (having possibly found
no entertainer, and therefore no dinner at all, the day
before) has been preserved for us by Aulus Gellius out
of a lost comedy which he attributes to Plautus,—

* See p. 44.

'The Bœotian,'—founded upon one of the same name by Menander:—

" The gods confound the man who first invented
  This measuring time by hours ! Confound him, too,
  Who first set up a sun-dial—chopping up
  My day into these miserable slices !
  When I was young, I had no dial but appetite,
  The very best and truest of all timepieces ;
  When that said 'Eat,' I ate—if I could get it.
  But now, even when I've the chance to eat, I must not,
  Unless the sun be willing ! for the town
  Is grown so full of those same cursed dials,
  That more than half the population starve." *

These persons are represented, of course, as having not only the habit of living as far as possible at other men's expense, but as bringing an insatiable appetite with them to their entertainers' tables—

  "'Tis not to gather strength he eats, but wishes
    To gather strength that he may eat the more." †

Neither host nor servants are sparing in their gibes as to the gormandising propensities of this class of self-invited guests. The cook in 'The Menæchmi' of Plautus is ordered to provide breakfast for three :—

  Cook.   What sort of three ?
  Erotium. Myself, Menæchmus, and his Parasite.
  Cook. Then that makes ten. I count the parasite
  As good as any eight.

Although the character of the Parasite is a direct importation from the Greek stage, it was likely to be a very common one also in Roman society. The rela-

* Aul. Gell., iii. 3.   † Fragment of Plautus.

tion of patron and client, which meets us everywhere
in the Roman city life of those days—when the great
man was surrounded with his crowds of hangers-on, all
more or less dependent upon and obsequious to him,
and often eating at his table—was sure to breed in
plenty that kind of human fungus.

Among the remaining characters common to this
Menandrian Comedy we meet with the waiting-maid,
more or less pert and forward—who, although a slave,
seems to have had considerable liberty of tongue, and
who maintains her ground upon the modern stage
with little more change in the type than has followed
necessarily with the changes of society. There is, again,
the family nurse, garrulous but faithful; and sometimes we have another of the household in the person
of the family cook. Lastly, there is the hateful slave-
merchant, the most repulsive character in the Greek
and Roman drama, and upon whose ways and doings
there is no need for us here to dwell.

The philosophy of Menander has been spoken of as
distinctly of an Epicurean character, and his morality
is certainly no whit higher than that of his age and
times. Yet fragments of his have escaped the general
wreck, which have in them a grave melancholy not
usually associated in our ideas with the teaching of
that school, and which have led a modern scholar, than
whom no one understood more thoroughly the spirit of
Greek literature, to remark that Menander after all
seems to have been "more adapted to instruct than
to entertain." *   Such a fragment is the following :—

* Walter Savage Landor.

" If thou wouldst know thyself, and what thou art,
   Look on the sepulchres as thou dost pass ;
   There lie within the bones and little dust
   Of mighty kings and wisest men of old ;
   They who once prided them on birth or wealth,
   Or glory of great deeds, or beauteous form ;
   Yet nought of these might stay the hand of Time.
   Look,—and bethink thee thou art even as they."*

We find also passages quoted as his, though their
genuineness is somewhat doubtful, which breathe a
higher tone still. The sentiment expressed in the following lines, attributed to the poet by Clement of
Alexandria, is almost identical with that of the grand
passage with which Persius concludes his second
Satire :—

" Trust me, my Pamphilus, if any think
   By offering hecatombs of bulls or goats,
   Or any other creature,—or with vests
   Of cloth of gold or purple making brave
   Their images, or with sheen of ivory,
   Or graven jewels wrought with cunning hand,—
   So to make Heaven well-pleased with him, he errs,
   And hath a foolish heart. The gods have need
   That man be good unto his fellow-men,
   No unclean liver or adulterer,
   Nor thief nor murderer from the lust of gain,
   Nay, covet not so much as a needle's thread,
   For One stands by, who sees and watches all." †

The same writer has quoted another line as from the
Greek dramatist, referring to the purification required

* Menand. Rel., 196.   † Clem. Alex. Strom., v. c. 14.

of the worshipper of the gods, which is a close parallel to the Christian teaching:—

" He is well cleansed that hath his conscience clean."

Another father of the Church has cited a terse apophthegm, which he attributes to Menander, as an argument to show the folly of idolatry:—

" The workman still is greater than his work." *

We owe the loss of Menander's plays most probably to the fierce crusade made by the authorities of the early Church against this kind of heathen literature. Yet it is plain that this feeling was not shared by the ecclesiastical writers who have been quoted; and it is singular that we have one sentence of his embalmed in the writings of a still higher authority—St Paul:

" Evil communications corrupt good manners."

A manuscript of some at least of these comedies was said to have been long preserved in the library of the Patriarch at Constantinople, but it seems to have escaped the search of modern scholars, and has probably in some way disappeared.†

How great the loss has been to the literary world cannot be measured, though something may be guessed. It may be said of him as was said of our own Jeremy Taylor—" His very dust is gold." The number of single verses and distiches caught up from his plays which passed into household proverbs show how widely his writings must have leavened the literary

* Justin Mart., Apol. i. 20.   † See Journ. of Educ., i. 138.

taste both of Athenians and Romans. The estima-
tion in which he was held by those who had access
to his works in their integrity is fully justified by
what we can trace of his remains. "To judge of
Menander from Terence and Plautus is easy but
dangerous," says M. Guizot; dangerous, because we
cannot tell how much he may have lost in the process
of adaptation to the Roman stage. Cæsar has been
thought to have spoken slightingly of Terence when
he called him "a half-Menander:" but the Roman poet
in all likelihood bore no such proportion to his great
original.

CHAPTER III.

ALL the writers of Comedy for the Roman stage, of whose works we have any knowledge, were direct imitators of Menander and his school. Plautus, however, was probably less indebted to him than were his successors, Cæcilius, Lavinius, and Terence. Of the two intermediate authors we know very little ; but Plautus and Terence have been more fortunate in securing for themselves a modern audience. Their comedies may not have been really better worth possessing than those of other writers who had their day of popularity : but theirs alone have been preserved, and it is from them that we have to form our judgment of the Comedy of Republican Rome.

Titus Maccius Plautus—the second would be what we should call his surname, and the last simply means "flat-foot" * in the dialect of Umbria, the district in

---

* Literary tradition in some quarters asserted that in one of his comedies he introduced a sketch—certainly not too flattering —of his own personal appearance :

> "A red-haired man, with round protuberant belly,
> Legs with stout calves, and of a swart complexion :
> Large head, keen eyes, red face, and monstrous feet."
>   —Pseudólus, act iv. sc. 7.

which he was born,—was a man of humble origin, the
son, according to some authorities, of a slave. But little
is known with any certainty on these points. He is said
to have made money in trade, and to have lost it again ;
to have then worked as a stage carpenter or machinist,
and so perhaps to have acquired his theatrical taste.
These early associations are taken also, by some critics,
as an explanation of some rudeness and coarseness in his
plays ; for which, however, the popular taste is quite
as likely to have been accountable as any peculiar
tendencies of the writer. Like that marvel of dramatic prolificness, Lope de Vega, who quotes him as
an apology, Plautus wrote for the people, and might
have pleaded, as the Spaniard did, that "it was only
fair that the customers should be served with what
suited their taste." The masses who thronged
the Roman theatres had not the fine intellect of the
Commons of Athens. Aristophanes could never have
depended upon them for due appreciation of his double-
edged jests, or appealed to them as critical judges of
humour. The less keen but more polished dialogue and
didactic moralising of Menander would have been still
less attractive to such an audience as that to which
Plautus had to look for favour. The games of the circus
—the wild-beast fight and the gladiators, the rope-dancers, the merry-andrews, and the posture-masters,—were
more to their taste than clever intrigue and brilliant
dialogue.

Plautus—we know him now only by his *sobriquet*—
began his career as a dramatist B.C. 224. He continued
to write for the stage, almost without a rival in popularity, until his death, forty years later. How many

comedies he produced during this long service of the
public we do not know: twenty remain bearing his
name, all which are considered to be genuine.   All,
with the exception probably of 'Amphitryon,' are
taken from Greek originals.   It is not necessary here
to give a list of their titles; the most interesting of
them will be noticed in their order.   With Greek
characters, Greek names, and Greek scenery, he gives
us undoubtedly the Roman manners of his day, which
are illustrated more fully in his pages than in those of
the more refined Terence.   Let the scene of the drama
lie where it will, we are in the streets of Rome all the
while.   Athenians, Thebans, or Ephesians, his *dramatis
personæ* are all of one country, just as they speak one
language; they are no more real Greeks than Shakspeare's Othello is a Moor, or his Proteus a "gentleman of Verona"—except in the bill of the play.   So
little attempt does he make to keep up anything like
an illusion on this point, that he even speaks of "tri-
umvirs" at Thebes, builds a "Capitol" at Epidaurus,
and makes his characters talk about "living like those
Greeks," and "drinking like Greeks," utterly careless
of the fact that they are supposed to be Greeks themselves.   He is as independent of such historical and
geographical trifles as our own great dramatist when
he makes Hector quote Aristotle, or gives a sea-coast
to Bohemia.   But he has the justification which all
great dramatists would fairly plead; that his characters,
though distinctly national in colour, are in a wider
sense citizens of the world ; they speak, in whatever
language, the sentiments of civilised mankind.

  However coarse in many respects the matter and

style of Plautus may appear to us, it is certain that good judges amongst those who were more nearly his contemporaries thought very highly of his diction. It was said of him by Ælius Stolo that "if the Muses ever spoke Latin, it would be the Latin of Plautus." Perhaps he was the first who raised conversational Latin to the dignity of a literary style.

His plays are in most cases introduced by a prologue, spoken sometimes by one of the characters in the play, and sometimes by a mythological personage, such as Silenus or Arcturus. The prologue generally gives an outline of the plot, and this has been objected to by some critics as destroying the interest of the action which is to follow. But a similar practice has been adopted of late years in our own theatres, of giving the audience, in the play-bill, a sketch of the leading scenes and incidents; and this is generally found to increase the intelligent enjoyment of the play itself. The prologues of Plautus frequently also contain familiar appeals on the part of the manager to the audience, and give us a good deal of information as to the materials of which the audience was composed. The mothers are requested to leave their babies at home, for the babies' sakes as well as for the sake of other people; and the children who are in the theatre are begged not to make a noise. The slaves are desired not to occupy the seats, which are not intended for them, but to be content with standing-room; protests are made against the system of *claqueurs*,—friends of some favourite actor, who gave their applause unfairly, to the discredit of others : and the wives are requested not to interrupt the performance with their chatter, and so annoy their husbands who are come to see the play. Remarks of this kind, addressed to the " house," are not confined, however, to the prologue, but occur here and there in the scene itself ; these last are evident relics of the earlier days of comedy, for we find no such in the plays of Terence.

CHAPTER IV.

THE COMEDIES OF PLAUTUS.

I.—THE THREE SILVER PIECES.

THE plot of this little comedy, which is confessedly borrowed from the Greek of Philemon, and is called in the original with perhaps more propriety "The Buried Treasure," is simple enough. Charmides, a rich citizen of Athens, has been half ruined by an extravagant son. He goes abroad, leaving this son and a daughter in charge of his old friend Callicles, begging him to do what he can to keep young Lesbonicus from squandering the little that is left of the family property. At the same time, he intrusts his friend with a secret. He has buried under his house a treasure—three thousand gold Philips.* This, even if things come to the worst, will serve to provide a marriage portion for his daughter, in the event of his not living to return to Athens. Callicles has striven in vain to persuade the young man to mend his ways; Lesbonicus has gone on in the same course of extravagance, until he has nothing left but a

* Gold coins struck by the Macedonian kings, and worth about two guineas apiece.

small farm outside the city, and the house in which he lives—and where the treasure is buried. This house at last he offers for sale : and Callicles is only just in time to buy it in for himself, and so to preserve for his absent friend the precious deposit.

The action of the piece is introduced by a short allegorical ' Prologue,' in which Luxury introduces her daughter Poverty into the house of the prodigal, and bids her take possession : a very direct mode of enforcing its moral upon the audience. This moral, however, is by no means carried out with the same distinctness in the catastrophe.

So much of the story is told at the opening of the play by Callicles to a friend, who seems to have called purposely to tell him some disagreeable truths—as is the recognised duty of a friend. People are talking unpleasantly about his conduct: they say that he has been winking at the young man's extravagance, and has now made a good thing of it by buying at a low price the house which he is obliged to sell. Callicles listens with some annoyance, but at first with an obstinate philosophy. Can he do nothing, his friend asks, to put a stop to these evil rumours ?

> I can,—and I can not ; 'tis even so ;
> As to their saying it,—that I cannot help :
> I can take care they have no cause to say it.

But, on his old friend pressing him, he yields so far as to intrust him with the whole secret.

A suitor now appears for the hand of the young daughter of the absent Charmides. It is Lysiteles, a young man of great wealth and noble character, the

darling of an indulgent father, who consents, though
with some natural unwillingness, not only to accept
her as a daughter-in-law without a portion, but even to
go in person and request the consent of her brother
Lesbonicus, who is known to be as proud as he is now
poor, and who is very likely to make his own poverty
an objection to his sister's marrying into a rich family,
though the lover is his personal friend. The father
has an interview with him, but can only obtain his
consent to such a marriage on condition that his friend
will accept with her such dowry as he can give—the
single farm which he has retained in his own possession
out of all the family estate, and from which his faithful slave Stasimus—the classical prototype of Scott's
Caleb Balderstone—is contriving to extract a living for
his young master and himself. This honest fellow is
present during part of the interview, and is horrified
to hear the prodigal generosity with which the ruined
heir insists, in spite of all the other's attempts to
decline it, upon dowering his sister with the last remains of his estate. At last he draws Philto—the
suitor's father—aside on some pretence, and the following dialogue ensues:—

Stasimus. I have a secret for your ear, sir—only you ;
Don't let *him* know I told you.
    Philto.   You may trust me.
    Stas. By all that's good in heaven and earth, I warn
        you,
Don't take that land—don't let your son set foot on it—
I'll tell you why.
    Phil.   Well,—I should like to hear.

Stas. Well, to begin with—(*confidentially*) the oxen,
      when we plough it,
Invariably drop down dead in the fifth furrow.
    Phil. (*laughing*).   Stuff! nonsense!
    Stas. (*getting more emphatic*).   People say there's devils
      in it!
The grapes turn rotten there before they're ripe.
    Lesbonicus (*watching their conversation, and speaking
      to himself*).   He's humbugging our friend
      there, I'll be bound!
'Tis a good rascal, though—he's stanch to me.
    Stas. Listen again—in the very best harvest seasons,
You get from it three times less than what you've sown.
    Phil. An excellent spot to sow bad habits in!
For there you're sure they won't spring up again.
    Stas. There never was yet a man who had that land,
But something horrible always happened to him;
Some were transported—some died prematurely—
Some hung themselves! (*pauses to watch the effect.*) And
      look at him, now, there—(*motioning towards
      his master*).   The present owner—what is he?
      —a bankrupt.
    Phil. (*pretending to believe him*).   Well, heaven deliver
      me from such a bargain!
    Stas. Amen to that!—Ah! you might say 'deliver
      me,'
If you knew all.   Why, every other tree
Is blasted there by lightning; all the hogs
Die of pneumonia: all the sheep are scabbed;
Lose all their wool, they do, till they're as bare
As the back of my hand is.   Why, there's not a nigger
(And *they'll* stand anything) could stand the climate;
Die in six months, they all do, of autumn fever.
    Phil. (*coolly*).   Ah! I daresay.   But our Campanian
      fellows
Are much more hardy than the niggers.   Still,

This land, if it's at all what you describe it,
Would be a fine place for a penal settlement,
To banish rascals to, for the public good.
    Stas. 'Tis just a nest of horrors, as it is ;
If you want anything bad,—there you may find it.
    Phil. No doubt ;—and so you may in other places.
    Stas. Now please don't let *him* know I've told you
        this !
    Phil. Oh—honour bright ! I hold it confidential.
    Stas. Because, in fact, you see, he's very anxious
To be well rid of it, if he can find a man
That's fool enough to take it.—You perceive ?
    Phil. I do : I promise you, it shan't be me.

Philto is unwilling either to accept the farm, or to hurt
the feelings of Lesbonicus by the refusal—he will leave
the two young friends, he says, to settle that matter
between them. And poor old Stasimus is quite satisfied that his pious falsehood has saved this remnant
of the family property.

Young Lysiteles is as reluctant to accept the offered
marriage portion as his friend is determined, for his
honour's sake, to give it : and the struggle between the
two young men, which almost leads to a quarrel, gives
occasion to a fine scene, though perhaps somewhat too
wordy for our English taste. Lysiteles is the more hurt
at his friend's obstinacy, because he has discovered his
intention of quitting Athens, now that his patrimony
is all gone, and taking service under some potentate
in the East, the great field which was then open to
young men of spirit and enterprise. Stasimus' despair,
when he too learns this last resolution on the part of
his young master, is highly comic : he will not desert
him, even if he could, but he has no taste for a mili-.

tary life—wearing clumsy boots, and carrying a heavy buckler, and a pack on his shoulders.

But Callicles has heard of the proposed marriage, and will by no means allow his absent friend's daughter to go to her bridegroom dowerless, when there is money stored away specially for that object. But how is it to be done without discovering to the public the secret of the buried treasure, which is sure to confirm the suspicion of his underhand dealings? and which treasure if the young spendthrift once comes to know of, the rest of it will very soon follow the estate. If Callicles gives the money as out of his own pocket, people will only say that he was now doling out a part of some larger fund, left in his hands in trust, and which the girl and her brother ought to have had long ago. He adopts the scheme of hiring one of those unscrupulous characters who hung about the law courts at Athens, as they do about our own, ready to undertake any business however questionable, and to give evidence to any effect required—"for a consideration." This man shall pretend to have just landed from foreign parts, and to have brought money from Charmides expressly for his daughter's marriage portion. The required agent is soon found, and his services engaged by Callicles for the "Three Silver Pieces," which gives the name to the play. He is equipped in some outlandish-looking costume, hired from a theatrical wardrobe, and knocks at the door of Charmides' house (a small apartment in which is still occupied by his son) as though just arrived from sea. But at the door he meets no less a person than Charmides himself, who has just returned from his long absence, has noticed this strange-looking personage on his way from the harbour, and is much astonished to find him knocking at his own door. Still more surprised is he to hear that he is inquiring for his son Lesbonicus, and that he is bringing him a letter from his father. The scene between the pretended messenger and the returned traveller whose agent he professes to be,—the man's astonishment and embarrassment when he finds that he is talking to Charmides himself, and the consummate effrontery with which he faces the situation to the very last, long after he knows he is detected, is one of the most amusing scenes in Plautus, though unfortunately too long for insertion here. The impostor has not been prepared for any kind of cross-examination, and has even forgotten the name of Lesbonicus' father, from whom he asserts that he brings the money. His efforts to recover this name—which he says he has unfortunately "swallowed" in his hurry; his imaginary description of Charmides, who stands before him in person; the account he gives of his travels in countries he has never seen,—are all highly farcical. One argument in proof of the reality of his mission he advances triumphantly—the thousand gold pieces which he carries with him; if he did not know Charmides personally, would he ever have intrusted him with the money? At last his inquisitor announces himself—"I am Charmides—so hand me over my money." The other is staggered for the moment : " Bless my life ! " he says to himself—"why, here's a greater impostor than I am ! " But he soon recovers his coolness. "That's all very well," he replies; " but you never said a word about your being Charmides until I told you I had the gold. You are only

Charmides for a particular purpose—and that won't do."
—"Well, but if I am not Charmides," says the father—
not very cleverly—"who am I?" " Nay," says his op-
ponent—"that's your business ; so long as you are not
the person I don't intend you to be, you may be anything
you please." As he is shrewd enough, however, to discover that Charmides is the person whom he claims to
be, and as the latter threatens to have him cudgelled
if he does not leave his door, he makes his exit at last
not in the least crestfallen, and congratulating himself that, come what will, he has safely pocketed the
Three Silver Pieces : he has done his best, he declares
(as indeed he has), to earn them fairly, and can only go
back to his employers and tell them that his mission
has failed.

The first person who meets Charmides on his return
home is Stasimus. He has been drowning his dread
of a military life in the wine-flagon, and has reached
the sentimental stage of intoxication. His maundering
moralities upon the wickedness and degeneracy of the
present age, and the wickedness of the world in general,
and his sudden recollection that while he is thus gene-
ralising upon questions of public interest his own
particular back is in great danger, for having loitered at
the wine-shop, are admirably given. His old master is
all the while standing in the background, listening with
much amusement to his soliloquy, and throwing in an
occasional remark aside, by way of chorus. When at
length he discovers himself, the joy of the faithful old
tippler sobers him at once, and he proceeds to tell his
master how affairs have been going on in his absence.
Charmides is shocked to hear of the continued extrava-

gance of his son, of his sale of the house, and the consequent loss of the buried treasure on which he had depended, and still more at the faithlessness of his friend,—who has not only taken no care to prevent this catastrophe, but has employed his knowledge of the secret to his own advantage in the most shameless manner, by becoming the purchaser of the house.

Of course such misunderstanding is soon cleared up. The father hears with joy of his daughter's approaching marriage, and thanks young Lysiteles warmly for his generous conduct, though he will not allow him—especially as he has made money during his absence abroad—to take into his house a portionless bride. But the young man has a favour to ask of much more importance : it is that Charmides will overlook and forgive the extravagance of his dear friend, his son,—who will, he assures him, do better in future. Somewhat reluctantly the father consents—he can refuse nothing at such a moment, and to so generous a petitioner. His judgment upon the offender forms a characteristic ending to the piece.

Charm. If you'll reform, my old friend Charicles
Here offers you his daughter—a good girl ;
Say, will you marry her ?
    Lesbon. (eagerly).   I will, dear father !
I will—and any one else besides, to please you.
    Charm. Nay—one's enough: though I *am* angry with ye,
I'll not inflict a double chastisement ;
That were too hard.
    Callicles (laughing). Nay, scarcely, for his sins—
A hundred wives at once would serve him right.*

* This is the only comedy of Plautus which has been presented by Westminster scholars of late years. When it was acted in

II.—THE BRAGGADOCIO.

The hero—if he can be so called who is the very opposite of a hero—in this comedy is one of those swaggering soldiers of fortune who have already been briefly described. His name, which is a swagger in itself, is Pyrgopolinices—"Tower of Victory." He is in the pay of Seleucus, for whom he is at present recruiting ; but he has also served, by his own account—

> "On the far-famed Gorgonidonian plains,
>   Where the great Bumbomachides commanded—
>   Clytomestoridysarchides's son."*

He is attended by his obsequious toady Artotrogus— " Bread-devourer "—who flatters his vanity and swears

1860, the humorous modern Latin Epilogue which now always follows the play (and which is really a short farce in itself) took an especially happy turn. A project was then on foot for removing the School to a different site, and Lesbonicus is introduced in this epilogue as offering to sell the old College premises ; while "College John," as the scholars' official is always called, in the character of the slave Stasimus, endeavours to prevent the sale by enlarging upon the horrors of the Thames water and the squalor of Tothill Fields. The negotiation is stopped by the entrance of the Ghost of Dr Busby, who informs them of a treasure which he had buried under the old foundations. They proceed eagerly to dig, and the treasure proves to be—a gigantic ROD ! which is exhumed and displayed in triumph to the audience. This is, the old Master declares, the real key to honours— the "golden bough" of classic fable—

> "Aurea virga tibi est, portas quæ pandit honorum."

* We need not go far to seek the original of the opening lines of ' Bombastes Furioso,' where the hero asks—

> " Aldibarontiphoskifornio,
>   How left you Chrononhotonthologos ?"

to the truth of all his bragging stories—"maintaining his teeth," as he says, "at the expense of his ears."' The Captain's stories are of such an outrageously lying description as to be somewhat too improbable for the subject of legitimate comedy, and we can only suppose that in this kind of fun the taste of a Roman audience preferred a strong flavour. He affects to believe that not only do all the men dread his prowess, but that all the women are charmed with his person : and his companion and flatterer does his best to persuade him that it is so.

> *Artotrogus.* You saw those girls that stopped me yesterday ?
>
> *Pyrgopolinices.* What did they say ?
>
> *Art.*   Why, when you passed, they asked me—
> "What, is the great Achilles here ?"—I answered,
> "No—it's his brother." Then says t'other one—
> "Troth, he *is* handsome !   What a noble man !
> What splendid hair ! "
>
> *Pyrg.*   Now, did they *really* say so ?
>
> *Art.* They did indeed, and begged me, both of them,
> To make you take a walk again to-day,
> That they might get another sight of you.
>
> *Pyrg. (sighing complacently).* 'Tis a great nuisance being so *very* handsome ! *

This hero gentleman has just carried off from Athens—by force, however, and not by the influence of his personal attractions—a young lady who is an object of tender interest to a gentleman of that city,

* So Le Capitan Matamore, . in Corneille's ' L'Illusion Comique '—

> " Ciel qui sais comme quoi j'en suis persecuté !
> Un·peu plus de repos avec‿moins de beauté."

who is at the time gone upon a voyage to Naupactus. His faithful slave Palestrio takes ship to follow him thither, but on his way falls into the hands of pirates, by whom he is sold, and, as it happens, taken to Ephesus and there purchased by Pyrgopolinices. He finds the lady shut up in half-willing durance in the Captain's house, and at once writes information of the fact to her Athenian lover, his master Pleusicles, who sails at once for Ephesus. On his arrival, he finds that an old friend of the family occupies the adjoining house : a jolly old bachelor, of thorough Epicurean tastes and habits, and quite ready to forward a lover's stratagem. By his good-natured connivance a door is broken through his house into the women's side of his neighbour's mansion, by which Pleusicles is enabled to hold communication with the object of his affections. But a servant of the Captain's, who has been specially charged to keep an eye upon the lady, happens to be running over the roof of the two houses in the pursuit of an escaped monkey, looks down through a skylight with the curiosity of his class, and is a witness of one of these stolen interviews between the lovers. How Philocomasium (for that is the lady's long Greek name *) has found her way into the house next door is what he does not understand ; but there she is, and he is determined to tell the Captain. First, however, he

---

* These Greek female names are anything but euphonious to English ears. But we must remember that what seems to us a harsh termination was softened away in the Latin pronunciation, and that in its Greek form it was a diminutive ; so that names ending in " ion " conveyed to their ear a *pet* sound, as in our Nellie, Bessie, &c.

takes into his counsels his new fellow-servant, Palestrio, and confides to him his discovery. Palestrio tries to persuade him that his eyes have deceived him, but finding him obstinately convinced of their accuracy, invents a story of a twin-sister, who by a curious coincidence has just come to Ephesus and taken the house next door, where she allows a lover of her own to visit her. The chief fun of the piece, which is somewhat of a childish character, consists in the ingenuity with which Philocomasium, with the aid of Palestrio, contrives by a change of costume to play the double part of herself and the imaginary twin-sister; much to the bewilderment of the Captain's watchful and suspicious retainer, who is ignorant of the existence of the secret passage by which at her pleasure she flits from house to house.

The catastrophe is brought about by the absorbing vanity of the military hero. He is persuaded by the ready Palestrio that a lady in the neighbourhood, of great charms and accomplishments, has fallen violently in love with him, and that if only out of charity it behoves him to have compassion on her. She has a jealous husband, and dare not invite him to her house, but asks to be allowed to call upon him at his own. In order to have the coast quite clear, he sends off Philocomasium for a while, in charge of the trusty Palestrio, who willingly undertakes to escort her— with her mother and the twin-sister, as he thinks — really with her lover Pleusicles, who, in the guise of a shipowner, carries her off to Athens. The fate of the Captain is that of Falstaff, in the ' Merry Wives of Windsor.' As soon as the love-stricken lady—who is only a lady's-maid employed for the occasion—is ascertained to be paying her expected visit to this professional Adonis, his bachelor neighbour, from next door, enters in the character of the jealous husband, with a band of stout slaves, and beats him to a jelly.

III.—THE HAUNTED HOUSE (MOSTELLARIA).

The Latin name of this play means something like "The Goblin;" but perhaps the English title here given to it will better express the nature of the plot. A worthy citizen of Athens has been away for three years on a trading voyage to Egypt, and during his absence his son Philolaches, though a young man of amiable disposition, has gone altogether wrong, kept very dissolute and extravagant company, and spent the greatest part of his father's money. In this he has been aided and abetted by Tranio, his valet and factotum, —one of those amusing rascals who seem to take delight in encouraging their young masters in such things, though they feel it is at the risk of their own backs.

The youth is just sitting down to supper with some of his friends (one of whom has come to the party already drunk), when Tranio, who has been down to the harbour to buy fish, comes in with the startling intelligence of the father's return from sea; he has just got a glimpse of him as he landed. Philolaches feels that the evil day has come upon him at last. His first idea naturally is to get rid of his friends, have the supper-table cleared away, and make things look at least as quiet and respectable as possible. But his friend Callidamates is by this time so very drunk and incapable that it is impossible to hope to get him safely off the premises in time; especially as, in his drunken independence, the only notice he takes of the news is first to "hope the old gentleman's very well;" secondly, to advise his son, if he doesn't want him, to "send him back again;" and, lastly, to offer to fight him, then and there.

Philolaches. Who's that asleep there ? Wake him up,
   do, Delphium !
Delphium. Callidamates! Callidamates—wake! (*shaking*
   him.)
Call. (*looking up drowsily*). I am awake—all right.
   Pass us the bottle.
Delph. Oh, do awake, pray do ! His father's come—
From abroad, you know ! (*Shakes him again.*)
Call. (*just opening his eyes*). All right—hope 's pretty
   well.
Phil. (*angrily*). He's well enough, you ass !—I'm very
   bad.
Call. Bad ! why,—what 's 'matter ?
Phil.   Do get up, I say,
And go—my father's come.
Call. (*drowsily*).   Father's come, is he ?
Tell him—go back again. What the deuce 's want
   here ?
Phil. (*in despair*). What shall I do ? Zounds ! he'll be
   here in a minute,
And find this drunken ass here in my company,
And all the rest of ye. And I've no time—
Beginning to dig a well when you're dying of thirst,—
That's what I'm doing ; just beginning to think
What I'm to do, and here's my father come !
Tranio (*looking at Call.*) He's put his head down and
   gone to sleep again !

Phil. Will you get up? (*shaking him.*) I say,—my father's
here !

Call. (*jumping up*). Father here ? where ? Give me my
slippers, somebody !

My sword, there !—polish the old gentleman off in no time
—Act ii. sc. 2.

But Tranio proves equal to the occasion. He desires
them all to keep quiet where they are, to let him lock
the house up and take the key of the street-door, and
go to meet his elder master with a story which he has
ready for him. The good citizen makes his appearance
in the next scene, congratulating himself heartily on
having escaped the perils of this his first—and, as he
is determined it shall be, his last—sea voyage.

Enter THEUROPIDES—*slaves following with his luggage.*
     TRANIO *looking round a corner, and listening.*

Theu. I do return you hearty thanks, good Neptune,
For letting me out of your clutches safe and sound,
Though scarce alive ; but if from this time forward
You catch me setting foot in your dominions,
I give you leave—free leave—that very instant,
To do with me—what you've just tried to do.
Avaunt ! Anathema ! I do abjure ye
From this same day ! (*looking back towards the harbour,
     and shaking his fist*). I've trusted to ye once,
But never will I run such risk again.

Tran. (*aside*). Zounds, Neptune, you've just made a
     great mistake—
Lost such a charming opportunity !

Theu. Three years I've been in Egypt : here I am,
Come home at last !—How glad they'll be to see me !

Tran. (*aside*). There's only one we had been more glad
     to see—
The man who brought us word that you were drowned.

[THEUROPIDES *advances to his own door, at which he knocks, and looks up at the closed windows. Tranio comes forward.*

Tran. Who's this? who ventures near this house of ours?
Theu. Why, this is my man Tranio!
Tran. O, dear master,
O, welcome home! I am so glad to see you—
Are you *quite* well?
Theu. Quite, as you see (*knocks again*).
Tran. Thank heavens!
Theu. But you,—are ye all mad?
Tran. Why so?
Theu. Because
Here you are walking about, and nobody in.
(*Knocks and kicks at the door.*) Not a soul seems to hear.
Will nobody open? (*Kicks again.*)
I shall kick the door down presently.
Tran. (*shuddering and shrieking*). O—O—Oh!
Don't ye do that, dear master—don't ye, don't ye!
—Act ii. sc. 2.

Then Tranio begins his story. The house is haunted. There is a ghost there, of a man who was murdered in it by the last owner for the sake of his gold, and buried under the floor. This ghost had come to young Philolaches in his sleep, nearly frightened him out of his senses, and warned him to quit his premises at once. Pluto would not admit him into the Shades, he said, because he had not been properly buried, and so he was obliged to live in this house, and he wanted it all to himself. So they had shut it up, Tranio tells the father, and left the ghost in possession; and, for the present, his son is gone into the country. Just in the agony of the tale, a noise is heard inside

—the party there are not keeping so quiet as they ought.

Tran. (*pretending to be frightened, and catching his master by the arm.*)

Hush-sh ! (*Listening.*)

Theu. (*trembling*). Eh ! what was it ?

Tran. (*looking aghast at Theu.*) Was it *him*, d'ye think ?

(*Listening at the key-hole.*) I heard a knocking.

Theu.   Eh ! my blood runs cold !

Are the dead men coming from Acheron to fetch me ?

Tran. (*aside*). Those fools will spoil it all, if they're not quiet.

Theu. What are you saying to yourself, sir—eh ?   .

Tran. Go from the door, sir, pray — run, do, I beg you !

Theu. (*looking round in terror*). Where shall I run to ? why don't you run yourself ?

Tran. (*solemnly*). Well—I've no fear—I keep an honest conscience.   .

Callidamates (*inside*). Hallo there, Tranio ! (*Theuropides runs off.*)

Tran. (*going close to the door, and whispering*). Don't call me, you fool !

(*Aloud, as to the ghost.*) Don't threaten *me*—it wasn't *I* kicked the door.

Theu. (*putting his head round the corner*). O dear ! what is it ? why do you shake so, Tranio ?

Tran. (*looking round*). Was it *you* called me ?—Well, so help us heaven,

I thought it was the dead man scolding me
For making all that rapping at his door.
But why do you stand there ? why don't you do
What I just told you ?

Theu. (*clasping his hands*). O dear ! what was that ?

Tran. Run, run ! don't look behind you—and cover your
    head up !
    [THEUROPIDES *runs off with his cloak over his head.*
                     —Act ii. sc. 2.

There may not be very much wit in the scene, but
it is a fair specimen of the style in which Plautus
seems to have excelled. It is full of bustle and spirit,
and would act, as is the case with so many of his
scenes, far better than it reads. If any reader will imagine the two characters in the hands of say Mr Keeley
and Mr Buckstone, he will perhaps admit that it would
be sufficiently laughable even if it were put exactly as
it is upon the stage of a modern minor theatre.

The " Ghost " is left, for the present, in undisturbed
possession. But Tranio's plan is nearly frustrated at
the outset ; for, as he is following his master down the
street, they meet a money-lender to whom the son is
indebted, and who is come to demand his interest.
The old gentleman overhears the conversation between
the creditor and Tranio, who vainly tries to prevent
him from bawling out his complaints of non-payment.
He succeeds, however, in persuading the father that
his son has only been borrowing in order to pay the
deposit-money upon the purchase of a house (which
he has been driven to buy in consequence of the
Ghost's occupation of the old one), and which is, as he
assures him, a most excellent bargain. Theuropides
is naturally anxious to see the new house at once ;
and Tranio, almost in despair, declares that it is that of
their next-door neighbour, Simo, whom he sees just
coming out of his door on his way to the Forum.
Tranio goes up to this person and requests permission

for his master to look over the house, which he wishes
to copy, as a model of admirable contrivance, in some
new buildings which he is about to make on his own
ground. The owner, much flattered, begs them to
walk over it "just as though it were their own ;" an
expression which rather amuses Theuropides, as he is
about to make it his own in reality by paying the rest
of the purchase-money. Tranio adroitly whispers to
him not to say a word about the sale, "from motives of
delicacy :" poor Simo, he assures him, has been obliged
to part with his family property owing to reduced circumstances, and the whole transaction is naturally a
sore subject to him. Theuropides takes the hint at
once, praising his servant at the same time for his
thoughtfulness and good feeling. He is charmed with
the house, with the terms of the purchase, and with
the business-like habits of his excellent son.

But the father's dream is speedily dispelled. He
meets in the street, near his own door, a slave of the
young gentleman who is at this moment sleeping off
his debauch in his son's apartments, and who has come,
in obedience to the prudent orders issued beforehand
upon such occasions, to convey his master home.
Theuropides would fain persuade him that there is some
mistake ; he must have come to the wrong house ; this
has been shut up and unoccupied for some time ; and
his son Philolaches is quite unlikely to keep the kind
of company to which this roysterer belongs. But the
slave knows his business better, and in defence of his
own assertions tears the veil somewhat rudely from
the old gentleman's eyes. If he could be supposed to
have any doubts remaining, they are removed by a

second interview with his neighbour Simo, who laughs at the notion of his house having been sold without himself being aware of it. It only remains for the deluded father to take vengeance on Tranio, and this he will set about at once. One favour he will ask of Simo—" Lend me a couple of stout slaves, and a good whip or two ;"—and, thus provided, he goes in quest of the culprit.

Tranio discovers that all is lost except his spirit. That still keeps up : and he appears to have propped it with an extra cup or two. His soliloquy, in the hands of a good actor, would no doubt be effective. He has succeeded in getting the revellers out of the house before the angry father comes into it ; but they have now lost all faith in him as an adviser, and what step he is to take next is by no means clear even to himself.

TRANIO (*solus*).

The man who loses heart when things go crooked,
In my opinion, he's not worth a rap—
What a " rap " means, now, blest if I can tell !
Well—when the master bid me fetch the young one—
Out of the country (*laughs to himself*), ha, ha ! Well, I
    went—
Not into the country—to the garden-gate ;
And brought out the whole lot of 'em—male and female.
When I had thus safely withdrawn my troops
Out of their state of siege, I called a council—
A council of war, you know—of my fellow-rascals;
And their very first vote was to turn me out of it.
So I called another council—of myself;
And I am doing—what I understand

> Most people do in awkward circumstances—
> Make 'em as much more awkward as they can.
>
> —Act v. sc. 1.

His master comes to look for him, followed by two slaves carrying whips and fetters, whom he keeps in hiding for the present in the background; but Tranio, quite aware of what is in store for him, takes refuge at the family altar, and will listen to no persuasions to come away. From this vantage-ground he holds an argument with his master; persuades him that his prodigal son has done nothing out of the way—only what other young men of spirit do; and when Theuropides vents his wrath against such a shameful piece of deception in a slave, gravely advises him to hold his tongue at all events on that point. With his grey hairs, he surely ought to have been wiser; if people once come to know how he has allowed himself to be duped, they will infallibly work him into a plot for the next new comedy.

Tranio gets off at last, by the intercession of Callidamates, who has sobered himself sufficiently to come forward and express repentance on the part of his young friend, and to entreat that all may be forgotten and forgiven; offering, handsomely enough, to pay off out of his own pocket the little debt to the money-lender. Tranio assures his master that he will not lose much by forgiving him this time—the whipping which he is longing to give now need only be a pleasure deferred, inasmuch as he is quite certain to do something to deserve one to-morrow. Which very characteristic witticism brings down the curtain.

Upon this comedy Regnard, who perhaps ranks next

to Molière of the French comic dramatists, founded
his play, in one act, of 'Le Rétour Imprévu;' and
Fielding's 'Intriguing Chambermaid' is little more
than a translation of it. But Dunlop remarks that
neither the French nor the English adapters have
availed themselves of the hint which Plautus left for
them, of a telling scene in which the previous occupant
of the "Haunted House" might be charged by the
excited father with the murder of his imaginary guest.

IV.—THE SHIPWRECK (RUDENS).

This is a play of a different character in many respects, and comes nearer to what we should call a melo-
dramatic spectacle than anything else. The Latin title
is simply "The Rope"—given to it because the rope
of a fisherman's net is an important instrument in the
dénouement. But the whole action turns upon a ship-
wreck, and this is the title preferred by some English
authorities.

The prologue, which is in a higher strain than Plautus commonly aspires to, is spoken in the character of
Arcturus,—the constellation whose rising and setting
was supposed to have very much to do with storms.
The costume in which he appears is evidently brilliant
and characteristic.

> Of his high realm, who rules the earth and sea
> And all mankind, a citizen am I.
> Lo, as you see, a bright and shining star,
> Revolving ever in unfailing course
> Here and in heaven: Arcturus am I hight.
> By night I shine in heaven, amidst the gods;

I walk unseen with men on earth by day.
So, too, do other stars step from their spheres,
Down to this lower world ; so willeth Jove,
Ruler of gods and men ; he sends us forth
Each on our several paths throughout all lands,
To note the ways of men, and all they do ; *
If they be just and pious ; if their wealth
Be well employed, or squandered harmfully ; '
Who in a false suit use false witnesses ;
Who by a perjured oath forswear their debts ;—
Their names do we record and bear to Jove.
So learns He day by day what ill is wrought
By men below ; who seek to gain their cause
By perjury, who wrest the law to wrong ;
Jove's court of high appeal rehears the plaint,
And mulcts them tenfold for the unjust decree.
In separate tablets doth he note the good.
And though the wicked in their hearts have said,
He can be soothed with gifts and sacrifice,
They lose their pains and cost, for that the god
Accepts no offering from a perjured hand.

After this fine exordium, so unlike the ordinary tone
of the writer that we may be sure he is here translating from a great original, the prologue goes on to set
forth the story of the piece. The speaker gives the
audience some description of the opening scene, and a
key to the characters. It is the tradition of the com-

---

* The same idea occurs in a well-known passage in Homer :—

    " Gods in the garb of strangers to and fro
      Wander the cities, and men's ways discern ;
      Yea, through the wide earth in all shapes they go,
      Changed, yet the same, and with their own eyes learn
    How live the sacred laws, who hold them, and who spurn."
               · Odyss. xvii. 485 (Worsley's Transl.)

mentators, and the wording of the prologue corroborates
it, that the mounting of this piece, both in scenery and
machinery, was very costly and elaborate. It opens,
like Shakspeare's 'Tempest,' with a storm—or rather
on the morning after.* The sea forms the background;
on one side is the city of Cyrene in the distance, on the
other, a temple of Venus, with a cottage near. This
cottage is the residence of Dæmones, once a citizen of
Athens, but who, having lost his property and met
with other troubles, has left his native country and
settled down here in retirement. He and his slaves
are come out to look to the repairs of their cottage,
which has suffered by the storm. A boat appears
struggling through the waves in the distance, which,
as it gets nearer, is seen to contain two girls, who after
great danger (described by one of the slaves, who is
watching, in a passage which a good actor would no
doubt make sufficiently effective) make good their land-
ing among the rocks, and meet at last upon the stage,
each having thought the other lost. One of them is
Palæstra : a free-born girl of Athens, but stolen and
sold, as she tells us, in her infancy. Pleusidippus, a
young Athenian, had seen her at Cyrene, fallen violently in love with her, and made proposals to the slave-
merchant for her ransom. But that worthy individual,
thinking that he could make a better bargain for such
wares in Sicily, had just set sail for that island, carrying Palæstra and her fellow-captives with him, when
the whole party are wrecked here on the coast, just
going out of harbour.

* Possibly the storm was represented on the stage during the
delivery of the prologue, before the action of the piece began.

The two girls, drenched as they are, take refuge in the Temple of Venus, where they ask the protection of the Priestess. That good lady is the very model of an ecclesiastical red-tapist. Though they tell their sad story, she objects that they ought.to have come in the proper garb of supplicants — in a white robe, and bringing with them a victim ; and is hardly satisfied with poor Palæstra's explanation of the great difficulty which a young woman who had narrowly escaped drowning herself would find in carrying a white dress and a fat lamb with her.

Labrax, the slave-dealer, whom every one hoped had been drowned according to his deserts, has also escaped from the wreck and got ashore. Not without the loss, however, of all his money, which has gone to the bottom, and with it a small case of jewellery, family tokens belonging to Palæstra, of which he had obtained possession. He hears that the two girls who are his property are hidden in the temple, and proceeds to drag them thence by force. He is met there, however, by a servant of young Pleusidippus, who is in search of his master, and who runs to Dæmones's cottage for help. The owner comes out with two stout slaves, rescues Palæstra and her companion, and leaves Labrax in custody, the slaves standing over him with cudgels, until the case can be investigated. Pleusidippus soon arrives upon the scene, his servant having hurried to inform him of the state of affairs — that his dear Palæstra has escaped from the wreck, and taken refuge in the temple, from which Labrax would have dragged her but for the timely interference of a very worthy old gentleman. The young man hauls the slave-dealer off, with very little ceremony, before the nearest magistrate, to answer both for his breach of contract and his attempt at sacrilege. And with this scene ends the third act of the drama.

Then there is an interval of time before the commencement of the fourth act. Gripus, one of Dæmones's slaves, has been out fishing. He has taken no fish; but has had a haul which will prove, he hopes, to be of more importance. He has brought up in his net a heavy wallet, and feels certain that it contains gold; enough, no doubt, to purchase his freedom, and to make him a rich man for the rest of his life besides. His soliloquy, as to what he will do with all his riches, reminds us not a little of the dream of Alnaschar.

Now, this shall be my plan—I'm quite determined :
I'll do it cunningly; I'll go to my master,
With just a little money from time to time,
To buy my freedom : then, when I am free,
I'll buy a farm—I'll build a house—I'll have
A great many slaves. Then I shall make a fortune
By my big merchant-ships. I shall be a prince,
And talk to princes. Then I'll build a yacht,
Just for a fancy, and like Stratonicus
Sail round the seaport towns.* When my renown
Spreads far and wide, then—then, I'll found a city ;
I'll call it "Gripè," in memory of my name
And noble acts ; I'll found an empire there.
I do resolve great things within this breast (*striking his
    chest*) ;

* Stratonicus was treasurer to Philip and Alexander, and probably thought himself a greater man than either of his masters. The allusion to Alexandria in "Gripè" is obvious.

But for the present, I must hide my windfall.

(*Takes his breakfast out of his scrip, and looks at it.*)
But more's the pity that so great a man
Must for to-day have such a sorry breakfast!

—Act iv. sc. 2.

Before he has time to hide his booty, Trachalio, the
slave of Pleusidippus, who has been watching all
Gripus's proceedings, comes up, and wants to claim
half-shares in the contents. The dialogue between the
two has some amusing points, though it is rather too
much spun out for modern taste. Trachalio declares
that he knows the person to whom the wallet formerly
belonged ; Gripus replies that he knows to whom it
belongs *now*, which is of much more importance—it
belongs to him. All that he catches belongs to him,
clearly ; nobody ever disputed it before. Trachalio argues
that this is not a fish. It *is* a fish, declares Gripus ;
"all's fish that comes to the net"—using our proverb in almost so many words. This sort of fish
doesn't grow in the sea, says the other. Gripus declares that it does—only the species, he is sorry to say,
is very seldom caught. He is a fisherman, and knows
a good deal more about fish, he should hope, than a
landsman. Trachalio protests it is with him a matter
of conscience : since he has seen the wallet fished up,
unless he goes and tells the owner, he shall be as great
à thief as Gripus ; but he is willing to share that responsibility, provided he shares the prize. They very
nearly come to blows about it ; but at last Trachalio
proposes to submit the dispute to arbitration ; and as
the cottage of Dæmones is close at hand, they agree that
he shall decide as to the disposal of the property—

Trachalio not being aware of Gripus's connection with the old gentleman, and Gripus hoping that his master will surely give an award in his favour.

When the wallet is opened, it is found to contain, besides valuable property belonging to Labrax, the precious casket containing Palæstra's family relics: and, by desire of Dæmones, she describes the articles which ought to be in it, in order to prove her claim to its ownership. To his joy and surprise, one of these relics, a small toy implement, bears his own name, and another that of his wife. Palæstra is their long-lost daughter, stolen in her childhood, and thus restored. Of course she is handed over to her lover Pleusidippus, a free woman.

The disposal of the claims to the rest of the wallet's contents hardly meets our notions of dramatic justice. Dæmones retains in his possession the prize which poor Gripus has fished up, in order to restore it to its owner; not only without any hint of salvage-money, but with the addition of a long moral lecture to his slave upon honesty. This is all very well; but the subsequent proceedings serve to show that if it was a characteristic of the slave to be always ready to cheat his master, the master had also his peculiar idea of honesty as between himself and his slave. Gripus meets Labrax lamenting for his lost wallet, and as a last hope of making something out of his good luck, agrees to inform him of the whereabouts of the missing treasure for the consideration of a talent of good money paid down. Dæmones, when he comes to hear of the arrangement, ratifies it so far as this: Gripus is his property; therefore, what is Gripus's is his. Labrax

has to pay the talent into the hands of Dæmones, who
applies half to the ransom of his daughter's friend and
companion in misfortune, and allows the other half as
the price of Gripus's freedom.   The reply which that
personage makes previously to his master's lecture on
morality seems to show that he took it for about as
much as it was worth.

> Ah ! so I've heard the players on the stage
> Rehearse the very finest moral sentiments,
> And with immense applause ; showing quite clearly
> All that a wise man ought to do : and then
> The audience would go home, and not a soul of 'em
> Would follow that grand preaching in their practice.*

The play called CISTELLARIA — "The Casket" —
turns upon the same incidents—the loss of a daughter
when young, and her discovery by her parents by means
of a casket of trinkets which had been attached to her
person.† The copies of this play are very imperfect, and
there is a want of interest in the scenes.   One passage,
in which Halisca, the slave who has dropped the casket
in the street and returns to look for it, appeals path-

---

* A portion of this comedy appears to have been performed
as an afterpiece in the Dormitory at Westminster in 1798, when
a very clever "Fisherman's Chorus," written in rhyming Latin,
by the well-known "Jemmy Dodd," then Usher, was introduced.
—See Lusus Alt. Westm., i. 177.

† Parents had no hesitation in "exposing" a child whose
birth was for any reason inconvenient ; leaving it to die, or be
picked up by some charitable stranger, as might be.   But it was
held a sin to do this without leaving something valuable on the
child's person : and jewels, or other articles by which it might
possibly be recognised afterwards, were often fastened to its
clothes.

etically to the audience, to know whether any of them have picked it up, and will restore it, and so save her from a whipping, may remind a modern reader of Molière's Harpagon looking among the audience for the thief of his money. The despairing taunt with which she turns away, after pausing for some reply—

"'Tis no use asking—there's not one among ye
Does aught but laugh at a poor woman's troubles "—

is strong presumptive evidence that the spectators at a Roman comedy were almost exclusively men.

V. —THE CAPTIVES.

This pretty little drama is quite of a different complexion from the rest. The author tells us, in his prologue, that we are not to expect to find here any of the old stock characters of comedy, who, as he is free to confess, are not always of the most reputable kind. The interest is, in fact, rather pathetic than comic, and the plot is of the simplest kind. Almost the only comic element is supplied by the speaker of the prologue, who has a joke or two for the audience, of a very mild and harmless kind. The principal characters in the play appear to have been grouped in a kind of tableau on the stage while the prologue was delivered, in this as in some other plays. The prologist informs the audience that the two captives who stand in chains on his right and left, are Philocrates, a young noble of Elis, and his slave Tyndarus. There is war between Elis and the Ætolians; and these two prisoners, recently taken in battle, have been purchased amongst others by Hegio, a wealthy citizen of Ætolia, whose

own son is now, by the fortune of war, a prisoner in
Elis.   The father is sparing no cost in purchasing such
captives of rank and birth as are brought to Ætolia and
sold as slaves, in the hope of being able thus to effect
an exchange for his son.   He feels the loss of this son
all the more, because his younger brother was carried
off in his infancy by a revengeful slave, and he has
never seen him since.   " Do you understand, now ?"
says the speaker to the audience—" I hear a gentleman
standing up at the back of the gallery say ' no.'   Then
come a little nearer, sir, if you please ; I'm not going
to crack my voice in bawling to you at that distance.
And if you've not money enough to pay for a seat,
you've money enough to walk out, which I recommend
you to do.   And now—you gentlemen that *can* afford
to pay for your seats,—have the goodness to listen,
while I continue my story."   He goes on, after the
fashion which has been noticed as common in such
prologues, to sketch in brief the whole plot.   He begs,
however, to assure the audience, confidentially, that
they need not be alarmed because there is a war
going on in this play between Elis and Ætolia.   He
promises them—quite in the spirit of Bottom and his
company of players—that they " will leave the killing
out ; " all the battles shall be fought behind the scenes.
It would never do for them, he says, a company of
poor comedians, to encroach upon the domain of tragedy.
If any gentleman present wants a fight, he must get
one up on his own account—and it shall go hard but
that the present speaker will find a match for him, if
he be so inclined.   He concludes by asking their favourable verdict in the dramatic contest :—

And so I make my bow. Sirs, fare ye well ;
Be gentle judges of our comedy,
As ye are—doubtless—valorous hearts in war.

The interest of the drama lies in the generous devotion
of the slave Tyndarus to his young master.   Hegio
has ascertained that his captive Philocrates is the
only son of a man of great wealth, and hopes that by
sending a message to the father he may enlist his
interest at Elis in making search for his own son
among the Ætolian prisoners there, and sending him
home in exchange for Philocrates.   But this latter has,
at the suggestion of Tyndarus, exchanged clothes with
him, and the slave, who is nearly of the same age, and
of noble presence, personates the master.   Under this
mistake Hegio sends the slave (as he thinks) to Elis to
negotiate there with the father of Philocrates the release of his son.   But it is really the young noble who
is sent, and Tyndarus who personates him remains a
prisoner in his place.   There is a fine passage in which
the disguised slave appeals to Hegio for generous treatment during his captivity.

As free a man as was your son, till now,
Was I ; like him, the hapless chance of war
Robbed me of liberty ; he stands a slave
Among my people, even as here I stand
Fettered before you.   There is One in heaven,
Be sure of it, who sees and knows all things
That all men do.   As you shall deal with me,
So will He deal with him.   He will show grace
To him who showeth grace ; He will repay
Evil for evil.   (*Hegio appears moved.*) Weep you for
     your son?
So in my home my father weeps for me.

The parting between Tyndarus and his master gives
rise to another scene which would be highly effective
in the hands of good actors. The two young men had
been brought up together, it must be remembered, from
childhood, had played the same games, gone to the
same school, and served in the same campaign. There
is an equality of feeling between them, which even the
miserable conditions of slavery have not been able
to prevent. Philocrates, speaking as Tyndarus, asks
the latter if he has any message to send home to his
father.

> *Tyndarus* (*as Philocrates*). Say I am well ; and tell him
> this, good Tyndarus,
> We two have lived in sweetest harmony,
> Of one accord in all things ; never yet
> Have you been faithless, never I unkind.
> And still, in this our strait, you have been true
> And loyal to the last, through woe and want,
> Have never failed me, nor in will nor deed.
> This when your father hears, for such good service
> To him and to his son, he cannot choose
> But give you liberty. I will insure it,
> If I go free from hence. 'Tis you alone,
> Your help, your kindness, your devoted service
> Shall give me to my parents' arms again.
> *Philocrates* (*as Tyndarus*). I have done this : I'm glad
> you should remember ;
> And you have well deserved it : (*emphatically*) for if I
> Were in my turn to count up all the kindness
> That you have shown to me, day would grow night
> Before the tale were told. Were you my slave,
> You could have shown no greater zeal to serve me.
>   —Act ii. sc. 3.

Hegio is touched by the affection shown by the young pair ; and Tyndarus is treated as liberally as a prisoner can be. But there is another prisoner of war of whom Hegio has heard, who knows this young man Philocrates and his family, and is anxious to have an interview with him, which Hegio good-naturedly allows. This man at once detects the imposture ; and though Tyndarus attempts for a time (in a scene which must be confessed to be somewhat tedious) to maintain his assumed character in spite of the other's positive assertions, he is convicted of the deception, and ordered by the indignant Hegio to be loaded with heavy chains, and taken to work in the stone-quarries ; which would seem to have been as terrible a place of punishment in Greece as we know they were in Sicily. In vain does Tyndarus plead his duty to his master : in vain does he appeal to Hegio's feelings as a father—

Tyn. Think, now—if any slave who called you master
Had done this for your son, how you had thanked him !
Would you have grudged him liberty, or no ?
Would you have loved him above all the rest ?
Nay—answer me.

    He.   I grant it.

    Tyn.   Oh, why then
Are you thus wroth with me for doing likewise ?

    He. Your faith to him was treachery to me.

    Tyn. What ! would you ask that one brief night and day
Should give you claim on a poor captive's service
Just fallen within your power, to cancel his
With whom I lived and whom I loved from childhood ?

    Heg. Then seek your thanks from him.—Lead him
        away.

In vain does his fellow-captive, whose evidence has

brought down Hegio's wrath upon him, plead on his
behalf.   Tyndarus is dragged off to the quarries, preserving his calmness of demeanour to the last.

Well—death will come—thy threats can reach no further;
And though I linger to a long old age,
Life's span of suffering is but brief.—Farewell !
I might find plea to curse thee—but—farewell !

—Act iii. sc. 5.

The *dénouement* comes rapidly.   There is a long supposed interval between the third and the two last
brief acts of the drama,—which in a modern play
would be rather termed scenes.   Philocrates returns
from Elis, and brings with him Hegio's son Philopole-
mus, whom he has ransomed from captivity.   But he has
not forgotten his faithful Tyndarus, and has come in
person to insure his liberation.   But this is not all.   He
has also met with the runaway slave who, twenty years
ago, had stolen from his home the younger son of
Hegio.   When this man is now cross-examined by his
old master, it is discovered that he had fled to Elis, and
there sold the child to the father of Philocrates, who
had made a present of him to his own boy, as was not unusual, to be a kind of live toy and humble playfellow.
It is this very Tyndarus, who now stands before his
father loaded with chains and haggard with suffering
of that father's infliction.   The noble nature displayed
by the captive is explained by his noble blood.

    No one will deny that it is a pretty little drama,
with a good deal of quiet pathos in it.   But (if we have
the piece complete, which may be doubtful) whatever
pathos a modern audience would find in these last

scenes would be due to such force of expression and by-play as could be thrown into them by clever actors; they are very bald indeed in the reading. The claim which the speaker of the brief epilogue makes for the play, that its morality is of the purest and simplest, is well deserved. It contains, strange to say, no female character whatever. For these and other reasons 'The Captives,' in spite of the lack of comic element, used to be a very favourite selection with English schoolmasters, in the days when the performance of a Latin comedy by the elder scholars seems to have formed part of the annual routine in most of our large schools. Yet, strange to say, there is no record of it having ever been performed at Westminster. Perhaps the absence of those distinctly comic characters and situations which are made so telling in the annual performance by the Queen's Scholars has been the reason of its neglect.

VI.—THE TWO MENÆCHMI.

This comedy deserves notice not so much for its own merits—for whatever they might have appeared to a Roman audience, they are not highly appreciable by our taste—but because upon it Shakspeare founded his 'Comedy of Errors.' It appears to have been the only work of Plautus which had at that time been translated into English, which may account for its being the only one from which Shakspeare seems to have borrowed. The plot is improbable in the highest degree, though admitting some farcical situations. It all turns upon the supposed resemblance between two twin-brothers — so strong as to deceive their servants, their nearest friends, and even their wives. Antipholus of Ephesus and Antipholus of Syracuse are but reproductions of Menæchmus of Epidamnus and Menæchmus Sosicles—the twins of Plautus's comedy, who were separated in their youth, and whose marvellous likeness, which makes it impossible to distinguish between them, leads to the series of ludicrous mistakes and entanglements which are at last set right by their personal meeting on the stage. Shakspeare has added the pair of Dromios, who, like their masters, are duplicates of each other : thereby increasing the broad fun of the piece, such as it is, and not materially increasing the improbability. The use of masks upon the Roman stage·made the presentation of the likeness comparatively easy ; whereas in the English play all has to depend upon exact similarity of costume and the making up of the faces of the two actors, which is not always satisfactory. The incidents in the Latin play are not so amusing as in Shakspeare's version of it, and the morals much more objectionable.

VII.—AMPHITRYON.

'Amphitryon' is also founded on a famous case of mistaken identity. It is termed by Plautus a "tragi-comedy;" which does not mean that there is anything in it to which we should apply the word "tragic," but merely that the introduction of gods amongst the characters gives it some of the features of classic tragedy. In saying that it is a dramatic version of the myth of Jupiter and Alcmena, enough has been said to indicate that the morality in this case is that common to pagan mythology. This did not prevent it from being acted at Westminster so late as 1792. There are well-known French and English imitations of it : the 'Amphitryon' of Molière and 'The Two Sosias' of Dryden. It must be said, at least, in favour of the great French dramatist, that the morality in his play is higher than that of the original. 'Amphitryon,' however, has some wit, which is more than can be well said for the 'Menæchmi.' Here, too, it is possible that we have the original of the two Dromios in Shakspeare's comedy. For, as Jupiter has assumed the character and likeness of Amphitryon, so he has directed Mercury to put on the resemblance of Sosia, Amphitryon's body-slave. The scene in which poor Sosia, sent by his master (who has just returned from his campaign) to announce his arrival to his wife Alcmena, is met at the door by his double in the person of Mercury, is very comically drawn. It has the defect of being, at least to our modern taste, somewhat too prolonged, and only a portion of it can be given here. Mercury insists upon it that he is the true and original Sosia, gives the other a drubbing as an impudent impostor, and threatens to give him a worse if he does not at once take himself off. Sosia becomes extremely puzzled as to his own identity when his rival, in reply to his questions, shows an intimate knowledge of all his master's movements during the late campaign, and especially in the matter of a gold cup presented to him out of the spoils, which is secured in a casket under Amphitryon's own seal— which seal, however, this duplicate Sosia can describe perfectly.

Sosia (aside). He beats me there. I must look out, it
    seems,
For a new name. Now where on earth could this fellow
Have been, to see all that ? I'll have him yet ;
Things that I did by myself, with no one near—
What I did in the tent—it can't be possible
He'll tell me that. (*Aloud.*) Now look—if you be Sosia,
What was I doing in my master's tent,
That day they'd such hard fighting in the front ?
Come—tell me that, my friend—and I'll give in.
    Mercury (slily). There was a cask of wine : I filled a
        pitcher—
    Sos. (*to himself*). He's not far out.
    Mer.   Filled it with good red wine—
As honest stuff as ever grew in grape.
    Sos. Marvellous !—unless this chap was *in* the cask !—
Fact—I *did* fill the pitcher—and drank it too.
    Mer. How now ? have I convinced you I *am* Sosia ?
    Sos. (*puzzled*). D'ye say *I'm* not ?
    Mer.   How can you be, if I am ?
    Sos. (*half crying*). I swear by Jove I *am* Sosia—it's no lie.
    Mer. I swear by Mercury it is : Jove won't believe you ;
He'd trust my word far sooner than your oath.
    Sos. Who am I then, I ask you, if not Sosia ?
    Mer. That I can't tell you—but you can't be Sosia,
So long as I am : when I've done with the name,
Then you may take it. Now be off with you,
Name or no name, unless you want a thrashing.
    Sos. Upon my life, now that I look at him,
And recollect myself—(I take a peep
Into my master's glass occasionally)
It strikes me that there *is* an uncommon likeness. (*Ex-
    amines Mercury furtively.*)
The broad-brimmed hat and surcoat—just the same ;
He looks as like me as I do myself !
Legs—feet—proportions—short-cropped hair—bull-neck—

Eyes—nose—lips—cheeks—the very chin and beard—
The whole of him is me ! the very ditto !
I wonder whether he's got whip-marks on his back—
If so, the copy's perfect.* (*Cogitating.*) Still—it seems,
When I consider on't, I must be I :
I'm the same man I was ; I know my master—
I know his house,—there 'tis. I've got my senses ;
(*Pinching himself.*) And I can feel. No ; I will *not*
      believe
A word this fellow says. I'll knock again. (*Goes up to
      the door.*)
    Mer. (*rushing up*). Hallo ! where now ?
    Sos.   Home, to be sure.
    Mer.   Be off—
Be off like lightning, if you'd keep whole bones !
    Sos. Mayn't I give master's message to his lady ?
    Mer. To his—by all means ; only not to ours :
If you provoke me more, I'll break your head.
    Sos. (*running away*). No—no ! I'll go ! Poor devil that
      I am !
Where did I lose myself ? when was I changed ?
How did I lose my corporal capacity ?
Did I forget myself, when I went abroad,
And leave myself at home here, by mistake ?
For he's got what *was* me, there's no doubt of it ;
All the outside, I mean, that I used to have.

* Molière has improved upon this passage, in the scene in
which Sosia tells his master of the beating which he has just received from his own double, and how he was at last convinced
that this latter was the real man :—

> " Longtemps d'imposteur j'ai traité ce moi-même ;
>   Mais à me reconnaître enfin il m'a forcé :
>   J'ai vu que c'était moi, sans aucune stratagème ;
>   Des pieds jusq'à la tête il est comme moi fait,—
>   Beau, l'air noble, bien pris, les manières charmantes ! "
>   —Amphit., act ii. sc. 1.

Well—I'll go back again and tell my master:
Perhaps *he* won't own me !   The gods grant he don't !
I shall be free then, even if I'm nobody.
                                                    —Act i. sc. 1.

The scene in which the pilot of the ship is unable
to decide between the false Amphitryon and the true,
when at last they are brought upon the stage together,
is probably only a "restoration" of the mutilated work
of Plautus.   Molière has substituted Sosia for the
pilot, and makes him decide in favour of the false pre-
tender.   The convincing argument which confirms him
in this decision has passed into a proverb, better
known perhaps in itself than in its context.   Jupiter,
in his assumed character of Amphitryon, is made to
reserve the disputed identity for the verdict of the
Thebans in full assembly :   meanwhile he invites all
the company present to dinner :—

"*Sosia.* Je ne me trompais, Messieurs, ce mot termine ¿
        Toute l'irrésolution;
        Le véritable Amphitryon
        Est l'Amphitryon où l'on dîne." *

VIII.—THE POT OF GOLD (AULULARIA).

The prologue to this comedy is spoken in the character of the "Lar Familiaris," as the Romans called him
—a sort of familiar spirit supposed to be attached to
every Roman household, who had his own little altar

* Dunlop shows, however, that this is really borrowed from
an older comedy on the same subject by Rotrou—'Les Deux
Sosies'—which the later author has laid under contribution
in other scenes.   Sosia's words in Rotrou's play are—"Point,
point d'Amphitryon où l'on ne dîne point."

near the family hearth, and whose business it was, if duly cultivated, to look after the family fortunes,—a private "Robin Goodfellow." He informs the audience that the owners of the establishment over which he presides at present have been a generation of misers. The grandfather had buried under the hearth a "Pot of Gold," intrusting the secret only to him, the Lar, and praying him to see to its safe keeping ; and too covetous, even at his death, to disclose this secret to his son. The son was rather worse than his father, grudging the Lar his sacrifices even more than the old man had ; and therefore, the Lar saw no good reason for discovering the treasure to *him*. And now the grandson, Euclio, is as bad as either father or grandfather. But he has a daughter ; rather a nice young woman, the Lar considers : she is constantly paying him little attentions, bringing incense, and wine, and garlands, and suchlike, to dress his altar : and as the Lar must have seen a good deal of her, and the audience is never allowed to see her at all, they have to take his word for her attractions. She will be expecting a husband soon : and the family guardian has fixed upon one for her—Lyconides, nephew to one of their next-door neighbours, Megadorus. But as he has some reason to know that the young man would not be acceptable to her father, he will contrive that the uncle shall ask the girl in marriage for himself, and afterwards resign in his nephew's favour. And he has made known to Euclio the secret of the buried treasure, in the hope that out of it he will provide a liberal dowry for the young lady who is so zealous in her household devotions.

But Euclio has no intention of using the gold in that or in any other fashion. It becomes his one delight, and his perpetual torment. He leaves it buried in its hiding-place : but he is in continual terror lest it should be discovered. He scarcely dares move from home, lest when he returns he should find it gone. Every noise that he hears, he fancies proceeds from some attempt to carry off his treasure. He leads his poor old housekeeper, his one slave Staphyla, a wretched life, from his perpetual worrying. When his neighbour Megadorus comes to ask the hand of his daughter in marriage, he is sure that it is because he has heard in some way of the gold. His continual protest is that he is miserably poor. One of the most ludicrous situations is the dilemma in which he finds himself placed, when upon some occasion a dole of public money is announced for the poorer citizens. If he does not attend and claim his share, his neighbours will think he is a rich man, and be sure to try to hunt out his money: if he goes to the ward-mote to receive it, and has to wait perhaps some time for the distribution, what may not have become of his darling " Pot " during his absence ? Acute critics have said, apparently with truth, that in Euclio we have the pure miser ; who has no desire to increase his store, no actual pleasure in the possession, no sense of latent power in the gold which he treasures, but who is a very slave to it in the terror of losing it.

Euclio, though much alarmed at first as to the probable motives of Megadorus's request, consents to give him his daughter ; still, however, under protest that he is a very poor man, which the other fully believes. He can give no dowry with her : but Megadorus is prepared to take her without; he will even provide out of his own purse all the expenses of the wedding-feast, and will send in to Euclio's house both the provisions and the cooks required for the occasion.

But the cooks, when they come, and begin to busy themselves in the house, are a source of continual agony to the miser. He hears one of them call for a " larger pot : " and he rushes at once to the protection of his gold. He finds his own dunghill-cock scratching about the house ; and he is sure that these new-comers have trained him to discover the buried treasure, and knocks the poor bird's head off in his fury. In the end he drives them all off the premises under a shower of blows, and only when he has in their absence dug up the precious pot, and got it safe under his cloak, will he allow them to come back again. When the bride-groom expectant, in the joy of his heart, invites him to drink with him, he feels satisfied that his intention is to make him drunk, and so to wring from him his secret.

The miser carries off the pot, and proceeds to bury it afresh in the temple of Faith, placing it under that goddess's protection. He finds that this proceeding has been watched by a slave belonging to Megadorus, and carries the gold off again to the sacred grove of Sylvanus, where he buries it once more. This time, however, the slave takes his measures successfully, by getting up into a tree ; and when Euclio is gone, he unearths the pot, and carries it off rejoicing. The discovery of his loss almost drives the miser frantic : and the scene is worth extracting, if only because Molière has borrowed it almost entire in the well-known soliloquy of Harpagon in 'L'Avare.' It shall be given in as literal a prose version as it will bear, in order to its more ready comparison with the French imitation.

EUCLIO (*solus, rushing on the stage*).

I'm ruined! dead! murdered!—where shall I run? Where shall I not run to? Stop him there, stop him!— Stop whom! Who's to stop him? (*Striking his forehead in despair.*) I can't tell—I can see nothing—I'm going blind. Where I'm going, or where I am, or who I am, I cannot for my life be sure of! (*Wringing his hands, and appealing to the audience.*) Oh pray—I beseech you, help me! I implore you, do! Show me the man that stole it! Ah! people put on respectable clothes, and sit there as if they were all honest! (*Addressing a spectator in the front seats.*) What did you say, sir? I can believe *you*, I'm sure—I can see from your looks you're an honest man. (*Looking round on them all.*) What is it? Why do you all laugh? Ah, I know you all! There are thieves here, I know, in plenty! Eh! have none of them got it? I'm a dead man! Tell me then, who's got it?—You don't know? Oh, wretch, wretch that I am! utterly lost and ruined! Never was man in such miserable plight. Oh, what groans, what horrible anguish this day has brought me! Poverty and hunger! I'm the most unhappy man on earth. For what use is life to me, when I have lost all my gold? And I kept it so carefully!—Pinched myself, starved myself, denied myself in everything! And now others are making merry over it,—mocking at my loss and my misery! I cannot bear it!

—Act v. sc. 2.*

The scene which follows between the miser and the

---

* Compare Molière's 'L'Avare,' act iv. sc. 7.

young man Lyconides, who has anticipated his uncle in the love of the miser's daughter, has also been borrowed by Molière. Lyconides comes to confess that he has stolen the young lady's affections ; but Euclio is so full of his one great loss, that he persists in interpreting all Lyconides's somewhat incoherent language to imply that he is the thief of the gold. The play upon the Latin word *olla*, which means " pot," and is also the old form of *illa*, " she," helps the *equivoque* materially. But the French version is far more amusing ; and the words of Harpagon, when, in reply to Valère's talk about "la passion que ses beaux yeux m'ont inspirée, he exclaims in bewilderment, " Les beaux yeux de ma cassette !" * has passed, like so many of Molière's lines, into a favourite proverb.

This play is imperfect, and we only know what the catastrophe was from the brief sketch in the metrical prologue, which Priscian the grammarian is said to have affixed to each of these comedies. The lover recovers the pot of gold for its owner ; and—by some miraculous change in the miser's nature—is presented with it as a dowry for the daughter. The later scenes have indeed been supplied by more than one ingenious " restorer ; " but such restorations are unsatisfactory at the best.

Besides the admirable adaptation of this comedy in the French, no less than three English dramatists, Fielding, Shadwell, and Wycherley, have each a comedy called ' The Miser,' the plot and materials of all which are borrowed more or less from Plautus.

* ' L'Avare,' act v. sc. 1.

IX.—THE TRICKSTER (PSEUDOLUS).

This comedy would deserve special notice, if only
because it was, if we may trust Cicero, the "darling"
of Plautus. An author, however, is not an infallible
judge of his own works; and though the action of the
piece is very busy and lively, and the tricks of Pseudolus fairly amusing, few modern readers would be
likely to select it as their favourite. Probably it might
act better than it reads. Its plot is the old story of
money which has to be raised in some way for the
ransom of a slave-girl out of the hands of the dealer,
and the humour consists entirely in the devices of
Pseudolus to procure it for his young master. But
one of the early scenes contains such a graphic picture
of one of these hateful traffickers in human flesh and
blood, that portions of it may be worth presenting to
the reader.

Enter BALLIO, *the slave-dealer, and four flogging-slaves,
all armed with whips : other slaves following.*

Come out, here ! move ! stir about, ye idle rascals !
The very worst bargain that man ever made,
Not worth your keep ! There's ne'er a one of ye
That has thought of doing honest work.
I shall never get money's worth out of your hides,
Unless it be in this sort (*lays about them with the whip*).
  Such tough hides too !
Their ribs have no more feeling than an ass's—
You'll hurt yourself long before you'll hurt them.
And this is all their plan—these whipping-posts—
The moment they've a chance, it's pilfer, plunder,
Rob, cheat, eat, drink, and run away's the word.

That's all they'll do.   You'd better leave a wolf
To keep the sheep, than trust a house to them.
Yet, now, to look at 'em, they're not amiss ;
They're all so cursedly deceitful.—Now—look here ;
Mind what I say, the lot of ye ; unless
You all get rid of these curst sleepy ways,
Dawdling and maundering there, I'll mark your backs
In a very particular and curious pattern—
With as many stripes as a Campanian quilt,
And as many colours as an Egyptian carpet.
I warned you yesterday ; you'd each your work ;
But you're such a cursed,—idle,—mischievous crew—(*gives
    one of them a cut at each word*)   .
That I'm obliged to let you have this as a memorandum.
Oh! that's your game, then, is it ? So you think
Your ribs are as hard as this is ? (*Shows his whip.*) Now,
    just look !
(*Turning to his whipping-slaves*). They're minding some-
    thing else !   Attend to this,
(*Striking one of the others.*) Mind this, now, will you ?
    Listen, while I speak,   _
You generation that were born for flogging ;
D'ye think your backs are tougher than this oow-hide ?
(*Lays about him with it.*) Why, what's the matter ? Does
    it hurt ? O dear !—
That's what slaves get when they won't mind their masters.
                    —Act i. sc. 2.

There was a highly comic element in this, we may be
sure, to an audience of Roman freemen.   Even if there
were, as it is certain there must have been, present in
the theatre, many who had been slaves themselves, and
whose fathers had been in slavery, and many who were
slaves still, we may feel only too sure that their laugh
was amongst the loudest.   Among the curses of modern

slavery has been the selfish disregard of human suffering which it encouraged not only amongst the masters
but amongst the slaves themselves ; and it is well
known that a negro overseer has often shown far more
cruelty towards those of his own colour than the
white owner of the plantation.

The slave Pseudolus, who is the hero of this piece,
and from whom Molière seems to have borrowed in
some degree his character of Mascarille in ' L'Etourdi,'
is somewhat of a more intellectual rascal than others
of his type who appear in these comedies.   He looks
upon successful roguery as a highly intellectual accomplishment.

> Just as the poet, when he takes his pen,
> Seeks things which upon earth have no existence,
> And straightway finds them, and makes that like truth
> Which is but very falsehood ; thus will I
> In my way be a poet ; these gold pieces
> Which are not, shall be ; genius shall create them.

The scene in which he meets his master Simo, who is
looking for him in order to make some inquiries as to
the late discreditable goings-on of his son, in which he
thinks with some justice that Pseudolus has been aiding
and abetting, is a good specimen of cool effrontery.
Simo is accompanied by his friend Callipho, and Pseudolus sees them coming.

> *Pseudolus (to himself).*   A bold behaviour in a doubtful
>   cause
> Is half the victory.   (*Bowing profoundly to Simo.*)   Sir,
>   my best respects—

They are my master's due. (*Bowing to Callipho.*) My
    second best,
Such as are left me, sir, I offer you.
    Simo (*gruffly*). Good morning. Where may you be
        going, eh ?
    Pseud. I'm standing still, sir, as you might observe
        (*striking an attitude*).
    Si. Look at the fellow's posture, Callipho !
Stands like a lord there !
    Callipho.   Well, he's not afraid ;
That's a good sign.
    Pseud.   I hold, sir, that the slave
Who has an honest conscience (*lays his hand on his heart*)
    should feel proud,
Especially in the presence of his master.
    Si. Hark to him ! Now he'll so philosophise,
And choke you with a flood of clever words,
You'd think he was not Pseudolus, but Socrates.*
    Pseud. You hold me in contempt, sir—that I know ;
You do not trust me ; ah ! you'd have me be
A rascal ; no, sir—I'll be honest still.
                          —Act i. sc. 5.

His master asks him whether he can answer honestly a few questions about his son: and Pseudolus assures
him that his replies shall be " as the oracles of Delphi."
His son has got into trouble ? Yes. Owes money ?
Yes. He, Pseudolus, is trying to procure it for him ?
Yes. Probably intending, by some tricks or cajolery,
to extract it out of his—the father's—pocket? Pseudolus confesses that he had such intention. And, after

---

* This reputation for " sophistry " seems to have followed
Socrates from the pages of Aristophanes to those of his brother
dramatist.

some satirical compliment from Simo upon his candour,
and thanks for having thus put him on his guard, he
coolly assures his master that he retains this intention
still, and is confident of succeeding in it. Nay, more
—when Simo challenges him to try, he will undertake
not only to get from him the money required for the
ransom of the young person upon whom his son has set
his heart, but to get her away from her present owner
without any ransom at all. It ends in a promise from
Simo to make him a present of the sum required, if he
succeeds in his design upon Ballio the slave-dealer. The
old gentleman, however, gets so uneasy on the subject,
that he succeeds in " hedging " his own stake in the
matter by telling Ballio of the plot which is laid for
him, and making a wager with him to the same amount
that Pseudolus will beat him in spite of all precautions.
He does ; and his master—who is evidently as proud
of possessing such a clever slave as some people are of
a specially mischievous child — hands him over the
money ; with the less reluctance, because he gets re-
couped at the expense of the wretched Ballio, who
loses both his slave and his wager. Pseudolus liberally offers to return his master half, if he will join him
at a supper which he has ordered in celebration of his
double triumph ; and Simo, in accordance with that
curious combination of familiarity and despotism which
has been remarked as pervading all the relations between master and slave, accepts the invitation at once,
although Pseudolus is very far from sober when he gives
it. Simo suggests that he should also invite the audience ; but Pseudolus replies that none of them have
ever yet invited *him.* If, however, they will now sig-

nify their approval of the comedy, he will give them an invitation—to-morrow.

The plays named 'EPIDICUS' and 'BACCHIDES' both turn upon incidents very similar to the preceding, the clever and unscrupulous slave being the leading character in both. They call for no particular notice here ; unless it be to mention that the 'Epidicus' must have been, like the play just noticed, a special favourite with its author, since he makes one of the characters in his 'Bacchides' say that he "loves it as well as his own life ; " * and that this latter play, like the 'Pseudolus,' appears to have suggested to Molière some points in his 'L'Etourdi.' One of its scenes † has also (as Thornton thinks) been imitated by him in 'Les Fourberies de Scapin.'

X.—THE YOUNG CARTHAGINIAN (PŒNULUS).

This play has an interest apart from any literary merit, because, written as it was during the Second Punic War, it has some Carthaginians introduced into it. We may conclude that the sketches were such as Plautus judged likely to meet the popular taste; and if so, they are creditable to the Roman contemporary estimate of their powerful enemies. With the exception of a joke or two about long trailing foreign dresses, and their being "pulse-eaters,"—just as we used to affect to believe that Frenchmen lived upon frogs,—and a hit in the prologue at the proverbial "Punic faith," which on a Roman's tongue meant Punic faithlessness, there is nothing derogatory to their national character

* Bacch., act ii. sc. 2.   † Act iii. sc. 3.

in this impersonation of the Carthaginians by the Roman
dramatist. The elder of the two, who is introduced
under a very historical name—Hanno—is a highly
straightforward and unselfish character, who at once
gives up to his cousin, Agorastocles, the " young Carthaginian," as soon as he discovers their relationship, the
property which had been left to himself by the young
man's father, in the belief of his son's death. Agorastocles himself is neither better nor worse than the Athenian (or, as they really are, Roman) youths who figure
in the comedies. And as for Adelphasium—Hanno's
lost daughter, with whom the hero of the piece has
fallen passionately in love in her position as a slave—
there is more character in her than in any one of the
heroines (the word must be used because there is no
other to be found) of Plautus or of Terence. It is difficult to separate her from the very disagreeable interlo-
cutors in the dialogues in which she takes a part : but
the quiet way in which she treats her sister's love of
finery, and her half-affected indifference to the flat-
teries of her lover, and disregard of all his raptures so
long as he fails in his promise of obtaining her freedom,
mark her out very distinctly from most of the female
characters in Plautus. There is an amusing scene in
which her lover, finding that she will not listen to him,
begs his servant Milphio, in whose rhetorical powers
he feels more confidence, to plead his cause with her.
Milphio consents to do it—warning his master, at the
same time, that he may possibly think his ambassador
too energetic. So the young man listens in the background, while Milphio, speaking on his behalf, entreats
Adelphasium, in the most approved style of lovers'

language, to have some pity upon his unfortunate
master. He throws himself so heartily into his com-
mission, that the Carthaginian listens to his rapturous
expressions with dismay, and at last can endure it no
longer. He rushes forward, and seizes his ambassador
by the collar, wholly regardless of the presence of the
lady and her sister, who look on with much amusement.

Agorastocles. Now am I not worth purchase at three
    farthings,
If I don't break that scoundrel's head.—Come here, sir!
    (*seizes Milphio.*)
There's for your "sweets,"—and "dears,"—and "pretty
    darlings"—(*beats him at each word*).
Here's "heart's delight" and "lovely charmer" for you!
    (*beats him again.*)
Milphio. Oh, master, master! it's rank sacrilege!
You're beating an ambassador!
    Agor.   I'll beat him
More yet.—"Kiss her all day," sir, could you?
I daresay! (*striking him again.*)   "Nestling of your
    bosom," is she?
    Mil. (*roaring and rubbing his shoulders*). Oh! that's
    enough!
    Agor.   Was that the fashion, sirrah,
In which I meant you to address the lady?
    Mil. Why, what was I to say, then?
    Agor.   Say, you rascal?
Why, this—"Light of my master's eyes—queen of *his*
    soul—
Breath of *his* life—joy of *his* heart,"—and so on:
Instead of that, sir, in your cursed impudence,
You've been calling her *your* darling all the time!
    Mil. Oh! now I see! (*goes up to Adelphasium, and
    begins again.*)

> I implore you, gracious madam,—
> Joy of *his* heart—but *my* abomination—
> Queen of *his* soul—but enemy of my ribs—
> His pet, my pest—his angel, but my devil—
> Light of his eyes—but black as night to me—
> Don't be so very cross to him,—if you can help it.
>   *Adelphasium (laughing and turning away).* Go hang
>   yourself! you and your master too!
>   *Mil.* I shall lead a precious life of it, I see, through you;
> I've got a back already in your service
> Whealed like an oyster-shell.
>   *Adel.*   It's your own back
> That you think most of, I suspect; not him,
> Or how he cheats me with deceitful promises.

When Hanno has discovered that these two sisters are
the long-lost daughters in search of whom he has
journeyed to Calydon, he determines to play upon their
feelings for a while—in the most unnecessary and unlikely fashion—by pretending to them that he merely
comes to claim them as his slaves. And here, again,
there are little touches on the part of Adelphasium
which almost redeem the scene from tediousness.
Hanno pretends to summon the girls before the magistrate, in order to prove his claim; and the lover, who
is present, and helps (though with evident impatience)
to humour the father's jest, asks him if he shall at once
make Adelphasium *his* prisoner. She has heard him
address the stranger as his "cousin;" and the fine
scorn with which, as she draws back from his eager
arm, she exclaims—

"Said you this person was your kinsman, sir?"

could not fail to be effective from the lips of a clever

actress. So, too, when she requests to know the nature
of Hanno's claim to her, and the lover, eager to put an
end to the *equivoque*, says that all shall be told if
she will but accompany the stranger, she scornfully
replies—

"What! does my own dog bark at me?"

it is not difficult to sympathise with the young Carthaginian's intense admiration of her as she stands there
defying him. He vows that for her sake Jupiter would
soon "send Juno packing;" and when at last she throws
her arms round her father's neck, he laments that Apel-
les and Zeuxis died too soon—they had never such a
subject for their pencil. These are by far the most
life-like pair of lovers in any comedy of either
Plautus or Terence. Granted that he is a little
foolish, and she something of a coquette,—that does
not make the characters either less natural or less
entertaining.

Nevertheless, all this absurd mystification on the
part of the father does make this scene tedious, as are
some others in the play. Hanno carries on his heavy
joke so long, that at last his young cousin, who is impatient for the recognition of his dear Adelphasium,
appeals to him by pointing to the audience :—

"Sir, cut it short—these gentlemen are thirsty."

There is no symptom of relenting disclosed on the
part of Adelphasium towards her suitor, even after her
true position as a free-woman has been secured ; but,
as Hanno unhesitatingly promises her hand in marriage
to her new-found cousin, and daughters in the comic

drama are very dutiful on such points, we are left to conclude that his constancy is rewarded.   Mr Dunlop —whose critical judgment is entitled to so much respect—has pronounced this to be the dullest of all the author's productions.   Plot there certainly is none ; and the heavy badinage of the excellent Hanno is enough to put any critic out of temper.   But there is certainly more point in the dialogue than in most of the comedies of Plautus.

The play has a special interest for scholars, independently of any literary merit.   It is supposed to contain the only existing specimen of the Carthaginian language, in which Hanno is made to speak when first he appears upon the stage.*   There are eighteen lines of it (some of them, however, containing a mixture of Latin words), besides a few scattered phrases.   This philological curiosity has naturally much exercised the ingenuity of the learned.   Scaliger, Petit, and others, consider the language to be merely a variation of Hebrew, and in Pareus's edition of Plautus the lines are printed in Hebrew characters.   Others have sought to identify it with Chinese, Persian, or Coptic.   Some modern philologers incline to consider it a mere unmeaning jargon, invented by Plautus for the occasion ; and the frequent admixture of Latin words and terminations in the last lines of the passage (as though the writer were tired of keeping up the farce) certainly lends some countenance to this view.   The vocalisation of some of the words bears no slight resemblance to

* Act v. sc. 1.

Welsh. But the question of the affinities of language is not one to be discussed here.

The remaining Comedies may be dismissed with brief notice. The stock characters—the parasite, the military swaggerer, and the cunning slave—reappear upon the stage in very similar combinations, and in less respectable company. 'Stichus,' which is in other respects deficient in interest, having no plot whatever, and which some authorities do not consider to have been written by Plautus, deserves notice as containing the pretty female character of Pamphila (or Pinacium, as she is called in some copies), the exemplary young wife who maintains her fidelity to her absent husband in spite of the strong probabilities of his death or desertion. In vain has her father urged upon her and his other daughter, in accordance, no doubt, with the feeling of society on such points, the propriety of unprotected young women in their circumstances marrying again. Their husbands have now been absent, ostensibly on a trading voyage, for above three years, and have sent no word home. But Pamphila will listen to no such suggestion, and encourages her sister in steady resistance to all temptations to such breach of their first vows. Of course both husbands return home in due time, enriched by the profits made in their foreign voyages ; and such is the whole story of this brief and inartistic drama, remarkable only for its pleasant companion pictures of the two young wives. Six more plays make up the list of Plautus's surviving comedies, and if these had not survived, we should certainly have had no loss. Their names are ' Casina '—which seems to have furnished Beaumarchais with part of the plot of his ' Mariage de Figaro '—' Curculio,' ' The Ass-dealer ' (Asinaria), ' The Churl ' (Truculentus), 'The Merchant,' and ' The Persian.' The morality of all these is of the very lowest, and the three last are stupid besides.

CHAPTER V.

A DRAMATIC generation elapsed between Plautus and Terence; for the latter was only ten years old at the date of Plautus's death. The great name which filled the interval in the annals of Roman comedy was that of Cæcilius; but of his works nothing remains except a few disjointed passages to be found here and there in the works of other authors. Horace mentions him with approval, while Cicero accuses him of bad Latin. Cæcilius, too, was a copyist from Menander, and a very indifferent copyist in the opinion of Aulus Gellius, who gives us an additional testimony to the genius of the Greek dramatist, when, in comparing a passage from one of his lost comedies with the imitation of it by Cæcilius, he says that the difference in brilliancy is that of the golden armour of Glaucus compared with the bronze of Diomed.

Such biographical record as we have of Terence is mainly derived from a source which is very apocryphal. There is a "Life" of him, ascribed to Suetonius, but more probably written by the grammarian Donatus: we do not know what authority the writer had for his details, and the anecdotes which it contains have a suspicious colouring.

Though the name by which he is known—Publius Terentius — is Roman, we are told that he was by birth a Carthaginian, whence came his *sobriquet* of "Afer" (the African), and that he was either born in slavery or had become a prisoner of war. He was brought up in the household of a Roman senator named Terentius, and, as was not uncommon among slaves when they obtained their freedom, took the name of his patron. That under these circumstances he should have had a liberal education need not discredit the story; for in many Roman families we know that such young slaves as showed ability were allowed ample opportunities of instruction. But other opportunities are said to have fallen to the lot of Terence such as few in his position could have hoped for. He was admitted, while yet a young man, to an intimate association with Scipio and Lælius; and this pair of accomplished friends were even said to have had a large share in the composition of the dramas which were brought out in the name of their humbler associate. There is a story that Lælius, being one evening busy in his library, and slow to obey his wife's summons to dinner, excused himself by saying he had never been in a happier mood for composition : and forthwith recited, as part of the result, a passage from what was afterwards known as 'The Self-Tormentor' of Terence. The dramatist himself, perhaps very naturally, seems partly to have encouraged the popular notion that he enjoyed such distinguished help; for though in his prologue to the comedy which was said to have been really the work of his aristocratic friend he speaks of this report as " a weak invention of the enemy," yet in the prologue to a subsequent drama, 'The Brothers,' he evidently treats it as a compliment, and does not care altogether to refute so flattering an accusation.

> For as to that which carping tongues report,
> That certain noble friends have lent their hand
> To this his work, and shared the poet's toil,—
> What they would fling at him as a reproach
> He counts an honour,—to be thus approved
> By those whom universal Rome approves.*

Cicero thought it probable.that his illustrious friends did help him, though it might have been only by judicious hints and corrections. It is also more than possible that the dramatist may have been indebted for much of the refinement of his dialogue, directly or indirectly, to the accomplished women whose society he enjoyed in the household of Lælius. The ladies of that family were all charming talkers ; and Lælia, the eldest daughter of Scipio's friend, is mentioned by her son-in-law Crassus, the famous orator, as reminding him, in the elegance of her language, of the dialogues of Nævius and Plautus.

It is said that when he offered his first play to the Ædiles, who as the regulators of the public games had to choose the pieces which were to enjoy the honour of public representation, he found the officer to whom he brought it to read seated at table. The young author was desired to take a stool at a distance, and begin : but he had scarcely got through the opening passage

* Prologue to the Adelphi, 15.

of 'The Maid of Andros' when the Ædile motioned
him to a seat by his own side, and there the reading
was completed.

The six comedies which follow are probably all that
their author ever put upon the stage. In the midst of his
dramatic career, he left Rome in order to travel in
Greece, and is said during his tour to have employed
himself in the translation of upwards of a hundred
of Menander's comedies. He seems never to have
returned, and tradition says that he was lost at sea on
his voyage homeward, and that his precious manuscripts perished with him. Another story is that he
himself escaped from the wreck, but died of grief for
the loss of his literary treasures.

His plays have far more elegance, but less action,
than those of Plautus. He is perhaps more adapted
for the library, and Plautus for the stage. Very much
of the fun of the latter is broad farce, while Terence
seldom descends below parlour comedy. But the two
writers had moved in very different circles : Plautus
had been familiar with life in the Suburra—the St
Giles's of Rome—while Terence had mixed in the
society of the Palatine. Their tastes had thus been
formed in very different schools. It is probable that
Terence gives us a better notion of what Menander was
than either Plautus or Cæcilius. A criticism of Cæsar
has been already quoted, in which he calls Terence a
" half-Menander." In the same lines he speaks of his
" pure diction " and " smoothness," and regrets his de-
ficiency in that lively humour (" *vis comica*") which
Menander seems to have succeeded in combining with

the Attic elegance of his style. There seems much justice in this criticism.

The brief prologues with which Terence introduces his plays, unlike those of Plautus, contain no kind of explanation of the plot. They are personal appeals of the poet to his audience, informing them honestly of the sources from which he has borrowed his piece (for to the honours of original invention no Roman dramatist of those days seems to have thought of aspiring), or defending himself against some charge of unfair dealing brought against him by his rivals. In this respect they bear a strong resemblance to the " parabasis," as it was called, introduced here and there between what we should call the acts, in the old Attic Comedy of Aristophanes and Cratinus.

CHAPTER VI.

THE COMEDIES OF TERENCE.

I.—THE MAID OF ANDROS.

' THE Maid of Andros '—the earliest in date of
Terence's comedies with which we are acquainted—
is confessedly founded upon two plays of Menander,
his ' Andria' and 'Perinthia ;' and the Roman dramatist
tells us, in his prologue, how certain critics complained
that in this adaptation he had spoilt two good pieces
to make a single indifferent one. How much truth there
may be in the accusation we cannot even guess. But there
seems to have been generally a lack of incident in the
comedies of his great original, which, supposing such
adaptation to be permissible at all, would quite justify
a writer who had to make his own work effective in
supplying himself with sufficient material from as
many separate pieces as he thought proper. Even as we
have the play, the incidents are so few and simple, that
its defect, if acted before a modern audience, would be
the want of sufficient interest in the plot. A lady
named Chrysis has come from the island of Andros to
Athens, and there, from lack of money or friends, after

a hard struggle to make an honest livelihood, has been driven to make a market of her beauty. Amongst the visitors to her house, one of the most constant has been the young Pamphilus, who may be considered the hero of the piece. But, whatever the lady's reputation, the relations between her and Pamphilus have been of the most innocent kind : and of this fact none are better convinced than his father Simo, and the freedman Sosia—who is, in spite of his humble position in the household, the confidential friend and adviser of both father and son. The scene between Sosia and his master gives us, as most of these comedies do, a very pleasant idea of the kindly relations which in a well-regulated Roman household might subsist between the head of the family and his dependants, even under the hateful conditions of slavery. For we must still remember that, though the scene is laid in Athens, the words, and in a great degree the manners also, are Roman ; though Terence is more careful on this point than Plautus. Simo tells his freedman that he wants his services in a matter which involves trust and secrecy —qualities in which he has not hitherto found him wanting.

Simo. You know that, since I bought you when a boy,
You found me as a master just and kind ;
Then from a slave I made you free ; and this
Because you had served me with a free goodwill ;
The greatest boon I had to give, I gave you.
   Sosia. I don't forget it.
   Si.   Nor do I repent it.
   So. If aught that I have done, or can do, pleases you,
It is my pleasure : if you thank me for it,

I thank you for the thanks.   But that you name it
Troubles me somewhat ; thus reminding me
Seems half to charge me with ingratitude ;—
Sir, in one word, what would you have me do ?

Simo will tell him.   It was true,—there was nothing
between his son and Chrysis ; his visits were really
not to her.   But Chrysis died a short time ago ; and
Pamphilus, as a mark of respect to an old acquaintance,
had followed amongst the mourners at her funeral.
Simo—one of the many idle old gentlemen who were
wont to be spectators on such occasions—had seen his
son actually wipe away a tear.   He was charmed, he
tells Sosia, at such a mark of true sensibility.   "If he
weeps, said I to myself, for a person who was a mere
common acquaintance, what would he not do for me—
his father !"   Suddenly a young woman, hitherto unknown, attracted his attention : of such a ravishing
beauty that the staid father of the family grows posi-
tively enthusiastic—rather to the surprise of the discreet
Sosia—in his description.   When the corpse is laid, according to Athenian custom, on the funeral pile, this
interesting young stranger, in the agony of her grief,
crept so close to it as to be almost caught by the flames ;
when a young man rushed forward, clasped her in his
arms with the tenderest expressions of affection, calling
her his "darling Glycerium," and led her off sobbing
very familiarly on his shoulder—quite as if she was used
to the situation.   And this young man was Pamphilus—
and his father looking on with his own eyes !   He had
gone home, as he tells Sosia, in such mood as might be
imagined after witnessing this outrageous conduct in

the promised bridegroom of his old friend's daughter.
Yet, after all, he continues—

> I had scarce ground enough, methinks, to chide him ;
> He might reply—"Have I deserved this, father ?
> What have I done ?   Wherein have I offended ?
> She would have thrown herself into the flames ;
> I hindered it—I saved her life !"—Such plea
> Sounds fair and honest.
>   *So.*   Marry, so it does ;
> For if you chide him that would save a life,
> What will you say to him that seeks to take it ?

However, the father is in great tribulation.   His friend
Chremes has heard of the matter, and is told that
Pamphilus is privately married to this young foreigner ;
and very naturally declines any longer to look upon him
as a future son-in-law.   But Simo is determined to find
out the truth, and to be satisfied whether his son has
really got into this disreputable entanglement.   He
means to pretend to him that the marriage with Chremes's daughter, so long meditated, is at last finally settled,
and is to come off at once, this very evening, the day
originally named.   Young men in Athenian society
must have been usually very obedient to their fathers
in such matters : for Simo has no doubt of his son's
compliance, unless he can show good and reasonable
cause to the contrary.   If this Andrian girl really
stands in the way, Pamphilus will make decided objec-
tions to the being disposed of in marriage, and then—
then, this indulgent father, who evidently dreads nothing so much as having to find fault with his son at
all, will know how to deal with him.   So Sosia is

charged to keep up the deception, and to assure every one that his young master is to be married this very evening.

But, if Sosia justly enjoys the confidence of his master, the young heir of the house has his confidant too. This is a slave named Davus—the best-known representative in classical comedy of the familiar character who has been described in a previous chapter.* He has considerably more cleverness than Sosia, but nothing of his honesty: except, indeed, a kind of spaniel-like fidelity to his young master's private interests, partly attributable to the mischievous pleasure which he finds in thereby thwarting the plans and wishes of the elder one. Davus has heard of this sudden renewal of the marriage-contract, and comes upon the stage soliloquising as to how this complication is to be dealt with. His master enters at the same time on the other side, listening.

Davus. Ah ! I was wondering where all this would end!
The master was so quiet, I suspected
He must mean mischief. When he heard that Chremes
Downright refused his girl, he never spoke
An angry word, nor stormed at any of us.
    Simo. (aside at the wing, shaking his stick at Davus).
      He will speak soon, and to your cost, you rascal!
    Da. (still aside). So, so! he thought to take us unprepared,
Lapping us up in this fools' Paradise,
To swoop upon us at the last, too late
To give us time to think, or opportunity
To hinder this curst wedding. (*Ironically.*) Clever man !
    Si. (trying to listen). What is he muttering?

* See p. 15.

Da. (*discovering Simo*).   Ha! my master there!
I had not seen him.

Si. (*coming forward*). Davus!

Da. (*pretending not to have seen him before*). Hey?
  what is it?

Si. Here, sirrah, come this way!

Da. (*aside*).   What can he want?

Si. What say you?

Da.   What about?

Si.   D'ye ask me, sirrah?—
They say my son has a love affair?

Da.   Good lack!
How folks will talk!

Si.   D'ye mind me, sir, or no?

Da. I'm all attention.

Si.   Well—to inquire too closely
Into the past were harsh—let bygones rest.
But now he must begin a different life;
New duties lie before him from this day:
And you—I charge you (*changing his tone*)—nay, indeed,
  good Davus,
I rather would intreat you, if I may,
Pray help to keep him straight.

Da. (*affecting surprise.*) Why—what's all this?

Si. Young men, you know, with such whims, do not care
To have a wife assigned them.

Da. (*carelessly*).   So they say.

Si. Then—if a young man have a knavish tutor
Who trains him in such courses, why, the evil
Will grow from bad to worse.

Da. (*looking stolid*).   Hercules help me!
I can't tell what you mean.

Si. (*ironically*).   No—really?

Da.   No;
I'm only Davus—I'm no Œdipus.

Si. You'd have me speak more plainly—is it so?

Da. Indeed I would.

Si.   Then, if I catch you scheming
To disappoint this match of ours to-day,
By way of showing your own curst cleverness,
I'll have you flogged within an inch of life,
And sent to the mill—on this condition, look you—
When I let you out, I'll go and grind myself.
Now, sir, d'ye understand me ?   Is that plain ?

Da. Oh, perfectly ! (*bowing*).   You state the case so
    clearly,
With such entire correctness of expression,
So free from ambiguity—it's quite charming !

But Davus is not deterred by these threats.   He
meets Chremes going about with a very gloomy face,
not at all like a happy father-in-law : he meets his foot-
boy coming home from market with a penny bundle
of pot-herbs and a dish of sprats—very unlike provisions for a wedding-supper.   He peeps into their
kitchen ; no culinary preparations whatever.   Moreover, there is no music, as there should be, before the
door of the bride's house.   He is satisfied that his
suspicions are correct ; that there is really no wedding
on foot, at least for the present ; that Chremes still
firmly refuses to allow his daughter to marry a young
man whom he believes to be married already ; and that
Simo is only using this pretended renewal of the engagement as a test for ascertaining how matters really
stand between his son and the fair Andrian.   He
goes in search of his young master to acquaint him
with this discovery, and to advise him to checkmate
his father by consenting at once to the proposed
marriage ; which, as there is no bride forthcoming, will

evidently pose the old gentleman considerably, besides
convincing him that his son is free from the entanglement which he suspects. There will be a respite
gained, at any rate : and in the meanwhile, Davus
hopes,—" something will turn up."

He finds Pamphilus in a state of great perplexity,
and very indignant against his father for proposing
to marry him off-hand at such very short notice ;
the perplexity not being lessened by his Glycerium presenting him with a baby on this his wedding-day that
is to be with another lady. Simo has heard a report
of this little stranger's arrival : but he believes it to
be a mere plot to impose upon him and Chremes, and
to confirm his friend in his resolution to refuse his
daughter.

Acting upon the advice of Davus, Pamphilus assures
his father at their next interview that he is quite ready
to take the wife suggested to him. But Davus has
been too clever by half. Simo goes straight to his
friend, assures him that all is over between Pamphilus and Glycerium, that his son will gladly fulfil
the contract already made for him, and begs of him,
by their long friendship, not to refuse any longer a
connection which will be for his son's advantage and
for the happiness of all. Chremes with some reluctance consents : and in the joy of his heart Simo calls
Davus, to whose good offices he thinks he is chiefly
indebted for his son's compliance.

Simo. Davus, I do confess, I doubted you :
I had my fears ; slaves—common slaves, I mean—
Will do such things,—that you were cheating me,
As to this matter of my son's.

Davus. (*with an air of injured innocence*). I, master !
    could you think it ? cheat ?—Oh dear !

Si. (*soothingly*). Well, well—I fancied so : and with
    that thought

I kept the secret which I tell you now.

  Da. What's that ?

  Si.   Well, you shall hear : for now at last
I almost think that I may trust you—may I ?

  Da. At last, sir, it seems, sir, you appreciate me.

  Si. This wedding was a mere pretence.

  Da. (*with feigned surprise*).   No ! really ?

  Si. A scheme of mine, to test my son and you.

  Da. Indeed !

  Si.   Yes, really.

  Da.   Look ye ! what a wit
Our master has ! I never could have guessed it.

  Si. Listen ; when I dismissed you, I met Chremes—

  Da. (*aside.*) We're lost—I know it.

  Si.   Listen ; straight I told him
What you told me, that Pamphilus was ready.
I begged and prayed that he would give his daughter ;
At last I moved him.

  Da. (*aside*).   Then I'm done for.

  Si. Hey ! did you speak ?

  Da.   I only said " well done," sir.

  Si. And I beseech you, Davus, as you love me,
Since you alone have brought about this wedding—

  Da. I ! oh dear, no ! pray—

  Si.   For my son I ask you,
Still do your best to regulate his morals.

  Da. I will, I will, sir—trust me.   [*Exit Chremes.*
      (*Throws himself on the ground and tears his hair.*)
                        O—h ! O—h !

I'm gone—a thing of nought. Why don't I go
Straight to the mill-prison of myself ?—Forgiveness ?
No hope of that, from any one. I've played

The very mischief with the total household ;
Cheated the master—got the son a wife—
This very night, much to the old gentleman's
Astonishment, and his son's disgust.—Ah ! well !
This comes of cleverness.   Had I held my tongue,
No harm had happened.—Hist ! here comes young master ;
(*Looking about.*) Is there any place here high enough, I
     wonder,
For a man to break his neck from ?

There is another lover in the plot,—which is perhaps
to our modern notions more complicated than interesting.
This daughter of Chremes, to whom Pamphilus has
been contracted by his father, has a favoured admirer in
his friend Charinus. Pamphilus has assured him that he
himself has no aspirations whatever in that quarter, in
spite of the arrangement between the two fathers : and
the young lover is naturally indignant when he discovers, as he thinks, the treacherous part which his
friend has played in the matter, in now coming forward
to fulfil an engagement which he had always professed
to repudiate.   There is a spirited scene between the
two young men, in which Pamphilus at last succeeds in
convincing his friend of his own unchanged views in
the matter—he will never marry the girl of his own
free-will. Poor Davus narrowly escapes a thrashing from
both, for his unlucky interference.   He undertakes,
however, if they will but have patience with him, to
set matters right yet : and his next step is to persuade
the nurse to allow him to lay Glycerium's baby down
at his master's door—a silent claim upon his grandfather—just as Chremes, full of his daughter's marriage,
is coming to call on his old friend. Chremes finds out

—as Davus intends that he should—whose child it is, and is more than ever indignant at the deception which is being repeated upon himself and his daughter. He goes straight to Simo and once more recalls his consent.

But meanwhile a stranger has arrived at Athens, who announces that this Andrian girl was really no sister of Chrysis, but a free-born daughter of Athenian parents, and that therefore Pamphilus will be bound by Athenian law to marry her—if they are not married already. When Davus comes to announce this news to Simo, the old gentleman's indignation at this new ruse on behalf of the conspirators—as he thinks it—knows no bounds; and poor Davus, who is now speaking the truth for the first time in the whole business, is for his reward tied neck and heels by order of his irate master, and carried off to prison. But the tale is true. An Athenian citizen had been shipwrecked upon the island with a little child; had died there, and left the infant to be brought up by Chrysis. This shipwrecked stranger turns out to have been Chremes's own brother, to whose charge he had committed his little daughter — this Glycerium, long supposed to be drowned, and now restored to her father. All difficulties are over; Pamphilus shall yet be son-in-law to Chremes—only the bride is Glycerium, not Philumena. The latter young lady, who never makes her appearance, and whose charms, like those of Glycerium, must be taken on report by the audience, is with dramatic justice handed over to her lover Charinus. Davus is released; he comes in rubbing his neck and legs, which are still suffering from the very uncomfortable kind of stocks—a veritable " *little-ease* "—which the Romans used to punish their slaves, but too good-humoured and light-hearted not to rejoice in the restored harmony of the family. He concludes the piece by begging the audience not to expect an invitation to the weddings, which will take place, he assures them, quite privately.*

II.—THE MOTHER-IN-LAW.

The plot of 'The Mother-in-law,' though it is an extremely pretty play, and its moral excellent, turns upon incidents which would justly offend the reticence of modern manners. Here it can only be sketched generally. A young wife, but a few months married and of really irreproachable character, fancies that she has so fatally compromised herself with her husband under circumstances in which she was really not to blame, that in his absence she leaves the roof of his father and mother, with whom she has been living since her marriage, and takes refuge with her own parents. Laches, her father-in-law, a choleric and despotic personage, fancies that his wife Sostrata, the "mother-in-law," must necessarily be the cause; although that gentle and kindly woman has really a sincere affection for the runaway, to whom she has always shown every kindness. The scolding which Laches inflicts upon his wife in one of the early scenes of the play, will serve to show how little originality

* Upon this play Michel Baron, the French dramatist, founded his comedy of 'L'Andrienne,' the two first acts being little more than a translation. Steele's 'Conscious Lovers' is also borrowed from it.

there is in those conjugal dialogues which have always been so popular an ingredient in modern farce. If humour of this kind cannot be said to be in the very best taste, it may at least claim a high classical antiquity.

Laches. Good heavens ! what a strange race these women
    are !
They're all in a conspiracy ! all just alike,
In what they will and what they won't ; not one of 'em
But sings to the same note ; with one consent
Each stepmother detests her daughter-in-law,
Each wife is bound to contradict her husband ;
There must be some school where they all learn wicked-
    ness ;
And my own wife must be head-mistress in it.
    Sostrata. Poor me, poor me ! I don't know what I
        am charged with !
    La. (*sneering*). Oh ! you don't, don't you ?
    Sos. On my life, dear Laches,
No—as I hope to live and die with you !
    La. The gods deliver me from such a prospect !
    Sos. (*sobbing*). Well, when I'm gone, you'll know how
        cruel you've been.
    La. Cruel, forsooth ! what words are strong enough
For your base conduct, madam ? You've disgraced
Me, and yourself, and all the family ;
You've ruined your son's happiness—made enemies
Of our best friends, who gave their daughter to us.
'Tis you, and only you, have done it all.
    Sos. I !
    La. Yes, you, madam ! What ! am I a stone ?
Have I no feelings, think you ? Do you fancy
Because I am in the country, I don't know
How you all go on here while I am away ?
Ay ! better than I know what goes on there.

Your conduct, madam, makes me common talk.
I knew my son's wife hated you—yes, long ago ;
No wonder—'twould be a wonder if she didn't.
But that for your sake she had taken a hatred
To the whole family,—this I did *not* know.
Had I only known it, I'd have packed you off,
And made her stay—I would indeed, my lady !
Look how ungrateful, too, is this behaviour ;
All to please you, I take a place in the country ;
I work like a horse there—more than at my years
I ought to do—to keep you here in idleness,
Spending my money ; 'twas the very least
You might have done, to keep a quiet house.

   Sos. 'Twas not my fault, indeed, indeed, dear Laches !

   La. I say it *was* your fault, and no one else's ;
You'd nought to do but make things pleasant here ;
I took all other burdens off your hands.
Shame ! an old woman like you to go and quarrel
With a poor girl !—You'll tell me now, 'twas her fault ?

   Sos. No, no ! dear Laches, I have never said so.

   La. Well, I am glad, for my son's sake, you've the grace
To confess that. You don't much harm yourself
By the confession ; in your precious character
A fault or two the more don't make much odds.

.   .   .   .

You mothers never rest until your sons
Get them a wife ; and then your whole delight
Is to make mischief between wife and husband.

Some of the scenes in this play are the most
dramatic of any which have come down to us from
the author's hands. The grief of the young husband
when, on his return from a voyage on business, he
finds that his wife has left his father's roof and gone
home to her own parents, and when she refuses him an

interview on the plea of illness ; when he believes
that there is some cause of quarrel which is concealed
from him between her and his mother, whom he dearly
loves ; and the struggle between his love for his wife,
and his sense of what is due to his own honour, when
he learns the real cause of her withdrawal, are all very
finely drawn.   So are the little passages in which poor
Sostrata, still believing that the cause of Philumena's
estrangement is some unaccountable dislike which she
has taken to herself, though conscious that she has
done her best to make her a happy home, proposes to
give up her pleasant town-house and retire into the
country, and so leave the young pair to themselves.
Laches himself is touched at last by her simple and
unselfish goodness ; and though the indications of this
are slight in the Roman play, compared with the fuller
and more gradual development which would be
thought necessary in a modern comedy, there is in the
short scene between them a simple pathos which, when
the characters were played by good actors, no doubt
touched the feelings of the audience as it was meant
to do.

La. Well, well ; we'll go into the country ; there
You'll have to bear with me, and I with you.
    Sos. (*throwing her arms round her husband and sobbing*).
        Husband, I hope we may !
La. (*disengaging himself awkwardly, and trying to hide
        his emotion*).   There, there !—go in ;
Get ready all you want—I've said the word.
    Sos. I'll do your bidding—aye, and gladly.
    Pamphilus (*who has entered unperceived*). Father !
    La.   Well, Pamphilus, what is it ?

Pam.   What means this ?
My mother leave her home ?   It must not be.
  La. Why not ?
  Pam.   Because I am not yet resolved
As to my wife.
  La.   You bring her back, of course.
  Pam. I wish it—it is hard to give her up ;
But I must do that which I feel is best.
She and my mother will be friends—apart.
  La. You can't tell that. Besides, what matters it ?
`Your mother will be gone. (*Turns away from his son,
    who tries to interrupt him.*) We're getting old—
We're only troublesome to younger folk ;
We'd best be moving on. (*Turning again to Pamphilus
    with a smile.*)   In short, my boy,
We're only "the old man and woman," now.

But everything is made right in the end.   Philumena goes back to her husband a wife without
reproach, and we are allowed to hope that Laches did
not wait for Sostrata's death to repent of his injustice
to her character.   The dramatist had not altogether lost
his pains, if he had done something to qualify the
vulgar notion of a "mother-in-law."   The play appears
to have met with no success when first brought out,
for it has come down to us with a "second prologue,"
written for what seems to have been its third representation, in which the author takes the opportunity
to remark on its previous failures.   He attributes these
in both cases to the more powerful attractions of the
rope-dancers and the gladiators.   On the second occasion the audience were so impatient for the appearance of these latter, that they would not even sit out
the comedy.

III.—THE SELF-TORMENTOR.

The comedy of 'The Self-Tormentor' is in great measure borrowed, as well as its Greek name of 'Heauton-timorumenos,' from a lost comedy of Menander, of which we have but some ten lines.   It has very much the same kind of *dramatis personæ* as the preceding play.   Two fathers and two sons,—a young lady for each, and a scheming slave, devoted to the interests of his young master—make up the leading characters. Chremes and Menedemus, the fathers, have for the last few months been neighbours in the country; engaged, as Roman gentlemen who preferred a country life commonly were, in farming; an occupation in which it must be confessed they were generally much more successful than the average English squire.   Chremes has noticed that since Menedemus bought his present farm, he has worked upon it himself from morning till night, as hard as though he were a slave instead of a master; in fact, that he does more work than any of his slaves, and that the time which he spends himself in manual labour might, so far as the interests of the farm are concerned, be much more profitably employed in looking after them.   He has no reason to suppose that his neighbour is poor; and he has a curiosity to learn the secret of this " self-tormenting."   He succeeds in doing so in the opening scene, though not without some difficulty.   Menedemus gruffly expresses his surprise that his neighbour should have so much leisure from his own affairs as to concern himself about those of others.

Chremes makes answer in those famous words, which can only be inadequately given in any English translation ; words at which, as St Augustine tells us, the whole audience, though many of them rude and ignorant, broke out into thunders of applause :—

> " I am a man ; nothing in human life
> Can fail to have its interest for me." *

Menedemus then tells him that he had once (he almost fears he can no longer say he has) an only son, who had fallen in love with a young Corinthian stranger of humble fortunes, who had come to Athens (the " Maid of Andros," in fact, under another title), and had wished to marry her. The father's pride had refused to consent ; almost any marriage with a foreigner was held, it must be remembered, to be a *mésalliance* for a citizen of Athens. He had spoken harshly to his son ; and the young man, not choosing to be so dealt with, had entered upon that field of adventure which was open in those times to all young men of spirit : he had taken service with a body of mercenaries, and gone to seek his fortunes in the East. Distracted at the consequences of his own severity, and the loss of a son whom he deeply loved, Menedemus had sold his house in Athens, and retired into the country, determined to punish himself for what he considers his unnatural harshness by a life of rigid asceticism. He will live no life of ease after driving his son into exile and poverty ; whatever he can save by self-denial shall

---

* " Homo sum ; humani nihil a me alienum puto."

be saved for him at his return—if ever that happy day should come.

It comes with the very next scene. Young Clinia has returned from the wars, and has just been received into the house of Chremes—introduced there by his son, Clitipho, who had been an intimate friend of the wanderer, though the father does not seem to have been aware of it. Clinia has begged his friend to send at once to his dear Antiphila, and,—if she has been as faithful to him in his absence as he hopes,—to entreat her to pay him a visit in his temporary domicile. And now the complication begins. Syrus,—the slave to whom young Clitipho intrusts his friend's errand, his confidant in all business, lawful or unlawful—determines to take the opportunity of doing his young master a special kindness. Clitipho has also, as Syrus is well aware, a love affair of his own upon his hands, with a very dashing and extravagant lady indeed, to gratify whose expensive tastes in the way of presents he has already taxed his father's good-nature to the uttermost. Syrus has hit upon the brilliant idea of introducing this lady into his master's household as a visitor, instead of the modest and quiet Antiphila, as the object of *Clinia's* affections ; that Clitipho may thus enjoy the pleasure of a few days in her society. Antiphila meanwhile is sent into the ladies' apartments—which were quite distinct from the other rooms in the house—there to be entertained by Sostrata, Chremes's wife. How Clinia is brought to consent to an arrangement which would give him very little opportunity for interviews with his dear Antiphila—or how husband and wife, in such a

modest establishment as this seems to have been, could
each have entertained a young lady guest for some
days (as seems to have been contemplated by Syrus)
without each other's knowledge, is not so clear as it might
be. But even on our modern stage we are continually
obliged, if we go to be amused, to swallow glaring
improbabilities ; and to expect to criticise the Athenian
or the Roman stage by the light of our modern ignorance, is an occupation, perhaps, more tempting than
profitable.

The hospitable Chremes is somewhat astonished at
the ways of the dashing lady to whom—all to oblige
his son's friend—he has given shelter. He meets
Menedemus the next morning, and warns him in a
friendly way that Clinia's wife that is to be seems an
extremely fast young person.

Chr. First, she's brought with her half a score of maids,
Tricked out, the jades, with gold and jewellery ;
Why, if her lover were an Eastern prince,
He couldn't stand it—how on earth can you ?
    Men. (*mildly*). Oh! is she here, too ?
    Chr.   Is she here, do you ask ?
(*Ironically*). Oh yes !—she's here. There's no doubt as
    to that.
I know it to my cost. They've had one dinner,
She and her party. If I give another
Such as last night, why—I'm a ruined man.
She's very curious, mind you, as to her wines ;
Knows the best brands,—and drinks them. "Ha !"
    she'd say,
"This wine's not dry enough, old gentleman—
"Get us some better, there's a dear old soul !"
I had to tap my oldest casks. My servants

Are driven almost wild. And this, remember,
Was but one evening. What's your son to do,
And you, my friend, that will have to keep her always ?
  Men. Let him do what he will : let him take all,
Spend, squander it upon her ; I'm content,
So I may keep my son.

Chremes sees that it is impossible to argue with the
remorseful father in these first moments of his son's
return. But it will be a very dangerous thing for
young Clinia to know that his father is thus offering
him *carte blanche* for all his own and his mistress's extravagances. He therefore begs his friend, instead of
openly supplying the money, to allow himself to be
made the victim of a kind of pious fraud. The amount
of expenditure for the present may not be of so much
importance, provided the son is not led to believe that
he has unlimited command of his father's purse.
Chremes will manage that the supplies required for
the lady's demands shall be drawn from Menedemus on some specious pretext. He has evidently a
great fancy for transacting other people's business ; for
though he has an arbitration case which he ought to
attend to-day, he will go and have it put off, that he
may have time to arrange this matter for his friend.
The happy father willingly consents, and is all impatience to be cheated.

    Syrus meanwhile is racking his wits to know how
he is to get money for his young master to lavish upon
the extravagant Bacchis. In this mood his elder
master meets him ; and knowing him to possess the
talent for intrigue and deception which is common to
his class, asks his help to impose some tale upon

Menedemus—whom he affects to abuse as "a covetous old wretch"—in order to make him a little more liberal to his unfortunate son, whom he has once already driven from home by his harshness. "That poor young man ought to have had some clever servant," says Chremes, "who would have managed the old gentleman for him." Syrus is astonished, as he may well be, at such a proposal from such a quarter; but it suits his own purpose exactly.

Syr. Oh! I can do it, sir, if you insist—
I have, methinks, some modest gifts that way.
   Chr. Egad! so much the better.
   Syr.   I'm not used
To so much lying—but——
   Chr.   Do it—you'll oblige me.
   Syr. But hark ye, sir, remember this, I pray you;
In case—I say in case—men are but men—
Your son should get in some such scrape hereafter.
   Chr. That case won't happen, I trust.
   Syr.   Nay, heavens forefend!
I trust so too. Don't think, because I mention it,
That I have any suspicion—not the slightest;
But still—he's young, you see—such things will happen;
And if they *should* (*bowing*), I shall know how to act,
By following your excellent instructions.
   Chr. (*laughing*). Well, well; we'll see to that, my
       worthy Syrus,
When the day comes; now go about this business.
                         [*Exit Chremes.*
   Syr. I vow I never heard my master talk
More to the purpose—never had I before
Free leave and licence given to be a rascal!

The behaviour of his young guests is somewhat

puzzling to Chremes, though he is quite unsuspicious as to the real state of affairs.   Clinia and the supposed object of his affections conduct their love-passages in the most calm and decorous fashion ; but young Clitipho, to the great annoyance of his father, who understands what is right and proper under such circumstances, insists upon thrusting his company upon them on all occasions.   He naturally grudges his friend all the *tête-à-têtes* with his own beloved Bacchis, which his good-natured father is so anxious to secure for them.   Clinia does not seem to mind these interruptions on the part of his friend ; but Chremes is indignant at his son's want of ordinary tact and good manners, especially as ·he has detected little acts of glaring flirtation between him and Bacchis, which seem to imply gross disloyalty to his friend.   He taxes him with this in an amusing scene, in the presence of Syrus, who is much alarmed lest his young master's want of self-command should lead to the detection of the imposture ; for he, too, has seen him very distinctly toying with Bacchis's hand.   Both of them beg him to go and leave the young couple to themselves.

Clitipho (helplessly). Where shall I go, sir ?
Syrus.   Go ? why, bless my life,
Go anywhere—only leave them—go for a walk.
Clit. Where shall I walk to ?
Syr.   Zounds ! why, anywhere—
There's plenty of walks—go this way—that way—any
    way.
Chremes. The man's quite right, sir,—go.
Clit. (moving off gloomily). Well, then—I'm going.
      (Shaking his fist at Syrus as he goes.)

Devil take you, rascal, for your interference !

Syr. (*aside to him*). You keep your hands to yourself,
  young man, hereafter. (*Watching him as he goes*
  off with apparent interest, and turning to Chremes.)
Indeed, sir, he's too bad. What will he come to ?
You had best give him very serious warning,
And keep him tight in hand.

Chr.   I will, I will.

Syr. Before it is too late.

Chr.   I will, I say.

Syr. I hope you will, sir. As for *my* advice,
(*Shrugging his shoulders.*) He minds it less and less, I
  grieve to say.

Chremes's wife has meanwhile made the discovery,
by the common test of a family ring, that the girl
Antiphila is a long-lost daughter whom she had sent
away immediately after her birth, in obedience to her
husband's threats that, in case one should be born
to him, he would never bring up such a troublesome
addition to his family. This, of course, makes everything clear for Clinia's marriage with her ; and that
young gentleman is accordingly made happy, by the
consent of all parties. But not before the busy Chremes
has been hoisted with his own petard, by Syrus's
contrivance. Acting very much upon the principle
recommended to him by his master himself, the cunning
rascal has extracted from him fifty pounds as an imaginary ransom for his own daughter Antiphila, whom
he declares to have been purchased in her infancy by
Bacchis : and the gold is actually sent to that lady by
the hands of his own son. There is some complication
in this part of the plot, fairly amusing as worked out

in detail in the original, but not worth analysis.   It
is very long before Chremes can be brought to believe
that it is his own son, and not Clinia, who is the real
lover of the dashing young lady whom he has been
entertaining out of complaisance, as he considered,
to his son's friend.   Menedemus, no longer a "self-
tormentor," is equally gratified to find that, after all,
he is to have such a modest and highly respectable
daughter-in-law, and amused at the collapse of his
scheming friend.

> MENEDEMUS (*solus, laughing to himself*).
>
> I don't profess myself to be a genius—
> I'm not so sharp as some folk—that I know :
> But this same Chremes—this my monitor,
> My would-be guide, philosopher, and friend,—
> He beats me hollow.   Blockhead, donkey, dolt,
> Fool, leaden-brains, and all those pretty names—
> They might suit *me ;* to him they don't apply :
> His monstrous folly wants a name to itself.

Poor Chremes grows very crestfallen in the closing
scenes, when he looks forward to the ruin which his
son's extravagant tastes, with the fair Bacchis's assistance, will bring upon him.   Menedemus retorts upon
him his own advice,—not to be too hard upon his
son—young men will be young men: but Chremes
fails to take the same philosophical view of his own
case as he had done of his friend's.   He vows at first
that he will disinherit his young prodigal, and settle
all his property upon his new-found daughter and her
husband ; but he is persuaded at last to alter this
determination.

Clitipho promises on his part to give up Bacchis altogether, and take to wife at once a neighbour's daughter, a most unobjectionable young lady—upon whom, with the facile affections of such young gentlemen, he seems to have had an eye already.

IV.—THE ETHIOPIAN SLAVE.

The comedy of 'The Ethiopian Slave,' which is partly taken, as the author tells us in his prologue, from Menander, introduces to us once more, under another name, our old friend Pyrgopolinices of Plautus. Captain Thraso, who has fought—or who says he has fought—under Seleucus in the East, and his toady Gnatho, are the most amusing characters in the play. The plot is more simple and well-defined than is usual in these comedies; and though it must be modified a little to suit either these pages or an English stage, it will not suffer much from such treatment. This Thraso,—a rich braggart, who takes Gnatho about with him everywhere to act as a kind of echo to his sentiments and to flatter his vanity,—is one of the suitors of a lady named Thais, who prefers a young gentleman named Phædria, though she does not care to discard altogether her rich lover. Poor Phædria is in despair, when the play opens, at having been refused admittance when he called on the lady the day before, because, as he understood, "the Captain" was with her. His slave Parmeno, who is much more of a philosopher than his master, gives him the very sensible advice to keep away altogether for a little while, when, if Thais really cares for him, she will soon call him back.   It is advice which he is not very willing to follow, until Thais herself entreats him to do something of the same kind.   She has particular reasons at this moment for not wishing to offend the Captain. He has just made her a very handsome present,—a slave-girl of exceeding beauty.   But this is not her value in her new owner's eyes.   Thais discovers that this poor girl, whom the Captain has bought in Caria, and brought home with him, was a child whom her mother had brought up, and who had been to herself as a younger sister.   The story was, however, that she had been originally stolen by pirates from the coast of Attica.   Upon her mother's recent death, the brother of Thais, intent only upon gain, had sold this girl— well-educated and very beautiful — once more into slavery ; and so she had come into the hands of Thraso. Thais—who, though a heartless flirt of the worst description, still has her good points—is anxious to rescue her old companion, and, if possible, to restore her to her friends, to whom she hopes she has already found some clue.   She fears that if her military lover believes her to prefer Phædria—as she assures that young gentleman she really does—he will break his promise, and not give her this girl.   Phædria, who has himself just sent her a present of a pair of Ethiopian slaves, consents, under many protests : he will not call again "for two whole days :" he will go into the country : but Parmeno tells him that he fully believes he "will walk back to town in his sleep."   The impassioned words in which the lover takes his unwilling leave, begging Thais not to forget him when in the company of his rival, have always been greatly admired, and often, consciously or unconsciously, imitated. Addison, in the 'Spectator,' calls them "inimitably beautiful : "—

> Be, in his presence, as though absent still ;
> Still love me day and night ; still long for me ;
> Dream of me, miss me, think of me alone ;
> Hope for me, dote on me, be wholly mine,
> My very heart and life, as I am thine.
>
> —Act i. sc. 2.

Gnatho is deputed by his magnificent friend to conduct the young slave girl to Thais's house. On the way he is met by Parmeno : and even that unimpressible old servitor is struck by the girl's wondrous beauty. The scene between the two officials of the rival powers is very good.

Gnatho (to himself as Parmeno comes up). I'll have a little sport, now, with this knave.
(*Aloud, making a low bow.*) My excellent Parmeno, is it you ?
Your most obedient.—*How* d'ye find yourself ?
Parmeno (coolly). I hadn't lost myself.
Gna.   You never do.*
Nothing unpleasant in this quarter—eh ?
          (*Pointing over his shoulder to Thais's house.*)
Par. There's you.
Gna.   *That* I can fancy. Nothing else ?

---

* This is not the literal joke in the original, but may serve to express it. Colman quotes an illustration of the same kind of humour from 'The Merry Wives of Windsor :'—

> "*Falstaff.* My honest lads, I'll tell you what I am *about.*
> *Pistol.* Two yards, or more."

Par. What makes you ask ?

Gna.   You look so glum.

Par. (*sulkily*).   Not I.

Gna. Don't—I can't bear to see it.   But this girl,
(*Whispering.*) The Captain's   present,—what d'ye think
   of her?

Par. (*affecting to eye her carelessly*).   Oh ! she's not bad.

Gna. (*aside*).   I've hit my friend on the raw.

Par. (*overhearing him*). Oh no, you haven't !

Gna.   But you must surely think
That Thais will be pleased with our new offering ?

Par. You've cut us out, you mean ? Well—wait a while;
Your turn to-day—it may be ours to-morrow.

Gna. For some six months, I promise you, Parmeno,
You shall have rest—no running to and fro
With notes and messages ; no sitting up
Till late at night to wait for your young master ;
Isn't that a comfort ?   Don't you feel obliged to me ?

Par. Oh, vastly !

Gna.   Well—I like to oblige my friends.

Par. Quite right.

Gna.   But I detain you—perhaps you've business ?

Par. Oh, not at all !

Gna.   Be so good then, if you please,
To introduce me here—you know the party.

Par. Oh ! such fine presents introduce themselves—
They're *your* credentials.

Gna. (*as the door opens*). Could I take a message ?
      [*Parmeno makes no reply, and Gnatho goes in with
         the slave-girl.*

Par. (*shaking his fist after him*).
Let me but see two days go by, my friend—
But two short days, I say—and this same door,
That opens now to your lightest finger-tap,
You may kick at all day, till you kick your legs off.
                                        —Act ii. sc. 2.

As he goes homewards, Parmeno meets the younger
son of his master's family,—Chærea, an officer in the
City Guard. He is in a great state of excitement,
raving to himself about some young beauty whom he
had seen in the street on his way from guard, and followed for some time, but has suddenly lost sight of.
The family servant is in despair, for he knows the temperament of the young soldier. Phædria, the elder
brother, is inflammable enough in such matters; but his
is mere milk-and-water passion compared with Chærea's.
It is love at first sight, in his case, with a vengeance.
He confides his whole story—a very short one—to Parmeno; reminds him of all the tricks they played
together when he was a boy; how he used to rob the
housekeeper's room to bring his friend in the servants'
hall good things for supper: and how Parmeno had
promised what he would do for him when he grew up to
be a man. Parmeno, with the usual inclination of his
class to oblige his young master in such matters, asks
him some questions about this interesting stranger: and
from Chærea's description of her companions—Gnatho,
and a maid-servant—and the fact of her having disappeared somewhere in this little by-street, he comes to
the conclusion that she can be no other than the beautiful slave-girl whom he has just seen pass into the house
of Thais. He begs Chærea to discontinue his pursuit:
the object is unworthy of him. But when the young
officer learns that Parmeno knows who she is, and
where she is to be found, he becomes still more eager
in his quest. At last Parmeno suggests a possible
mode of introduction—if Chærea likes to black his
face, and change clothes with the Ethiopian whom his

brother is going to send as a present to Thais, he, Parmeno, who has instructions to convey the pair to her house on this very day, will venture to introduce Chærea in this disguise.   He makes the proposal, as he declares, more in jest than earnest: but the young man, as may be supposed, catches at it eagerly, and insists upon it being carried at once into execution.

The next act of the play opens with a highly amusing scene between the Captain and his obsequious friend.   Thraso wishes to know how the lady has received his present.

Thraso. I say—was Thais very much obliged?
Gnatho. Immensely.
Thra.   She was really pleased, you think?
Gna. Not with the gift so much as that you gave it;
'Tis that she's proud of.
Thra.   I've a happy way—
I don't know how—but everything I do
Is well received.
Gna.   I've noticed it myself.
Thra. Yes.   Even the King himself, after an action,
Would always thank me in person.   'Twas a thing
He never did to others.
Gna.   Well, with gifts like yours,
A man gets double credit, while poor souls
Like us work hard, with nobody to thank us.
Thra. Egad, you have it!
Gra.   Ah! no doubt his Majesty
Had his eye on you, always.
Thra.   Well,—he had.
I may tell *you*—I was in all his secrets—
Had the whole army under me, in fact.
Gna. (*with deep interest*). No—really!

Thra. Yes. And then, when he was tired
Of seeing people, or grew sick of business,
And wanted to unbend him, as it were,—
You understand?

Gra. I know—something, you mean,
In what we call the free-and-easy line?

Thra. Just so—he'd ask me to a quiet dinner.

Gna. Indeed! his Majesty showed fine discernment.

Thra. That's just the man he is—one in a thousand—
There are few like him.

Gna. (aside). *Very* few, I fancy,
If he could stand *your* company.*

Thraso goes on to relate to his friend some of the
excellent jokes which he made during the time he enjoyed this intimacy with royalty; jokes at which the
parasite (who was paid for it in good dinners) laughs
more perhaps than the reader would. Here is a specimen.

Thraso. Did I ever tell you
How I touched up the Rhodian once at dinner?

Gna. Never! pray tell me—(*aside*) for the hundredth
time.

Thra. This youth was dining with us; as it chanced,

---

* A fragment preserved by Athenæus from a lost comedy
of Menander—'The Flatterer'—from which this play is partly
taken, has the following passage. [Bias is the original of
Thraso, and Strouthias is his "flatterer."]

    Bias. I have drunk off, in Cappadocia, Strouthias,
    A golden goblet that held full ten quarts—
    And three times filled.
    Strouthias. Why, sir, you must have drunk
    More than the great King Alexander could!
    Bias. Well—perhaps not less—by Pallas, no!
    Str. Prodigious!

There was a lady there, a friend of mine;
He made some joke about it; "What," said I—
"What, you young puppy, have you learnt to bark?"
 Gna. (*laughing*). Ha, ha,—ho, ho! O dear!
 Thra.   You seem amused.
 Gna. (*roaring still louder*). Oh! good indeed! delicious!
  excellent!
Nothing can beat it!—Tell me now, though, really—
Was that your own? I thought it had been older?
 Thra. (*somewhat disconcerted*). What?—had you heard
  it?
 Gna.   Often; why, it's reckoned
The best thing out.
 Thra. (*complacently*). It's mine.
          —Act iii. sc. 1.

The new Ethiopian slave, Phædria's gift, is introduced by Parmeno, and even Thraso, who is present, is obliged to confess that, black man as he is, he is a very good-looking young fellow. Parmeno assures them that his person is his least recommendation; let them test his accomplishments in literature, in music, in fencing—they will find them such as will make him a most valuable addition to a lady's retinue.* And Parmeno hopes that Thais will show a little kindness to his young master in return for his well-chosen present; which, however, in the Captain's presence, she will by no means profess herself inclined to do.

But this new servitor soon causes a terrible scandal in

---

* "*Viola.* I'll serve this duke;
Thou shalt present me as an eunuch to him:
It may be worth thy pains; for I can sing,
And speak to him in many sorts of music."
     —Twelfth Night, act i. sc. 2.

the household. Before morning it is discovered that the fair slave whom Thraso had so recently presented to Thais has eloped with the Ethiopian. The virtuous indignation of every waiting-gentlewoman in the establishment is roused by such an outrageous breach of all the proprieties, and they rush on the stage with voluble outcries—"Eloped! and with a black man!" A friend of Chærea's has been considerably astonished at meeting him hurrying along the street in a strange costume and with his face blacked; but the young man makes him his confidant, and obtains from him a change of clothes. Phædria,—who, as his slave Parmeno had foretold, has found it impossible to remain even two days in the country away from the object of his affections, and who has returned to the city and is lingering about Thais's door,—hears the story, and goes off to his own house to see if anything has been heard there of the fugitives. He finds the real Ethiopian hidden there in Chærea's clothes, and hauls him off, under a shower of blows, to be cross-examined by Thais and her domestics. But they all agree that this is not at all like *their* Ethiopian, who was a much better-looking fellow : and Phædria extracts at last from the terrified man that this is some trick, which promises to have serious consequences, of his madcap brother's.

The Captain meanwhile has quarrelled with Thais, believing that after all she prefers Phædria to himself; and not altogether satisfied with the private interviews which she has lately been holding with a young gentleman from the country—a somewhat rustic sort of personage, but whom Thais seems for some reason to treat

with very marked attention. As niggardly as he is
jealous, Thraso comes to demand back again from his
lady-love the expensive present he has made to her,—
this young slave, whom it is not agreeable or convenient,
for more reasons than one, for Thais to give up. She
flatly refuses ; and Thraso determines to take her from
the house by force. The " young man from the country,"
who is at this moment paying a visit to Thais, is really
the brother of this girl, who has been stolen in her infancy; and Thais now calls upon him to stand by her
in defence of his sister. He would much prefer to go
and fetch the police ; but there is little time for that,
for Thraso is seen approaching with a party of followers,
and Thais, who with all her faults has plenty of spirit,
barricades her door and defies him.

The scene must have been sufficiently effective,
especially if artistically arranged, upon so wide a stage,
when the gallant Captain leads his forces to the attack.

Enter THRASO, *with his sword drawn, at the head of a
motley retinue of hangers-on and household slaves.*

Thra. You, Donax, with the crow-bar, lead the centre ;
Simalio, you command on the left wing ;
Syriscus, you the right.   Bring up the reserve !
Where's our lieutenant, Sanga, and his rascals ?
They can steal anything—from a loaf to a woman.

Sanga. Here, Captain, here am I !

Thra.   Why, zounds ! you dolt,
Have you come out to battle with a dish-clout ?

San. Brave sir, I knew the mettle of my Captain—
I knew his gallant men ; this fight, quoth I,
May not be without blood—I'll stanch the wounds.

Thra. (*looking round doubtfully on his troops*).
Where are the rest of ye ?

San.   Rest ? we're all here—
We've only left the scullion to keep house.
    Thra. (to Gnatho). Form them in line ; my post is in
        the rear ;
Thence will I give command, and rule the fight.
    Gna. (half-aside to the others). Most admirable tactics !
        we to the front ;
He takes the rear-guard—to secure retreat.
    Thra. It was the plan great Pyrrhus always practised.
                                        —Act iv. sc. 7.

Thais soon discovers, as she says, that the champion
whom she has called in as her protector has more need of
a protector himself—for he is a fair match for Thraso in
cowardice.   However, he plucks up spirit enough to
threaten that gallant officer, from the safe vantage of
an upper window, with all the terrors of Athenian
law, if he ventures to lay a hand upon his sister Pamphila—a free-born woman of Athens, as he openly
asserts her to be ; and since Thraso, somewhat daunted
by this double peril, confines his hostile operations to
a battle of words, the lady and her party very naturally
get the best of it.   By the advice of Gnatho—who
has also more appetite for dinners than for fighting—
the Captain determines to await the surrender of his
enemy, which Gnatho assures him will follow next day,
and withdraws his army ;   reminding his lieutenant,
the cook, that for him, as for all good soldiers, as there
is a time to fight, so also

    " There is a time to think of hearth and home ;"

a sentiment which Sanga fully reciprocates—

    " My heart has been in the stew-pan long ago ;"

and which, appealing to their business and their bosoms, the whole body cheer vociferously as they move off.

There is not much worth notice in the comedy after this scene. If this girl Pamphila, whom Chærea has carried off, is really an Athenian citizen, as she is soon proved to be, there is no difficulty as to his marrying her, and he does so with his father's full consent. Indeed we are allowed to suppose that the quiet old gentleman, as well as the trusty Parmeno, must have been glad to see such a scapegrace respectably settled in any way. Phædria and the Captain are left rivals for the good graces of Thais as before, but Gnatho contrives to patch up the quarrel between them for the present; doing this good office, as he assures them, from the most unimpeachable motives—his own personal interest, inasmuch as he hopes to get many a dinner from both of them.

This is said to have been the most popular of all the author's productions; he received for it from the Ædiles (who had to provide the dramatic entertainments for the people) something like sixty pounds. Not a large sum, but more, it is said, than had been paid for any comedy before. It must be remembered that the ancient theatres were open only at festivals, for a few days at a time, and therefore no piece could have a long "run," as on the modern stage.*

---

* Upon this comedy were founded 'Le Muet' of Brueys, 'L'Eunuque' of Fontaine, and Sir Charles Sedley's 'Bellamira.' It has furnished Shakspeare with a quotation which he puts into the mouth of Tranio, in the 'Taming of the Shrew,' act i. sc. 1,— "Redime te captum quam queas minimo." Johnson, however, thinks that he went no farther for it than Lilly's Grammar.

V.—PHORMIO.

The play called 'Phormio' is taken also from a Greek original, not, however, by Menander, but by Apollodorus, a prolific writer of the same school. Here the principal character is the parasite—Phormio ; a fellow with an enormous appetite, consummate impudence, a keen eye to his own interest, and a not over-scrupulous conscience, but by no means a bad heart. He and the slave Geta have between them all the brains which carry on the plot ; for these gilded youth of Athens, who are the lovers in these comedies, are not, it will be observed, more largely furnished in this particular than their modern successors, and the fathers are commonly the easy prey of the adroit and unscrupulous slave who—from pure love of mischief, it would seem, and often at the risk of his skin—assists the young heir in his attack upon the paternal purse. The respectable victims in this play are two brothers—Chremes and Demipho—who have both gone abroad on business, and left their sons under the guardianship of Geta, the confidential slave of the younger brother. Their confidence is not very well repaid. The youths give the old man so much trouble, that he soon grows tired of asserting an authority which in his position he has no means of enforcing ; in fact, as he complains in the opening scene, his wards lay the whip about his back whenever he interferes. He finds it more to his interest to humour them in everything to the top of their bent. And it has come to this ; that Phædria, the son of Chremes, has taken a fancy to a little music-girl whom he insists on ransoming from her rascally master, who of course raises his price to an exorbitant figure as soon as he finds out the young gentleman's infatuation. Antipho, his cousin, had for a long time given promise of great steadiness : but these still waters run deep, and he plunges all at once into a romantic passion for a beautiful Cinderella, whom he discovers with bare feet and in a shabby dress, mourning over a dead mother who has left her a portionless orphan. And, finding that she is of free birth, he actually marries her. His acquaintance Phormio — whose friendship is at any young man's service who can give a good dinner—has suggested to him a plan by which he may in some degree escape his father's anger at this very imprudent match. There is a law at Athens which, like the old Levitical law, obliges the next of kin who is available to marry an orphan of the family. Phormio undertakes to appear before the proper court on behalf of the girl, and to bring evidence that Antipho is her nearest unmarried male relative : and, since the young lover of course makes no attempt to disprove it, the court gives judgment that he is to make her his wife, which he does forthwith.

All this has taken place before the action of the piece begins. And now a letter has arrived from Demipho to say that he is coming home, and both the son and Geta are in great alarm as to how he will take the news which awaits him. Antipho, like others who have married in haste, is beginning to feel something very like repentance at leisure ; he feels, he says, in the position of the man in the proverb who has "got a wolf by the ears—he can neither hold her nor let

her go." Geta is conscious that he has no very satisfactory account to render of his stewardship, and has
prophetic visions of the stocks and the mill-prison.
The son has made up his mind, by Geta's advice, to
meet his father with something very much like bluster;
but the moment the old gentleman makes his actual
appearance, his courage evaporates, and he makes off,
leaving his cousin Phædria, with Geta's assistance, to
make such apologies on his behalf as they can.

The father's indignation, though it does not spare
either Geta or Antipho, is chiefly directed against the
parasite Phormio,—this disreputable Mentor of youth,
who has trumped up such an imposture. But Phormio
is equal to the occasion; indeed, his nature is rather
to rejoice in these kind of encounters with his angry
dupes, in which he feels confident his natural audacity
and shrewdness will carry him through. "It is a
tough morsel," he says—drawing his metaphor from
his familiar sphere of the dinner-table—"but I'll
make a shift to bolt it." Geta, who regards him with
a kind of respectful envy, as a knave of higher mark
than himself, wonders how, considering all the more
than doubtful transactions he has been engaged in, he
has hitherto escaped the meshes of the law.

Phormio. Because, my friend, no fowler spreads his net
For hawk or kite, or such-like birds of prey;
'Tis for the innocent flock, who do no harm;
They are fat morsels, full of juice and flavour,
Well worth the catching. Men who've aught to lose,
Such are in danger from the law; for me—
They know I've nothing. "Nay, but then," you'll say,
"They'll clap you up in jail." Oh! will they? Ah!

(*Laughing and patting himself.*) They'd have to keep me
      —and they know my appetite.*
No—they're too wise, and not so self-denying,
As to return me so much good for evil.

The father has taken the precaution to provide himself with no less than three lawyers to back him in his
interview with Phormio.   It must be remembered that
all interviews, even of the most private character,
according to the conventionalities of the classic stage,
take place in the public street.   Should this seem to
shock our notions of the fitness of things, we have only
to remember the absurd anomalies of our own attempts
at realistic scenery,—where the romantic forest which
forms the " set " at the back has a boarded floor and a
row of footlights in the front.   Phormio and Geta see
their adversaries coming round the corner of the street,
and at once engage in a spirited controversy between
themselves, purposely intended for the other party to
overhear.   Phormio professes to be shocked at the want
of common honesty on the part of his friend's father.
What! will he really repudiate the connection? disown
his excellent relative Stilpho (which is the name of the
pretty Phanium's father), merely because he died poor?
Well! what will not avarice lead to !   Geta, like a
faithful servant, defends the character of his absent
master: and the pair appear to be coming to actual
blows on the question, when Demipho steps forward
and interrupts them.   Phormio meets the old gentle-

----

* The creditor, both at Athens and at Rome, though he had
the right to imprison a debtor who failed to pay, was bound to
maintain him while in confinement.

man's remonstrances with perfect coolness. It is no use to tell *him*, that a man does not remember his first cousin; Demipho has evidently a convenient memory. If poor old Stilpho had left a large fortune behind him, he would have routed out the whole family pedigree. If he is not satisfied with the award of the court, he can appeal, and have the cause tried over again. But law, he must remember, is an expensive luxury; his own advice would be, that Demipho should try to make himself comfortable with his new daughter-in-law—who is really a very nice young person. If he turns her out of his house, he, Phormio, as her father's friend, will feel it to be his duty to bring an action against him. And so he wishes him a very good-morning.

When Demipho turns to his legal friends for advice, he scarcely finds wisdom in the multitude of counsellors. For these counsellors by no means agree. The first delivers it as his opinion that what the son did in such a matter, in the absence of the head of the family, is void in law. The second holds that the judgment of the court cannot now be overruled, and that it would not be for Demipho's credit to attempt it. The third, the oldest, and as cautious as the most doubting of English Lord Chancellors, wishes to take time to consider. So the client dismisses them, each with their fee, declaring that their valuable advice has left him more bewildered than ever.*

* This scene, with the three lawyers seems to have given Molière the hint for several scenes in which he has introduced legal consultations,—*e. g.*, in 'Le Mariage Forcé,' sc. ix., where he makes Sganarelle say, "L'on est aussi savant à la

Young Phædria adds to Geta's troubles by coming to beg him to extract from his uncle Demipho, by some contrivance or other, the sum needful for the purchase of his dear music-girl from her master—only a poor hundred guineas. "She's a very dear bargain," remarks the old servitor. Phædria insists, of course, that she is cheap at any price; and Geta promises to do his best to get the money.

The return of Phædria's father—Chremes, the elder of the two brothers — from the island of Lemnos, threatens to complicate matters : but it turns out that he brings with him the key to at least the great difficulty. He has been to the island on some private business, the nature of which is known to his brother Demipho, but which is kept a strict secret from his wife Nausistrata, of whom he stands in considerable awe. The secret is partly disclosed in the scene between the two brothers on his return. Chremes had contracted, in his younger and more imprudent days, while visiting Lemnos, a private marriage (under another name) with a person in that island, the issue of which was a daughter. He had broken off this connection for some years ; but the object of this last voyage had been to make some inquiries about this duplicate family. He has formed a plan, with his brother's approval, to marry this unacknowledged daughter, now grown up to womanhood, to her cousin Antipho ; and is therefore as anxious as his brother to get this present unfortunate marriage, which they both look upon as contracted under false pretences,

fin qu'au commencement;" and in 'M. de Pourceaugnac, act ii. sc. 13, where the "Deux Avocats" chant their opinions.

annulled if possible. So when Phormio comes and
offers to take the young lady off everybody's hands
and marry her himself, if Demipho will give her a
dowry of a hundred guineas, Chremes persuades his
brother to close with the offer, and even advances
great part of the sum : which Phormio hands over
to his young friend Phædria for the ransom of his
mistress.

Chremes has learned that, while he was on his voyage
to Lemnos, his deserted wife has meanwhile come over
to Athens in search of him, and brought the daughter
with her. He is soon further enlightened upon this
subject. As he is crossing the street from his own
house to his brother's, he sees a woman coming from it.
It is Sophrona, the old nurse of this foreign girl whom
his nephew has married, and who is now stowed away
somewhere in her unwilling father-in-law's house. The
nurse has been there to try to discover what turn
affairs are likely to take, now that the old gentleman
has come home.

    Chremes (*looking at her stealthily*). Eh ! bless me !
      Yes—or do my eyes deceive me ?
Yes—this is certainly my daughter's nurse !
    Sophrona (*to herself, not seeing Chremes*). And then,
      to think the father can't be found !
    Chr. What shall I do ? Shall I speak first, or wait
Till I hear more ?
    Soph.   Oh ! if we could but find him,
All might go well !
    Chr. (*coming forward*). 'Tis she, no doubt ; I'll
      speak.
    Soph. (*hearing his voice*). Who's that ? I heard a voice
      there !

Chr.   Sophrona !

Soph. He knows my name !

Chr.   ·   Look at me, Sophrona.

Soph. (looking close at him). Oh ! gracious heavens !
     What ! are you Stilpho ?

Chr. (making signs to her to be silent). No.

Soph. Can you deny it ?

Chr.   Hush-sh ! come further off !—
A little further from the door, good Sophrona—
And never call me by that name again !

Soph. Why, by that name we always knew you!

Chr. (pointing to the door opposite).   —Sh !

Soph. What makes you afraid of that door ?

Chr. (coming near her, in a half-whisper). Why, because
It's got my wife inside—an awful woman !
That's why I took another name, you see.
For fear lest you might blab my real one,
And she *(pointing to the door)* should hear it.

Soph.   'Twas no wonder, then,
We could hear nothing of you here in Athens.

                               —Act v. sc. 1.

He learns from the old nurse that his Lemnian wife
is dead, and that his daughter is just married to his
nephew Antipho. In the bewilderment of the moment
he fails to identify the fair subject of the lawsuit with
his own daughter : and perhaps only those who have
seen this play acted by Westminster scholars can
appreciate the comic earnestness with which the uncle,
with his own double relations strong in his mind, and
fancying that his young nephew is in the same predica-
ment, asks of Sophrona—

     " What—has *he* two wives ? "

When he finds out that the two wives are one and the

same, and that his Lemnian daughter is really married, by a happy accident, to the very husband he had designed for her, he blesses the gods for his good fortune, and it is plain that all Antipho's difficulties are over.

But Chremes, unluckily, joins his brother in an attempt to recover from Phormio the gold pieces which he has got from them under pretence of dowry. They don't want him to marry Phanium now, of course; and they see no reason for his not returning the money. But Phormio, with his usual cleverness, has made himself master of the whole story. He declares *his* willingness to complete at once *his* part of the bargain, and protests, with considerable show of justice, that he will not be cheated out of wife and dowry too. He threatens Chremes that unless he holds his tongue about the money, he will tell his wife Nausistrata all about that little establishment at Lemnos. This impudence is more than Demipho can stand, and he calls his slaves to carry off the parasite to jail. The noise he makes brings in Nausistrata, and though both the brothers try to stop his mouth, he carries his threat into execution. Nausistrata, of course, is in a considerable fury at first : but as her rival is dead, and this unnecessary daughter safely disposed of, she is satisfied with the rod which Phormio has put into her hands to be wielded over her husband in any future connubial disagreement ; and, partly out of gratitude for this acquisition of power, and partly to annoy her husband, invites him at once to supper. The parasite foresees that there will always be a knife and fork ready for him at her table as well as at Phanium's.

VI.—THE BROTHERS.

This comedy, like 'Phormio,' has always been a favourite with the Westminster actors. It is taken partly from a play of Menander, and partly from one by another Greek dramatist, Diphilus. It was acted lately at Westminster with great success, and it may be permissible to borrow, as a familiar rendering of the early portion of the story, a few verses from the clever sketch of the "Plot" which was handed round on that occasion for the enlightenment of the less classical among the audience :—

" Two brothers once in Athens dwelt of old,
    Though widely did their dispositions differ ;
One loved the country, was a churl and scold,
    The other bland and gentle as a zephyr.

Demea, the churl, had once a wife, since dead,
    And, as it seems, he did not much regret her ;
Micio, the bland, had not been so *miss*-led,
    And never took a wife, for worse or better.

Now Demea had two sons ; but he did predicate
    That one was quite enough ; and gave the other—
The elder of the two—to rear and educate,
    In short, to be adopted, by his brother.

The youngest, Ctesipho, at home was taught,
    Was duly lectured, disciplined, and scolded ;
Rose early—read—walked—and, as Demea thought,
    Into a rural innocent was moulded.

But Micio loved the city, and, forsooth !
  Ne'er thought of looking after his adopted ;
But if he told the truth, and all the truth,
  Whatever prank was played, he never stopped it."

Demea has protested from time to time against his
brother's very lax system of discipline ; and when he
finds that young Æschinus's not very steady course has
just culminated in a tremendous and notorious row—
that he has broken open the house of a slave-dealer,
beaten the master, and carried off a young woman—
he lectures his brother severely on the results of his
ill-judged indulgence.

But Ctesipho, who has been kept in stricter leading-
strings by the father, is not quite the pattern youth
that the old gentleman thinks him. He is really
the person most concerned in the brawl which caused
so much scandal ; for the girl who has been thus
forcibly carried off from her owner is a young music-girl
with whom he has fallen in love—who claims, however,
as usual, to be free-born and entitled to all the rights
of citizenship. Æschinus, not standing so much in
fear of his good-natured guardian as the other does of
his father, and having, besides, no great reputation to
lose, is content to take upon himself all the blame
of the late burglary and abduction ; though Ctesipho
has been really the principal in the affair, in which
his brother has only aided and abetted out of pure
fraternal affection. There is the usual intriguing
slave, Syrus, who is of course in the secret ; and who
persuades the father that Ctesipho is gone down
to the country grange, whither Demea follows him,
quite persuaded that he shall find his exemplary son

deep in farming operations. He is, in fact, at this moment taking care of his prize in Æschinus's apartments
in his uncle's house, whither she has been conducted.

Syrus, delighted to have such an opportunity of
exercising his wit upon Demea, whose principles of
education he altogether dislikes, compliments him
highly upon his son Ctesipho's irreproachable conduct.
He declares that the good youth has been quite shocked
at his elder brother's iniquity, and has reproached him
with the discredit he was bringing on the family.

Syrus. Æschinus, quoth he, I am ashamed of you—
You waste not money only, but your life.
 Demea. Heaven bless him ! he'll be worthy of his fore-
   fathers.
 Syr. I'm sure he will.
 Dem.   Syrus, he's had good teaching.
 Syr. Ah ! he had those at home who understood it.
 Dem. I *do* take pains ; I omit no single item :
I train him well ; in fact, I bid him study,
As in a mirror, all the characters
He sees around him, and draw from them lessons
For his own guidance : copy this, I say—
 Syr. Ah ! capital !
 Dem.   This, again, avoid—
 Syr.   Just so.
 Dem. This act, I say, is praiseworthy—
 Syr.   Quite right.
 Dem. That was a fault—
 Syr.   I see.
 Dem.   And then, besides—
 Syr. I beg your pardon—I could listen all day—
But I'm so busy : there's some splendid fish—
I must not let them spoil : for this, you see,
In my vocation, sir, would be a sin,

Just as, with gentlefolks, neglect of morals :
Indeed, in my poor sphere, I train my knaves
Exactly on your worship's principle. Look here,
I say, that dish 's too salt ; this roast is burned—
That's not washed clean ; that fricassee is good—
Just the right thing—be sure the next is like it.
The best advice that my poor wit affords
I strive to give (*looking gravely at Demea, and copying
     his manner*). In short, I bid them study
As in a mirror, every dish I make,
Thus to draw lessons for their own instruction.
'Tis but a humble school, I feel, I train them in ;
But we must do our best—man can't do more.—
(*Bowing demurely*). Can I oblige you, sir, in any way ?
  Dem. (*angrily*). Yes—mend your manners.*
                      —Act iii. sc. 3.

The elder of the young men has in truth perplexities
enough of his own to have justified him, if he had been
less good-natured, in declining to involve himself in
those of his brother. He has an unacknowledged wife,
and just at this time the not very welcome addition
of a baby. The news of his having been engaged in
this brawl, and having carried off the singing-girl to
his uncle's house, soon reaches the ears of Sostrata,
his very respectable mother-in-law : who comes to the
natural conclusion that Æschinus is faithless to his
poor wife at this interesting crisis, and intends to repudiate her altogether, instead of presenting her to
his uncle, as he had promised, and obtaining his sanction to their public union. By the advice of Geta, an
old and trusty servant, who has remained with them
in their reduced fortunes (for there are faithful slaves,

---

* Horace had probably this dialogue in his mind, Sat. I. iv. 103.

in these comedies, as well as the more common type of dishonest ones), they lay the case before an old friend of the family, the excellent Hegio, who undertakes to represent to Micio the great wrong which is being done by his ward to his unfortunate young relative. On his way to Micio's house he falls in with Demea, who is an old acquaintance, and informs him of this new enormity on the part of young Æschinus, at which the father can only lift up his hands and eyes, and lament over this still more convincing proof of the sad results of such a training as the youth has had from his uncle.

But on his way to his country-house he meets a workman who tells him that his own dear Ctesipho has not been seen there since he left. So he goes back to make inquiry about him at his brother's,—inquiry which, under present circumstances, is somewhat awkward to meet. Yes,—he has been there, Syrus tells him, and points to his own bandaged head as evidence. The good youth was so indignant at his brother's conduct that he took him to task roundly, and ended by beating the music-wench, and breaking poor Syrus's head. "He ought to be ashamed of himself," says the latter whimpering,—"a poor old man like me, that nursed him!"—"Not at all," replies the unsympathetic Demea; "'tis you ought to be ashamed of yourself— you nursed his brother in wickedness!" He next inquires of the slave where his brother Micio is; for he wants to expostulate with him about this unfortunate business. He is not at home, Syrus assures him; but he will give him full directions where to find him. He must go through the portico behind the shambles, down the next street, then to the right, then up the next, then to the left, past the chapel, through the narrow lane where the wild fig-tree stands, straight on to Diana's temple, then to the right; then he will see a mill, with a joiner's shop opposite, where his brother is gone to order an oak table: and with these very particular directions, which will give the old gentleman a good long afternoon's walk through the suburbs, he gets rid of him for the present. The two young men are in the house all the time, having a little dinner in celebration of the successful rescue of Ctesipho's fair friend; and Syrus, having got rid, for some hours at least, of this inconvenient visitor, will take the opportunity of this festive occasion to get royally drunk.

Æschinus soon learns the misconstruction which has been put upon his conduct; for when he next goes to his lodgings to visit his young wife, he is refused admittance. Neither she nor her mother will have anything more to do with such a villain. But in the crisis of his distress he is encountered by his good-natured guardian, to whom Hegio has told the whole story, and who has gone at once to see for himself what kind of people these new connections are: and he—after playing for a little while with the young man's anxiety—throws him at last into ecstasies of joy and gratitude by magnanimously promising to recognise his wife, and desiring him to bring her home to his house as soon as he thinks proper.

Demea returns from his long walk in search of his brother, very hot and very angry. He has not been able to find the "joiner's shop," and half suspects that Syrus has been fooling him: for he meets Micio just coming out of his own house. He attacks him with the story of this new escapade of his precious ward Æschinus; but his brother listens with a composure which is exceedingly irritating.

Demea. He's got a wife!

Micio.   Well—better he than I,

Dem. She's got a baby!

Mic.   Doing well, I hope?

Dem. The jade's an absolute beggar!

Mic.   So I hear.

Dem. You mean you'll take her in without a sixpence?

Mic. I do.

Dem.   What's to become of them?

Mic.   Of course
They must come here.

Dem. (ironically).   Why, you seem quite delighted!

Mic. No—not if I could alter it.   Look ye, brother,
Man's life is as it were a game of tables;
If that the throw we want will not turn up,
Skill must correct such luck as fortune gives us.

                              —Act iv. sc. 7.

It is the better side of the Epicurean philosophy, put into few and terse words; and we shall probably not be wrong in assuming the lines to be pretty closely translated from Menander, who may not improbably have had the idea from Epicurus himself.

Another precious example of his brother's domestic discipline meets Demea as he comes away from this unsatisfactory interview. It is Syrus, so drunk as to have lost even the semblance of respectful demeanour.

Syr. (staggering up against Demea). Oho! you're back again, are you, Mr Wisdom?

Dem. (pushing him away). If you were *my* slave,
sirrah—

Syr.   You'd be lucky—
You'd have a (*hiccup*) treasure—save you half your income.

Dem. (shaking his stick at him). I'd make an example
of ye !

(*Enter Dromo, another slave, running from the house.*)

Dro.   Hallo—Syrus !
Ctesipho wants ye !

Syr. (aside to him). Hush-sh ! away, you fool !

Dem. Ctesipho !—here ?

Syr.   N-no, n-no, sir !—it's not him,
It's—it's—another young man—a little parasite—
Of the same name.—You know him, don't you, sir ?

Dem. I very soon will, at any rate (*making for the
house*).

Syr. (trying to hold him back). Stop, sir, stop !

But the father has heard enough to open his eyes.
He rushes in, spite of Syrus's drunken efforts to stop
him, and makes at last full discovery of how he has
been deceived. Micio succeeds in soothing him in
some degree, by assuring him that his own fortune is
ample enough to supply both the young men's wants ;
that he will give a dowry also to Ctesipho with his
beloved, and see him married respectably.

The failure of his own system, and the placid
triumph of his easy brother, work an odd transforma-
tion in Demea's behaviour. He meets this "irony of
events" by a curious irony of his own. Since easy
temper is the mode, he will at once adopt it. He
begins by shaking hands with Syrus, and thanking
him for his admirable conduct—he will certainly do
something for him. Then he meets Geta, and shakes

hands with him (who certainly deserves it better); he will do something for him too. He persuades his brother to give Syrus his freedom, with a sum of money to set him up in life, "by way of encouragement to honest servants," as he ironically puts it. He will have him make a deed of gift of a snug farm to Hegio, who has acted the part of a good relation so manfully; and he ends by persuading the old bachelor himself to marry the excellent Sostrata, his ward's mother-in-law—a lone woman, much in want of a protector. The good-natured Micio does make some wry faces at this last item in the arrangements, but his brother's arguments as to the great duty of pleasing everybody are too strong for him. If complaisance with other people's fancies, and reckless liberality, are the right thing, Demea is determined to give his brother full opportunity to put in practice this new-fangled virtue.

In obedience to an ordinance contained in the Charter of Queen Elizabeth, the Westminster Scholars present every year, on three nights just before Christmas, a Latin play. The performance, which takes place in the Dormitory of the College, with appropriate scenery and costume, is perfectly unique of its kind, and is the only relic of an ancient custom once common to all our great schools. Although, as has already been noticed, a comedy of Plautus has occasionally been selected, Terence has always been the favourite. Four of his comedies—'The Maid of Andros,' 'The Ethiopian Slave,' 'Phormio,' and 'The Brothers'—

are usually taken in rotation ; and a Queen's Scholar who shows any dramatic talent is not unfrequently an actor in two or three of these plays successively. The performance is preceded by a Latin prologue, in which such events of the year as have affected the school are briefly touched upon : and followed by an epilogue in elegiac verse, which of late years has assumed almost the dimensions of a farce, in which the current topics or follies of the day are satirised under an amusing disguise of classical names and associations.

END OF PLAUTUS AND TERENCE.

PRINTED BY WILLIAM BLACKWOOD AND SONS, EDINBURGH.

EDUCATIONAL WORKS

PUBLISHED BY

WILLIAM BLACKWOOD & SONS,

EDINBURGH AND LONDON.

———◆———

English Language.

AN ETYMOLOGICAL AND PRONOUNCING DICTIONARY OF THE ENGLISH LANGUAGE. Including a very copious selection of Scientific, Technical, and other Terms and Phrases. Designed for use in Schools and Colleges, and as a Handy Book for General Reference. By the Rev. JAMES STORMONTH, and the Rev. P. H. PHELP, M.A. Crown 8vo, pp. 760, 7s. 6d.

THE SCHOOL ETYMOLOGICAL DICTIONARY AND WORD-BOOK. Combining the advantages of an ordinary Pronouncing School Dictionary and an Etymological Spelling-Book. By the Rev. JAMES STORMONTH. Fcap. 8vo, pp. 254, 2s.

THE HANDY SCHOOL DICTIONARY, PRONOUNCING AND EXPLANATORY. Also containing Lists of Prefixes and Postfixes; Rules for Spelling correctly; Words same in Sound but different in Spelling and Meaning; Common Abbreviations; and Common Quotations from the Latin, French, &c. For Use in Elementary Schools. By the Rev. JAMES STORMONTH. 16mo, pp. 268. 9d.

A MANUAL OF ENGLISH PROSE LITERATURE, Biographical and Critical: designed mainly to show characteristics of style. By W. MINTO, M.A. Crown 8vo, 10s. 6d.

"Is a work which all who desire to make a close study of style in English prose will do well to use attentively."—*Standard.*

"Here we do not find the *crambe repetita* of old critical formulæ, the simple echoes of superannuated rhetorical dicta, but a close and careful analysis of the main attributes of style, as developed in the work of its greatest masters, stated with remarkable clearness of expression, and arranged upon a plan of most exact method. Nothing can be well conceived more consummate as a matter of skill than the analytical processes of the writer as he lays bare to our view the whole anatomy—even every joint and sinew and artery in the framework —of the sentence he dissects, and as he points out their reciprocal relations, their minute interdependencies."—*School Board Chronicle.*

"An admirable book, well selected and well put together."—*Westminster Review.*

CHARACTERISTICS OF ENGLISH POETS, FROM CHAUCER TO SHIRLEY. By WM. MINTO, M.A., Author of 'A Manual of English Prose Literature.' One vol. crown 8vo. 9s.

PROGRESSIVE AND CLASSIFIED SPELLING-BOOK. By HANNAH R. LOCKWOOD, Authoress of 'Little Mary's Mythology.' Fcap. 8vo, 1s. 6d.

ENGLISH PROSE COMPOSITION: A PRACTICAL
MANUAL FOR USE IN SCHOOLS. By JAMES CURRIE, M.A.,
Principal of the Church of Scotland Training College, Edinburgh.
Tenth Edition, 1s. 6d.

" We do not remember having seen a work so completely to our mind as this,
which combines sound theory with judicious practice. Proceeding step by step,
t advances from the formation of the shortest sentences to the composition of
complete essays, the pupil being everywhere furnished with all needful assistance in the way of models and hints. Nobody can ▮▮▮ through such a book
as this without thoroughly understanding the stru▮▮▮re of sentences, and
acquiring facility in arranging and expressing his thoughts appropriately. It
ought to be extensively used."—Athenæum.

Geography.

NEW AND GREATLY IMPROVED EDITION.

A MANUAL OF MODERN GEOGRAPHY, MATHE-
MATICAL, PHYSICAL, AND POLITICAL. By the Rev. ALEXANDER
MACKAY, LL.D., F.R.G.S. Crown 8vo, pp. 676. 7s. 6d.

This volume—the result of many years' unremitting application—is
specially adapted for the use of Teachers, Advanced Classes, Candidates for the Civil Service, and proficients in geography generally.

THIRTIETH THOUSAND.

ELEMENTS OF MODERN GEOGRAPHY. By
the Same. Thirteenth Edition, revised to the present time. Crown
8vo, pp. 300. 3s.

The 'Elements' form a careful condensation of the 'Manual,' the
order of arrangement being the same, the river-systems of the globe
playing the same conspicuous part, the pronunciation being given, and
the results of the latest census being uniformly exhibited. This volume
is now extensively introduced into many of the best schools in the
kingdom.

This day is Published,

THE INTERMEDIATE GEOGRAPHY. Intended
as an Intermediate Book between the Author's 'Outlines of
Geography' and 'Elements of Geography.' By the Same.
Crown 8vo, pp. 208, price 2s.

SIXTY-NINTH THOUSAND.

OUTLINES OF MODERN GEOGRAPHY: SIX-
TEENTH EDITION, REVISED TO THE PRESENT TIME. By the Same.
18mo, pp. 112. 1s.

These 'Outlines'—in many respects an epitome of the 'Elements'—
are carefully prepared to meet the wants of beginners. The arrangement is the same as in the Author's larger works. Minute details are
avoided, the broad outlines are graphically presented, the accentua-
tion marked, and the most recent changes in political geography exhibited.

FORTY-EIGHTH THOUSAND, REVISED TO THE PRESENT TIME.

FIRST STEPS IN GEOGRAPHY. By the Same.
18mo, pp. 56. Sewed, 4d. In cloth, 6d.

GEOGRAPHY OF THE BRITISH EMPIRE.
From 'First Steps in Geography.' By the Same. 3d.

Geographical Class-Books.

OPINIONS OF DR MACKAY'S SERIES.

MANUAL.

Annual Address of the President of the Royal Geographical Society (Sir Roderick I. Murchison).—We must admire the ability and persevering research with which he has succeeded in imparting to his 'Manual' so much freshness and originality. In no respect is this character more apparent than in the plan of arrangement, by which the author commences his description of the physical geography of each tract by a sketch of its true basis or geological structure. The work is largely sold in Scotland, but has not been sufficiently spoken of in England. It is, indeed, a most useful school-book in opening out geographical knowledge.

Saturday Review.—It contains a prodigious array of geographical facts, and will be found useful for reference.

English Journal of Education.—Of all the Manuals on Geography that have come under our notice, we place the one whose title is given above in the first rank. For fulness of information, for knowledge of method in arrangement, for the manner in which the details are handled, we know of no work that can, in these respects, compete with Mr Mackay's Manual.

ELEMENTS.

A. KEITH JOHNSTON, LL.D., F.R.S.E., F.R.G.S., H.M. Geographer for Scotland, Author of the 'Physical Atlas,' &c. &c.—There is no work of the kind in this or any other language, known to me, which comes so near my *ideal* of perfection in a school-book, on the important subject of which it treats. In arrangement, style, selection of matter, clearness, and thorough accuracy of statement, it is without a rival; and knowing, as I do, the vast amount of labour and research you bestowed on its production, I trust it will be so appreciated as to insure, by an extensive sale, a well-merited reward.

G. BICKERTON, Esq., Edinburgh Institution.—I have been led to form a very high opinion of Mackay's 'Manual of Geography' and 'Elements of Geography,' partly from a careful examination of them, and partly from my experience of the latter as a text-book in the EDINBURGH INSTITUTION. One of their most valuable features is the elaborate Table of River-Basins and Towns, which is given in addition to the ordinary Province or County list, so that a good idea may be obtained by the pupil of the natural as well as the political relationship of the towns in each country. On all matters connected with Physical Geography, Ethnography, Government, &c., the information is full, accurate, and well digested. They are books that can be strongly recommended to the student of geography.

RICHARD D. GRAHAM, English Master, College for Daughters of Ministers of the Church of Scotland and of Professors in the Scottish Universities.—No work with which I am acquainted so amply fulfils the conditions of a perfect text-book on the important subject of which it treats, as Dr Mackay's 'Elements of Modern Geography.' In fulness and accuracy of details, in the scientific grouping of facts, combined with clearness and simplicity of statement, it stands alone, and leaves almost nothing to be desired in the way of improvement. Eminently fitted, by reason of this exceptional variety and thoroughness, to meet all the requirements of higher education, it is never without a living interest, which adapts it to the intelligence of ordinary pupils. It is not the least of its merits that its information is abreast of all the latest developments in geographical science, accurately exhibiting both the recent political and territorial changes in Europe, and the many important results of modern travel and research.

Spectator.—The best Geography we have ever met with.

Geology.

" Few of our handbooks of popular science can be said to have greater or more decisive merit than those of Mr Page on Geology and Palæontology. They are clear and vigorous in style, they never oppress the reader with a pedantic display of learning, nor overwhelm him with a pompous and superfluous terminology; and they have the happy art of taking him straightway to the face of nature herself, instead of leading him by the tortuous and bewildering paths of technical system and artificial classification."—Saturday Review.

INTRODUCTORY TEXT-BOOK OF GEOLOGY.
By DAVID PAGE, LL.D., Professor of Geology in the Durham University of Physical Science, Newcastle. With Engravings on Wood and Glossarial Index. Tenth Edition. 2s. 6d.

"It has not been our good fortune to examine a text-book on science of which we could express an opinion so entirely favourable as we are enabled to do of Mr Page's little work."—Athenæum.

ADVANCED TEXT-BOOK OF GEOLOGY, DE-
SCRIPTIVE AND INDUSTRIAL. By the Same. With Engravings, and Glossary of Scientific Terms. Fifth Edition, revised and enlarged. 7s. 6d.

"We have carefully read this truly satisfactory book, and do not hesitate to say that it is an excellent compendium of the great facts of Geology, and written in a truthful and philosophic spirit."—Edinburgh Philosophical Journal.
"As a school-book nothing can match the Advanced Text-Book of Geology by Professor Page of Newcastle."—Mechanics' Magazine.
"We know of no introduction containing a larger amount of information in the same space, and which we could more cordially recommend to the geological student."—Athenæum.

THE GEOLOGICAL EXAMINATOR. A Progres-
sive Series of Questions, adapted to the Introductory and Advanced Text-Books of Geology. Prepared to assist Teachers in framing their Examinations, and Students in testing their own Progress and Proficiency. By the Same. Fifth Edition. 9d.

SYNOPSES OF SUBJECTS TAUGHT IN THE GEO-
LOGICAL CLASS, College of Physical Science, Newcastle-on-Tyne, University of Durham. By the Same. Fcap., cloth, 2s. 6d.

THE CRUST OF THE EARTH: A HANDY OUT-
LINE OF GEOLOGY. By the Same. Sixth Edition. 1s.

"An eminently satisfactory work, giving, in less than 100 pages, an admirable outline sketch of Geology, . . . forming, if not a royal road, at least one of the smoothest we possess to an intelligent acquaintance with geological phenomena."—Scotsman.
"Of singular merit for its clearness and trustworthy character."—Standard.

GEOLOGY FOR GENERAL READERS. A Series
of Popular Sketches in Geology and Palæontology. By the Same. Third Edition, enlarged. 6s.

"This is one of the best of Mr Page's many good books. It is written in a flowing popular style. Without illustration or any extraneous aid, the narrative must prove attractive to any intelligent reader."—Geological Magazine.

HANDBOOK OF GEOLOGICAL TERMS, GEO-
LOGY, AND PHYSICAL GEOGRAPHY. By the Same. Second Edition, enlarged. 7s. 6d.

" The only dictionary of Geology in the English language—modern in date, and exhaustive in treatment."—*Review.*

CHIPS AND CHAPTERS. A Book for Amateurs
and Young Geologists. By the Same. 5s.

THE PAST AND PRESENT LIFE OF THE
GLOBE. With numerous Illustrations. By the Same. Crown 8vo. 6s.

THE PHILOSOPHY OF GEOLOGY. A Brief Re-
view of the Aim, Scope, and Character of Geological Inquiry. By the Same. Fcap. 8vo. 3s. 6d.

"The great value of Mr Page's volume is its suggestive character. The problems he discusses are the highest and most interesting in the science —those on which it most becomes the thinkers and the leaders of the age to make up their minds. The time is now past for geologists to observe silence on these matters, and in this way to depreciate at once the interest and importance of their investigations. It is well to know that, however they may decide, questions of high philosophy are at stake, and therefore we give a hearty welcome to every book which, like Mr Page's, discusses these questions in a fair and liberal spirit."—*Scotsman.*

Physical Geography.

INTRODUCTORY TEXT-BOOK OF PHYSICAL
GEOGRAPHY. With Sketch-Maps and Illustrations. By DAVID PAGE, LL.D., Professor of Geology in the Durham University of Physical Science, Newcastle. Seventh Edition. 2s. 6d.

" The divisions of the subject are so clearly defined, the explanations are so lucid, the relations of one portion of the subject to another are so satisfactorily shown, and, above all, the bearings of the allied sciences to Physical Geography are brought out with so much precision, that every reader will feel that difficulties have been removed, and the path of study smoothed before him."— *Athenæum.*

"Whether as a school-book or a manual for the private student, this work has no equal in our Educational literature."—*Iron.*

ADVANCED TEXT-BOOK OF PHYSICAL GEO-
GRAPHY. By the Same. With Engravings. Second Edition. 5s.

" A thoroughly good Text-Book of Physical Geography."—*Saturday Review.*

" It is not often our good fortune to meet with scientific manuals so cheap and so excellent in matter, and so useful for the practical purposes of education, as this admirable work, which is beyond all question the best of its kind." —*Evening Standard.*

EXAMINATIONS ON PHYSICAL GEOGRAPHY.
A Progressive Series of Questions, adapted to the Introductory and Advanced Text-Books of Physical Geography. By the Same. Second Edition. 9d.

COMPARATIVE GEOGRAPHY. By CARL RITTER.
Translated by W. L. GAGE. Fcap., 3s. 6d.

Zoology.

OUTLINES OF NATURAL HISTORY, for Beginners; being Descriptions of a Progressive Series of Zoological Types. By HENRY ALLEYNE NICHOLSON, M.D., F.R.S.E., F.G.S., &c., Professor of Biology and Physiology, Durham University College of Medicine and Physical Science, Newcastle. 52 Engravings, 1s. 6d.

"There has been no book since Patterson's well known 'Zoology for Schools' that has so completely provided for the class to which it is addressed as the capital little volume by Dr Nicholson."—*Popular Science Review.*

BY THE SAME AUTHOR.

INTRODUCTORY TEXT-BOOK OF ZOOLOGY, FOR THE USE OF JUNIOR CLASSES. With 127 Engravings. A New Edition, 2s. 6d.

"Very suitable for junior classes in schools. There is no reason why any one should not become acquainted with the principles of the science, and the facts on which they are based, as set forth in this volume."—*Lancet.*

"Nothing can be better adapted to its object than this cheap and well-written Introduction."—*London Quarterly Review.*

TEXT-BOOK OF ZOOLOGY, FOR THE USE OF SCHOOLS. Second Edition, enlarged. Crown 8vo, with 188 Engravings on Wood, 6s.

"This capital introduction to natural history is illustrated and well got up in every way. We should be glad to see it generally used in schools."—*Medical Press and Circular.*

A MANUAL OF ZOOLOGY, FOR THE USE OF STUDENTS. With a General Introduction on the Principles of Zoology. Third Edition. Crown 8vo, pp. 706, with 280 Engravings on Wood, 12s. 6d.

"It is the best manual of zoology yet published, not merely in England, but in Europe."—*Pall Mall Gazette, July 20, 1871.*

"The best treatise on Zoology in moderate compass that we possess."—*Lancet, May 18, 1872.*

A MANUAL OF PALÆONTOLOGY, FOR THE USE OF STUDENTS. With a General Introduction on the Principles of Palæontology. Crown 8vo, with upwards of 400 Engravings, 15s.

"This book will be found to be one of the best of guides to the principles of Palæontology and the study of organic remains."—*Athenæum.*

INTRODUCTION TO THE STUDY OF BIOLOGY. Crown 8vo, with numerous Engravings, 5s.

EXAMINATIONS IN NATURAL HISTORY; being a Progressive Series of Questions adapted to the Author's Introductory and Advanced Text-Books and the Student's Manual of Zoology. 1s.

History.

EPITOME OF ALISON'S HISTORY OF EUROPE,
FOR THE USE OF SCHOOLS. Sixteenth Edition. Post 8vo, pp. 604. 7s. 6d. bound in leather.

ATLAS TO EPITOME OF THE HISTORY OF EUROPE.
ELEVEN COLOURED MAPS. By A. KEITH JOHNSTON, LL.D., F.R.S.E. In 4to, 7s.

THE EIGHTEEN CHRISTIAN CENTURIES. By
the Rev. JAMES WHITE, Author of 'The History of France.' Seventh Edition, post 8vo, with Index, 6s.

"He goes to work upon the only true principle, and produces a picture that at once satisfies truth, arrests the memory, and fills the imagination. It will be difficult to lay hands on any book of the kind more useful and more entertaining."—*Times.*

HISTORY OF FRANCE, FROM THE EARLIEST TIMES.
By the Rev. JAMES WHITE, Author of 'The Eighteen Christian Centuries.' Fifth Edition, post 8vo, with Index, 6s.

"An excellent and comprehensive compendium of French history."—*National Review.*

FACTS AND DATES; or, The Leading Events in
Sacred and Profane History, and the Principal Facts in the Various Physical Sciences: the Memory being aided throughout by a Simple and Natural Method. For Schools and Private Reference. By the Rev. ALEX. MACKAY, LL.D., F.R.G.S., Author of 'A Manual of Modern Geography,' &c. Second Edition, crown 8vo, pp. 336. 4s.

THE LIFE AND LABOURS OF THE APOSTLE
PAUL. A continuous Narrative for Schools and Bible Classes. By CHARLES MICHIE, M.A. Second Edition, Revised and Enlarged. Fcap. 8vo, cloth, 1s.

"The details are carefully collected and skilfully put together, and the outcome is a succinct, yet clear and comprehensive, view of the life and labours of the great Apostle. The story of Paul's life, so replete with spirit-stirring incidents, is told in a manner extremely well fitted to arrest the attention of advanced pupils, and we can with confidence commend this little work as an admirable text-book for Bible-classes. The narrative is enriched by footnotes, from which it is apparent that Mr Michie is well posted up in the literature of the subject. These are subjoined without any pretence or parade of learning, and only when required to elucidate or illustrate the text. The map at the close will enable the reader to trace the course of the Apostle in his various missionary tours. We give this handbook our warm commendation: it certainly deserves a wide circulation."—*National Education Gazette.*

A COURSE OF HISTORICAL STUDY, FOR THE
USE OF SCHOOLS AND FOR PRIVATE READING. In Three Parts, comprising—Ancient History, Middle Ages, Modern History. By MADEMOISELLE REYNAUD. *[In the Press.*

School Atlases.

By A. KEITH JOHNSTON, LL.D., &c.
Author of the Royal and the Physical Atlases, &c.

ATLAS OF GENERAL AND DESCRIPTIVE GEO-
GRAPHY. A New and Enlarged Edition, suited to the best Text-Books; with Geographical information brought up to the time of publication. 26 Maps, clearly and uniformly printed in colours, with Index. Imp. 8vo. Half-bound, 12s. 6d.

ATLAS OF PHYSICAL GEOGRAPHY, illustrating,
in a Series of Original Designs, the Elementary Facts of GEOLOGY, HYDROGRAPHY, METEOROLOGY, and NATURAL HISTORY. A New and Enlarged Edition, containing 4 new Maps and Letter-press. 20 Coloured Maps. Imp. 8vo. Half-bound, 12s. 6d.

ATLAS OF ASTRONOMY. A New and Enlarged
Edition, 21 Coloured Plates. With an Elementary Survey of the Heavens, designed as an accompaniment to this Atlas, by ROBERT GRANT, LL.D., &c., Professor of Astronomy and Director of the Observatory in the University of Glasgow. Imp. 8vo. Half-bound, 12s. 6d.

ATLAS OF CLASSICAL GEOGRAPHY. A New
and Enlarged Edition. Constructed from the best materials, and embodying the results of the most recent investigations, accompanied by a complete INDEX OF PLACES, in which the proper quantities are given by T. HARVEY and E. WORSLEY, MM.A. Oxon. 21 Coloured Maps. Imp. 8vo. Half-bound, 12s. 6d.

"This Edition is so much enlarged and improved as to be virtually a new work, surpassing everything else of the kind extant, both in utility and beauty."—*Athenæum.*

ELEMENTARY ATLAS OF GENERAL AND
DESCRIPTIVE GEOGRAPHY, for the Use of Junior Classes; including a MAP OF CANAAN and PALESTINE, with GENERAL INDEX. 8vo, half-bound, 5s.

NEW ATLAS FOR PUPIL-TEACHERS.

THE HANDY ROYAL ATLAS. 46 Maps clearly
printed and carefully coloured, with GENERAL INDEX. Imp. 4to, £2, 12s. 6d., half-bound morocco. A New Edition, brought up to the present time.

This work has been constructed for the purpose of placing in the hands of the public a useful and thoroughly accurate ATLAS of Maps of Modern Geography, in a convenient form, and at a moderate price. It is based on the 'ROYAL ATLAS,' by the same Author; and, in so far as the scale permits, it comprises many of the excellences which its prototype is acknowledged to possess. The aim has been to make the book strictly what its name implies, a HANDY ATLAS—a valuable substitute for the 'Royal,' where that is too bulky or too expensive to find a place, a needful auxiliary to the junior branches of families, and a *vade mecum* to the tutor and the pupil-teacher.

Keith Johnston's Atlases.

EXTRACTS FROM OPINIONS OF THE PRESS.

SCHOOL ATLASES.

"They are as superior to all School Atlases within our knowledge, as were the larger works of the same Author in advance of those that preceded them."—*Educational Times.*

"Decidedly the best School Atlases we have ever seen."—*English Journal of Education.*

" . . . The 'Physical Atlas' seems to us particnlarly well executed. . . . The last generation had no such help to learning as is afforded in these excellent elementary Maps. The 'Classical Atlas' is a great improvement on what has usually gone by that name; not only is it fuller, but in some cases it gives the same country more than once in different periods of time. Thns it approaches the special value of a historical atlas. The 'General Atlas' is wonderfully full and accurate for its scale. . . . Finally, the 'Astronomical Atlas,' in which Mr Hind is responsible for the scientific accuracy of the maps, supplies an admitted educational want. No better companion to an elementary astronomical treatise could be found than this cheap and convenient collection of maps."—*Saturday Review.*

"The plan of these Atlases is admirable, and the excellence of the plan is rivalled by the beauty of the execution. . . . The best security for the accuracy and snbstantial value of a School Atlas is to have it from the hands of a man like our Anthor, who has perfected his skill by the execntion of much larger works, and gained a character which he will be careful not to jeopardise by attaching his name to anything that is crude, slovenly, or superficial."—*Scotsman.*

"This Edition of the 'Classical Atlas' is so much enlarged and improved as to be virtually a new work, surpassing everything else of the kind extant, both in utility and beauty."—*Athenæum.*

THE HANDY ROYAL ATLAS.

"Is probably the best work of the kind now published."—*Times.*

"Not only are the present territorial adjustments duly registered in all these Maps, bnt the latest discoveries in Central Asia, in Africa, and America, have been delineated with laborions fidelity. Indeed the ample illustration of recent discovery, and of the great groups of dependencies on the British Crown, renders Dr Johnston's the best of all Atlases for English use."—*Pall Mall Gazette.*

"This is Mr Keith Johnston's admirable Royal Atlas diminished in bulk and scale so as to be, perhaps, fairly entitled to the name of 'Handy,' but still not so much diminished but what it constitutes an accurate and useful general Atlas for ordinary householda."—*Spectator.*

" The 'Handy Atlas' is thoroughly deserving of its name. Not only does it contain the latest information, but its size and arrangement render it perfect as a book of reference."—*Standard.*

Arithmetic.

THE THEORY OF ARITHMETIC. By DAVID MUNN, F.R.S.E., Mathematical Master, Royal High School of Edinburgh. Crown 8vo, pp. 294. 5s.

"We want books of this kind very much—books which aim at developing the educational value of Arithmetic by showing how admirably it is calculated to exercise the thinking powers of the young. Your book is, I think, excellent —brief, but clear; and I look forward to the good effects which it shall produce, in awaking the minds of many who regard Arithmetic as a mere mechanical process."—*Professor Kelland.*

ELEMENTARY ARITHMETIC. By EDWARD SANG, F.R.S.E. This Treatise is intended to supply the great desideratum of an intellectual instead of a routine course of instruction in Arithmetic. Post 8vo, 5s.

THE HIGHER ARITHMETIC. By the same Author. Being a Sequel to 'Elementary Arithmetic.' Crown 8vo, 5s.

FIVE-PLACE LOGARITHMS. Arranged by E. SANG, F.R.S.E. Sixpence. For the Waistcoat-Pocket.

TREATISE ON ARITHMETIC, with numerous Exercises for Teaching in Classes. By JAMES WATSON, one of the Masters of Heriot's Hospital. Foolscap, 1s.

Botany.

A MANUAL OF BOTANY, ANATOMICAL AND PHYSIOLOGICAL. For the Use of Students. By ROBERT BROWN, M.A., PH.D., F.R.G.S., Lecturer on Botany under the Science and Art Department of the Committee of the Privy Council on Education. Crown 8vo, with numerous Illustrations, 12s. 6d.

Agriculture.

CATECHISM OF PRACTICAL AGRICULTURE. By HENRY STEPHENS, F.R.S.E., Author of the 'Book of the Farm.' A New Edition. With Engravings. 1s.

PROFESSOR JOHNSTON'S CATECHISM OF AGRICULTURAL CHEMISTRY. A New Edition, edited by Professor VOELCKER. With Engravings. 1s.

PROFESSOR JOHNSTON'S ELEMENTS OF AGRICULTURAL CHEMISTRY AND GEOLOGY. A New Edition, revised and brought down to the present time, by G. T. ATKINSON, B.A., F.C.S., Clifton College. Foolscap, 6s. 6d.

Miscellaneous.

A TREASURY OF THE ENGLISH AND GERMAN LANGUAGES.

Compiled from the best Authors and Lexicographers in both Languages. Adapted to the Use of Schools, Students, Travellers, and Men of Business; and forming a Companion to all German-English Dictionaries. By JOSEPH CAUVIN, LL.D. & PH.D., of the University of Göttingen, &c. Crown 8vo 7s. 6d., bound in cloth.

"An excellent English-German Dictionary, which supplies a real want."—*Saturday Review.*

"The difficulty of translating English into German may be greatly alleviated by the use of this copious and excellent English-German Dictionary, which specifies the different senses of each English word, and gives suitable German equivalents. It also supplies an abundance of idiomatic phraseology, with many passages from Shakespeare and other authors aptly rendered in German. Compared with other dictionaries, it has decidedly the advantage."—*Athenæum.*

INTRODUCTORY TEXT-BOOK OF METEOROLOGY.

By ALEXANDER BUCHAN, M.A., F.R.S.E., Secretary of the Scottish Meteorological Society, Author of 'Handy Book of Meteorology,' &c. Crown 8vo, with 8 Coloured Charts and other Engravings, pp. 218. 4s. 6d.

"A handy compendium of Meteorology by one of the most competent authorities on this branch of science."—*Petermann's Geographische Mittheilungen.*

"We can recommend it as a handy, clear, and scientific introduction to the theory of Meteorology, written by a man who has evidently mastered his subject."—*Lancet.*

"An exceedingly useful volume."—*Athenæum.*

A GLOSSARY OF NAVIGATION.

Containing the Definitions and Propositions of the Science, Explanation of Terms, and Description of Instruments. By the Rev. J. B. HARBORD, M.A., Assistant Director of Education, Admiralty. Crown 8vo, Illustrated with Diagrams, 6s.

DEFINITIONS AND DIAGRAMS IN ASTRONOMY AND NAVIGATION.

By the Same. 1s. 6d.

ELEMENTARY HANDBOOK OF PHYSICS.

With 210 Diagrams. By WILLIAM ROSSITER, F.R.A.S., &c. Crown 8vo, pp. 390. 5s.

"A singularly interesting Treatise on Physics, founded on facts and phenomena gained at first hand by the Author, and expounded in a style which is a model of that simplicity and ease in writing which betokens mastery of the subject. To those who require a non-mathematical exposition of the principles of Physics a better book cannot be recommended."—*Pall Mall Gazette.*

Crown 8vo, pp. 760, 7s. 6d.,

AN ETYMOLOGICAL AND PRONOUNCING
DICTIONARY
OF
THE ENGLISH LANGUAGE.

INCLUDING A VERY COPIOUS SELECTION OF

SCIENTIFIC, TECHNICAL, AND OTHER TERMS AND PHRASES.

DESIGNED FOR USE IN SCHOOLS AND COLLEGES,

AND AS

A HANDY BOOK FOR GENERAL REFERENCE.

BY THE REV. JAMES STORMONTH,

AND THE

REV. P. H. PHELP, M.A.

OPINIONS OF THE PRESS.

" This will be found a most admirable and useful Dictionary by the student, the man of business, or the general inquirer. Its design is to supply a full and complete pronouncing, etymological, and explanatory Dictionary of the English language ; and, as far as we can judge, in that design it most completely succeeds. It contains an unusual number of scientific names and terms, English phrases, and familiar colloquialisms ; this will considerably enhance its value to the general searcher after information. The author seems to us to have planned the Dictionary exceedingly well. The Dictionary words are printed in bold black type, and in single letters, that being the form in which words are usually presented to the reader. Capital letters begin such words only in proper names, and others which are always so printed. They are grouped under a leading word, from which they may be presumed naturally to fall or be formed, or singly follow in alphabetical order—only so, however, when they are derived from the same leading root, and when the alphabetical order may not be materially disturbed. The roots are enclosed within brackets, and for them the works of the best and most recent authorities seem to have been consulted. The meanings are those usually given, but they have been simplified as much as possible. Nothing unnecessary is given ; but, in the way of definition, there will be found a vast quantity of new matter. The phonetic spelling of the words has been carefully revised by a Cambridge graduate—Mr Phelp ; and Dr Page, the well-known geologist, has attended to the correctness of the various scientific terms in the book. The Dictionary altogether is very complete."— *Greenock Advertiser.*

" This Dictionary is admirable. The etymological part especially is good and sound. We have turned to 'calamity,' 'forest,' 'poltroon,' and a number of other crucial words, and find them all derived according to the newest lights. There is nothing about 'calamus,' and foris,' and 'pollice truncus,' such as we used in the etymological dictionaries of the old type. The work deserves a place in every English School, whether boys' or girls'."—*Westminster Review.*

OPINIONS—*continued.*

"That which is now before us is evidently a work on which enormous pains have been bestowed. The compilation and arrangement give evidence of laborious research and very extensive scholarship. Special care seems to have been bestowed on the pronunciation and etymological derivation, and the 'root-words' which are given are most valuable in helping to a knowledge of primary significations. All through the book are evidences of elaborate and conscientious work, and any one who masters the varied contents of this Dictionary will not be far off the attainment of the complete art of 'writing the English language with propriety,' in the matter of orthography at any rate."—*Belfast Northern Whig.*

" This strikes us as likely to prove a useful and valuable work. . . . The number of scientific terms given is far beyond what we have noticed in previous works of this kind, and will in great measure render other special dictionaries superfluous. Great care seems also to have been exercised in giving the correct etymology and pronunciation of words. We trust the work may meet with the success it deserves."—*Graphic.*

"On the whole, we may characterise Mr Stormonth's as a really good and valuable Dictionary; and with the typical exceptions we have pointed out, we frankly allow his claim to have laboured earnestly and conscientiously in the production of it."—*Journal of Education.*

" I have examined Stormonth's Dictionary minutely, and again and again with satisfaction on points where other Dictionaries left me hopeless. It is an elaborate and splendid work, and with its great fulness, its grouping of words, and its meanings of phrases, should be the *vade mecum* of every student. It is a book I would like very much to see in the hands of all my advanced pupils."—*David Campbell, Esq., The Academy, Montrose.*

"I am happy to be able to express—and that in the strongest terms of commendation—my opinion of the merits of this Dictionary. Considering the extensive field which it covers, it seems to me a marvel of painstaking labour and general accuracy. With regard to the scientific and technical words so extensively introduced into it, I must say, that in this respect I know no Dictionary that so satisfactorily meets a real and widely felt want in our literature of reference. I have compared it with the large and costly works of Latham, Wedgwood, and others, and find that in the fulness of its details, and the clearness of its definitions, it holds its own even against them. The etymology has been treated throughout with much intelligence, the most distinguished authorities, and the most recent discoveries in philological science having been laid under careful contribution."—*Richard D. Graham, Esq., English Master, College for Daughters of Ministers of the Church of Scotland and of Professors in the Scottish Universities.*

" For clearness of printing, neatness of arrangement, and amount of information, this Dictionary leaves nothing to be desired; while its correctness and condensed form giving all that is necessary with no redundance, will prove of great service to all who want a work of complete and easy reference, without having recourse to a Cyclopedia. In all cases where I have referred to the etymology, I have found it most satisfactory; once or twice after being unable to find a word in another Dictionary, I have met what I wanted in this one."—*John Wingfield, Esq., M.A.*

THE SCHOOL ETYMOLOGICAL DICTIONARY

AND WORD-BOOK.   Combining the advantages of an ordinary Pronouncing School Dictionary and an Etymological Spelling-Book. By the Rev. JAMES STORMONTH.   Fcap. 8vo, pp. 254, 2s.

" This is mainly an abridgment of Mr Stormonth's larger Etymological Dictionary, which has already been favourably criticised in 'The Schoolmaster.' The Dictionary, which contains every word in ordinary use, is followed up by a carefully prepared list of prefixes and postfixes, with illustrative examples, and a vocabulary of Latin, Greek, and other root-words, followed by derived English words.   It will be obvious to every experienced teacher, that these lists may be made available in many ways for imparting a sound knowledge of the English language, and for helping unfortunate pupils over the terrible difficulties of our unsystematic and stubborn orthography.   We think this volume will be a valuable addition to the pupil's store of books, and, if rightly used, will prove a safe and suggestive guide to a sound and thorough knowledge of his native tongue."—*The Schoolmaster.*

" For these reasons we always advocate the good old practice of teaching children English to a large extent by means of lists of spellings, all but the most elementary classes learning spellings with 'meanings.' Mr Stormonth, in this admirable word-book, has provided the means of carrying out our principle in the higher classes, and of correcting all the inexactness and want of completeness to which the English student of English is liable.   His book is an etymological dictionary curtailed and condensed. . . .   As a dictionary the book is very carefully compiled, and much labour has been expended on the task of economising words and space with as little actual loss to the student as possible.   The pronunciation is indicated by a neat system of symbols, easily mastered at the outset, and indeed pretty nearly speaking for themselves."—*School Board Chronicle.*

"A concise handy-book of this kind was much wanted in schools, for most pocket-dictionaries are by no means reliable guides.   Besides the word and its meaning, the pronunciation is given in each case, together with the kindred or root words in other languages.   The work seems very complete."—*Educational Times.*

"The derivations are particularly good."—*Westminster Review.*

" This cheap and careful abridgment of Mr Stormonth's larger Dictionary, which has met with so cordial a welcome in all quarters, will be received as a boon by all interested in the education of the young. . . .   We heartily endorse its claim to be 'a thoroughly practical school-book, and fitted for daily use by the pupil in and out of the school-room, in the preparation of the English lessons.'"—*Aberdeen Herald.*

" The work is admirably adapted for teaching the meanings of words, since after the meanings of the various postfixes have been learnt, the pupil will obtain excellent exercise in the formation of words derived from those given in the Dictionary."—*Mechanics' Magazine.*

ANCIENT CLASSICS

FOR

ENGLISH READERS

BY VARIOUS AUTHORS.

EDITED BY

REV. W. LUCAS COLLINS, M.A.

Author of ' Etoniana,' 'The Public Schools,' &c.

OPINIONS OF THE PRESS.

"We gladly avail ourselves of this opportunity to recommend the other volumes of this useful series, most of which are executed with discrimination and ability."—*Quarterly Review.*

" These Ancient Classics have, without an exception, a twofold value. They are rich in literary interest, and they are rich in social and historical interest. We not only have a faithful presentation of the stamp and quality of the literature which the master-minds of the classical world have bequeathed to the modern world, but we have a series of admirably vivid and graphic pictures of what life at Athens and Rome was. We are not merely taken back over a space of twenty centuries, and placed immediately under the shadow of the Acropolis, or in the very heart of the Forum, but we are at once brought behind the scenes of the old Roman and Athenian existence. As we see how the heroes of this 'new world which is the old' plotted, intrigued, and planned ; how private ambition and political partisanship were dominant and active motives then as they are now ; how the passions and the prejudices which reign supreme now reigned supreme then ; above all, as we discover how completely many of what we may have been accustomed to consider our most essentially modern thoughts and sayings have been anticipated by the poets and orators, the philosophers and historians, who drank their inspiration by the banks of Ilissus or on the plains of Tiber, we are prompted to ask whether the advance of some twenty centuries has worked any great change in humanity, and whether, substituting the coat for the toga, the park for the Campus Martius, the Houses of Parliament for the Forum, Cicero might not have been a public man in London as well as an orator in Rome?"—*Morning Advertiser.*

" It is difficult to estimate too highly the value of such a series as this in giving 'English readers' an insight, exact as far as it goes, into those olden times which are so remote and yet to many of us so close. It is in no wise to be looked upon as a rival to the translations which have at no time been brought forth in greater abundance or in greater excellence than in our own day. On the contrary, we should hope that these little volumes would be in many cases but a kind of stepping-stone to the larger works, and would lead many who otherwise would have remained in ignorance of them to turn to the versions of Conington, Worsley, Derby, or Lytton. In any case a reader would come with far greater knowledge, and therefore with far greater enjoyment, to the complete translation, who had first had the ground broken for him by one of these volumes."—*Saturday Review, Jan.* 18.

Now complete, in 20 vols., fcap. 8vo, 2s. 6d. each,

Ancient Classics for English Readers.

1.—HOMER: THE ILIAD. By THE EDITOR.

2.—HOMER: THE ODYSSEY. By THE EDITOR.

3.—HERODOTUS. By GEORGE C. SWAYNE, M.A.

4.—THE COMMENTARIES OF CÆSAR. By ANTHONY TROL-LOPE.

5.—VIRGIL. By THE EDITOR.

6.—HORACE. By THEODORE MARTIN.

7.—ÆSCHYLUS. By REGINALD S. COPLESTON, B.A.

8.—XENOPHON. By SIR ALEXANDER GRANT, Bart., Principal of the University of Edinburgh.

9.—CICERO. By THE EDITOR.

10.—SOPHOCLES. By CLIFTON W. COLLINS, M.A.

11.—PLINY'S LETTERS. By the Rev. ALFRED CHURCH, M.A., and the Rev. W. J. BRODRIBB, M.A.

12.—EURIPIDES. By W. B. DONNE.

13.—JUVENAL. By EDWARD WALFORD, M.A.

14.—ARISTOPHANES. By THE EDITOR.

15.—HESIOD AND THEOGNIS. By the Rev. J. DAVIS, M.A.

16.—PLAUTUS AND TERENCE. By THE EDITOR.

17.—TACITUS. By W. B. DONNE.

18.—LUCIAN. By THE EDITOR.

19.—PLATO. By CLIFTON W. COLLINS, M.A.

20.—THE GREEK ANTHOLOGY. By LORD NEAVES.

45 GEORGE STREET, EDINBURGH; 37 PATERNOSTER ROW, LONDON.